I0726495

GODDESS OF WAR

THE JESSICA KELLER CHRONICLES VOLUME 4

BLAZE WARD

KNOTTED ROAD PRESS

Goddess of War
The Jessica Keller Chronicles: Volume 4
Blaze Ward
Copyright © 2016 Blaze Ward
All rights reserved
Published by Knotted Road Press
www.KnottedRoadPress.com

ISBN: 978-1-943663-22-4

Cover art:

© Philcold | Dreamstime.com - Far Planets Photo

Cover and interior design copyright © 2016 Knotted Road Press

Never miss a release!
If you'd like to be notified of new releases, sign up for my newsletter.

I will never spam you or use your email for nefarious purposes. You can also unsubscribe at any time.

http://www.blazeward.com/newsletter/

This book is licensed for your personal enjoyment only. All rights reserved. This is a work of fiction. All characters and events portrayed in this book are fictional, and any resemblance to real people or incidents is purely coincidental. This book, or parts thereof, may not be reproduced in any form without permission.

ALSO BY BLAZE WARD

The Science Officer Series

Start with: The Science Officer

The Jessica Keller Chronicles

Start with: Auberon

CS-405 (Command Centurion Kosnett, part of Jessica)

Start with: Queen Anne's Revenge

First Centurion Kosnett (sequel to Jessica)

Start with: Encounter at Vilahana

Additional Alexandria Station Stories

Alexandria Station Collection

Handsome Rob (Alexandria Station Universe)

Start with: Can't Shoot Straight Gang

=====================

Corsac Fox

Start with: Flight of the Corsac Fox

Operation Marrakesh

Start with: Trial by Leviathan

Captain Daring

Start with: Revoked

The Hunter Bureau

Start with: Mirrors

Fairchild

Start with: Fairchild

Last Stand

Start with: Lost Dreams

The Lazarus Alliance

Start with: Escape

Shadow of the Dominion

Start with: Longshot Hypothesis

Star Dragon

Start with: Birth of the Star Dragon

Kincaide's War

Start with: The Eden Package

Star Tribes

Start with: Winterstar

Blaze also writes Action-Adventure Here

AUTHOR'S NOTE

I've mentioned this before. Jessica kind of snuck up on me and took over. The ideas behind the middle act of Queen came to me over a decade ago as part of a larger story, but I didn't have either end to go with it. Just that amazingly weird space battle over a planet with a bunch of pirates.

And then Jessica tapped me on the shoulder and introduced herself one day. At that moment, I had the entirety of the first three books (I can't say trilogy, even as they are, because it will be a very large series and you're holding book four) in my head and ready to go. Writing them was mostly just the time to actually type the words and make sure I had them all right before going on.

I always knew there would be more of her story, about the time I finished book 1. Somewhere in the middle of book 2, I knew what the rest of the entire series would look like. I won't bother explaining it now, but somewhere around book 5, the astute reader ought to be able to go back to the exact sentence in Queen of the Pirates where everything else crystalized, like rock candy in hot water.

I certainly knew.

I have noticed that I tend to write female characters that appear to be out of tune with traditional publishing. They aren't bad-ass, super-wizard, demon-hunting, super-models single-handedly saving the universe from evil. I find that kind of character just as unreasonable as the broken, helpless waif who requires Prince Wonderstud to come rescue her from a bad manicure.

She won't appreciate it, but one of my reviewers out in the real world paid me the highest compliment she could, as she was trying to insult me. I had all these interesting and powerful female characters running around, but the book she read was "just another space opera war-story." She was insulted that I wasn't committing high, feminist literature.

And that's because she doesn't know what that is.

Joss Whedon was once asked why he kept doing powerful female characters. His response was because people kept asking him that question. They didn't take for granted that a woman could be her own self, rather than being defined by her relationship to a man or to her mother, which seems to be the default choice ninety percent of the time.

So I had all these powerful women running around, but they were being characters, rather than feminist icons. I don't believe feminism will achieve its goals until the gender of the character doesn't matter. If Jessica was male, and possessed of a grander libido, she'd probably be compared to Jim Kirk. Because if you erase gender from the page, she's rather just like many of the male action-figure characters you have read about.

That's on purpose.

She's a woman, sure. But she's not defined by being a woman. *Fribourg* would love to do that, and they frequently make that mistake, because to them a woman is a frilly, lesser creature who can't be trusted to handle her own affairs. Even today, we fall into that trap. When a woman does something any number of men have done, how often does the media focus on her gender rather than her accomplishments? What does that imply? Why have we failed?

So remind your daughters and your nieces that they don't have to settle for whatever crumbs a man deigns to share with them. They can take their own slice of life and crack the long bones for the marrow without having to have a man do it for them.

Jessica Keller is, for me, a feminist icon of a woman who will do things her way, rather than how a man thinks she should behave. She's not a Bond sex kitten. She's not a man-hating harpy. She is a fully-realized human being, who happens to be smarter than most of the people around her, and driven to achievement by her own demons.

Stop thinking that a woman has to be a bimbo, and start appreciating them as people.

Okay, rant over. Raw nerve.

This is Book Four: Goddess of War. The first three were a single tale, covering what we might call The Rise of Jessica Keller. She is a Fleet Lord now, and she is going to take the war to *Fribourg*. At present, I expect that there will be something around nine novels in Jessica's arc, plus a number of side characters and events I want to explore in short stories and novellas that will serve to fill in gaps and provide depth. (I have an encyclopedia of notes. Literally. 15,000 words right this moment, and over 100 pages.)

I have already started writing book five as you read this, and that is where things get really interesting. All the rest of the titles and plots have been worked out at this point, at least in broad enough detail to do an elevator pitch.

It's not that I write into darkness. I do, but I always have the end points in my head and then it's just a matter of getting there. Jessica will be no different, because I know how the overall plot will go across the last five novels beyond this one. It will be the little details that surprise and delight me.

With any luck, I will have delighted you enough that you join me.

shade and sweet water,
blaze
West of the Mountains, WA

OVERTURE: SEVENTH SON

IMPERIAL FOUNDING: 175/03/21. SEVENTH SON. ABOVE THURINGWELL

Seventh Son was old, as freighters went. Well-used, but well-loved at the same time. Oversized corridors instead of something cramped. Too many lights, but power was cheap and it was worth the time and effort to keep the ship bright inside.

Merryn settled into the left-hand bridge seat and studied her blinking console as the ship came out of final jump. *Thuringwell* was right where it was supposed to be, a yellow and green and blue marble hanging on a spackled, black background. She brought the big engines on line and felt the slightest shiver in the gravplates as the little freighter re-routed a sudden overabundance of power.

Seventh Son probably could have made do just fine with only one of those two engines back there, but Merryn liked being able to outrun damned near anything in space. Not all of her destinations were nice, boring, little, Imperial industrial colonies like *Thuringwell*. Hell, a place like this she didn't even need to have Tyler manning the gun turret.

"*Thuringwell* Traffic Control," she pushed the record button on the comm. "This is TCL-100893471AJQ. Requesting lane assignment for docking. Cargo of mixed goods including sector mail from *Kittras*."

A ping and the message was away. If they were on the ball over there, forty-five seconds for a reply. It was mid-day Tuesday. Otto should be on duty. He was always a professional, unlike Lo or Michael.

Merryn looked around the bridge as she waited. The starship was over a century old, but still in reasonably good shape. She probably had another three years before she needed to strip and repaint all the crew compartments. The hallways everywhere else were still a soothing, airy green, occasionally decorated with flowers and horses she had painted when she was a teenager with aspirations to high art.

Back when she still thought her father would be around forever.

The electronics, at least, were state of the art. Every spare bit of cash went into keeping the internal systems and engines sharp. More than once she had outrun a wanna-be pirate on the edges of the *Rhios II* gravity well.

The local officials there were far more corrupt than here. *Thuringwell*'s current Duke was a patriot and a stickler for rule of law. So he just perverted the laws in his favor rather than ignoring them like they did everywhere else.

And then brought in men like Colonel Dieter Haussmann to enforce them. Merryn shivered just a little, remembering her last encounter with Imperial Security's local Operations Commander.

She had been pretty sure he was going to open that second-to-last shipping container on the last trip.

Smuggling narcotics probably would have gotten her twenty years on a prison colony. The guns in that crate would have gotten her executed.

And it wasn't like she was a revolutionary, or anything. If these people didn't like their Duke, that was their issue. She was just going to make a good amount of money on the side providing them illicit materials.

Come to think of it, the Duke might have preferred it if she brought some of the softer narcotics. Not having anything to take the edge off of life on a crappy, dead-end world like this was part of what was driving the angry men to contemplate doing stupid things.

Stupider things.

Of course, Duke Waltev Damsell rarely came to *Thuringwell* to see that for himself, preferring life in the salons of the Imperial Capital, *St. Legier*.

"*Seventh Son*, this is Traffic Control," Otto's voice broke through her reverie. "Dock 14 is reserved. Lane assignments attached. See you in a few hours."

Merryn lined the beast's great nose up with the distant station and let the engines pulse.

From the outside, *Seventh Son* looked like one of the great aquatic rays that had been brought to space from the Homeworld during the great terraforming era and seeded in so many oceans. She was a wide, flat ellipse, thick in the middle, with the bridge where the creature's eyes would be, wings that sloped subtly down, and a nasty stinger in the tail, right where she needed it when she was being chased by bad men.

Even if today she was going towards them.

CHAPTER I

DATE OF THE REPUBLIC DECEMBER 1, 395
BRANI, LADAUX

THAT ORNATELY-DECORATED, white door probably would have intimidated her, once upon a time. Terrified her, even.

But that was before.

Nothing could intimidate Jessica Keller today. All capacity for that had been burned out of her. Purged forever in the fires of battle at *First Petron* and *First Ballard*.

Today, she was even poised on the verge of returning to space, to starship command, for the first time since she had been formally relieved of duty above *Ballard*. Even the Court Martial for losing half of her squadron, both *Auberon* and *Rajput* too damaged to even make it home, had been a mere formality, Fleet Lords comparing the tonnage of losses for the *Republic of Aquitaine* Navy that day against the horrendous damage inflicted on the *Fribourg Empire* in a single afternoon of withering combat.

Today, she was nearly ready to go home. Back to space. Back to command. Back to the Eternal War she intended to win.

But first, a surprise visit into an even scarier place than the First Lord's office at Fleet HQ. After all, she had been there several times now. And if she and a man like Nils Kasum weren't going to be peers, they were certainly comrades in arms.

She could relax on that knowledge.

The door ahead was a more disconcerting puzzle.

Jessica took a moment as the hired skimmer dropped her at the top of the formal circular driveway, on a curb lined with well-manicured grass and artistically shaped hedge. She was surrounded by the evening air, redolent with rose gardens and an orchard of fruit trees nearby, planted long ago and slowly expanded by each office holder.

Jessica found the air comforting, even if she preferred the carefully processed air aboard a starship. Right now, she needed to catch her breath, center herself. This was a social event, not two war fleets maneuvering, or politicians that needed to be battled across a tabletop. Probably.

Who could have ever imagined that at twelve years old and holding the admission letter welcoming her to the Fleet Boarding School, that one day she would be looking at the front door of the President of the Republic? Had it really been twenty-six years?

Jessica pulled the invitation from the inside pocket of her jacket, just to read it once and experienced again the thrill. The heavy linen paper felt so imposing in her hands.

So far she had come, and yet so far remaining before her.

She smiled and tucked the letter back into her jacket. The language had been unusually specific. No uniforms. No Plus-One. A private dinner. Semi-casual cocktail attire, whatever that meant.

For Marcelle, her long-time steward and personal dog-robber, it had meant a budget to go shopping, and then time for a team of expert seamstresses to work their utter magic and dreams into fabric.

The result was a form-fitting belted tunic in indigo, with sleeves down to just past her elbows and a shallow-V collar in a lighter purple, over a gray patterned skirt that came down to the top of cute, little, chocolate-dark, lace-up boots. Marcelle, but more to the point Indira, Jessica's mother, had insisted on a light-weight gray-black jacket over that, cut somewhere between her normal, hip-length dress jacket and a bolero, done in a rough herringbone texture.

She no longer doubted the eyes of Marcelle, Indira, or Moirrey Kermode, when it came to fashion. The mirror an hour ago had made her look amazing.

And Jessica was no longer itchy wearing civilian clothes. Twenty-two months groundside, doing the rounds of politicians and finishing a Class II degree at Fleet Command School, had finally gotten her comfortable in mufti. A long visit home to *Petron* had done wonders, as well.

Home? Petron?

She could see duty. Jessica Keller was all about duty. But the trip to *Petron* four months ago, with Desianna Indah-Rodriguez, technically merely the senior government minister to David Rodriguez, Desianna's son and Jessica's Regent, but more importantly, her friend, had unlocked something, some painful knot in her soul.

She took a deep breath and faced a new dragon's den. This woman tonight was merely the President of the *Republic of Aquitaine*. How scary could someone like Calina Szabolcsi be, after standing before her own throne on *Petron* again?

THE PRESIDENTIAL PALACE was mostly a museum these days, rather than a working office. The Presidency itself was largely ceremonial and formal, with true power residing in the Senate.

That being said, it still came with perks.

Jessica was met at the door by two members of the Palace Guard in formal, rather dressy uniforms evoking an earlier age, backed by four other men and women with harder faces and heavily armed, lurking quietly in the corners.

The man on the right checked her invitation with diligence and ceremony before passing her with a warm smile to an usher. The latter was a young woman, possibly still a university student with family connections. Jessica followed her through a set of secured doors out of the museum and into the Personal Quarters.

These rooms were warmer, homier. Jessica could feel Madame Szabolcsi's touch in the decorations, the colors, the very air. Carpets here were a warm green, walls a softer blue. Art on waist-high pillars regularly represented the best of the Republic: ceramics, bronzes, exotics of all kinds.

The young woman walked Jessica to a closed door, pulled it open outward into the hallway, and gestured for Jessica to proceed.

"Madam President awaits, ma'am," she said with an impish grin and a twinkle in her eyes.

Jessica smiled back and stepped through the door.

Now, she would find out what was really going on.

Jessica entered the room, not quiet keyed up for a combat drop, but a little more wired than normal. The inhabitants put her on an ever-sharper guard even as she knew she was supposed to relax.

At a glance, there were only four people in the room, and she knew every single one of them, at least by sight and reputation.

Standing to her left, holding a tall goblet of something purple, First Fleet Lord Petia Naoumov. Flag Officer of the Star Controller *Athena*, SC-005. Commander of Home Fleet. The senior serving officer in the *Republic of Aquitaine* Navy. Jessica's line boss in just about all things.

Petia was tall, taller even than Jessica's aide Marcelle, with long black hair done up in an elaborate, formal braid, and Japanese ancestry in her skin and the bones of her gorgeous face. Tonight, she wore a flowing dress in taupe and sand colors, accentuated with bright green as she smiled in Jessica's direction and nodded.

Jessica made a point to memorize everything she saw, knowing she would be grilled mercilessly by three fabric experts tomorrow.

Standing next to the First Fleet Lord was Hennigan McCandless, fourth generation of McCandless and Daughters, one of the largest and most important ship foundries in the Republic, and technically her own father's boss, Miguel Keller now being one of five active Master Builders at the firm.

Hennigan was a small woman, with blond hair buzzed short on the sides and spikey on top. Her eyes always reminded Jessica of sapphires, or perhaps tanzanite. She was wearing dark blue slacks and a matching jacket over a crimson shirt. Not quite a power suit, but appropriate for a shark like Hennigan, even such a girlie shark.

Hennigan stepped close and engulfed her in a hug, and stood on her toes to plant a warm kiss on both cheeks.

"It's good to see you, Jess," she said with a warm smile.

"You too, Henn," Jessica replied with an evil grin, leaning back but not breaking contact. "Is my ship done, yet?"

The smaller woman's smile grew larger and she laughed throatily.

"I am not at liberty to divulge such state secrets, Keller," she teased.

Hennigan turned her head to indicate the other pair of women in the room and gestured with one hand.

"Ask them."

Jessica stepped clear of the hug and looked to her right.

Closer, standing next to a small bar tucked into the corner, was Senator Judit Margrét Chavarría, Premier of the Senate, political head of the Republic. They had never met formally, but Jessica had sat in occasional briefings with the woman.

She was a short, stocky fireplug of a woman, no taller than Moirrey Kermode, but she felt twice as massive. Her mahogany skin and black eyes stood out against a yellow dress that looked like the cold-weather descendant of a Sari, all wraps and long, flowing pieces going hither and yon.

Jessica started to say something when her brain finally registered who it was standing behind the waist-high bar, pouring drinks.

Calina Szabolcsi. Madame President.

She was tall, with an erect carriage that made her seem a head taller than Jessica's barely average height. Her shoulder-length hair had long since gone silver-gray, but the piercing green eyes and bronzed skin had lost nothing with age. There was a charm, a charisma about the woman that was nearly magnetic. She was dressed in the most basic black: cotton dress, leather belt, onyx stone pendant set in a silver necklace.

The President gestured to the array of bottles around her with a smile.

"What will it be, Madam Keller?" she solicited.

Jessica's normal default in these situations was a white wine. Usually something light, and barely consumed, but at least polite. Useful in unsure circumstances.

Tonight had a very different feel to it. Lighter, almost playful. Someplace Jessica Keller rarely visited.

"Champaign cocktail, please," Jessica replied.

"Anything particular?" the President asked with a sly smile.

Jessica shrugged.

"Surprise me."

The evening was already a surprise on many levels. She would let these women set the tone.

Something else she was learning to do. Let go. On occasion.

The President worked some invisible magic beneath the counter and handed Jessica a goblet that was an even deeper indigo than the First Fleet Lord's, and far more fizzy.

Jessica took a sip and let the bubbles tickle her nose.

Political events were always serious events over wine. Fleet parties tended towards either harder alcohols or coffee, depending. This tasted vaguely like grape juice, cranberries, and champagne, heavy on the juice.

"Ah," the President said with a bright voice, "our last voice is arrived."

Jessica turned to consider the final guest, and received a greater surprise.

Dr. Wakely Okafor. Jessica had taken a master class in Imperial Governance from her during Fleet Command School. And plotted assorted mayhem with the woman over tea afterwards.

Wakely was a native of *Zanzibar*, one of the founding worlds of modern civilization and a member of the fabled Story Road that ran through deep space to *Ballard*.

Her idea of cocktail attire was a bright red tabard, slashed to the hip over matching pants short enough to be called capris and a tight blue, long-sleeved top. In the middle of her chest, and once she turned to speak to Petia, her back, a blue cross fleury, musketeer-style. It showed off the defined muscles in her arms and shoulders. Wakely's lines might have been better than the President's, a woman who was herself a retired professional athlete. Their muscles were almost as good as Jessica's, a master of *Valse d'Glaive*.

Her skin was the healthy brown of a good hot chocolate, with eyes like brown dwarf stars, hot and subdued. Dr. Okafor's hair was almost shaved on the sides, and standing more than a hand-span tall on top, like some fierce, tribal mohawk atop a Maasai warrior from her ancient homeland, or a Samurai from Petia's.

Jessica stood to one side as Wakely waded carefully into the room, far less at home in these rarified chambers. A glass of wine appeared and seemed to relax her.

"My friends, now that we are all here, I give you a toast," President Szabolcsi intoned formally, holding her glass in the air. "The Republic."

Jessica joined the ringing of glasses and took a drink.

"I suppose you are wondering why I have asked you all here tonight," she continued with a merry laugh. "I realize that sounds like a bad mystery novel, but I will lay all the blame at Judit's feet and absolve myself of all responsibility save bartending."

This was not how Jessica expected an evening with this group of people, these women, to unfold. By any stretch of the imagination.

The Premier took a moment to eye each of them silently, carefully before she spoke.

"They will ask," she began, in a dark and ominous tone. "In those Imperial Halls of Planning, those Intelligence wonders. They will speculate, when you go home and chat about a lovely, lively evening of drink and good food. They will draw the obvious conclusion."

Judit took a drink and encouraged each of them to do the same.

"They will be wrong," she continued with the faintest sneer in her tone and lips. "Because they are fools, they will believe what we want them to see."

"Fools, Premier?" Wakely asked in a voice dripping with the kind of sarcasm that would be more appropriate on first-year freshmen.

Jessica kept her ideas on the topic to herself. She knew the reputations of some of the men involved on the other side. Many would be fools. How many depended.

"Fools, Dr. Okafor," the Premier replied. "And please, at least for tonight if not longer, call me Judit. All of you."

"Judit," Wakely replied warily. "Fools?"

"*Fribourg* is governed by an entire class of aristocrats wedded to the idea of their innate masculine superiority," Judit continued.

Jessica could see an angry fire burning at the back of the Senator's eyes. It was one she frequently shared.

"Admiral Emmerich Wachturm has tried to kill Jessica Keller a number of times," Judit said, pointing. "Because he has failed, he has been demoted, retired by command of the Emperor himself. Now he is a Distinguished Scholar at their own fleet academy, teaching a new generation of students, but no longer a personal threat to the borders. They do not consider that she might be better than him. She cannot be, simply because she is a woman."

"I still do not see the greater connection to foolishness. Judit."

Wakely had migrated slowly into something like an orbit of Jessica, close and perhaps drawing strength from the person she knew best in the room.

Judit smiled like a shark.

"They will see six powerful women meeting," Judit concluded, holding up a hand and gesturing around the room. "And many of them will decide that we spoke of nothing more serious, more significant, than getting our nails done, a topic, you will note, for which I am already famous in some quarters."

The whole room chuckled. Judit Chavarría was indeed famous on *Ladaux*, and much of the Republic, for hosting mani/pedi parties. Jessica suddenly wondered how much of that was a cover for evenings like this one. Suddenly, several other things about Judit's reputation and success as a politician made more sense.

Wakely's eyes narrowed and grew canny, but she held her own counsel.

Jessica decided to step in and rescue her friend, however little rescue a woman like Wakely Okafor needed.

"So what shall we discuss over cocktails, Judit?" Jessica asked carefully.

"You," Judit replied, pointing a finger at her that looked remarkably like a gun. It slid sideways like a turret to point at Wakely next. "And your co-conspirator."

Jessica said something like "Erp?"

Judit smiled.

"Specifically, *Operation Harbinger*."

Ah.

It was Jessica's turn to clam up and listen, lest she say something stupid to the very women that might approve it. Or deny her request.

"Petia is here as the Fleet's resident tactical and strategic expert," Judit continued. "One who can give me an opinion not coloured by the obvious affection Nils Kasum has for one of his favorite students."

Jessica nearly bit her tongue rather than speak.

Judit continued to gesture around the room like a bull fighter, slowly drawing them in with a highball glass instead of a cape, but no less effective.

"Hennigan is building the lance that will lead the charge."

"Wakely was the inspiration behind the plan." Judit waved a hand to dismiss Jessica and Wakely's attempt at a reply. "I have read the paper Jessica wrote for your class, Wakely. And little birdies have whispered in my ear."

Judit speared Jessica with a keen eye. Jessica understood now how this woman had come to be at the pinnacle of power. She was that sharp, that dangerous.

That good.

They all were, else they wouldn't be here. But still.

"The President and I represent the Republic," Judit continued, gesturing to herself and Calina. "History and circumstance have put the six of us in this position, that we can initiate a crusade that just might challenge the very tenets of the *Fribourg Empire*, and possibly rock it to its core."

The rest of the room seemed to disappear into Judit's eyes as she and Jessica stared at each other for several moments.

"Jessica," Judit said, barely above a whisper. "If any other officer had proposed this idea, I would have laughed them out of the room. And seen them to shore afterwards."

Judit took a breath. All of the other women took a breath with her. The air hung heavy and still, like the most dangerous parts of the water.

"Will it work?"

Jessica fought down the gleeful giggle that threatened to erupt out of her mouth. It would be inappropriate. Probably.

She took a drink of her champagne instead, into a suddenly dry throat.

Cocktail parties were still a new thing to her. Apparently, they were very much like her usual tactical puzzles to solve on the fly, maneuvering a fleet in six axes.

This was strategic planning. This was her area of expertise among these women. Among most humans.

"Can it?" Jessica began. "Yes. Will it? We cannot know until we try. But I believe that not making the attempt would be a mistake."

"Why?"

Judit's eyes were fire now.

The other four women became shadows around Jessica, because only one mattered. One woman would determine if she would be given this chance.

Right here. Right now.

She was reminded of the opening notes to the aria that was the battle that would be known to human history as *First Ballard*. The implicit promises made for battle with the Red Admiral.

Death or glory.

"Everybody agrees," Jessica stated flatly. "It is impossible to actually conquer and hold a hostile planet for any meaningful length of time."

"And yet," Petia stepped into the conversation now from Jessica's left. "You think you can succeed."

It was not a question.

Jessica was reminded of the recent defense of her Master's thesis against a panel of experts similar to this group, on this very topic. Far less enthusiastic experts, who had still granted her a Class II Degree over it.

She nodded at her friend.

"Something Dr. Okafor, Wakely, said during one of her early lectures," Jessica replied. "Something about the manner in which Imperial worlds are governed at the local level, in contrast to how we do it. She and I have spoken extensively about it since then, and I did my thesis on what we now call *Operation Harbinger*."

Jessica felt three pair of eyes drift past her to her left suddenly. She could almost feel the strength and calm power Wakely projected back at the others, another woman not to be trifled with.

A rock that could not be broken.

Judit's eyes never left her.

"I have identified five Imperial planets," Jessica continued. "Each is slightly different, but all of them exhibit the same level of fragile rigidity that I believe could be fractured by application of the right leverage."

Jessica took a deep breath and finished her tiny cocktail.

"If we did it right," she said simply, handing the glass back to the President of the Republic for a refill. "They will conquer themselves. And when the word spreads, other worlds might do the same."

Judit's fire was banked, perhaps.

"Do you honestly believe that you could unravel the entire *Fribourg Empire*, Keller?" she asked.

"Judit," Jessica replied, letting some of her own fire come to the fore finally. "That is my job, my mission, my oath. To destroy *Fribourg*."

"Are you willing to put your reputation, your entire career, behind that statement?" the Premier asked carefully. "To go down with it if it fails?"

"Judit, I do that every morning when I put on that uniform. The difference here would be the number of men and women who might get killed or wounded if I'm wrong."

"No, Jessica," Judit continued. "If this fails, your career will be effectively over. Are you willing to accept that?"

Jessica bit back the first retort that crossed her tongue. And the second one. They were past that point. This was for everything.

"Yes."

COCKTAIL PARTIES apparently frequently included dinner.

Jessica had snacked earlier, unsure what to expect. Now she sat at a cozy round table with the five other women, as men and women of the Household Staff cleared dinner plates and delivered dessert tarts on cute little chilled tiles.

Jessica had never really been a fan of oversized, sharable trays of Chinese food. After tonight's adventures, she was going to have to have a chat with her chef, Nicolai Aoiki, Master of the Wardroom.

She looked at the five other faces, bright with excitement as they had let her do most of the talking, with occasional questions for Wakely or Petia. They seemed to be on her side, so far.

Judit's face grew serious, though, as she contemplated the enormity of the proposed undertaking. Jessica grew still first.

"Wakely," the Premier said carefully. "I've done my research. I know you believe that this can be made to work."

"And yes," Wakely replied. "It is an enormously risky, dangerously fragile task we would undertake, Judit."

"I would propose one change," Judit continued. "It is a small one, in the overall scheme, but I think it would have vast implications, both politically as well as militarily."

Jessica felt the whole room grow silent, grow still. This entire evening might have been arranged to come to this moment. She had made her case, backed solidly by research and experience. She was willing to put herself on the line to do this.

But her intuition and reputation would only get her so far. Judit and Calina had to get behind it and push.

It wasn't enough to acquiesce. They needed to be seen championing the affair, if it was going to work.

"Wakely," Judit said with quiet gravity. "I would like you to be there, representing the Senate."

Jessica watched her former professor's face fall slack.

"What?" Wakely asked sharply.

"Jessica will be in command," Judit replied. "The historical term is *Margrave*. But the campaign calls for a political specialist on the ground, filling the role of *Palsgrave*, or *Palatine*. Jessica proposed several officers, many of them highly-qualified former students of yours. I want a civilian on the ground, acting as Governor to the local administration. You are the single most qualified person in the Republic to handle that task."

Jessica held her breath. Wakely being on board would make so much of what she needed to do easier, since the woman had helped craft much of the scheme.

Her refusal might doom it.

They all watched, hypnotized, as Wakely took a sip from her glass.

"I'm not Fleet," she offered carefully.

"And you will not propose military solutions, Wakely," Jessica said quietly. "I will have ten thousand experts on organized warfare handy, offering me advice. We only get one chance to do this right."

Wakely turned to stare at her. The rest of the room faded into a fog as Jessica calmly returned the look. Gone were professor and student, hashing out options and probabilities over beer. Gone were friends talking over dinner.

They had come to the crux. Jessica knew she could win the war in her lifetime. Wakely's help right now might shave a decade off the task.

For a moment, Jessica envisioned herself on a bridge somewhere, watching the skies of the Imperial Capital at *St. Legier* as bombs and missiles rained down on that world.

Something of it must have shown in her eyes.

"Jessica?" Wakely asked.

After two semesters together, and all the time after, they had reached that level of shorthand.

"There is nobody I want more for this, Wakely," Jessica replied.

Wakely scanned the rest of the room, settling on Judit.

"*Palsgrave?*" she inquired heavily, almost formally. "That is a term that has very specific legal and political implications, Judit."

Judit smiled. Jessica had seen others with that smile. Sharks smelling fresh blood in the water, just waiting to pounce upon some injured foe.

"Yes it does, Wakely," the Premier grinned, pointing at the President and then herself, and the other women. "A woman President and a woman Premier. In a warship manufactured by a woman, in a Navy led by a woman. A campaign commanded by two women. In the

Republic, we would think nothing of it. Find the best man or woman for the task and send them off."

"But the Empire does not think that way," Wakely concluded. "On top of everything else, this will strike at the foundations of their culture, their civilization, their assumption of masculine superiority. This is Níðhöggr gnawing at the very roots of Yggdrasil."

"I owe those bastards for *Ballard*," Jessica growled quietly. "For what they did to Moirrey and Arlo and Suvi. For *Alexandria Station*. I want Karl to sleep nervously for the rest of his life, fearful that the beams beneath his empire have rotted and will give way without warning."

Wakely took a deep breath, but Jessica could already see the commitment in her eyes.

"Yes, Judit," she said quietly. "I will do this thing."

Jessica smiled with the other women. This was just the first of many rude surprises *Fribourg* had coming.

CHAPTER II

NILS SMILED TO HIMSELF.

Being First Lord of the Fleet had many perks, but today was one of the rare moments when he truly got to enjoy himself.

Ships were commissioned and decommissioned almost constantly, as construction met age and battle damage. He could not attend every ceremony personally, but he would not have missed this one for the world. That he was seeing the fruits of his own decade-long labors to get the Navy to this point was just icing on an otherwise lovely cake.

Nils looked around the Locking Station on this space dock. The space enclosed was huge, even by the standards of Fleet Headquarters. But it was both necessary and fitting.

Looking through the big bay window in the middle of the far wall, two meters tall and nine meters long, he could see the newest addition to the *Republic of Aquitaine* Navy getting ready to slip the reins and take to deep space.

No more Builders Trials. No more Acceptance Inspections. She had passed every step with flying colors, and stood ready. Poised. Dangerous.

Spacers were a superstitious lot. A ship did not get her name painted on the bow until she was ready to be *Accepted Into Service*, lest the gods and demons of deep space take offense.

Indeed, while her hull number was one of the first tasks on the list, a ceremony completed almost as soon as the first two planks were welded together, nothing more was done along those lines. Construction crews would only ever refer to her by that number after that.

Until she had a name.

Just an hour ago, a special crew, filled with some of the most senior staff at the foundry, had finished that last ceremonial touch. Nils was reasonably confident that Master Builders did not ever handle such tasks personally, regardless of their seniority, but today was special. That man had a personal connection to this project far and above the normal.

He had earned it.

For more than a year, she had been officially nothing more than hull number SC-006, the sixth Star Controller the *Republic of Aquitaine* Navy had built. They were the largest warships in space, combining the firepower of a Dreadnaught with the entire flight wing of a Fleet Carrier. With their escorts, they were pocket fleets unto themselves, able to do literally that, control the space around a star.

An hour ago, Miguel Keller had finished *Naming* this vessel, as far as the foundry was concerned. She could now be sent on her way.

Now the Navy took over. In the far distant past, the tradition had apparently been to shatter a bottle of champagne across the bow of a ship when commissioning her. That made sense in an era of water and wood. In the frozen depths of space, it was a waste of good champagne and an icy mess to clean up.

These days, the ship's Sponsor opened the official bottle, pouring the first glass for the Command Centurion who would take charge. For the last nine months, Denis Jež had been the senior officer in charge of construction oversight. That had been part of his reward for the years of service when he had been overlooked on the frontiers.

Before Jessica.

Nils looked around the crowd that had gathered, tearing his eyes away from the great, gray beast floating so close.

He missed standing on a deck in command, some days. Especially days like this. But there were other rewards.

The dock was filled with people, mostly Navy but with a significant civilian population as well. Today was something special for everyone.

He couldn't see Jessica, but that wasn't unexpected. She would be keeping a very low profile. This day belonged to Jež and she was a stickler for making sure her people got their chances to shine.

Jež himself was back in one corner, heads together with several other command centurions. Jessica's Merry Men, from what he could see. Dangerous conspirators, but only to Imperials.

Premier Chavarría was in another corner of the space, chatting with Tadej Horvat and several Senators and their families. That was where most of the civilians were keeping themselves.

Most of the space around him were uniforms. Nils had tried to keep as much of the crew of the old ship together as he could, retirements and promotions notwithstanding. He had done a pretty good job at it, since most of these people wanted to be here. There were even two extremely Senior Chiefs in engineering that had put off retirement specifically so they could be plank-holders, members of the first crew of this proud, new vessel.

A sound brought Nils back to the present from his wool-gathering.

A door had opened along one wall and the traditional Fife-and-Drum team was playing a marching tune as they slowly filed into the room, taking center stage, facing the now-silent crowd. Behind them, several rows of officers and crew lined up in formation as well.

Today was obviously going to be something more interesting than the normal ceremony.

Instead of the usual assortment of department chiefs facing the audience, the first row were all marines in dress uniforms, with polished swords in their hands instead of guns, led by Command Marine Centurion Phillip Crncevic, known universally around the fleet as *Navin the Black*. His skin was only dark brown, so Nils had always presumed he was nicknamed for some lost ancient pirate. He made a note to ask, sometime.

At the other end of the front row was newly-commissioned Centurion Vo Arlo, one of the heroes of *First Ballard*, and other, more recent adventures. Nils had read the file regarding the *Order of Baudin* award on the man's chest, and what had been required to receive it. Today, afterwards, would be Nils's first chance for a personal word with the man, a thank you for service so far above and beyond the call of duty.

But that was later. Right now belonged to Jež. He was content to remain down in the audience. That was another part of Denis's reward.

But Nils realized quickly that someone had choreographed the traditional Acceptance Ceremony in a very different direction.

Normally, a Fleet Lord would officially take possession of a new construction, formally inducting it into Naval Service. For a new Star Controller, Nils would be within his rights to claim the task himself.

But the man standing up there deserved this moment.

Nils knew that history would largely overlook Denis Jež. That was the downside of standing so close to someone like Jessica Keller. Tomas Kigali and Alber' d'Maine would be remembered as more than footnotes. And even, to a lesser extent, later heroes like Robbie Aeliaes.

But only hard-core historians and naval veterans would understand how much of her success relied on the competence and professionalism of the man who had been her First Officer during those fateful days.

Nils knew. He had read the reports after *First Petron* and *First Ballard*.

So Denis got today.

As the Fifes and Drums built, Denis Jež came out from the side, led by Tomas Kigali in his newly-adopted role as Mercury, Messenger for the Gods, and trailed by Alber' d'Maine and Robbie Aeliaes.

It was strange, seeing Jež as a Command Centurion, even today. But now he was their equal, their peer, in uniform as well as in service.

And today, their superior. Just as it seemed that everyone in the Navy was a Centurion together, all Command Centurions were created equal. What distinguished them was the vessel they commanded and her place in the line.

d'Maine and Aeliaes had already taken over newer commands and would be there with Jessica.

And Kigali couldn't be blasted out of *CR-264* to be promoted to a bigger vessel, threatening instead to simply resign and walk away if pushed. And that man would.

But Denis was taking command of something bigger. Something grander.

The music trailed away to silence.

From the left, a figure emerged from a small crowd and made her graceful way to the center of the room.

President of the Republic Calina Szabolcsi, today in formal robes that just made her even more beautiful, carefully carried a very old, very valuable bottle of champagne that had come from Tadej Horvat's personal cellars, specially picked for this occasion.

She was almost as tall as Jež normally. Eight-centimeter heels made her tower over almost everyone present. As if anyone could outshine the smile on Denis's face right now.

"Command Centurion Jež," she said formally, loud enough for the entire space to hear her. "It is my great pleasure to deliver to the Navy our latest vessel, SC-006. May she bear you well and far and always bring you home safe."

Denis nodded formally to her, almost a bow as he reached into a pocket and pulled out a sheet of heavy paper that he unfolded. His voice was uncharacteristically emotional as he spoke the words, but that could be forgiven, considering their weight.

'By will of the Republic of Aquitaine Navy and First Lord Nils Kasum, the undersigned, Command Centurion Denis Jež, is hereby ordered to report aboard the RAN Auberon at the earliest opportunity and take command, subject to the normal rules and regulations. He will exercise excellence and demand the same of his crew, that the whole reflect the greatest acclaim in serving the needs of the Republic and the will of the Senate.

SIGNED *on the Date of The Republic February 16, 396 by First Lord Nils Kasum and countersigned February 16, 396 by Denis Jež.'*

The crowd erupted in a loud round of applause and cheers.

Nils had been to many such ceremonies. Normally, they were sedate affairs, almost quaint. This was already far and away the loudest he could remember. These people brought out the emotion in such affairs.

Denis was much beloved and respected by his fellow officers, even the ones with a personal distaste for Jessica Keller. And everyone recognized what that giant vessel in the background represented.

Yesterday, the *Republic of Aquitaine* Navy had three Star Controllers in service: *Athena*, *Archimedes*, and *Amaravati*, commanding Home Fleet, First War Fleet, and First Border Fleet respectively.

RAN Auberon would anchor First Expeditionary Fleet.

After so many years on the defensive, everyone understood that the war had turned. Jessica Keller wasn't personally responsible for that. It came from the combined efforts of millions of men and women, but the Navy knew that she would be taking the war to the *Fribourg Empire* for them shortly.

The tip of the spear.

The *Fribourg Empire* knew that as well.

As the sound died down, the ceremony went sideways.

He should have expected that, with those four men in charge of planning.

Nils watched Denis turn to Alber' d'Maine with a smile and a very formal nod, before stepping back into line with the other officers.

d'Maine took four steps forward and scowled at the crowd, slowly, deliberately.

Gods, that man could scowl.

Something softened his look into merely a harsh smile. Nils was reminded of a drill instructor inspecting crew who were about to graduate from basic training. A proud hawk of a parent, thinking to himself what a fine crop of children he has molded.

"Training company," d'Maine commanded at the top of his lungs. "STAND TO!"

It had been more than thirty-five years since Nils had graduated from the Academy.

That didn't matter one bit.

Automatically, his hands snapped to his sides and his feet came together, shoulders back, head up. Just like he had then.

"Sir, yes, sir!" he called back, one of hundreds of such voices in perfect cadence and unison.

Some things went bone deep.

Alber' d'Maine actually smiled at the room at that point.

Nils didn't know the man *could* smile. Certainly, he couldn't remember ever having seen it happen.

d'Maine turned back to Denis Jež, grinning ear to ear.

"Command Centurion," d'Maine barked. "You have the deck."

d'Maine returned to his spot on the front row with the other three trouble-makers.

Jež stepped forward again. He looked out over the crowd for a moment before turning back and looking out the big window at the mighty warship parked so close.

He turned back and took a deep breath.

Nils was close enough to the man to see how close Jež was to tears at the emotion of the moment.

"Friends and fellows," Jež continued solemnly. "I want to thank you for joining me here today. For joining us."

He gestured back to encompass the three men immediately behind him, as well as the rows of assembled officers and crew behind them.

"We have been through the fires together," Denis continued. "At *Ballard*, we lost *Auberon* and *Rajput*, and many friends and fellows. Today we celebrate a new *Auberon* joining the fleet, a new beginning."

Denis paused and turned to look Nils directly in the face across the space. He nodded as the room grew very still.

"We are here because *Auberon* is a warship, and we are warriors," he continued. "But there is one other task we need to attend to today. Command Centurion Kigali, you have the deck."

Nils found himself holding his breath, along with eight hundred others.

Kigali stepped forward out of line and turned sideways as Jež returned to it.

"Color Guard, to your stations," he said simply, across a room that had grown deathly silent.

This wasn't anywhere in the Book of Ceremonies. Nils was certain of that. Over the last three years, he had personally seen to a generational review of those regulations.

It probably would be, tomorrow.

These people did that.

The Fifes and Drums started up again, slowly and quietly. It was a quiet, formal tune, almost a fighting song, compelling and penetrating at the same time.

The assembled crew split down the middle and turned inward, creating a hollow space surrounded on three sides by *Auberon*'s marines and open to the rest of the Navy and the Republic at the front.

"Draconarius," Kigali continued, his voice growing louder and heavier. "Present the colors."

Nils held his breath. *Draconarius* was an Army term, not something the Navy ever used.

Before today.

A compact female marine, no taller than Moirrey Kermode, but much broader and darker complected, stepped out of line and into the space at the center of the universe.

Nils knew Nadine Orly by reputation. She had been the smallest marine on the old *Auberon*, and, by reputation confirmed by Navin the Black and others, possibly the toughest and meanest. She had been *CVS Auberon*'s Flag Marine. Apparently she would hold the same role on *SC Auberon*.

She had been holding a rod in one hand instead of a sword, down by her side, when she entered, apparently, because it was there now and Nils hadn't seen where it came from.

Orly pushed a button on the side of the rod. It telescoped upward from just under one meter to nearly three with a sound like ten thousand dragons snapping their fingers.

She reached inside her jacket next and pulled out a bundle of cloth, reddish-gray and carefully folded. Nimbly, she pulled a corner of the cloth and attached it to the top of the pole, adding another corner a second later.

Yeoman Orly turned the flagpole back upright and planted it hard on the floor with a hollow thump.

Nils didn't need to see it splayed out in the wind to know that the triangular pennon displayed was *Auberon*'s battle flag. When Jessica had taken command of the old Strike Carrier, she had used that ship's flag as her own, operating as her own semi-unofficial flag officer on the borders.

Using it here, now, was a declaration of war, if he had ever seen one.

The rest of the room felt it as well. There was a powerful, unsettling energy everywhere suddenly. Like the whole universe was suddenly watching.

Orly nodded silently at Kigali.

He turned and looked over the rest of the room for several seconds before he spoke.

"Ladies and gentlemen," he commanded simply. "*RAN Auberon*."

The shocked silence was utterly deafening.

"Boss," Kigali said to one corner of the room with a brief nod and what Nils could only classify as an evil smile. "We're ready."

Movement on his left caught Nils's eye.

He hadn't seen Jessica earlier because she was apparently wearing a long, gray cloak over her uniform, making her appear like one of the civilians tucked back in that corner of the room.

She removed it now and handed it to her mother and father, standing with her.

Nils heard the whole room gasp.

He would have liked to have said she was out of uniform right now. But that would be untrue.

A *RAN* Centurion wore a simple uniform. Black slacks fit snug in order to get quickly into an emergency suit. Dark green tunic top, hip-length, with a black fabric stripe across the chest and onto the upper arms, and then dark green forearms. A chaos green undershirt showed two centimeters of mock turtleneck above the collar.

On the outer side of the left shoulder, the person's unit badge, be it flight wing, vessel, or station.

On the right arm, one bold stripe in white for a Centurion, two for a Senior Centurion, three for a Command Centurion.

For a Fleet Lord, as Jessica Keller was now, the uniform would be very similar to that of a regular Centurion. The tunic of a Fleet Lord was longer and generally tailored, with two vents on back on the corners. There would be white epaulets with bullion fringe on the shoulders and white cuffs. For the rank insignia, a single broad white stripe, twice the size of a Centurion's stripe, on the right arm.

Jessica Keller was not wearing a Fleet Lord's uniform today.

Black leggings and ship slippers. Those hadn't changed in centuries, a combination of tradition and functionality.

Jessica's tunic was identical to that of a Command Centurion, without any of the braid or accoutrements of a Fleet Lord, but done in pure white with dark green for the sides and upper arms, offset by white cuffs. On her left arm, *Auberon*'s badge. On her right arm, four green stripes encircled the muscles.

Because the *Republic of Aquitaine* Navy was a traditional place, the chapters on formal uniforms were never removed, just appended and expanded as styles and culture changed. The uniform for a Fleet Lord, and a First Fleet Lord, like the titles themselves, dated back just over seventeen decades, even as the Republic approached its fifth century.

Every morning, on his way to his office, Nils passed two portraits in what the Navy liked to call the *Hall of Heroes*, a long arcade with oil portraits of famous commanders. Membership on those walls was by accolade of the Navy, not command of the Senate.

Jessica was wearing the same uniform as those two men.

Nils Kasum might have promoted her to the rank of Fleet Lord as a preparation for what she was going to do next, but Jessica Keller had gone almost primordial in the process, back to the dawn of the Republic.

She was something the Navy hadn't seen in a very long time.

Nils Kasum could tell people, years from now, that he had been there when the next revolution occurred.

Instead of a Fleet Lord, Jessica Keller was announcing to the galaxy that she was warrior from the old days.

She was a Fleet Centurion.

CHAPTER III

DATE OF THE REPUBLIC FEBRUARY 16, 396
FLEET HQ, LADAUX SYSTEM

THERE WAS a tension to the room that had been absent thirty seconds ago.

Jessica took her spot at the right end of the front row with a smile, in line with Denis, Tomas, Alber', and Robbie. Calina stood some distance farther to her right, smiling warmly.

In front of her, the key players in the Republic, as well as the Navy. Among the civilians, Judit and Calina had known it was coming. Jessica's own mother, Indira, had known as well. It was she who had sewn the outfit in the strictest secrecy. And the boys had planned the entire sneaky affair for maximum effect.

The effect on the crowd and the photographers was electric.

For just a moment, Jessica smiled, sure that the Navy gossip tomorrow would be almost as intense as the planetary fashion boards, for the same reasons.

As the whispering finally died down, Jessica stepped forward out of line. Every eye in the place was on her.

"Forty-four months ago," she began, drawing those men and women into her orbit. "First Lord assigned me to the Strike Carrier *RAN Auberon* and tasked me with causing the *Fribourg Empire* grief."

She took a breath to order her thoughts. We have come so far, and yet we have only begun.

"It began at *2218 Svati Prime*," Jessica continued, pitching her voice to modulate both power and warmth, something else she had learned to do at Fleet Command School. "Surprise, as they teach us, occurs in the enemy commander's mind. It does not require you to kill planetfuls of people to defeat them."

She turned to pick out Nils in the crowd before her, and then Judit in the corner, and finally Calina, standing just to her right, but beyond a tremendous gulf of intent and experience from the men to her immediate left and the willing crew behind her.

"At *Petron*, we did defeat them," she said, letting some of the pain in her soul bleed out. She husbanded it carefully, so that she never forgot Daneel, but the entire Republic needed to know. Many in this room already did.

"At *Ballard*, we faced the greatest test yet," she remembered. "Their best, coming to attack the very bones upon which the Republic was founded."

She gestured behind her with her left arm, encompassing the two-hundred-odd marines and crew that represented the new *Auberon*, selected from veterans of that battle.

"The cost was atrocious, as these people can attest to," Jessica let her voice modulate down, drawing a thousand people tighter into her eyes, leaning forward and straining to hear her words.

"We killed two Imperial frigates and a light cruiser in that battle. Another frigate was badly wounded, along with a battlecruiser and Emmerich Wachturm's own *Blackbird*. *Rajput* had to be dismantled in orbit afterwards, broken nearly in two. *Auberon* retained just enough power to maneuver into a permanent orbit, a new museum to replace the famous university known as *Alexandria Station* before it was destroyed. Only luck and courtesy, Imperial as well as our own, kept the casualties of that day from reaching six figures."

Jessica turned to face the men and women behind her. Those faces were calm, serious, committed. Ready to go into the fires with her once more.

Hers.

"Today," she announced, speaking directly to her crew, but loud enough that her words would bounce off the bulkhead and be heard by everyone in the room. And possibly in a small, private chamber on the Imperial capital world, *St. Legier*. "We are going to take the war to the *Fribourg Empire*."

The room erupted into polite applause, the crew maintaining a dignified silence, but smiling.

When it quieted, she turned back to the rest of the Republic.

"Madame President," she announced. "Premier. First Lord. Assembled friends. If you will follow us, we have prepared a reception on *Auberon*'s Flight Deck. Command Centurion d'Maine, you have the deck."

She took her spot in the line next to a smiling Denis.

"*Auberon*," Alber' roared. "Left face. Color Guard, take the van."

Orly and her six escorts, the Fife and Drum team, went first. Engineering, Flight Deck, Operations, and various officers were mixed somewhat randomly in the next several lines.

The marines were the last to leave, followed only by the four Command Centurions and then Jessica. That was correct, in her mind, for those marines would be the first into the next battle, right behind her.

CHAPTER IV

EVERYTHING HAD BEEN A SUCCESS. The Acceptance Ceremony, the reception, the mingling.

But it was done now, and Jessica had a more important task today.

One of the few places she had taken advantage of her personal connections to the designers and builders of this grand vessel had been in modifying the secondary gym to fit her needs and desires.

The rest of the crew still had a grand space available, with dozens of machines clumped together like strange metal trolls exposed to dawn's light. There was still an attached pool in which to do laps, complete with airlock seals to contain it if the vessel ever lost power for the gravplates. Runners could still do laps on a six-lane track with transparent walls on the inside edge to the other folks exercising.

The crew of this ship deserved no less.

But she had pulled rank to have a few bulkheads shifted around. Just enough to create a proper training dojo. Old school. Sand packed tightly into flat, heavy, taupe, canvas bags and pounded down with human heels until it had all the texture and firmness of the one at the fleet training academy. Wood walls painted by hand with love.

Home.

Just inside the door, the clear space was two meters deep and ran the entire width of the space side to side. Here the floors were simple hull metal, painted the same bland off-white as the walls. Nothing to distract the eye when practicing, when centering.

The practice floor was up a half step, a lip that left no doubts as to your standing. Inside or outside.

Again, home.

Jessica was not the superstitious kind. And yet…

This would be the first time she dueled with her personal fighting robot aboard this vessel. She had not even brought it aboard until now.

In her heart, she knew that she kept fearing that the dreams would return. That she would fall back into that place where she had been after Daneel died. After the Goddess of War touched Jessica's soul and left her four-palmed mark.

She had not claimed this space as hers until now.

She could not.

It had required something greater first.

Not until her father had returned through the airlock and handed her the welding gun he had used to name this vessel, this *Star Controller Auberon*, did she believe that she wasn't dreaming.

Not until Orly planted her flag on the deck was it real.

She was a Fleet Lord now.

Not just a Command Centurion out fighting the war with the *Fribourg Empire*, subject to whatever trade winds and political machinations might drive her hither and yon.

No, she would shape it now.

Fleet Centurion was a statement of purpose. Another glove thrown down in Emperor Karl VII's path. A challenging slap ringing off both his cheeks.

Do your worst, Fribourg.

She had faced the Red Admiral. She and the Goddess had danced death with the man more than once and won.

She was still here, still breathing, still dangerous.

Jessica took a deep breath and pushed all that nervous energy down and in.

Other schools trained you to push it all out of yourself to find calm. *Valse d'Glaive*, the Waltz of Swords, took a different tack.

Energy was power. Pushing it out of yourself robbed you of it.

No, pull it in. Drag it down with your breathing. Force it to your very center.

Compress it like a fire diamond held three centimeters behind your navel. Let it power your movements, holding all of your anger, all of your loss.

Jessica let the fire fuse itself inside her.

There.

She took one moment to check herself before stepping onto the mat.

Bare feet to learn to feel the movement of the ground beneath her. Ankle-length forest green leggings tight across her muscles to keep them warm and keep her sweat from splashing. Running shorts in black. An old chaos green uniform undershirt that was too large for her. She had mostly worn it out and wore it to sleep in occasionally. Blood red ribbon to tie back her slowly-graying hair into a French braid that hung between her shoulder blades. Matching red cloth rolled up and tied across her forehead to keep sweat out of her eyes.

Jessica held both her blades loosely and let her muscles flow as she shifted her weight back and forth and popped her neck once. In her left hand, she held a long, straight, single-edged sword, what the combatants called a *saber*. Instead of something more exotic, it was made of simple steel. Tradition. In her right hand was a much shorter blade, also steel, but heavier, and with a reinforced cross-guard instead of the saber's basket protecting her fingers: the *main-gauche*. She had acquired this pair during her Academy days and kept them ever since.

Had it really been nearly twenty years ago?

Across the mat, her opponent awaited her with the patience that only a non-intelligent fighting robot could muster. It was humanoid in shape, male in size, armed with a long blade and a short one, just as she was. Right-handed to her left, as most of her opponents would be.

The robot's blades were dull, plastic affairs, excellent at leaving a good training welt or bruise, without drawing blood. Jessica's training blades were dull as well, but only because any edge put to them would be banged off quickly as she struck the thing's metal hide.

It was faceless and nameless. Much like her foe, the *Fribourg Empire*.

Karl VII had a name, as did Admiral of the Red Emmerich Wachturm, but neither of them was her opponent now. Karl was safe at home in his palace at *St. Legier*. Emmerich had been retired after the battle known as *First Ballard*, and was an Emeritus Professor of

Tactics at their equivalent of the *Republic of Aquitaine*'s Fleet Academy. His students, young and old, would be her adversaries tomorrow.

Jessica had already stretched and warmed up before she'd stepped into the room.

She shrugged and dropped into a fast squat once, bouncing back up to make sure everything was still flexible.

"Fighting Robot activate," she called across the space. "Challenge Rating Five."

Five was enough today.

Jessica didn't have anything to prove to the robot. Only to the universe. She was not working out aggression nor sadness.

No, today, she was dedicating this space to the art of arms. Making it a Temple of War, a sanctuary for the Goddess of War herself.

Kali-ma.

Plus, she wanted to make sure she beat the damned thing the first time she fought it aboard her brand new starship.

Okay, maybe a little superstitious.

After all, Challenge Rating Six was for experts. Her on a good day. Seven was for masters of the blade and the dance. The man who had first introduced her to *Valse d'Glaive* has assured her that the number of people capable of regularly taking on a fighting robot above Rating Seven could be counted on two hands, not including himself in that number.

At one point, two years ago, after *First Petron,* she had been good enough to take the robot nine falls in fifteen at Challenge Rating Eight for a good run of time. Theoretically, it went all the way up to Ten, but she had never met anyone capable of actually beating it at that level.

She had only tried Nine a handful of times, when she was at her very best.

At the time, Jessica had been unwilling to dedicate her entire life to the kind of training regime necessary to maintain that level of skill. She had lost Daneel, and that rage had only fueled her for so long.

No, be honest, you do spend that much time thinking about it, training for it. But not for the fighting robot. For Karl. For Fribourg. *A different kind of hatred, but no less felt.*

Jessica smiled to herself. She did work that hard, but it was now on the strategic planning and tactical modeling necessary to win the Eternal War, not just to beat a simple fighting robot.

In that field, she was already at Challenge Rating Nine.

"Combat Mode initiated," a soothing woman's voice replied. "Challenge Rating Five confirmed."

Jessica pushed it all down into the fire diamond in her belly, gripped the stone like death itself, and let her movements become automatic.

CHAPTER V

DATE OF THE REPUBLIC FEBRUARY 17, 396
BRANI, LADAUX

"I AM BEING SERIOUS," Wakely replied, somewhat indignantly. "It will be perfectly safe."

"Mom, you're going to be in a war zone," Thana retorted.

Her daughter couldn't get too worked up, with a six-month-old boy quietly nursing at one breast, but she could still convey a wealth of emotion with just her tone and her eyes. And stubbornness, but she got all that from her father's side of the family.

Okafors were all meek and retiring creatures, didn't you know?

Thana's living room was small and cozy, with an overstuffed sofa covered in gray where Wakely sat and a century-old wooden rocking chair where Thana held her son Viri, rocking as the little man had his lunch.

"And I will be protected by a huge fleet AND Jessica Keller, Thana," Wakely said.

They had already gone over this several times. And her eldest was just as stubborn as she was.

Maybe Thana got some of the stubbornness from her mother after all, and not just Torvald.

After all, Dr. Torvald Kijek had his own students to look after, and had taken a phlegmatic approach to her planned, year-long sabbatical into the Empire. There hadn't been enough time for him to apply for a leave of absence, so he would stay home and watch over the grandkids.

"Mom, it's Jessica Keller," Thana said with exasperation. "Isn't she the boogie-man to these people?"

Technically? Probably. Although they would consider themselves too sophisticated to admit it in public.

Certainly the creature from their worst nightmares. And she was coming for them.

But Wakely had also studied as much as she could of the *Fribourg Empire*. There were very stringent rules around how the two sides would behave in these circumstances, magnified by the fact that Jessica was involved.

If they managed to drive Jessica Keller off and retake the planet, Wakely Okafor would be operating under long-agreed-upon rules of civilian management. Depending on the circumstances, they might actually leave her in place as a ruling Governor for as much as a year, while they sorted out how they wanted to reorganize things.

Weirder things had happened. Granted, usually it had been a new Imperial overlord installed over an existing Republic government, after a world had fallen. But there were rules.

At worst, a year as a visiting professor on *St. Legier* while negotiations went on.

And that assumed anyone could defeat Jessica Keller. She could tell her daughter that, but it wouldn't make any difference. This was her oldest child suddenly without her mother. Wakely had sent her own mother an invite to come for an extended stay on *Ladaux* to spend time with the grandchildren and great-grands, but Wakely would be gone before her mother arrived.

That was one thing about the military. When they decided to move, there were no extended committee investigations that might wind on for years before a presentation to the Provost.

Decide. Go.

"And she would not be able to do this without me," Wakely said simply.

Truth.

Jessica was brilliant. Wakely had known that before her very-famous student first set foot in that classroom. Determined in ways that set her apart even from the other Command Centurions who were her peers.

And damaged.

Wakely had read certain reports compiled by the First Lord's office, spoken with the man himself on two occasions to brief him on the status of his favorite charge. Things she would never tell Jessica, but enough to know what would be safe ground, and how to establish some borders that might help the woman heal, at a time when she might have simply given up and walked away.

Not that Wakely could ever imagine Jessica surrendering to life, but she had seen it in the younger woman's eyes now and again. Less so, today, but there, nonetheless.

"Guilt?" Thana probed, bringing Wakely suddenly back to the present.

"No, Thana," she replied. "Opportunity."

"How so?"

What to tell her *very civilian* daughter? How to put her mind at rest, with a fussy newborn?

She leaned close, carefully touching foreheads with her eldest.

Things whispered in secrecy.

"It was my idea, child," she said quietly. "Jessica Keller might be the sword, but I planted that seed. I was the one who suggested to her how it might be done. Showed her where. I should be there to watch that flower bloom."

"But you're a civilian, mom."

"Does that make me any less of a patriot?" Wakely snapped quietly. "Would you like to live in a place like *Fribourg*, a woman in a man's world? And let us not forget that they are aristocrats there. You would be gravel beneath the feet of some important Duke or noble, were the roles reversed."

Things you never even tell your husband.

Thana's eyes got big.

"You're serious," she whispered, carefully adjusting her son to her other breast.

"There was a time, daughter," Wakely quietly agreed. "I could have gone to the Academy and been a fleet officer instead of going into academia. It would have been a very different life for me. I might have been Jessica Keller, Thana."

No. There was only one Jessica Keller.

That woman was one in a century. But there could have easily been a Command Centurion Okafor out there today. Possibly even Fleet Lord.

No, Fleet Centurion.

Jessica was going to remake *Aquitaine* in her own image.

Her co-conspirators should pay attention to the little details if they were going to help her.

35

CHAPTER VI

DATE OF THE REPUBLIC MARCH 2, 396 FORT GUTHRIE, PEILLON, LADAUX

"CHIEF," a man's voice called as Dashyl leaned on the split-rail fence and stared at the new daystar that had just appeared in the otherwise-empty, eastern afternoon sky. It was quickly growing larger as she watched. Probably wasn't a good omen. "Do we know when whatever's supposed to be happening?"

She turned to look at the soldier, her Patrol Decurion, walking towards her across the corral. Tariq Azarola was a tall man, taller than even her own lanky height, and built pretty average for a man, compared to her own skin, bones, wires, and attitude problems. But his black eyes didn't miss much, which was frequently why they were all still alive.

Dashyl tilted her hat back enough that the sun could sneak past the brim and light up her face as she wiped one hand down to clear some of the dust off of it. Currying her roan mare, Göll, was always a dusty affair. She really wanted a shower right now, but figured that the ship coming in wouldn't let her.

Instead, she pointed behind him at the light growing brighter.

"Probably," she said laconically to the man. "Right about now."

He turned to look over a shoulder, grunted something vaguely obscene, and set his fists on his hips.

"Suppose the Primus Pilus or the Legate knows?" he asked after a moment.

"You volunteering to go tell them, Azarola?" she asked with a tease.

"No, sir, Patrol Centurion," he grinned back. "That's stuff for officers. I'm going to go get first in line for dinner. Y'all will have to have a friendly meeting, and be all formal-like for a bit. Hopefully I can get the first food, the first shower, and a quick nap before the flag goes up."

He smiled at her and began to move quickly in the direction of the main barracks.

Patrol Centurion Dashyl Mitja made a face, straightened everything out, and brushed off her uniform as much as she could after a day of hard field exercises, then started to walk the other direction. Fourth Saxon Legion had only been on *Ladaux* for a little over three weeks. Enough time for the horses to settle and start getting frisky, not so long that her troopers were at risk of doing the same.

Overhead, the first roar of engines as the star began to resolve itself into a DropShip.

That brought her up a little short. First off, people normally came to visit in Administrative Shuttles. Much smaller. Easier to fly. Better equipped. Much more refined for the tastes of Fleet Lords and Legates and Senators.

Second, what fool painted a DropShip bright red?

DASH LOOKED around the main briefing room with a hard eye. The newcomers were sure to make life far more interesting than she would have imagined when she got out of bed this morning to muck out stalls with her Patrol.

And the Legate hadn't chased her off, even if the meeting was really supposed to be for himself and the four Cohort Centurions. She had kind of fallen in with the other group, the strangers, when they landed and then come along with them for the ride.

It wasn't like she needed sleep that bad. And she might as well get it all from the horse's mouth.

Plus, the strangers were about as odd a group as she liked to expect.

It was plumb obvious who Fleet Lord Keller was, except she was Fleet Centurion Keller now, according to all the gossip, and had all the important folks in a right lather.

And Dashyl recognized Command Centurion Hường Haukea, commander of the Assault Carrier *Abbotsford*, the big ship that was kind of Fourth Saxon's personal taxi these days.

The rest were a mixed bag.

By uniform, the gigantic black guy with a shaved head and a gray van dyke was a fleet marine. High ranking if three stripes meant Command Centurion, like she thought she remembered. Dash was tall for a girl. She might have come up to the guy's jawbone. And weighed maybe a third of what he did. Monster from a nightmare, with a warm and friendly smile, like he could read minds. Which might have made it worse.

Next to him was a compact Korean woman, maybe a meter-fifty-five, meter-sixty, who probably outweighed Dashyl despite only coming up to *her* mouth. But that looked like it was all muscle. Probably gristle and bile, too, considering the uniform patches meant Heavy Armor. Lumbering turtles who could never find anything without her scouts going out and hunting it down for the big jobbers to shoot.

Loud, stinky, and annoying. And their tanks were worse.

In the middle of the group was a woman who looked like a native of Zanzibar: tall, chocolate, and athletic. Fierce. She was a civilian, but somehow managed to look like a unicorn in a herd of donkeys rather than a dandelion in a bouquet of roses. Considering all the uniforms, her presence said something very interesting, Dash just didn't ken what yet.

The others were staff and support, like the other big marine Centurion, almost the size of his boss, plus a couple of bodyguards trying to look innocuous and paranoid at the same time.

The only one that looked halfway interesting was the bald guy with the ginger handlebar mustache. He was tall and skinny, just like her. Keller had introduced him simply as *Gaucho*. And he was wearing a cowboy hat similar to what her unit wore, which was absolutely not standard issue on a starship. Plus, the hat was beat to hell, so it was something he wore a lot.

To top it all off, he was the crazy sombitch that flew that crimson DropShip.

And he was kinda cute.

JESSICA COULDN'T HELP but smile at the image. Fourth Saxon Legion's Legate had the erect carriage and bowed legs of a lifetime spent in the saddle. Ten thousand years of star flight, and the *Republic of Aquitaine* still fielded an entire legion of men and women riding horses into battle.

And not just horse infantry, the kind that used the big beasts merely as transport.

No, Fourth Saxon was an actual, dedicated Hussar, a term she'd had to dig up and translate from the ancient texts Suvi had once saved from being lost forever.

But for what Jessica had in mind, they were exactly what she wanted.

The Legate sat across from her now, with the rest of the two staffs mixed randomly, rather than fussing over pack hierarchy and seniority issues. That was a good sign. And one of the reasons she had picked Fourth Saxon in the first place.

Jessica let the man study her for a few moments. Ground forces ranks were not immediately comparable to the *RAN*, but the two of them were nominally peers, and all of his Cohort Centurions would be roughly equivalent to her Command Centurions.

But there would be no doubt of his place in the pecking order. The orders she had in her pocket declared her *Margrave*, and Wakely *Palsgrave* for the coming mission. Military Commander of the System and Civilian Governor.

Legate Declan Burdge would be in command of his own troops, and the attached heavy armor element, once they were on the ground and in the field.

Jessica knew, from studying his extensive campaign record, that she could trust his judgement. He needed to know he could trust her. That was why she had flown down here, to his turf, rather than ordering him to call upon her aboard *Auberon*, as nice as that might have been.

Apparently, he saw something he liked.

"Fleet Centurion," Burdge drawled with a relaxed nod. His glance around to his people let them know, as well.

"Legate," Jessica answered. She knew all of the faces in the room. She turned to look at the one that probably didn't belong, considering the rest, before she returned to Burdge.

"Should Patrol Centurion Mitja be here?" Jessica asked the man.

Jessica watched the woman blink in surprise.

"Dash is Scout Patrol, First Cohort, Fleet Centurion," the man answered. "She'll be the tip of the spear when we get there. Wherever there is."

Jessica knew that. She already had memorized the names and faces of all of the three Cohort's Patrol Centurions, as well as the leaders of *LVIII Armored Ala Heavy*, starting with Cohort Centurion Rebekah Kim, who had ended up on the other side of Vo Arlo from where Jessica sat now.

Good enough.

Jessica nodded.

"For operational security, there will be a full briefing packet available once the Legion is loaded aboard *Abbotsford* and we transition to JumpSpace," Jessica said. "For now, let me say that we'll be hitting and occupying an Imperial world for an extended period. The terrain is rough, and I expect the local security forces to fade into the bush and undertake a guerilla war."

The faces around her had been serious. Now they were intense, almost images graven in stone.

"Infantry is good for holding ground, and we'll have some with us aboard *Auberon*," she continued. "But there are no roads in most places, and a great many trees and mountains, so wheeled and tracked Heavy Scouts and Rapid Assault forces would be a sub-optimal solution."

She took a moment to fix each of them with a hard smile.

"This place was made for horses."

"I would have to check, Commander," the woman at the left end of the table spoke up with a soft tone and a beguiling smile. "But I don't remember Fourth Saxon ever operating with heavy armor before."

Jessica smiled back at the implied dig at what would be the Fourth Cohort when it was formally attached. First Cohort Centurion Eko Tri was *Primus Pilus* for the Fourth Saxon, literally *First Spear*. She was the field commander for the Legion. *LVIII Heavy* would come under her orders.

She was a small woman, lush with curves and black hair, and a debutante manner, according to the personnel files. But she could make dock-workers blush and teach them new profanities when she was pissed, according to some of the people Jessica had asked.

It might be fun to watch her and Rebekah angry at one another.

Jessica already knew from personal experience that the tank commander was abrasive and opinionated on topics she considered herself expert in.

And less than happy about being attached to a horse unit, herself.

Oil and water. Maybe with fire thrown in.

"It has only happened once, Primus Pilus," Jessica fired back, just as sweetly. "One hundred and twenty-six years ago, for a single campaign season."

"It seems such an unnatural combination," Tri smiled politely at Rebekah Kim.

As if putting honey on the blade somehow made the razor cuts less painful.

Jessica could almost hear Kim grind her teeth, but the woman kept her peace. She and Rebekah had already discussed in good detail what was likely to happen at this meeting.

Fourth Saxon were an ancient, proud, independent, and very hard-headed group.

"On the contrary, Tri," Jessica fired back, just as nice. "It makes perfect sense. The cavalry runs them to ground. They will be dug in like ticks on the back of a hound, so using artillery to take them down will be an expensive and time consuming undertaking. But a Squadron of sixty-six millimeter particle cannons, sitting on a distant ridge, will be just the way to kick the door in."

The Primus Pilus subsided after a moment with a nod, allowing Jessica the point. Fourth Saxon could be prickly, but they were all professionals. Kim managed not to say anything that would require smoothing out later.

Jessica let the air bleed out of the room for a moment before she continued.

"I wanted to introduce you to two members of my staff who will be working in close concert with Fourth Saxon in the field," she continued, pointing at the two men in question.

"*Gaucho* is the pilot of *Cayenne*, the DropShip that brought me down here today," she said. "You're going to work with my Flight Deck engineers to reconfigure her to haul horses into hot drops and provide close support and resupply."

It wasn't a question. She didn't want them to think this was optional. She had promised *Gaucho* more excitement on this campaign.

"Is he any good?" the Legate fired back, ignoring everyone but her.

"How's about you bring all eight of your pilots off *Abbotsford* and the whole gang off *Achaemenes*," Gaucho smiled back. "And we'll have a rodeo to see. M'okay?"

Jessica grinned slightly. *Gaucho* could fend for himself. There might be one or two pilots in those groups that could match him for pure flying skill. And maybe another couple that matched him for crazy.

But those weren't the same pilots. *Gaucho* was *Gaucho*.

The Legate saw it as well. He grinned knowingly back. The Primus Pilus wasn't as convinced, nor was Mitja. They'd probably have to find out the hard way. Jessica made a note to have *Gaucho* pack extra air-sickness bags. She wondered if horses puked.

"This is the other," Jessica continued, pointing. "Centurion Vo Arlo. He'll be handling tactical communications to the fleet and air elements. I want him trained up as a full cavalry trooper so he can be on point with your teams."

Jessica had made Arlo wear his formal dress uniform today, instead of his field uniform. There were two medals that got everyone's attention when they turned to look at him. The Republic Cross was the second highest medal the *Republic of Aquitaine* Navy awarded. It could only be won in combat, and was frequently posthumous. It was also known as the First Lord's medal, since that luminary had to personally sign off on the award.

It was the other one that she wanted them to notice. Rather than a simple ribbon they might not identify at first glance, he was wearing the full medal for the *Order of Baudin*, the second highest *civilian* award the Republic offered. The smaller version was a metallic red circle with Henri Baudin's tiny face etched on, hanging from a green ribbon. Today's version, the larger, formal one affixed to his chest, was the size of Arlo's palm, and Baudin's smiling face could be clearly recognized.

It was not a common thing to see in military circles. The Legate might be awarded one as a reward for a lifetime of service when he retired. That was one of two ways, and usually the more common.

Dashyl Mitja broke the ice.

"So how did you get the *Order of Baudin*, Arlo?" she asked laconically.

Jessica watched Vo size up the woman. She didn't flinch, even though the look on his face might have been used to polish stone. Nobody at this table was likely to flinch.

"Shooting pretty girls," Vo finally replied in a heavy voice.

Not the way Jessica would have described Arlo's adventures on *Quinta*, but probably closer to how he actually felt about the affair. She'd have to work on that.

Because she was already looking that direction, Jessica caught Kim's glance at the big man, and the small smile and nod that accompanied it.

"Can you ride a horse?" Mitja countered. It wasn't hostile, but it was certainly their measure of worth.

"Not today, Patrol Centurion," he said simply. "I will by the time it becomes necessary."

Nothing more, just that simple promise. The riders in the room all nodded to themselves and turned to Jessica at the same time.

"Can you depart in seven days?" Jessica asked the Legate.

His face got a mischievous look to it.

"Four, if'n you're in a hurry, Fleet Centurion," he replied with a long drawl.

"Make it six, then," she said. "*LVIII Heavy* is already mounted up, but we'll need to lay in a freighter full of hay to keep Fourth Saxon happy. And then we're going hunting, ladies and gentlemen."

CHAPTER VII

DATE OF THE REPUBLIC MARCH 3, 396 SC
AUBERON. LADAUX SYSTEM

THE WEE LITTLE whistles were really the silliest part of the whole thing, if Moirrey had to pick out just one. Not that she prolly coulda.

One whole engineering bay had been converted to what her team called the playroom, twenty-five meters long and nearly half that wide, emptied to the bulkheads, and then filled back in with an honest-to-goodness toy train set. Filled with wee, little trains going hither and yon at her beck and call as she sat in one corner over a control board that looked lots like a sound board in a dance hall.

It were hard not to giggle maniacally at the power. Almost as good as getting out the glitter gun.

Still, time to get back to work.

Moirrey shut everything down and watched the four-centimeter engines and cars come to a sudden halt in their little town. In the real world, they'd like to coast a ways afore friction caught up.

She'd hadta had a couple of her girls work out a computer program to practice the fine art of getting up a head of steam and letting a stack of cars go softly. It were kinda like the ancient sport o' curling, but without the ice or the brooms. And way bigger booms when your rocks collided.

And damned if Oz didn't have seven of the top ten scores. It were not fair how good that man was.

Still, she was the undisputed master of stripping and rebuilding the prototype ion-electric locomotive they had built in the next bay over. Nobody could touch her times. Not even Oz.

Moirrey stood up and studied the layout of the track one last time. Her team had built it from drawings she had worked up, but only she an' her boss, Command Engineering Centurion Ozolinsh, *Oz*, had seen the actual super-secret airborne pictures of the place, to know that the big switching yard were more than just a fancy.

They'd all finds out soon enough. Right sure.

Then the funs would begin.

OUTSIDE, Engineering were in a fine pickle this morning when Moirrey emerged from her break and put her officerness back on. Yeoman Robles had that look on her face.

Moirrey walked up and tried to estimate it, based purely on the amount of fidgeting her assistant couldn't contain.

It were a mixed bag. Hard to tell.

"Oz?" she hazarded a guess. If it were big, Oz woulda pinged her, but he might wait fer now and have Saana standing right here.

"Digger," the woman replied, her short red hair bobbing.

Crap. Nothing Moirrey could foist off on anyone else. Oz had foisted Digger and his men off on her in the first place.

"Here or there?" Moirrey asked.

"He would greatly appreciate your calling on him in Marine Bay Six at your earliest convenience," Saana repeated, mimicking Digger's tone almost perfectly, if up nearly an octave.

Six? They must be playing with the big toys.

Still, Oz had put her in charge of it. And Lady Keller were counting on her to make everytin' smooth-like.

"Right," Moirrey said. "No time like d'present. Let's go bug Digger and make him buy us beer."

"Right behind you, sir," Saana smiled as Moirrey started moving. Yeoman Robles were at least half a head taller, and it were all legs, so she could keep up, even when Moirrey's shorter legs were churning in a blur.

Marine Bay Six were huge. And a mess. It took her stopping four of Digger's people at different times and getting re-directed afore she found the man.

She shoulda knowed to find him in the *John Henry*. It were his baby. All the other heavy earthmoving equipment in the bay come in a distant second to his first love.

"Digger," she yelled as she came through the hatch in the big boring machine's butt.

Another one of Digger's people stuck a head out of an engine room and waved her closer.

Digger had apparently heard her coming. He managed to get out of the engine compartment he had been face down in and was standing by the time she and Saana entered the compartment.

She smiled up at him. Unlike her tinyness, he were average height. And average build. And average looks. And off-the-charts smart, like 3D puzzle-box solver.

All kinds a'sexy.

"Senior Centurion Wolanski," Moirrey oozed sweetness all over his name. "You rang?"

"Very funny, Moirrey," he said, grabbing a towel off a counter and wiping *something* off of his hands.

Better not asking.

"I appreciate operational security," he continued, trying to act serious-like. "But we're all loaded and not going anywhere. You could tell us what kind of terrain we'll be encountering so we can change out the cutting face on the boring machine."

Old bulldog, slobbered-all-over-bone. Still, he had managed to go two whole days since the last time he asked.

"Not my place, Digger," Moirrey replied with a grin. "Lady Keller wants to tell everyone at once, and not all the cowfolk gots loaded yet."

"It will take a week to tune, Moirrey," he pleaded unconvincingly.

"And it'll take at least four weeks ta gets there, Digger," she fired back.

"But you know where we're headed?" he got a sly tone to his voice. "What we'll be doing?"

"Building roads, bridges, and tunnels, Digger," she let some of her exasperation show. "Is why we loaded a whole Construction Ala in addition ta all the marines we'd normally take. More'n'at, I'm no at liberty to discuss. Anything else?"

He still had that sly look. That *up-to-no-good* look she recognized from th'mirror.

"Well," he drawled sideways, all relaxed and circumspect alls of sudden-like. "I was about to head for chow and maybe a pint. Care to join me and discuss other matters?"

Moirrey thought about letting that one go.

Still…

"Oh, what the hell," she replied, turning to Saana. "Hungry?"

"Oh, no, sir," Saana said quickly, stepping back out the door and half turning. "I have a bunch of paperwork that needs doing."

"Paperwork, Robles?"

"Aye, sir," Saana smirked at her just before vanishing from sight. "With you officers partying all the time, someone's gotta keep things running."

And then she were gone.

And all Digger's folks were suddenly clustered around the hole in the floor, all serious and intense-like. Totally ignoring the two of them.

What were he up to?

CHAPTER VIII

DATE OF THE REPUBLIC MARCH 4, 396 CAX
SHIVAJI. LADAUX SYSTEM

THE WORDS WERE SO wrong-headed that Alber' had a hard time making sense of them.

"Do you ever get tired of flying experimental warships, d'Maine?" Fleet Centurion Keller asked him, as they stood on the bridge of *RAN Shivaji*. The prototype for a prospective whole new class of warships.

His bridge.

And possibly the most dangerous warship in the fleet. Not just kilo for kilo, either.

Take a Founder Class Heavy Cruiser. Strip out the missile racks and storage. Fill all that sudden emptiness with auxiliary generators and batteries. Lots of them. Mount a turret midship, like a frog sitting on a crocodile.

Fill said turret with a twin Type-4 mount.

Station-class weaponry. An order of magnitude bigger than the Type-3's and bigger than the Primaries. Greater range and ferocity than anything else that moved, except Mobile Defense Platforms.

Alber' looked over at his commander. He understood that she was a warrior in the pure sense, but some days she obviously just did not get him.

With the heavy destroyer *Rajput*, he had killed a light cruiser in single combat. *Shivaji* might be able to duel with a battleship. He looked forward to the chance.

"Never," he settled for, unwilling to insult the woman who helped him commit his deadly art in space.

She nodded up at him with a knowing grin.

Up?

It was always odd to realize how small Fleet Centurion Keller was in person. In height, merely average for a woman.

Alber' was a little below average for a man, and much broader, but she still barely came up to his eyes in person.

In his mind, she was always so much bigger, grander. One of the Norse Giantesses that the gods fell in love with in all the stories. A force of nature, perhaps, more than a person.

And not his type at all. But then, he didn't have a type.

He had an *obsession*.

Alber' knew that *RAN* folks whispered stories about Fleet Centurion Keller. At least those who didn't *know*.

Alber' knew the truth. Knew that underneath the stories and legend was a woman who was still mostly human.

At one time, he had probably been human as well, but Alber' had given up trying to be normal a very long time ago.

The person closest to actually understanding him was probably Tomas Kigali. That man understood what a Vow of Excellence was, what it meant.

What it cost.

For Kigali, feats of navigation that made the history books.

For Alber', warfare.

If he followed any Siren, it would probably be Otrera, Goddess of War, and not one of the softer, weaker deities.

Mere moments had passed. Fleet Centurion Keller was studying his face, possibly reading his soul.

She was rumored to have that power.

"*Simeon*," she said simply, referencing a planetary system, but more importantly, a state of mind. An important shorthand among Command Centurions.

The Navy's primary training facility. Capable of handling everything from the smallest Extended Range Patrol Vessels up to full battle fleets.

"Lane Seven?" he asked, trying to suppress the hope in his voice.

Shivaji had run Lane Three several times when they were working out how to best handle a vessel with such extreme range and far less close-in firepower. It had been an interesting test, evaluating all the theories and then adjusting them for reality. And a good test for as much of his old crew from *Rajput* as he had been able to bring with him.

Silly Naval Architects tended to be far too conservative in their estimates. Yet another reason to bring warriors.

Fleet Centurion Keller did smile this time.

"Yes, Alber'," she said. "Lane Seven. Double arrowhead on the destroyers. *Nyamboya*, then *Shivaji*, then *Auberon*, with *Ishfahan* and *Ballard* on the rear flanks."

Something sour must have shown in his face.

Keller didn't speak. Just raised an eyebrow at him, like a teacher waiting for an apt pupil to speak up.

"A third arrowhead would be more effective," Alber' said quietly. "Put *Ishfahan*, with all those missile racks, on the hot corner up front as a shield, and *Ballard*, with her sensor suite and defensive guns, on the other side. *Shivaji* trailing a battlecruiser like *Nyamboya* will range on a single target at the same time, which nobody will be expecting. Three of the destroyers are Escort Carriers. Nine fighters there, plus *Auberon*'s eighteen and the heavy wing. Plus all the GunShips we have. Plus *Gaucho*. Tsunami."

"Most of the commanders in the Navy would also send the flight wings down a different Lane for training," Keller proposed. It sounded like a test.

"There won't be separate battles at *Thuringwell*, Fleet Centurion," Alber' observed quietly.

"No there won't," Keller agreed with a sure nod. "If we're lucky, there won't be anything heavier than a corvette."

"On the contrary, Fleet Centurion," he said with a feral smile. "If we're lucky, there will be an entire Imperial battle squadron there that's just big enough to think they can stop us."

CHAPTER IX

DATE OF THE REPUBLIC APRIL 1, 396 SC
AUBERON. SIMEON SYSTEM

THE OLD *AUBERON* hadn't had the sorts of true Flag facilities to host a proper event like this. But she had been a Strike Carrier, modified up from a Heavy Cruiser hull to use every cubic centimeter of interior space for the flight wing.

For Jessica, that was one of the most interesting parts of this new *Auberon*.

This mammoth ship, this beast, was a Star Controller. A monster of a ship. All of a Dreadnaught's guns and shields. All of a Fleet Carrier's Flight Wing capacity. They were the biggest warships in space by sheer enclosed volume. The *Fribourg Empire* had never built anything to this scale, preferring to spend their time on mere battleships instead.

Lane Seven had been just as much excitement and fuck-up as she had been expecting, with a whole new team of ships and crews that had never worked together before.

Still, that was why she'd ordered that run. To learn.

They would run it again tomorrow, and the results would be better. Or else.

Jessica looked over the crowd of people standing around with wineglasses, nearly filling the grand ballroom, and smiled. Most *Fleet Lords* would have only invited the nineteen Command Centurions to something like a cocktail party, putting them together as a group so they could let their hair down and chat as elite peers.

As a Fleet Centurion, she had specifically limited the invitation to the number of people that could fit onto a single administrative shuttle. And Kigali had apparently been pushing the envelope on the life support rating of his, to see people keep emerging from it like some sort of clown car.

Jessica smiled internally.

Lane Seven was programmed to be a bitch. She needed Kigali.

And she was very, very happy that Kigali had refused to let himself be promoted out of *CR-264*. Not just because she had won a bet with Calina. Having the little escort in front of her today, as always, like the horn on a unicorn, had kept them from being hit at least four times, any of them hard enough to have been crippling.

First Lord had tried to promote Tomas Kigali to a bigger vessel, several times. Jessica had to give Nils credit for tenacity. His mistake had been trying to offer the man a Survey Cruiser like *Ballard*. She might be brand new, and certainly capable of the sorts of sailing and navigation feats that *CR-264* was famous for, but she had one problem.

"Survey Cruisers don't kill things," Kigali has apparently stated flatly, almost rudely, when interviewed informally on the topic by the First Lord, followed by a raft of profanities Kigali had picked up on various planets along the way.

Command Centurion Haukea had taken a very liberal interpretation of the invitation as well, flying sixty folks over in one of her DropShips instead of an administrative shuttle. Still, that meant all of the centurions from Fourth Saxon were here, mingling with tankers from *LVIII Heavy*, Wolanski's Construction teams, and a mess of *RAN* crew and pilots.

At least Jessica had warned the mess hall to expect locusts.

Jessica took the last sip of wine from her glass and nodded to Enej Zivkovic, her Flag Centurion, standing close by.

He smiled back and put his thumb and middle finger in his mouth. Jessica had never learned how to make a sound like an air-raid siren with her mouth. She didn't need to. Not with Enej around.

The room fell to stillness quickly, followed by the rustling of cloth as everyone tuned to face her.

How many Fleet Lords did she know who would spend twenty minutes making speeches right now, working themselves and their command centurions up into a false lather of excitement?

That wasn't her style. The mob in front of her had gotten thirty minutes of mixing and drinks under their belts already. The cooks had made good use of the extra time.

She pointed at double doors opening in the far wall.

"Ladies and gentlemen," she called. "The buffet has been prepared. The Chief of the Wardroom has assigned seating randomly, and there will be briefing packets, waterproofed, on the tables, waiting for you."

That got a laugh. Working dinners were common in the *Republic of Aquitaine* Navy, and notoriously messy.

"Our target is the Imperial planet of *Thuringwell*," Jessica continued. "This is not a hit and run raid, but a full invasion with the intent to hold the planet for an extended period of time. Possibly forever. *Operation Harbinger*. We'll do Q&A after dessert."

Navin the Black took charge at this point. It might be her party, but it was his house. And nobody was going to argue much with that man, except maybe Moirrey.

Jessica would put her money on the female engineer in that conflict.

Quickly, the crowd turned and began to move away from her, like a bathtub where the plug has been pulled.

Jessica took a deep breath.

She had spent over a year planning this project. And she'd had help from experts like Wakely and a host of Navy Librarians too big to name.

Now she was going to turn it over to a mob of cowgirls and tankers, and let them figure out how to execute it.

She finally understood why Nils's hair had gone white.

<hr>

"WHY *THURINGWELL*?" a voice asked from one of the tables to her right.

Jessica turned that direction, trying to pick out the speaker from a mob of faces, some of which she knew, most of which were newcomers.

Centurion Mitja halfway raised her hand to take credit for the question. She looked a little nervous.

Still, it was a good question. And it was better than some of them she might have expected with a group this large and diverse.

Things like: *Are you nuts? Invade an entire planet?*

What the hell good do you think horses will be, anyway?

And is the fleet going to abandon us if somebody screws up?

All of those were likely questions, but perhaps not something someone would just yell out in this setting.

Maybe.

But the Patrol Centurion had gotten to heart of the matter.

Why Thuringwell*? Why not someplace more interesting, more useful, more central? More militarily relevant?*

"The list is as long as my arm, Dashyl," Jessica replied, making it more personal and informal by treating it as a conversation between Centurions. "But let me share a couple of them with everyone."

She took a sip of juice from her glass to settle her thoughts. The campaign would hinge on these people understanding what the stakes were. On them being able to execute on all the things she hadn't been able to foresee.

"Until recently, the top Imperial Admiral facing us was Emmerich Wachturm," Jessica began. "A cousin of the Emperor, and a brilliant strategist. I lost to him once, beat him once, and fought him to a draw at *Ballard*."

"A draw?" Dashyl asked, obviously confused.

"Draw," Jessica reiterated. "He set out to destroy *Alexandria Station* and kill Suvi. It was also a trap designed to kill me."

Jessica let that settle in. The latter wasn't widely known. Spies didn't like coming into the sunlight.

"He destroyed the station, as you know," Jessica continued after a moment. "He did not kill Suvi. He did cause the loss of the Strike Carrier *Auberon* and the Heavy Destroyer *Rajput*. Neither Alber' d'Maine nor I were killed, but both vessels did suffer serious casualties, men and women who were friends and comrades."

Again, a moment of silence. The rest of the room hung on her words, a trick Nils had taught her in phrasing and intonation.

The voice of leadership.

"The real reason Wachturm went to *Ballard* was to attack the psychological foundation of the Republic," Jessica stated. "Baudin started out there, on the Story Road, before he went on to found the *Republic of Aquitaine*."

Dashyl nodded at her, but did not speak. Those were history lessons every girl learned in school.

"So, why *Thuringwell*?" Jessica let her gaze wander the room, marking Alber', Denis, Robbie, and Tomas from their spots around the grand space. "At *Ballard*, it was good for the goose. It will be good for the gander."

Again, silence. More stunned confusion than anything. They had expected military rationalizations, perhaps. The effect on the *Fribourg Empire* from losing an entire planet that seemed to exist as a company town producing raw ores for ship-building. The psychological blow from a strike into Imperial territory by *Aquitaine*'s demonic woman commander, facing down an entire Empire of men.

No. This went deeper.

"The *Fribourg Empire* is an inherited aristocracy of birth," Jessica said firmly, repeating the first words out of Wakely's mouth in that very first lecture, so long ago.

Jessica smiled at Wakely, seated in a back corner with Vo Arlo on one side and Rebekah Kim beyond that. Wakely grinned at her and nodded back, recognizing the words.

"Men lead because they were born as the Duke of the planet, not because they were raised up on the shoulders and support of their fellow citizens, as we do it," Jessica continued, repeating the lecture she had recorded and listened to so many times.

"Not all Imperial worlds are happy citizens of the greater *body politic*," she said, again drawing the conversation intimate with Dashyl, and the nearly-two-hundred eavesdroppers listening in. "Especially if you have absentee landlords, unscrupulous financiers, and a population heavily tilted towards men with little chance of being long-term colonists, men who are exploited workers struggling to make enough money to control their own destinies."

"Rebellion?" Dashyl asked, giving voice to the rest of the folks who didn't dare interrupt.

"It would never work, Dash," Jessica replied. "Once we left, the Imperial Security Bureau would just round up all the troublemakers and shoot them. Instead, we're going to convince them to join the Republic of their own free will."

"How?"

"We're going to put them in charge of things," Jessica stated. "Let them run the planet as owners, and not as serfs."

"But what good will that do?" another voice called from her left. Enfys El-Amin, *Wombat*'s Command Centurion.

Jessica didn't bother to look at the woman asking. Dashyl would have asked the same question a beat later.

"What happens if all Imperial worlds suddenly demanded a say in how things are run? If they were no longer happy to be merely ruled, but wanted to participate in the decision-making process?" Jessica asked, turning and looking at all of her commanders, her warriors, her comrades.

"The Empire would come apart at the seams," Enfys El-Amin replied forcefully.

She was the Command Centurion of *RAN Wombat*, a specialist minesweeper Jessica had brought along with her Support Force. The ship could also lay mines, an almost-invisible web of deadly surprises she could weave in the skies above *Thuringwell*, for when the Imperials made their attempt.

That Command Centurion was a quiet woman. A craftsman intent on a very delicate task that required care and precision. She was a plain-looking woman, if you were to meet her on the street. Nothing would strike your memory, except perhaps the way she moved. Slow and deliberate. Nothing interesting, unless you spoke with her, perhaps over coffee.

Then her words would register.

Enfys El-Amin never put a syllable wrong, like she never put a domino wrong. Jessica could imagine this woman building one of those giant domino runs, small colored tiles, one by four by nine, that you then knocked over and watched them tip the next in line, and the one after, in complicated sequences, like Rube Goldberg machines. Moving artwork.

You could not make a mistake in that game, either, unless you wanted to start completely from scratch after all the tiles had finished falling over.

"If it does, El-Amin," Jessica replied, fixing her with a stare. "Then the Eternal War is over. We'll have won."

The room gasped as the implications of her words sunk in. There were a few, like d'Maine, who might miss a lifetime of warfare, but there were thousands of worlds full of people who would live better lives, not looking constantly over their shoulders for the war to land in their backyard.

Now Jessica just had to pull it off.

If she could.

CHAPTER X

JESSICA TOOK a deep breath as the countdown edged to zero.

For just a moment, she was suddenly back on the Flag Bridge of the old *CVS Auberon*, getting ready for that first raid on *2218 Svati Prime*, backed by nothing but *Rajput* and *CR-264*, and her own belief that she could whack the Empire and Emperor in the shins with a long stick, desperately out of scope with the actual amount of damage she intended to do.

Surprise occurs in the enemy commander's mind.

She wondered what the poor unfortunate soul at the other end was going to think about today.

Jessica wasn't sure that *surprise* was a large enough word to encompass what was about to drop into his lap.

The last hop had been short, barely two light years out from an otherwise irrelevant system that existed more as a navigation hazard in JumpSpace than anything else. Get everyone organized and primed. Dinner. Potty breaks. Fresh coffee.

Standard Fleet tactics for a force this size called for the entire force to drop out of JumpSpace well outside of the planet's gravity well as a block, launch fighters, and march carefully to the guns. Jessica sneered at the memory of First Fleet Lord Loncar treating *Third Iger* that way. A textbook screw-up.

Hopefully, enough Republic spies had planted enough seeds in the current of rumor that the *Fribourg Empire* expected her to try for what would have been labeled *Fourth Iger*, had she gone there instead. It was also a good target, but more heavily defended.

A key anchor point for the entire frontier.

Hopefully, there was an entire battle fleet poised at *Iger*, hiding and waiting for her. Like moray eels down in the rocks for a swimmer to come overhead. And they would stay put when the news of *Thuringwell* arrived, convinced that this was just a distraction to pull them out of position before she jumped them.

What the hell would anyone want with a place like *Thuringwell*, anyway? What did it gain the Republic?

What, indeed?

Emergence.

Like diving into a warm swimming pool. One moment dry, the next wet. The whole universe flinched around her.

All the projections came live at once.

Instead of a single projection in the middle of the big conference table, like the old *Auberon*, she had the big hologram in the center, and eight more smaller ones around it, plus an entire conference tabletop of flat screens displaying whatever information she needed behind their waterproof screens.

She was still nervous to set down a mug of coffee, even after Marcelle, her aide, had turned over a cup of coffee on it, just to prove a point.

Jessica smiled, and turned to look at Marcelle, comfortably waiting in a nearby corner jumpseat for Jessica's orders or needs.

Marcelle smiled back knowingly.

Would she have ever gotten here without that woman's help?

"Contact," Enej called.

Where he used to have a trio of enlisted assistants on the Strike Carrier, he now had a whole dedicated Flag Staff, fourteen people tracking things in this room, plus more in another cabin, talking to everyone, making sure nothing rolled off the table when it got messy out there.

An Imperial fleet would have had three times as many people at hand, in a much larger room. But Republic fleets were not commanded from the Flag Bridge.

They were directed.

Everyone knew the plan, and their place in it. They were

professionals. But here, they were given flexibility to adapt to circumstances without clearing it with the Fleet Centurion first.

Loncar would be ranting and frothing at the mouth right now. It was only one of the reasons he would never command again. After all, he hadn't actually been convicted of treason, only implicated and allowed to resign his commission and return to his estates in disgrace. Not like some of the others who had been involved.

Nils Kasum had let Loncar slide off the hook, but that was more of a favor to the Noble Lords of the fleet. He still needed their support, even if many of them would have gladly watched Loncar hang once his behavior became public.

"Give me the dispositions, Enej," Jessica called across the room, loud enough that everyone could hear.

He might not even be the one to handle the task, but someone would update the screen with the things she needed. Another thing this crew did better.

RAN Ballard had gotten here first and sat quietly for several hours, listening to the traffic and watching like a gargoyle from the distant edge of the system. It was one of the best things a Survey Cruiser did, scouting quietly.

It was better than Jessica had hoped. And worse.

Farther down the gravity well, one of the enormous ore freighters had just started her descent into the planet's atmosphere. They were monsters that collected all the minerals from the surface and hauled them off to one of the planets that specialized in steel mills. Being on the ground when she got here, Jessica could easily capture it and fill it with ore to haul off.

Jessica sneered to herself. A Republic world would have put the mills closer, here on *Thuringwell*'s surface or on an orbital platform. But that wasn't how the Imperial economy worked.

Thuringwell was a monoculture economy world, like so many of them were. Almost an old-fashioned company town, as she had understood the term from her studies of ancient history. The only industry was the mining of truly exotic minerals from a planet with a random overabundance of them, apparently having been born in the neighborhood of several ancient supernovae.

You could work in the mines, or support the miners.

Even with nearly ten million inhabitants, there was almost no agriculture on a scale larger than a few farmers markets supplying fresh vegetables, from what almost amounted to victory gardens.

Plus, there were very few women here, and those were mostly professional entertainers of various flavors, rather than wives starting families.

Everything was shipped in from elsewhere, leaving the men below her trapped in their circumstances: dead-ended, broke, and unhappy.

The central projection lit up with a full schematic of *Thuringwell* and nearby space.

Two smaller bulk freighters in orbit, probably unloading shipping containers of food and consumables to one of the orbital platforms owned by the Imperial Navy or the Duke. A variety of smaller country craft, locals without JumpSails just getting into orbit or onto the surface.

The Imperial Navy station came into view.

Again, that stark reminder of *2218 Svati Prime*. These things were almost exactly alike, usually built in pieces at a central yard and transported to station for assembly. An even dozen fighter craft for emergencies. A pair of local patrol boats for rescue and customs duty. Less firepower combined than either of her destroyer squadrons.

Again, why the hell would anybody want a place like *Thuringwell*?

"Squadron, this is the Flag," Jessica intoned formally, knowing her words were automatically routed to all of the ships in the area. "Prepare for final jump."

Screen Seven showed *Auberon* at the center of a sphere. Behind her, the Assault Carriers, *Abbotsford* and *Achaemenes*, with *CR-264* close by like a sheepdog herding them.

Outside that, the Battlecruiser *Nyamboya*, with Robbie Aeliaes commanding; the Heavy Cruiser Experimental *Shivaji*, with Alber' d'Maine at the helm; the Light Missile Cruiser *Ishfahan*, under Dorian Matveev; and the Survey Cruiser *Ballard*, with Cosmina Lungu.

Further in, the Escort Force. Her and Robbie's old command, *Brightoak*, and her squadron mates, *Vigilant* and *Rubicon*, protecting a trio of Escort Carriers: *Andover*, *Albena*, and *Advocate*, each of them a modified destroyer capable of fielding a trio of fighters. A whole other squadron of melee fighters.

Well up the gravity well, Jessica's Support Force. Two fast Fleet Replenishment Freighters: *Duncan*, and Jessica's old cohort from

Ballard, *Mendocino*. The Support Carrier *Andorra*, hauling an entire flight wing in cold storage and replacement pilots for extended campaigns. The Minesweeper *Wombat*, filled with deadly, little eggs like a spider. And the most revolutionary concept in modern warfare: the Troop Transport *Ladysmith*, reconfigured and loaded up with cattle, pigs, and sheep.

Thuringwell had been terraformed, once upon a time, millennia ago. Much of her surface today was grass-covered plains and a good mix of deciduous and evergreen forests.

Rabbits, beavers, squirrels, and lots of other small animals had been added, along with predators to keep them in check. Deer, elk, and bighorn had been turned loose, along with a few cattle, pigs, and sheep.

What she was bringing were new herds to expand bloodlines and see if she could make the entire planet self-sufficient for food.

It was a very good use of some of the treasure she had inherited as Queen of *Petron*, along with pallets and pallets of seeds of all kinds and entire orchards of young fruit trees in half-barrels.

The Command Centurion of *Ladysmith*, Guiomar Zelenko, hadn't been pleased to find out her latest mission, until she sat down and really dug into the ramifications of *Operation Harbinger*. At that point, she had cackled madly and thrown herself and her crew into the task with a fervor.

Jessica smiled broadly.

Revolutions were won down in the scrum, doing the little things that made it easier for the ball carrier to break loose and get all the glory scoring. Like flying the galaxy's largest farm animal truck into battle.

"All vessels, execute Plan Epsilon," Jessica said formally. "Make your jumps. Engage as you bear."

Alpha had assumed an enemy fleet too large to engage, followed by a rapid retreat into JumpSpace.

Beta, *Gamma*, and *Delta* would see the fleet engaging progressively smaller forces.

Now the fun would begin.

Epsilon was fox in the hen house. Any of the three cruisers could destroy the station, if that had been her plan. Hopefully, overwhelming force would cause the Imperial side to politely strike their colors and nobody would be killed today.

Tomorrow, if all went well, the hard part of governing, and the heads-cracking-together of a polite revolution.

Jessica rolled the dice.

CHAPTER XI

IMPERIAL FOUNDING: 175/04/28.
THURINGWELL ORBITAL CONTROL

OTTO WATCHED the signals as the Imperial Ore Carrier *TCH-101251071MBQ* settled into her glide descent and began to slowly circle her way down to Yonin Port on the surface below.

Everything was on the beam.

He took a sip of stale coffee and checked the boards. Nobody else was scheduled until tomorrow late shift, so he could mostly put his feet up and let the systems quietly listen to deep space murmuring. Another thirty minutes and *MBQ* would be on the ground. He could pull out a book at that point.

Calm. Quiet. Proper.

The arrival signal was jarring. That was intentional.

A ship dropping out of JumpSpace that wasn't registered should immediately get the attention of the Traffic Control Officer. It was the signal for a customs intercept, ninety percent of the time. Occasionally, it meant pirates, but *Thuringwell* was protected enough to keep them at bay.

A second chime sounded.

A third.

Oh, schiesse.

Otto watched the signal board light up with arrivals.

Fourteen signals were active by the time he could bring his brain to engage.

Fourteen?

And then a cloud of smaller signals erupted. Melee fighters. Hordes of them. None of them displaying an Imperial identification signal.

Otto unlocked the little rocker control at the top of his board and took a deep breath before he pushed it to the lock position.

"All hands to battle stations," he said into the comm, fighting to keep his voice calm. "Enemy invasion fleet inbound."

The room's lights went red. A siren wound itself up, sufficient to wake the dead.

Why the hell would anybody want a place like Thuringwell?

THE ALARM BROUGHT Dieter to his feet automatically.

"All hands to battle stations," the man's voice said. "Enemy invasion fleet inbound."

How many years had he planned for this moment? Prepared with every ounce of his being? Waited to be vindicated?

"Traffic Control, this is Colonel Haussmann," he keyed the comm live.

"Channel Two, Colonel," Otto Vollelk replied immediately.

Good, that man was on the ball. One of the others would have wasted precious seconds arguing protocol with him. Otto had already sent him the scan logs.

Mother of God. That's an entire battle fleet. And those two are Republic Assault Carriers. This really is an invasion.

Dieter took a moment to memorize everything, and then transmitted it to the surface for safe-keeping.

He switched to a second comm channel.

"Go ahead, Colonel Haussmann," Captain Arnholdt said immediately.

The station commander had a very calm voice. Dieter could already hear the resignation of defeat in it.

Fool.

"What are your plans, Captain?" Dieter asked anyway.

As if there was any doubt.

"Strike on honorable terms, Colonel," the man replied. "They outgun us by at least two orders of magnitude. Combat would be simple suicide at this point. I suggest you do the same."

Suggest? You do not offer suggestions to the Imperial Security Bureau, Captain.

"As you will, Arnholdt," Dieter said simply. "I will escape and carry on the fight from the surface."

Dieter cut the channel before the man could reply.

The man had nothing useful to say.

It was one thing to fight off a squadron of small raiders. This station would be overwhelmed in less than an hour. Possibly, they would be destroyed. More likely, everyone would be taken prisoner and used to assist the invasion force.

That would not do.

Dieter typed in the twenty-seven digit code that wiped out his board's memory. In fifteen minutes, if he didn't override it, it would do the same to the station's memory core.

And then it would activate the scuttling charges.

Dieter scowled at the universe.

He had warned them on *St. Legier* that this day might come. They had laughed and sent him to a distant backwater planet as a punishment.

He would show them.

There weren't many of his security officers on the station. Most were located on the planet's surface, playing cat to the many mice hiding in the brush and the granary. Dieter sent a signal to them, activating the correct sequence of contingency plans.

Those cowards in the Imperial Fleet might be about to surrender. Imperial Security never would.

Dieter pulled the key to his safe from a necklace under his tunic and opened the armored box in the bulkhead behind his desk. Papers could not be intercepted, could not be corrupted. And they burned nicely.

The red notebook went into a satchel kept in the safe for just this moment, along with a bundle of currency, a handgun, and two spare powerpacks.

A seven-digit code activated the timer on the flash charge to destroy everything else inside. He closed the safe door most of the way, grabbed a small go-pack from the bottom drawer of his desk, and stepped to the outer door to his office.

"Why do you want an office so far from the central complex, Colonel Haussmann?" they had asked, time and again.

Dieter smiled cruelly to himself as he walked directly across the hallway and opened the hatch to the emergency escape pod.

He stepped in, sat down, stowed his gear, and felt the system come alive and embrace him. Five seconds later, it launched him straight down to the surface of *Thuringwell*.

Let us see how well your invasion pans out, Aquitaine.

CHAPTER XII

DATE OF THE REPUBLIC APRIL 28, 396 SC
AUBERON. ABOVE THURINGWELL

JESSICA STARED at the display in quiet shock. At least for a moment.

Surprise occurs in the enemy commander's mind.

Mine.

Move.

"Enej," she called sharply. "What the hell just happened?"

In the primary projection, the icon that had been *Thuringwell*'s orbital command station had just exploded.

Well, fizzled, really. That part that had been the Imperial Fleet's fighter squadron base had vented plasma through the lock shields. A tremendous lot of it.

The rest of the station didn't appear to be in much better shape.

As she watched, tertiary explosions continued to wrack the place, like an earthquake in pudding.

Jessica had an image in her head halfway between an orange being ripped in two by an ogre, and a snowball in the face of a blowtorch.

"Engineering suggests someone tried to blow the station up from the inside," her Flag Centurion replied after a moment. "Not all the scuttling charges went off."

He checked his readout closely.

"Both cutters appear to have survived. No fighters made it out."

Jessica considered the options. None of them were good. Nothing she had planned had taken this chain of events into account.

"Squadron, this is the Flag," she said, knowing the message would be transmitted everywhere and obeyed. It better be obeyed. "All units stand down hostilities unless fired on. Repeat do not fire unless fired upon first. Transmit that order in the clear, just to make sure everyone in the system hears it."

She took a deep breath and trusted the fates.

"Enej," she said formally. "Contact the two Imperial cutters and order them to begin rescue operations immediately. Launch *Gaucho* right now to assist, and then coordinate getting as many DropShips and EVA teams as we can over there to pick up survivors. Back them with all the GunShips in case anyone feels frisky, but anybody on our side who fires first better hope the Imperials get to them before I do."

"Aye, sir," he replied. "Stand by."

Jessica watched the man lean forward and speak rapidly into a sound-deadening microphone.

Eighteen months planning. And nobody had ever suggested something as amazingly stupid as destroying the space station when *Aquitaine* showed up.

Apparently, I need to hire a couple of twelve-year old boys for better ideas in juvenile delinquency, next time. Maybe I should ask Marcelle's nephews.

CHAPTER XIII

DATE OF THE REPUBLIC APRIL 29, 396 SC
AUBERON. ABOVE THURINGWELL

"GENTLEMEN, WELCOME," she said quietly. "I am Fleet Centurion Jessica Keller, of the *Republic of Aquitaine* Navy."

Two new faces had joined her staff of projections around the table, to go with the thirty-odd who were physically present in the room. Lieutenants Walsh and Koppanen, commanding the two Imperial cutters, *CML-1596* and *CML-1688*, respectively.

Both men were in shock, but handling it well. Hearing her name seemed to at once jar them, and then relax them. Apparently, she was the succubus in the night to many Imperial folks, but she still had a reputation for honor within the Imperial Navy.

She hoped.

She turned to Denis Jež, physically present, while many of the rest were projections.

"Present count, Denis?" she asked.

"Fifty-three crew initially rescued," he replied without checking his notes. "Medbay suggests thirty-four will discharge in two days. Another three in a few weeks. Very little prognosis on the remainder."

"Thank you."

Jessica took a moment to say a silent prayer. Dying in battle was one thing. Being blown into deep space without adequate survival gear was something entirely else. Something she wanted to talk to someone about.

In a most unfriendly way.

She turned to the two Imperial officers. Her next words would be public record in both *Aquitaine* and *Fribourg*, so she needed to handle this very delicately.

Wakely smiled encouragingly. She had written most of the speech.

"Lt. Walsh and Lt. Koppanen," she began. "You have struck your colors properly and served your parole with honor. Most of the men rescued from the station are alive because of the efforts of your crews. I will transmit you to *Ladaux* with a recommendation that you be commended by our own Navy as well as by our Senate for your efforts. I have no doubts that you will be well-kept, and quickly traded home, where I will make sure that the Imperial Fleet receives a record of your activities. Thank you."

Walsh blushed. Koppanen smiled. Both had apparently expected her to act like a pirate.

She was a Pirate Queen, after all.

Jessica suppressed the smile that threatened to break out.

This was a moment to be dour and taciturn.

"Command Security Centurion," she said, locating Navin the Black among the projected faces. "Take charge of the prisoners. I would like them to joins us for a formal dinner of Command Centurions before they depart."

The giant black man nodded once, never one for many words.

"Denis," she continued. "Pull together prize crews for both vessels and begin the process of familiarization as soon as possible. We'll continue to use them for inspection duties for the time being, while we work out how to handle the loss of the station."

Koppanen actually raised his hand.

"You're keeping them?" he asked in obvious dismay.

"This is an invasion, Lieutenant," she said flatly. "Not a raid. I plan to be here for a very long time."

"Oh…" he started to say, when his projection froze.

"Flag, this is *Ballard*," a woman's voice cut through as Enej waved his hand to get her attention.

"Go ahead," she said, checking that all the other faces appeared active. Only the Imperials had been locked out.

"Flag, we're picking up explosions on the surface, centered on the port at Yonin," the woman continued.

It took a moment to place the voice. Senior Centurion Elzbet Aukley, First Officer and Science Officer aboard *Ballard*.

Almost as good as Tomas Kigali.

"Somebody just blew up that ore freighter that was landing when we first crashed the party," she said. "Major damage to the port. Secondary explosions as well."

Jessica watched her lovely plan continue to evaporate in front of her eyes.

So much for planetary surrender under *force majeure*. Peaceful occupation as she started the task of undermining the entire Imperial Edifice from this peaceful, irrelevant speck of a planet.

"Navin and Denis, get the cutters in hand immediately," she ordered, shifting gears quickly. "Haukea and Zviadi, I need Fourth Saxon and *LVIII Heavy* on the ground now. Stitch Yonin up as fast as you can before they do anything else crazy or stupid down there. Wakely, you'll be governor as soon as I get those idiots to stop shooting, but I'm going down with you to get their attention."

"Do you think that's a good idea, *Margrave*?" Wakely replied, implying that all of this would be played back for the Senate at some point, hopefully not at another Court Martial.

"No, I do not," Jessica replied. "But we have to kill or isolate as many of the dead-enders as we can. And we have to do it quickly. Most of the people down there just want to keep working and drawing a paycheck. Right now, we're firefighters."

No plan survives contact with the enemy. That was why he was the enemy.

But she'd be damned if she was going to let his plan work, either.

CHAPTER XIV

DATE OF THE REPUBLIC APRIL 30, 396 YONIN, THURINGWELL

LVIII HEAVY WAS the sledgehammer field commanders used when everything else failed.

Cohort Centurion Rebekah Kim knew that. Lived it.

Thrived on it.

She didn't really appreciate being detached from the Ninth Pohang Legion, but it was a fact of life in the modern Army. Every legion had four anchor cohorts, plus headquarters, and each one of those units was regularly rotated around to serve with other units as missions and needs evolved.

So here she was on *Thuringwell*, getting ready to wipe the lazy asses of Fourth Saxon. At least she would be able to do the job her way today, and not wait for them to get around to maybe riding out on their silly horses and finding the bad guys.

After all, there was no rain to stop them.

The ramp on the DropShip slammed down with a terrible ringing. The crew, and especially the loadmaster, had learned not to take their time getting things pretty when dealing with Cohort Centurion Kim.

She smiled harshly.

"Move out," she called, but her driver was already ahead of her, engines roaring and transmission screaming as the big beast known as *Freefall* lurched into motion and down the ramp.

It was an old nickname. As a rookie Patrol Centurion, she had once driven her tank off a ramp that had frozen halfway down, partly in an attempt to dislodge it, partly because she wasn't about to lose points on an exercise due to someone else's equipment failure. Tanks could easily drop at least their own length, with a very good chance of surviving.

She could testify to that.

Today, *Freefall* ran down ramp like an angry avalanche.

Horses might out-accelerate her, for maybe the first thirty meters, but they couldn't reach one hundred kph on a flat surface. Nor hold it for an hour, shooting every step of the way.

Freefall could.

Rebekah checked her command readout. Behind her, the rest of her team was moving. This DropShip was crammed tight, with the three tanks of *1-1-1*, First Lance/First Squadron/First Patrol, plus the three tracked vehicles of First Patrol's Support Lance. But everyone was in motion.

Rebekah checked the map display against the map in her head and the recent scans of the starport. *Auberon* didn't carry as much infantry on this mission, most of her space being given over to a full Construction Ala, but Keller had already put an entire rapid-deployment fireteam down in various locations around the west side of the port, where they could cut off traffic to the city and hopefully keep the saboteurs isolated.

There had been two more explosions on the ground before all the local ships had taken off like their tails were on fire. Sky-side, they were Keller's problem. Locally, they were nobody's problem unless they looked like they were about to start a strafing run on her.

Then they would discover what the particle cannons could do. The hard way.

"*LVIII Heavy*, this is the Flag," Keller's voice came over the comm.

"Go ahead," Rebekah replied.

This was always when the Fleet Lords took it upon themselves to meddle in things they didn't understand, like mud and rain. Why should Keller be any different?

"Kim, *Auberon*'s marines intercepted a local force after they dropped," Keller continued. "That force was headed towards the port, and heavily armed."

Rebekah's readouts suddenly filled with images of a convoy of men in big trucks. They weren't wearing blue Imperial Army uniforms, but gray.

Imperial Security.

Bullies with guns.

The montage was fast. Lightly armored trucks with pintle-mounted heavy weapons running headlong into a barrage of anti-tank rockets and ground fire from a small group of Republic marines that had gotten there first and dug in.

It was brief, harsh, and deadly, and then the Imperials fell back and scattered into the sidestreets.

"What are your orders, Flag?" Rebekah said as she digested the technical specifications that went with the footage. Counts, gear, directions, theories.

"My marines have the cork in the bottle, Kim," the Fleet Centurion replied. "Fourth Saxon's dropping around the perimeter of the port and pushing inward rapidly to control the situation and protect local fire and rescue efforts. I want you to pivot into the city and drive those bastards hard in front of you. They have very little weaponry that can take on heavy armor."

Rebekah waited for the other shoe to drop.

"That's it?" she blurted after a second. "Sir."

"That's it, *LVIII*. Find them, fix them. Kill them if necessary. I need the city pacified. Now."

Rebekah smiled. No silly orders about not damaging buildings, not hurting civilians, not disrupting anyone's High Tea. Just get in and crack skulls together.

She might like working for this Keller.

"First Support Lance, laager here and wait for instructions," Kim said into her comm. "This might be our starting point for anchor bases."

Behind her, three of the vehicles began to pull off the road, probably planning to backtrack a little to that park they had passed, and set up shop: a Recovery tank, a Logistics tank, and an Air Defense behemoth with twin autocannons and several tons of ammunition.

"*StealthLlama*, *Geulipon*, and *Nun*, form on *Freefall* and unlock all weapons. If it waves, smile. If it shoots, shoot back. We're going hunting."

REBEKAH FOUND herself pretending to be the local sheriff, which was absolutely bizarre on an otherwise-Imperial planet. She had to work not to giggle at the image in her head.

Yonin was a typical small city. Population about seventy-five thousand, mostly geared towards either the central planetary government, what they needed of such a thing, or supporting the port. Keller had said that everything was pretty much trucked in from somewhere else.

And things had gotten eerily quiet.

There were still explosions behind her, in the port. Someone had set fire to a row of warehouses, but Fourth Saxon and the fire department had it mostly under control by now.

Freefall rumbled down the center of a major boulevard that was otherwise empty. There weren't many private vehicles on *Thuringwell* to begin with, from the intelligence reports, and all business traffic had come to an absolute halt, except for emergency vehicles trying to help, and the occasional something running like hell in the distance.

The latter she had let go. Anything in line of sight could be hit with the particle cannon, but people running away from her weren't a threat.

There weren't many threats to heavy armor. Not on this planet.

Movement caught her eye.

Rebekah dialed in the scanners.

A man, standing in the middle of the street, waving both hands over his head to get her attention.

Older, maybe mid-fifties. Dark skin. Not quite dark enough to be a *Zanzibar* native. Maybe closer to *Ballard*. Probably some planetary equivalent on this side of the border.

Dressed in a business suit and very expensive shoes. Totally out of place in the middle of a potential warzone.

"Team, hold here," Rebekah said into the comm. "*Freefall* will scout."

Behind her, the other three vehicles would spread out and pivot to watch the flanks, *StealthLlama* in dark gray paint like a giant rock, *Geulipon*, Korean for *Gryphon*, wearing all brown, and *Nun*, the Korean word for Snow, looking like a giant Dalmatian in white and gray splatter camouflage.

Freefall came down to a walk. She had a good team.

"Hold at one hundred, Choe," she ordered.

In one of her screens, she saw her driver nod as he maneuvered the big beast.

Rebekah let Soun, her gunner, line the big cannon up with the civilian. There was a co-axial light autocannon, in case she needed it. Against an unarmed, middle-aged man in the middle of the street.

Right.

Rebekah flipped a switch and activated the public address system.

"*LVIII Heavy* Ala, Grand Army of the Republic," she said with a grin, like a waitress taking an order at a restaurant. "How can I help you today?"

Seriously, who could see her in the services industry?

The man flinched under the bombardment of sound. He pursed his lips and took a deep breath.

"Speak normally, I can hear you from there."

Another flinch. He looked like an insurance salesman.

"Imperial Security troops have taken over the Hall of Government," he said, mostly in a conversational voice, as if he frequently had conversations with armoured land whales. "They have barricaded themselves in and begun to shoot randomly out of windows and set fires."

Yup. Dead-enders. The smart ones were in trucks and flats right now, running like hell for the edge of town, where they could fade into the brush. Rebekah didn't figure that many of them would be able to just take off their uniforms and pretend to be civilians.

Imperial Army, maybe, not Imperial Security Bureau. Nobody liked those bastards.

"Hostages?"

"It is the Sabbath, madame," he replied, just a touch indignant. "Perhaps a few custodians were working. The rest would be Imperial Security troops guarding the building."

"Who are you?" Rebekah asked harshly.

She wasn't really listening. Soun had the big guns lined up for an ambush. Rebekah was watching the scanners for someone to jump out with a missile.

"Miles Gunderson," he replied.

Rebekah blinked in surprise. What was the mayor of Yonin doing here?

She called up the briefing files and compared pictures. Sure enough.

Huh.

Probably useful to have him in hand, right about now.

"Choe," she said on an interior channel. "Close up and pass him on our right."

"Got it," her driver replied as he pushed the tank into motion smoothly. Like a walrus on fresh pack ice.

Rebekah dialed down the speakers as she got closer. No reason to blast him deaf.

Today.

"Mr. Mayor," she said formally over the outside speakers. "I think it would be useful for everyone involved if you joined me and showed us where these people are."

She popped the hatch and surfaced with a pistol in one hand, about as far from Botticelli as you could get.

Nobody jumped out at her.

The mayor was a tall man. Dignified.

Rebekah climbed down onto the front fender to give him a hand up as the tank came to a halt.

Well, lift him bodily. He was skinnier than he looked and she was a lot stronger.

He had a look of surprise when he got to his feet atop the tank.

"Why is there Republic armor landing on an Imperial Planet, madam?" he inquired sternly.

"It's not an Imperial world anymore, Gunderson," she replied flatly. "It's my world. Now, let's go see about your juvenile delinquents."

"FLAG, THIS IS *FREEFALL*," Jessica heard Cohort Centurion Kim's voice come over the command channel.

"Go ahead, Kim," she replied almost immediately.

Jessica had never monitored a land battle from her Flag Bridge, safely in orbit. She was almost fidgeting with energy, with nothing to do about it.

She made a note to go have another good session with the fighting robot later.

"Bad just got worse, Flag," Rebekah said.

Jessica suppressed another flinch. Her fingers barely moved.

A screen lit up with an image of an impressive, granite building overlooking a large plaza. Windows had been shattered out. Three land vehicles were burning. As were a pair of flitters.

At least one of them had been moving when someone killed it. Parts were scattered across a corner and had shattered the façade of another building next door.

As Jessica watched, someone popped out from cover and opened fire with an energy rifle in the camera's general direction, before disappearing under cover.

"What's the problem, Kim?" Jessica asked, surprised that *LVIII* hadn't raked the building with their big guns.

You didn't negotiate with terrorists and snipers. You hit them with a big hammer. Rebekah Kim, for example.

A new feed came through, live. The same building, from farther back. The tank closest to the mess was the one called *Snow. Nun.*

At least four men were taking useless potshots at the tanks, as if goading them to shoot back. Others had apparently set fires, causing a haze of smoke to ooze out of shattered windows on the ground floor and from the eighth story roof.

Jessica hated fanatics.

"That's the Hall of Government for *Thuringwell*, Flag," Kim replied.

Ah.

Jessica checked the coordinates Kim was transmitting.

"And I have someone here who wants to talk to you, Fleet Centurion," Kim continued. "Go ahead."

Jessica watched the camera view swap to show Cohort Centurion Kim and a civilian, her standing up out of her hatch and him crouched behind the turret.

"Fleet Lord Keller, my name is Miles Gunderson," the man said with grand dignity. "I am the Mayor of the city you are destroying."

Wakely's head came all the way around from whatever she had been doing to stare at the projection.

Jessica glanced in Wakely's direction, got a nod in return.

"My troops aren't setting fires or shooting down civilian transports, Sri Gunderson," Jessica replied.

Briefly, she considered dropping a fireteam of marines on the roof to clear the place. The costs would probably be tremendous. Probably not worth it.

Yet.

"If you attack that building," Gunderson said. "You risk destroying all the paper records for the entire colony, Keller. Tax Records. Land Titles. Court Documents."

In other words, utter barbarism. Goths at the gates of the city.

Jessica leaned back as Wakely waved a hand to get her attention.

Jessica paused the channel and raised an eyebrow. This was verging over into Civilian Affairs, and she had an expert on the topic who wanted to say something.

She already knew what Kim's recommendation would be.

"He is absolutely correct, Jessica," Wakely began. "You would utterly decapitate this planet's entire government if we significantly damaged that building."

What Jessica didn't understand was the mischievous gleam in Dr. Okafor's eyes as she spoke.

"Okay?" Jessica hesitated to commit herself to anything.

"Think about the records he's referring to, *Margrave*," Wakely continued. "Who owes the state taxes and how much? Who owns the all the property? Who has been in trouble with the Imperial authorities?"

Wakely paused to consider the image.

"That smoke is probably *Securitat* troops burning all their records."

"Possibly," Jessica said. "So?"

"Jessica, the entire planet is basically the personal fief of the Duke. People owe *him* taxes. *His* police throw people in jail or ship them off to labor colonies. If we burn it, *he* loses everything, even if they evict us later. He would have to spend a decade recreating those records. If he even could."

"And if we hold the planet?" Jessica asked, suddenly realizing where Wakely's mind was going.

Creator. Could she commit that level of vandalism and pull it off? This would be something she would be answering to the Senate for, one way or the other.

Huns. About to cross the frozen Rubicon with a howl of savage glee fit to chill the blood.

"You would absolutely have to nationalize everything immediately, in the interests of orderly government, Jessica," Wakely said, apparently almost verging on a fit of giggles. "Ports. Transport. Industry. Everything."

"And then turn around and sell it to locals," Jessica breathed. "Who would be personally invested in keeping it up, expanding it, making a profit from it. Sweat equity in new corporate structures, with the *Republic of Aquitaine* as eventual minority partner."

Jessica could measure the pure insanity of the idea from the looks of bewildered shock on the faces around her. Men and women of her Flag Staff, jaws hanging open. All except Wakely.

But then, *Queen of the Pirates*.

Jessica turned to her Flag Centurion.

"Get me some Shore Patrol marines down there immediately, Enej," she said. "I want Miles Gunderson politely transported up here to keep him from meddling."

He nodded.

Jessica reopened the comm channel to the ground.

"Cohort Centurion Kim," she ordered forcefully. "You will take Mayor Gunderson into custody and secure him safely away from danger. *Auberon* is sending troops to transport him out of Yonin. Let me know when we have a secure signal."

Even gruff, no-nonsense, pain-in-the-ass Cohort Centurion Kim's mouth fell open a little. Gunderson turned white. Well, less chocolate brown. More burnt umber than anything.

Still, two minutes later, Kim was buttoned up inside *Freefall*. The crew of *StealthLlama* had taken the mayor, and were holding him a block away.

"Go ahead, Flag," Kim said warily.

"Kim, that building is a concrete and steel shell, faced with local granite, correct?"

"Affirmative, Flag. Not sure what they're burning over there. Probably furniture."

"No, Rebekah," Jessica replied. "Most likely they are burning paper files. The building is a major records repository."

"Paper records?"

Rebekah sounded aghast. Culture shock.

"That's the *Imperial Way*, Cohort Centurion," Jessica hammered the point home. "Metal filing cabinets and rooms filled with boxes, all filled with paper. Permanent records of government."

Jessica took a deep breath. This went against everything she had ever believed about law and order.

"Kim, I am ordering you to open fire on the building with the particle cannons on your tanks until you have crushed all resistance coming from that building. Exercise maximum care for your forces, pouring more fire into the building until you are absolutely certain the Imperial Security forces inside have been destroyed."

"And if they want to surrender?"

"They would have done that twenty minutes ago, Kim."

A light dawned in the woman's eyes.

"Paper records. You want me to commit arson, Flag?"

"Kim, I want you to burn every single piece of paper you can reach from there. The building won't collapse, but His Imperial Majesty's Government of *Thuringwell* just might."

"Roger that, Flag."

Jessica could hear the savage glee in that woman's voice.

Alber' d'Maine never got that happy, but the two of them were certainly kinfolk, under the skin.

Jessica stared at Wakely for a moment.

"This is insane, Okafor," she said.

Wakely nodded sagely.

"It is a clean slate, Keller."

Jessica nodded back.

She was about to destroy this planet as a working civilization, gambling that she and Wakely could rebuild it tomorrow.

Assuming it didn't get her Court Martialed.

Again.

CHAPTER XV

DATE OF THE REPUBLIC APRIL 30, 396 YONIN, THURINGWELL

VO ARLO WATCHED the DropShip *Cayenne* lift back into the sky and quickly run for the stars. He looked around for a moment to get his bearings.

It was a gray, cool, almost miserable day at this latitude. At least it wasn't raining, even if it smelled strange.

Every new planet smelled strange for at least a week. And that was without horses.

Somehow, he had gotten himself attached to Scout Patrol, First Cohort, as a liaison to the ground forces. That meant city boy was riding on the back of a horse in the middle of a planetary invasion.

Seriously?

A monstrously big, black gelding named Shevi who didn't look too smart, but was two hands taller than all the other horses around him.

That's how these people measured horses. Not meters and kilograms. Hands and Stone.

Weird.

And he felt like a fool. In mufti, no less.

Well, not mufti.

Army gear.

Heavy pants with thigh pockets and a reinforced seat. Baggy. Loose. Strange after his normal uniform, where everything had to be planned to fit under an emergency lifesuit in a hurry.

Button-up shirt instead of a tunic, with a button-up, rain-proof jacket over that and a heavy, armoured vest over that.

Big, floppy hat, a darker brown than the tan-speckled pattern of everything else.

At least he got to keep his boots.

They had wanted to raise a stink about that. They all wore boots with pointy toes on them, to slip into the stirrups easily.

No, thank you. Make me bigger stirrups, I'm keeping my boots.

They relented, eventually. It would have taken the Fleet Centurion to get him to change his mind on that one. They even figured that out all by themselves.

And he had been issued slug-throwers, instead of energy weapons.

Who the hell fights with slug-throwers?

And a six-shot, 12mm revolver? And a matching 12mm carbine rifle?

And a lariat. Let us not forget the lariat.

Seriously, these people took this cowboy thing way too seriously.

Of course, the single-edged saber on his belt was deadly. Nearly a meter of yataghan. Not quite the ancient-style katana he had mastered aboard *Auberon* under Navin the Black's eye, but serious business.

Vo looked up and realized that Patrol Centurion Mitja was smiling at him.

It was a warm smile. Not as nice as the one she usually had for *Gaucho*, but not threatening or disappointed.

City boy, who had never even seen a horse in person two months ago.

Now he was supposed to play cowboy with these people?

"You'll do fine, Arlo," she reassured him.

His horse seemed to disagree. Or maybe sneeze. Hard to tell, beast this big. Almost as big as him.

Vo wiggled his butt to get used to the hard leather saddle and shrugged. He was prepared to punch the monster, if Shevi turned to take a bite at his foot again.

Horse seemed to understand that. Finally.

"What's first?" he replied.

Dashyl pointed at the houses in the near distance. A few faces could be seen peeking out windows, but nobody was brave enough to actually stand in their front yard and wave.

Cayenne had set them down in an open ninety-hectare field, on the edge of one of the nicest neighborhoods in Yonin, a suburb called Aarhus.

Money.

Mansions that verged on castles from fairy tales.

Just the sort of place to ride up like a medieval knight on horseback, looking for the Holy Grail.

Seriously. How had he gotten here?

"First," Dashyl replied. "A sweep through the neighborhood to make sure everyone here understands we mean business. Later, we'll spread out and keep the peace. Local gendarmes aren't particularly heavily armed, but they're Ministry of Interior troops, not cops. Nothing *protect and serve* about them. They all get shipped sky-side, if they behave."

"And if they don't?" Arlo asked.

He had a pretty good idea what was likely to happen, but he wanted to see how a woman like Dash approached it. She was Tip-of-the-Spear crazy. Kinda like *Gaucho*, come to think of it.

"That's why we brought the whole patrol, Arlo," she replied seriously, gesturing to the mob of ninety-odd horseback troopers around them.

"PeeCee," a woman said from close by. Patrol Centurion. Dashyl. "Spotter call from *Gaucho*. Armed troops in a park not far from here. I've got coords."

Curator Aoibhín Hult, pronounced *EE-ven*, regardless of however weird she spelled it. Cornicen. Patrol communications. Technically, the person he was supposed to be spending the most time with.

She looked eighteen. Waify brunette. Her body language had suggested she might not be above an occasional tumble in the hay, if he wanted.

Vo couldn't bring himself to want to.

Not after last year.

Keep it professional, soldier boy.

He turned to her and cleared his throat. Too much horse dust in the air.

"Contact *LVIII Heavy* and see what units they have that can meet us there," he commanded.

Dash gave him a hard look.

"You don't think we can handle it?" she asked with a hard sneer.

A bunch of the troopers nearby similarly growled under their breaths.

Vo went to a dark place in his head before he spoke.

"My orders were simple, Patrol Centurion," he said with a blunt, sledge-hammer tone everyone close enough could hear. "Civilians who behave get left alone. Armed resistance gets crushed. If that means calling down orbital strikes from *Auberon* and the fleet, and leaving this city a smoking crater, that's the cost of doing business today. Any questions?"

That seemed to get through to the men and women around him.

Scout Patrol, First Cohort, was apparently used to operating on their own, utterly self-sufficient. They needed to be reminded occasionally that there was a whole fleet backing the Legion.

And a man willing to call down the fires of the apocalypse.

It had been one hell of a year for Vo.

"CC Kim says she's got a lance close enough to help out," the Cornicen replied after a minute.

Vo just looked mutely at Dash, unwilling to usurp her command, her experience, here on the ground.

"Vector them in on a pincer, Hult," Dashyl commanded. "Second Squadron on the right, Third on the left. Move out, troopers."

Apparently, Vo's horse was better trained at this than he was. Shevi immediately lurched into a trot with the rest of the force, nearly tossing Vo ass over teakettle.

He grabbed the saddlehorn and got his weight centered again.

Tomorrow, he was going to hurt, but he was damned sure not going to embarrass himself today.

———

IT WAS A PARK: big and green and artificial. That much Vo was sure of.

The rest was less obvious.

There was a big, square, concrete pond, almost in the middle. More than a wading pool, but not much more.

Concrete pathways ran in curves instead of straight lines, something utterly anathema to the Imperial mindset. It looked almost inviting.

A few trees dominated sparingly, leaving mostly hedge-like bushes here and there. Nothing at all like cover.

Scout Patrol was coming in from the south. The open space was approached by several wide, tree-lined boulevards on a precise, Imperial grid. It probably covered two hundred hectares, all in all, nearly as flat as a snooker table.

Along the northern part were a set of what looked like monuments. At least from here, through powerful binoculars.

Big, granite edifices. Strange shapes, almost geometric.

The big clues were the two obelisks on the ends. Black stone. Polished but not shiny. Flat tops. Big bronze-looking statues of soldiers atop those, facing each other, rifles out like they were charging over the top of a hill, bayonets fixed for serious business. Each four meters tall.

It was in the middle that he saw the problem.

That piece was a big, gray box of a monument. Looked kinda like an ancient altar from a church.

In front of it were four men.

At least they were dressed for the weather.

Each wore a long navy-blue coat, almost a cloak, but with sleeves. Kepis with cloth on the back protected their necks from the chill, as did scarves wrapped around their necks and tucked in.

All four were armed.

Long arms. Big, decorative rifles, minus the bayonets. Probably close by if necessary.

Two men stood at the near corners of the big monument, while the other two walked a very formal pattern in front of it.

Vo lowered the glasses and looked around him.

They were at least a kilometer away, at the far end of the park, but you couldn't hide an entire squadron of cavalry approaching in terrain like this.

Nobody over there had reacted. Or maybe they didn't care.

Dash had everyone still mounted, but he knew that there was a Ballistae team with each of the nine lances. Mostly, light machine guns and sniper teams, but there was at least one pair of troopers equipped with shoulder-launched anti-tank missiles.

Patrol Squadron, First Cohort was used to being the tip of the spear.

A sound on his left brought his head around and the binoculars back up.

A lance of heavy tanks, *Solenopsis* models with the big, sixty-six millimeter particle cannons, emerged from a side street on the other corner closest to them with a noisy rumble and a hint of burning diesel.

Three big, green Fire Ants.

Cataphracti.

The big guns.

Vo was pretty sure that the combined force could take on four men armed with single-shot rifles in a park.

Now, what the hell were they up to over there?

Nobody could miss this. And they hadn't reacted at all. Two men marching. Two men standing.

Vo laughed.

"Something funny, Arlo?" Dashyl asked from close by.

"Dunno," he said with a smile. "Think we can take them?"

"It'll be close," she replied with a matching smile. "Good thing you brought in that heavy armor to cover our flank."

The lance closest laughed as well.

Vo spurred Shevi into motion. The big horse blinked at him over a shoulder before he got up to speed.

"What are you doing, Arlo?" Dash asked as she spurred her own roan mare, Göll, into motion. Other horses started to move as well.

"Going to talk to them," he replied. "Don't need the whole squadron. And you'll probably make them nervous."

"Squadron halt," Dash called.

Shevi wanted to stop, too, but Vo heeled him once, maybe a little too hard, and the big gelding got back up to a canter. With an equine grumble.

Göll came alongside as well. When Vo glanced back, two others rode behind them, Curator Hult, and Curator Charpentier, the big man who was the Squadron's Draconarius, their standard-bearer. He had that flag out on the end of a spear.

Seriously, a spear.

"You sure you should be doing this, Dash?" he asked.

"Mags can run things just as well as I can," she replied, waving a hand behind them to encompass Centurion Borislavov and the rest of the group.

Nine lances settled. Vo could see the various weapons teams setting up, including the two lunatics with AT missiles.

This could get interesting.

They cantered across the open space, looping left-hand around the pond, the four of them.

The four men over there finally reacted when they got within a hundred meters.

Vaguely.

The two in the middle stopped marching and turned to face them. Nobody had taken the rifles off their shoulder slings, but they weren't going for cover either.

Vo glanced over and considered what would happen if even one of the particle cannons fired this direction. He shrugged.

This was probably a stupid idea, but so was getting out of bed this morning.

He brought Shevi down to a walk at about fifty meters out, and then pulled on the reins at about thirty.

Dash out-ranked him, but she was letting him ride lead on this one. She would have probably just opened up with the big guns at five hundred meters, followed by a massed charge. She had that kind of reputation.

Vo got a good look at the four men.

If he was reading their uniforms right, they were all fairly high-ranking enlisted men, without any officers present. Something equivalent to a Curator or a Decanus. Maybe a Decurion. And if the stripes on the right forearm each meant three years' service, like he thought he remembered, the baby in that group had been in for at least eighteen years.

So, veterans. Long serving-ones.

Everybody stared at each other for a few moments.

Vo dismounted and handed his reins to Hult. It put him down on their level, instead of towering over them. Plus, he could move faster if he needed to.

Let the rest be centaurs.

He took a few steps closer.

The man with the most stripes, both on his forearm and upper arm, got a hard look on his face.

Oh, what the hell.

Vo'd actually studied the right textbooks for this. Recently, too.

"My name is Centurion Vo Arlo," he said, gesturing around him. "This is the Fourth Saxon Legion, *Grand Army of the Republic of*

Aquitaine, and this planet has been placed under martial law under the recognized Rules of Warfare.”

Several seconds of silence.

At least nobody shot at him.

Vo figured the best thing to do would be to stand very still and drop to the ground, considering the amount of fire that Patrol Squadron was likely to pour into this area if they decided to.

Sergeant. That was the rank the guy had. Master Sergeant, maybe, if Vo was counting the stripes right.

“So?” the Master Sergeant said after a few seconds.

It wasn’t rude, or angry, or anything. Just a statement of fact.

Hard man.

Vo liked him immediately.

“So my job is to politely round you up, disarm you and your troops, and send you off to a camp where they’ll eventually trade you home.”

Master Sergeant considered the words for several seconds.

“No,” he said.

Again, not angry, not sneering.

Just not giving a shit.

“I beg your pardon?” Vo asked.

This had not been covered in the Rules of Warfare classes. Everybody played nice. Wars were fought in space, not on planets.

Of course, you raided planets. Nobody actually invaded them.

Until today.

Master Sergeant gestured to the big stone thingee behind him.

“We are under orders from the Emperor himself to provide a permanent Honor Guard for the Division Colors,” Master Sergeant replied simply. Cold. Hard. Honest.

Silence.

“Which Emperor?” Charpentier spoke up suddenly.

Vo glanced back at the man on the horse behind him, and the Cohort’s flag on the spear’s cross bar.

Master Sergeant looked over as well, studying the Draconarius closely for several seconds before he spoke.

Vo sensed a kinship between those two men. Veterans entrusted with the Colors.

“Karl the Fourth,” Master Sergeant replied after a moment.

Karl IV? Really? They've been here for eighty-something years, doing this?

Vo made a note to look up the unit when he got back to a library. Something impressive must have happened, back then.

"You may have invaded *Thuringwell*, Centurion," Master Sergeant growled at him. "You will not prevent us from doing our duty."

Seriously, Vo was surprised that nobody opened fire on the Imperials at that point. In the movies, that was when the music suddenly got ominous. And he knew there was somebody over yonder with the Narwhal, listening.

It was a lovely tool, the Narwhal. A passive sensor package you put on a telescoping flagpole and stuck in the air. Emitted no radiation signatures for anyone else to track, but could listen on conversations a ways away, in addition to sensors: optical, radio, and a number of interesting frequencies.

Patrol Squadron knew what the guy said just as well has Vo did. The Cataphracti were probably also dialed on the audio as well.

Four of them in Imperial Blue were gonna take on a lance of tanks and a full squadron of cavalry, in an open field, with rifles.

This Imperial had brass.

And it was going to get him killed.

Vo could smell trigger fingers getting twitchy. His were.

"And you will not surrender and be disarmed?" Vo asked.

Things were formal at this point. Like, explaining in a Court Martial to a group of Legates and Fleet Lords formal, why he had slaughtered these men.

Them being assholes wasn't going to be a particularly useful defense. Regardless of how accurate it might be.

"Never, Centurion," Master Sergeant stated.

At least none of the four Imperials reached for his rifle. Three seconds later, there wouldn't be enough pieces left to bury, if they did that.

Everybody seemed to understand that.

Stalemate.

Unless…

"What was your exact commission, Master Sergeant?" Vo asked carefully.

His brain had gone sideways. This was probably one of the reasons Navin the Black and the Fleet Centurion had picked him for this job.

Master Sergeant picked up on it. He probably didn't want to die today, either. Nobody really did.

"Karl the Fourth ordered the 189th Division to maintain a permanent, *armed*, Guard of Honor here," the man said carefully. "To protect the Division Colors."

Vo nodded slowly. Not a lot of wiggle room there. For a barracks lawyer.

Street punk from *Anameleck Prime* thought different.

"Armed?" he asked carefully.

Vo could see a wedge of daylight.

Master Sergeant nodded, just as carefully.

Vo could tell the man expected Vo's next words to be his death sentence.

He had brass.

"Nothing about rifles," Vo said, equally carefully, negotiating mentally with this total stranger. "What about swords?"

Master Sergeant blinked.

He blinked again.

"Uhm, no," the man said finally, utterly at a loss.

Good. Maybe nobody had to be splattered today.

"Master Sergeant…What is your name, anyway?" Vo asked

"Master Sergeant Edgar Horst," the man replied, puffing his chest a little. "Color Sergeant for the 189th Division."

"Master Sergeant Horst," Vo continued. "I cannot leave you and your men armed with rifles during this invasion. Would honor be satisfied if you stood your watch bearing swords instead?"

Master Sergeant blinked again.

Good. Anything to get through the man's iron hide.

Horst nodded slowly.

"Good," Vo said.

He reached down and unlatched his saber from his belt and turned to the other three.

"Gimme yours, too," he said with a cheerful smile.

Dash looked at him like he'd lost his mind. Hult wasn't much better. Charpentier grinned at him and grabbed his with the hand not holding the spear.

The two girls relented and surrendered theirs a moment later.

Vo turned back to the Master Sergeant, carrying four of Fourth Saxon's cavalry sabers in scabbards like he would a baby.

"Hult, tell everyone not to do anything stupid, please?" Vo asked breezily.

She nodded and started talking into a sound-deadening mic.

Master Sergeant nodded as Vo got close.

"Color Guard," he ordered loudly. "Stack Arms."

These man handled the task with the serious professionalism of a performance troop. The outer two left their corner posts in perfect cadence and marched to the fore. All four men came together at the center and grounded their rifles into a little triangle thingee that left them standing outright, leaning on each other like a house of cards.

Or a squad of men relying on each other to survive.

Master Sergeant first, followed by the others, each stepped forward, took a saber, and clipped it to his belt.

They returned to their posts, two on the corners, two facing him.

"Now what, Centurion Arlo?" Horst asked finally.

"Now, you make sure your team understands what the rules are, Master Sergeant," Vo said. "No guns, and nobody has to get shot. We'll make sure the troops assigned to this district know what's going on and to leave you alone."

Vo could hear the sound of nearly a hundred horses suddenly lurching into motion and coming this way, plus that scream a tank's transmission makes when you slam the sticks to the forward stops.

"No," Horst said, gesturing to the avalanche of military superiority coming towards him. "What is all this?"

"An invasion."

"No," Master Sergeant said. "Seriously."

"Seriously, Master Sergeant," Vo smiled back at him. "The *Republic of Aquitaine* has invaded *Thuringwell* and we're keeping this planet."

"Are you insane, Centurion?"

Vo gestured to the man, the sabers, the stack of rifles next to his foot, and the racing tide of troops coming over.

He grinned.

"Yup."

"Oh," Master Sergeant said.

CHAPTER XVI

IMPERIAL FOUNDING: 175/05/02.
THURINGWELL WILDERNESS

"REST PERIOD IS OVER," Dieter announced, looking around the clearing.

Twenty-three men came alive and stood up.

All but two of them were taller than Dieter. Big men. Well-honed violence.

The two small ones were probably the most dangerous ones here, relying on brains instead of using their brawn. Well, second and third most dangerous.

Dieter smiled cruelly.

"Sergeant Stoltberg," he called. "Contact the other teams and remind them that we are still on schedule to rendezvous in two days."

He waited long enough for the man to nod, then picked up his heavy backpack and slung it across his shoulders. The others might think they were tough. Dieter set out at a pace that would probably leave most of them gasping in another hour.

"All teams confirm, Colonel Haussmann," Stoltberg responded a few minutes later. "Team Six is behind schedule because they believe they were spotted by Republic troops and are moving off path to distract them and try to draw them into an ambush."

Dieter grunted noncommittally.

The original plan had called for only six of the ten teams to be able to coalesce in the deep woods after five days. Three hundred men.

Right now, he looked to have closer to five hundred men, armed to the teeth when they arrived at the secret weapons cache established several years ago in an unmarked valley.

With that much force, he could wreak untold damage on the invaders.

For a moment, Dieter regretted not having any personal transports, but that would have just led the Republic to his bolthole.

Better this way. Plus, these men needed toughening up. Garrison duty had left the rest of them so slack that a forty-seven-year-old desk officer was marching them into the ground.

As it should be.

CHAPTER XVII

DATE OF THE REPUBLIC MAY 3, 396 YONIN, THURINGWELL

"IT COULD BE WORSE," Wakely heard Jessica venture brightly over the hum of the DropShip's engines.

Wakely wasn't sure how.

The view below was hideous.

Starports were always supposed to be pretty places. Well organized.

Clean.

Yonin's was oversized for the planetary population, but that was because the place catered to a group of massive heavy freighters that hauled ore off-world on a regular schedule. And hauled in almost all the consumables needed.

Wakely traced the line of parallel railroad tracks that disappeared over the horizon.

Below the DropShip, those tracks vanished into a pile of rubble and bits.

The engineers had agreed that someone had sabotaged the engines of the monstrous freighter, almost three kilometer long and nearly half that wide. At least they had done it on the ground, so the ship had just exploded, throwing fiery wreckage everywhere, instead of when it was in the air and it would crash into the ground or the city like a meteor.

Even then, the experts had assured her, they could have the damage fixed in under a week.

The people would take longer.

Wakely turned to look at Jessica, hovering close.

"What does this do to the plan?" she asked.

Jessica shrugged.

They were functionally alone. Everyone else was conspicuously watching other screens, seated well away, and letting the two of them have some illusion of privacy if they talked quietly.

"No plan survives contact with the enemy, Wakely," Jessica said. "We adjust, we improvise, we improve."

"Just like that?" Wakely responded. "Chuck it out and start over?"

"Gods, no," Jessica said. "Moirrey and Digger will go on as planned. You will still run things down here for the civilians. In many ways, this represents an opportunity we couldn't have dreamed of."

How, exactly?

Jessica saw the question before she actually asked it.

"If we have to rebuild the rail yards anyway, we can make improvements. City and Planetary government will have to be reconstituted, but there won't be any records of how things used to operate. *Tabula Rasa.* A blank sheet of paper. Golden opportunity."

"Golden," Wakely sneered quietly.

"Wakely, look at me," Jessica urged fiercely. "They are in shock right now. If you hit them hard and fast you can force them to dance to your tune."

Dance?

"No records means no budget means no money," Wakely realized, hearing lock tumblers click into place. "Means they have to come to me if they want things. Means they are at my mercy, our mercy. Can we actually make this work, as screwed up as it is?"

Jessica smiled.

"Governor," she looked like a hawk. "You've staked your reputation on it. I've staked my entire career."

CHAPTER XVIII

IMPERIAL FOUNDING: 175/04/29. CAMP INDEPENDENCE, THURINGWELL

"FRASER," a voice brought him up from his brooding. "You need to see this."

He sat up and turned to see Conrad's head stuck through the tent's leather door, making the tiny, dirty space seem even smaller today.

Fraser grunted and ran his hand back through his hair. What there was of it. This wasn't the city, where he could amble down to the barber whenever he felt like it. Out here, they kept themselves shorn like sheep. Everything coming in now was gray, anyway.

He fixed his second-in-command with a hard glare. This was supposed to be his quiet time. Frequently, he would be napping about now. Would have been. Wasn't. Still no excuse to roust him, unless the world was ending.

"What?" he growled.

Conrad's energy was a little too much sometimes. Partly, that was the age gap. Conrad was still in his early thirties, that emotional and physical peak when all seemed right with the world.

Today, Fraser felt every day of his forty-seven years.

"All hell just broke loose in Yonin, Captain," Conrad's voice at least modulated down so he wasn't yelling any more.

Or maybe Fraser was just back in this world.

The other one had been nicer. Jeannine was there, as warm and beautiful as she had always been, short brown hair rippling in the spring breeze. Until…

"Yonin?" Fraser's brain finally engaged. "What?"

"Come look."

And the head disappeared.

Fraser considered going back to sleep, for half a second. But Conrad wouldn't intrude without a reason he thought was worth being yelled at.

Fraser levered himself mostly upright, still hunched over in the semi-darkness so he didn't bang his head on the cross-beam that held the dirt-covered roof aloft. The camp was crude and rough, but invisible to scanners and overflights.

They were all rebels against Imperial order here.

Not that Imperial Security usually cared enough to chase them, once they got far enough beyond the perimeter of town and stayed away. Still, you kept to the habits that kept you alive.

Outside, the afternoon weather was cool. Rain threatened. Possibly a late-season snow at this elevation.

All the more reason to stay laagered in and warm.

Fraser crossed the little gap of brush and pathetic trees to where a small group of his men were standing. Laying, perhaps, on the bank of a dry creek bed, peeking over and down the hillside.

Even before he got close, Fraser knew they had been right to wake him.

There were over a dozen craft in the air over Yonin, visible even at this distance. Small, fast ones. Dangerous looking insects seeking a victim to sting.

The lines were all incorrect. It took a moment for his brain to register the wrongness. Those weren't Imperial craft. Any of them.

Fraser flopped into line on the right end, next to Conrad, who passed him a set of passive, glass optics. Nobody wanted to be emitting a radiation signature today.

Yonin was on fire.

No. Parts were burning, not the whole city.

And the port was…what?

Flames everywhere. Massive destruction. Orbital strikes?

"What do we know?" Fraser called as he scanned slowly back and forth.

"Massive explosion on the ground at the port, sir," Roald called from the other end of the line. He must have had the watch this afternoon. "Couple of hours after the big freighter landed."

"Us?" Fraser asked grimly. You never knew if one of the other liberation movement teams might take matters into their own hands.

"Negative," Conrad interjected. "I've been listening to what radio signals I can understand. Looks like someone blew up one of the ore freighters."

"And you let me sleep?" Fraser growled.

He felt Conrad's shrug, shoulder to shoulder with him.

"Not a lot we could do from here, Captain."

"Then what?" Fraser continued.

It looked like hell had opened up down there and vomited out an army of demons. Those pulses of light from the center of the city were energy weapons reflecting off buildings. There were a lot of them.

"Speculation only, Captain," Conrad said quietly.

It was funny, when he thought about it. Neither of them had ever served in the military, unlike most of the rest of the troop of misfits Fraser commanded, but they had both fallen into the other men's habits of speech as readily as their habits of bivouac.

"Speculate, Lieutenant," Fraser replied.

"Sir, I think we're seeing a planetary invasion."

Fraser dropped the lenses to stare at the man beside him, sure he had misheard.

"A what?"

All conversation stopped as a shockwave of sound rolled over them and hammered them face down into the dirt, coming up from behind the five men. It took several seconds for the sound to fade.

Fraser watched the tail of the small fighter craft that had passed over them low enough to be felt, almost fast enough to break the sound barrier on this planet.

"I'm pretty sure that's a *Republic of Aquitaine* M-6 *Gungnir*, Captain," Roald spoke up in the raw silence.

What the hell would the Republic be doing here?

Fraser studied the men with him. On the one hand, anything that broke the hold of Imperial Security. On the other, would they just be changing masters and villains?

Fraser still thought of himself as a patriot in the loose sense. The men and women in his troop, and the other troops he was aware of, had been driven to criminality by the Duke and his bully-men. Minor infractions merited significant punishments. Men and women were jailed by Imperial Security for speaking out.

Jeannine rebuffed the sexual advances of a mid-ranking officer. So they had shot her instead as an example. Right there in the street.

Conrad's only crime had been to organize the men in one of the satellite mines to strike for better working conditions than the near-slavery they faced daily. He still had the scars and burns on his back to show for it.

And Fraser had a major bounty on his head.

Killing would-be rapists tended to piss people off. At least, the bullies. The regular citizenry didn't exhibit the same sort of rabid Imperial fanaticism about that sort of thing.

"Orders, Captain?" Conrad asked quietly.

How screwed are we? the man was really asking.

Fraser's crystal ball refused to clarify that one. He turned back to look at the wide, broad valley below them.

There were a LOT of craft dropping from orbit right now. From the amount of messiness on the ground already, this was the second run for these ships. Maybe the third.

How many divisions of troops would *Aquitaine* bring?

Fraser wanted to go back to sleep. Back to dream. Back to Jeannine. She had nicer things to say, then.

Unlike now.

My love, there will be bad men coming soon.

He already knew that. Imperial Security weren't the kinds of men that would meekly surrender in the face of a planetary invasion. They would do the same thing that Fraser's and the other troops had done.

Fade into the bush and mount guerilla operations.

The chessboard had just gotten very, very complicated.

CHAPTER XIX

DATE OF THE REPUBLIC MAY 3, 396
DESIGNATION LIMA-THREE, THURINGWELL

IT DINNA SMELL RIGHT. That were the problem today.

Sure, fresh-turned dirt and ripped up sod and stuffs, but no choking fumes of diesel'n'things having over it all.

Moirrey could smell wilderness over her shoulder.

It weren't right.

Still, Digger's teams were using big monster machines that didn't require liquid fuel at regular intervals, unlike the rest of this daffy planet.

She had a lovely view o'th'field from the big, prefab watch-tower thingee they had built first, over on one side of what would be a whole new starport in a couple o'days.

And it would be big. Them freighters the Impi's was using were likes ta be three kilometers long and half that wide. Granted, never more than one of them on the ground at a time, but that were the old days. Today, the field was being leveled smoother'n a baby's bottom fer four of the big beasties to be serviced at once.

If yer gonna do it, overdo's it the first time.

Off to her right, three of the construction Ala's big DropShips were settled, like great, big hyenas in a row, or monkeys seeing no evil, speaking no evil, nor hearing none.

Two days on the ground, and they was already unloading the first railroad engine that were gonna revolutionize this place som'tin' fierce.

Big stonking cranes had grabbed both sides like hands and lifted her up and rolled her out on a long arm. Crews was busy linin' up her wheels with the first length of rails they's puts down on the fresh-leveled ground.

Revolutions might be happening two hundred kilometers away in the capital city, but she were sitting atop one right here, right now. A nasty, bucking bronco patiently standing in the stall waiting his turn to gets all silly.

And he were gonna.

Saana's voice echoed up the open, metal stairwell.

"Moirrey," she hollered, sounding like a mom calling the chitlins to dinner. "Digger's headed this way and wanted to make sure you were ready."

Moirrey smiled benevolently out over the field. Her job were to keep Digger on track and run interference back fleet-side fer him. He was the one that were gonna build a new starport out here in the boonies, right next to a huge rail yard three times the size this planet needed.

Needed today.

And right next to a huge valley with a lovely river and dirt so's fertile you could toss seeds out the window of yer flitter and harvest more food than you knowed what to do with tomorrow.

Them bankers in Yonin might'a had a snake's grip on folks yesterday, but today, things were gonna be a might more interstin'.

"Boss?" Saana mommed at her.

"Coming."

Moirrey grabbed a jacket and a weapon belt off the hook as she stood.

Middle'o'nowheres they might be. Lady Keller'd left her with very strict instructions about being armed at all times when she were on the ground. She checked the pistol, confirmed it were loaded, clean, and safety on as she settled it around her snake hips.

And if the cute, little, tooled-leather belt holding the holster weren't fleet issue, t'weren't her problem, now, were it? After all, Quartermaster just dinna grasp the fundamental importance of glitter. Certainly not the recommended daily allowance thereof, no sir.

Downstairs, Moirrey presented herself to Saana's critical mom eye like a daughter going out on a first date. Ground boots warm and polished. Warm, baggy pants with oodles of pockets and loops and things. About five layers of shirt between skin and wind, including a hood she could pull up if'n the big, bad wolf came a-huffin'. Messenger bag fer stuff, stuffed with stuff, including lunch.

And the glitter gun, a'course. 'Cause you never knew when you'd need a glitter gun.

Outside, a pair of medium-sized AirShips, big, flying, radio trucks, were just landing. Digger'n the boys and girls were off fer a morning of field work.

After all, something that might be flat as snooker table on paper might be all marsh and crap once ya sunk hip deep in it without realizin'.

Ground transports would make more sense later, once people actually had ta walk the ground, but today they could stay low and fly over the plains on pretty, quiet repellors.

Both trucks were identical. Grasshopper-class combat transports. Just the sort of thing fer a morning jaunt on a maybe-hostile planet.

Three meters wide, eight long. Crew of three with a pilot, navigator, and the girl standing up inside the twin-bore autocannon turret. Big radio truck back end, almost an RV but not as posh and way more armoured. Big table in the middle with jumpseats down both sides that could flip up fer hammocks if need be.

Moirrey waited for a back hatch to open and Digger to stick his head out and wave at her before she crossed the fresh-mowed grass.

Inside were Digger and his Two, Centurion Musial, a broad, strong man barely half a head taller than her. He still felt like he massed her at least three times over, even though it were probably only twice. And she weren't that skinny. Not waify like Nina Vanek, up on *Auberon*, a thistle fearing a strong breeze. Nope, just short.

The other three were folks she dinna know, but they had that armed-to-the-teeth thing going that reminded her of Vo Arlo, so she knowed whats they was about, if nothing else.

"Ready?" Digger asked with a grin.

"A-yup," she replied, settling into a jumpseat on the left side with the best view of the big screen on the front bulkhead. This being Digger and his folks, she took a moment to strap herself in. Not her day to bounce all over the inside of the place if they decided to maneuver all sudden-like.

But the pilot weren't nearly as crazy as *Gaucho*. Almost sedate-like. Friendly, even. Of course, Moirrey knowed all about gift horses full o'Greeks. She kept her belt tight.

"What's first?" she asked the two men in charge.

Not that Musial would talk much. He were even worse than Digger about always wanting to be face down inside a machine tinkering.

Digger smiled at her from his seat across the table.

"There's a river we'll need to bridge," Digger replied, pulling out a topo map from an overhead compartment and laying it flat on the table. "Plus a few spots we'll need to think about tunneling. We've got materials to bore up to three kilometers of tunnel right now."

"Digger," Moirrey retorted. "If we have to tunnel that much, we picked the wrong spot to put the starport."

"I know," he sighed. "But we've got the *John Henry* all set up and ready to go. Be a shame not to use it."

Moirrey suppressed the giggle before it could escape. Big boys. Big toys.

"You can always put a subway under the port, ya know," she said.

And that were *exactly* the wrong thing ta tell these two. She knew it as soon as they looked at each other and their eyes got all glittery-excited-like.

It were like standing under a tree as the lightning storm crept closer.

Digger had a dangerous smile on his face. Musial had gotten positively reckless. Fer him.

Not good. Bring them back to the table afore they gots silly.

"So what about the first bridge?" she said sternly.

"Huh?"

"The bridge ya needs ta build me, Digger."

"Oh, right."

At least some of the air liked ta bled off the two men at that point.

"We'll need to span at least sixty meters, possibly ninety," he said, shifting back into technician mode and out of mad-scientist. At least fer now.

Seriously? It were gonna be herding goldfish with these two, weren't it?

CHAPTER XX

IMPERIAL FOUNDING: 175/05/06.
BACKCOUNTRY, THURINGWELL

IT HADN'T BEEN necessary to maintain absolute silence, but everyone pretty much had done so anyway. After all, the bad guys were on the far slope, across the valley, more than three kilometers away. And they would be just as interested in remaining hidden over there as his folks were over here.

Still, Fraser didn't have to tell his people not to move around, not to make noise, not to point any glass optics at the Imperial platoon over there. Being outnumbered was only part of it.

Fraser had eight men and three women with him today on this patrol sweep. Twelve of them. At least there were weapons for everyone, even if it amounted to two shotguns, six rifles, and four pulseguns. Not enough to keep them alive if they got into a tussle with the men in gray across the way. Not twenty-four Imperial Security troops.

He knew who they were, even from this distance. They might have encoded radios, but they were still on Imperial frequencies making squelch and noise. And they were on foot.

That had been the biggest surprise over the last week.

Fraser had been expecting low-flying repulser armor, or wheeled scouts. He hadn't believed the first reports until he had seen for himself that *Aquitaine* had horsemen here.

It was insane. It was archaic.

It was genius.

Horses could move across country much faster than either his team or those Imperials across the way. And much quieter. Any aircraft were at significant risk in terrain this heavy. Somebody getting low enough to see anything was in range of energy weapons and shoulder-launched missiles.

Someone had given a lot of thought to this planet before landing. That did not bode well.

More food for thought.

It had been an hour now since he had first spotted the Imperials, before his force was seen. An hour of sitting in a thorn bush thinking green thoughts.

The last Imperial stragglers had finally vanished around the lee of a hill and out of sight. It was a serious, armed force over there, much more heavily armed than his own, if those backpacks were any sign.

Fraser had been willing to risk a quick scan with the glasses, buried deep in the shadows of a dead tree and hiding pretty much under a giant bramble of blackberries. It was too early for berries, but late enough for leaves to give them cover.

Conrad wriggled close enough to talk in a normal voice.

"What do you think, Captain?" he said.

What did he think?

Fraser had heard the radio chatter from Yonin. Nationalization. New starts. Amnesties for the bush men and women willing to turn themselves in and register under *Aquitaine* law.

He wasn't sure he believed any of it.

It all fell into the too-good-to-be-true category his mother had always warned him about.

Still, was it worth risking?

"Captain?" Conrad sounded a little concerned. Or maybe grumpy that the old man had fallen asleep on him.

Time to Captain.

"I think that Haussmann's goons are up to no good," Fraser finally said.

"Anything we can do about it?" Conrad countered.

"We? No, Conrad. You," Fraser finally said.

Being Captain meant making hard decisions. It wasn't enough to keep everyone alive and fed. That was actually pretty easy to do, if they didn't chase after of the fixings of home. *Thuringwell* was habitable, temperate, and bountiful enough for humans to survive in the wilderness.

No, this was why they had put him in charge.

"Me?"

"You," Fraser said sternly.

He turned enough to face his Lieutenant, rather than just talking across the cool, wet, thorns. It was important that he convey to the man the gravity of what was coming next.

"You'll take Elizabeth with you," Fraser continued. "Take a rifle and a shotgun and enough food."

He watched Conrad's eyes get big, and then clamp down to slits. The man was smart. Probably smart enough.

Fraser waited for a nod of understanding and pointed at the horizon southwest of them, roughly parallel to the track the Imperials were following, but diverging slowly.

"I want the two of you to get well away from here," Fraser ordered in a deep voice. "When you think you've given us enough head start, call *Aquitaine* and ask for someone to come pick you up."

"Surrender?" Conrad asked sharply.

"No. You're there to negotiate. We might be willing to come in. You know where an Imperial strike force was headed. That ought to be enough coin to get their attention."

"And if they just open fire?" Conrad asked with a cold voice. "Or throw us in a camp to rot?"

"There are risks in warfare, Lieutenant," Fraser fixed him with an even colder eye. "Part of the weight of command lies in acknowledging it."

Conrad nodded, deep in thought.

Fraser nodded as well, but more to himself. He stood, wiping leaves and grime off his butt and legs as he slung one of the precious pulseguns over his shoulder. Command was lonely, hard, and miserable. Why had they picked him?

"Everyone," he called louder. "Gather up. Change in plans."

Fraser watched the men and women appear from the underbrush like pixies from some fairy tale his grandmother had told him. They carried with them an air of fragility he often found alien. It found no track in his granite soul.

Maybe that was why.

CHAPTER XXI

DATE OF THE REPUBLIC MAY 7, 396 YONIN, THURINGWELL

SMOKE.

Just a trace.

Barely a taste at the back of Jessica's mouth.

A hint, hidden under the musk of people, their own funk mostly filling the big meeting hall with the mauve walls. Her marines around the outside wall, contrasting with the rest of the room sharply in their green; heavily armed and scowling professionally at the civilians. Locals sitting in the middle in uncomfortable-looking suits, like a herd of sheep being rounded up by angry, growling dogs.

Jessica looked out over the room and hoped that the smell in the air wasn't a harbinger of failure.

After all, it had been her orders that caused the bottom third of this building to be subject to the sorts of ravening, destructive fires as had been necessary to cauterize the wound left behind by the crazies. The Imperial Navy were professionals, acting in accordance with long-understood rules of behavior and an understanding that, whenever possible, it was better to live to fight another day, than to throw one's own life away in futile gestures.

Le Beau Geste. A term that predated starflight, and had stayed with mankind for thousands of years.

No. The *Fribourg Empire*'s Naval Arm was staffed with professionals. Predictable, reasonable, understandable.

It was Imperial Security that recruited the hard-headed, the crazy, the fanatic.

Hopefully, the men before her today would be reasonable.

Jessica turned her attention back outward.

She was atop a small riser, behind a long, wooden, running desk that wrapped around in a quarter circle in the large room. Once upon a time, the Citizen's Council of Yonin had met here to hear complaints and make recommendations to the Mayor, who might or might not pass them along to the planetary governor.

That was the limit of democratic trappings to be found on *Thuringwell*.

Today, it served at least a symbolic purpose.

Jessica sat next to Wakely, with the other three chairs empty.

Again, symbolism.

Before them, down on the level, forty-odd locals, almost all men, save for two women that represented a local secretarial organization and the local prostitution guild.

Again, an Imperial thing. Colonies like this, like their fleet, were all men. Nine men to every woman. There was a need to provide female entertainment in an organized manner. Port prostitutes, to put a not-too-fine point on it.

Those two women represented between them all the middle and lower class females to be found on *Thuringwell* who weren't wives of the businessmen in front of her.

The rest were men.

Businessmen. Bankers. Merchants. Actuaries. Lawyers. Shippers. And the two heads of the local mining guild. Those latter were probably the most dangerous. Certainly the most important.

There had been enough pause that they were starting to get restless.

Jessica tugged the sleeves of her best dress uniform into place and took a quick breath. She cleared her throat.

"Gentlemen," she began with a serious tone. *"Force Majeur.* Nothing more. Nothing less. As of Twenty-Nine April, the *Thuringwell* system is under Martial Law dictated by the Senate of the *Republic of Aquitaine* and enforced by her Navy in the form of her dedicated *Margrave*, myself, Fleet Centurion Jessica Keller."

She paused to let the men gasp and murmur and twitch. Her name alone guaranteed a certain level of panic out there. At the same time, a specific respect. They knew who she was, at least by reputation. That was something she could work with.

It took only a few moments for the locals to calm down and stop fidgeting. Now she could get to the interesting parts of the speech Wakely had written for her.

The dangerous parts.

"As of now, *Aquitaine* will also nationalize a significant portion of the local economy, specifically, all Imperial holdings and all of the personal property of the Ducal family."

A man in the back started to say something. It didn't look friendly and inviting.

His eyes caught fire. His mouth opened. One hand came up to interrupt her.

Jessica's finger pointed at him like a gun cocked. Her scowl could have etched glass.

Fortunately for him, the man closed his mouth before he said something as insulting as she would expect from a powerful male official in an Empire where women were second-class citizens at best.

"*Aquitaine* will establish a local civilian administration to replace the one being removed," she continued. "Removed. This planet is now being administered by the *Republic of Aquitaine*. None of this is subject to negotiation."

That got through, both to the man in back, and to the rest. This wasn't a simple raid. This wasn't a mission to kidnap some important figure and hold him for ransom, nor to assassinate someone dangerous.

There was, literally, a new Sheriff in town.

Her.

Jessica smiled serenely from her platform. Some of these men might subscribe to the silly ideal that no woman was capable enough to rule over men. It had religious overtones with men like this.

She would enjoy disabusing them of that notion.

"Allow me then to introduce your new Governor," Jessica said. "Dr. Wakely Okafor."

The next round of gasps from the men was priceless, especially after all the reorganizing she had been required to do after everything blew up in their faces a week ago.

"The legal term," Jessica emphasized, adding even-greater gravitas to her words, "is *Palsgrave*. You might be more familiar with the Imperial term: *Palatine*. Wakely?"

Yes. That level of shock. The *Fribourg Empire* frequently used *Palatine Counts* to administer its holdings.

There had never been a woman *Palatine*.

Ever.

Until now.

———

SHOCK.

Perhaps also tinged with dread.

That was the phrase she would use to describe the looks on the faces below her.

Wakely kept her own face stern and emotionless.

Many of the men below looked like they expected to be running through a chute into a slaughterhouse in the near future.

That would be up to them.

Besides, these men probably had the least to worry about. All of them had voluntarily shown up in response to the calls she had put out, the flyers, the announcements over audio and video channels. They were the ones with either enough local patriotism, or clear-enough consciences, that they were willing to risk being here.

Of course, there would likely be a handful of sociopaths and narcissists convinced that they could talk their way out of any situation, regardless of any damning evidence to the contrary.

She would have a wonderful surprise for them, all by herself. *Aquitaine* wasn't about birthright and power. Judges in the local courts would be closely vetted before being appointed, and then there would be elections to replace them all in nine months anyway.

Let the locals exercise their own voice on who they wanted to faithfully execute the laws around here. Not the men who were bestest-pals with the governor. Nor the Duke's second cousin.

Ha.

Wakely fought to keep her predator smile subdued.

The old Governor had simply disappeared, but nobody had been willing to discuss if he had managed to get off-planet somehow, fled into the bush with Imperial Security, or suffered the kind of accident that had happened to a few of the less-popular locals over the last week at the hands of old rivals.

She listened to Jessica speak. Watched the words roll over these men like tidal waves, drowning some, pulling others into deep water. One looked like he wanted to challenge the heavens and the tides, at least until Jessica let her anger show.

Her cue.

Wakely did smile now.

Jessica had spoken from her seat, so Wakely did as well. It was a bit unnatural, as she was so used to pacing across the front of the classroom while shaping minds.

But this wasn't a lecture hall, with twenty rows of nervous freshmen furiously taking notes.

"Gentlemen," Wakely said simply.

She had learned how to use her voice as a weapon years ago. Irresistible, penetrating, dominant. Tired students trying to stay awake on too-little sleep and too much caffeine.

They would hear her now.

"You represent the civilian infrastructure of Yonin, and by extension, the rest of the planet."

Wakely took their measure slowly, in cadence with her words. Build them up. Give them hope. Reassure them that the hammer of doom would fall somewhere else, as long as they behaved.

As long as they behaved.

That was almost a smell she could put into the room for them to unconsciously sniff.

"*Aquitaine* will rule without challenge for a time," Wakely said sternly. "As many of you know, rogue elements of the previous regime caused significant damage to the Hall of Government before they were annihilated."

Use a colorful word. *Annihilated*. Not *stopped*. Not *killed*.

Utterly destroyed.

We're talking about cockroaches here, not people.

Nobody liked Imperial Security.

"During the fighting, the tax records of the colony were destroyed," Wakely smiled. "As a result, I will be directing the inspectors who have chosen to retain employment to re-assess everything as rapidly as possible, using any old notes they had handy, and then cross-checking against my own personal assessments."

That would make the men down there perk up. They were the ones who saw the taxes paid directly, as opposed to being taken from pay stubs or deducted at the point of sale. And more than half of the previous Imperial staff had chosen to stay on. Of course, with a mono-culture economy like this, the only other real choice was going to work in the mines.

Or going rogue.

The men began to look devious now. Obviously, there were edges to exploit.

"In the interim, I will direct everyone to make their next quarterly payment based on a good-faith estimate of value, after we publish new levy rates."

And the crushing of hope. This woman was serious.

Wakely made a mental note of the various responses before her. Who looked hopeful. Who looked sly. Who should probably be subject to surprise inspections shortly.

Nobody liked tax inspectors. Honest ones were even worse, for certain classes of businessmen.

A man off to her right, about midway back, started to raise his hand tentatively, like one of her students wanting her to refine a point. He immediately put it back down in his lap, blushing furiously as he did.

Wakely gave him her first warm smile today and pointed at him.

He was a middle-aged man, dressed quietly but well. Money, but not noisy about it. Short, brown hair, round face with a second chin, sharp eyes, a bit pudgy around the middle.

"You had a question, Sri?" she asked invitingly.

Let these men know she could be approached. Jessica's job was to be aloof and volatile, as needed.

She watched his eyes grow big and his jaw ground as his lips pursed. He gave her the faintest shake of his head.

"It's okay to ask," she continued. "That's why you are here today."

Now, did he have the temerity to take her up on it?

MERDE.

Now you've gone and done it. Brought attention to yourself.

What were you thinking?

Ulaffson Redyert wasn't even sure he belonged in this room, especially not considering the likes of the men around him. Justin Hender, up two rows and surrounded by several cronies in the middle of the room, could probably buy him outright from petty cash, had Ulaffson been willing to sell.

Of course, that was before somebody blew up one of his freighters on the ground.

I wonder if his insurance is up to date. Be a shame to lose something that expensive and not have the Emperor reimburse you.

Still, Ulaffson made a public show of being a patriot. Mostly. Within the limits of what was normally acceptable behavior.

Stolid, but not showy.

And now, these two dangerous women. And everybody in the room turning around to stare it him, the only one with the gumption to actually ask a question, Jose Wardson's near explosion at Keller notwithstanding.

Make it good.

"Madam Governor," Ulaffson began a bit shaky, and with a nod, as if meeting her on a sidewalk.

What a strange and barbaric term.

"If the government has fallen, will you continue to honor existing contracts for services?"

There. Safe ground. Simple question. Deflect everyone onto financial and legal questions, and away from politics.

Ulaffson had an image of himself at one end of a line of men, in front of a wall, about to be executed by masked soldiers with rifles.

Yesterday, those men had been wearing Imperial Security gray. Today, it was *Aquitaine* green.

It was apparently a good question. The black woman with the graying ringlets leaned back and smiled warmly at him. Keller continued to scowl, but she was Zeus atop Olympus. That was to be expected.

"I cannot speak to your specific contracts, Sri," Governor Okafor replied after a moment. "And, in fact, it would speed things if you could bring me a copy of yours for review."

Her eyes got serious of a moment. Deadly serious. Monster in the closet serious, but she let that evil glow flow over the rest of the men, being warm and friendly when she got back to him.

It still didn't help his state of mind.

"I will be reviewing all contracts, mind you," she continued. "Good ones will be renegotiated on similar terms. Suspicious ones will be… *audited*."

That did not sound like a pleasant experience, by any stretch of Ulaffson's imagination.

"And you are, Sri?" she dangled at him.

"Herr Ulaffson Redyert, Governor," he replied with another nod, amazed at how calm his own voice sounded. "I have a variety of import licenses, generally for non-industrial goods."

Anything too petty for Hender and his cronies to bother with. And nothing that threatened their stranglehold over this colony.

"Oh, and the Imperial Mail Service."

Although, that one might just be curtailed after all this. They weren't Imperials anymore. And he would need to arrange a very private meeting with Merryn Teke. *Seventh Son* would be due in a week or ten days.

And she would be running into a nest of angry hornets, probably with no warning.

"Please make arrangements with my staff for a meeting as soon as is convenient, Sri Redyert," she said smoothly.

It still felt like a dragon's maw opening before him.

Ulaffson nodded and let a banker in the second row ask the next question. Up until now, most of his little swindles had been minor affairs, the sorts of things gentlemen in business did as a matter of course.

With the exception of importing armaments for dangerous men who didn't like the Duke.

Ulaffson didn't either, but he was just a businessman.

Now, the stakes had gotten very high.

Who was going to drown in these new tides?

CHAPTER XXII

IMPERIAL FOUNDING: 175/05/07.
BACKCOUNTRY, THURINGWELL

CONRAD FIGURED he had gone far enough. The Old Man had gotten about a half-day head start, headed back and away, towards their semi-permanent camp further up the mountains. That left Conrad and his scout down in a valley a whole ridge line away, following game trails that headed vaguely towards Yonin.

Elizabeth was good company. She had grown up backwoods. That much was obvious, even though she was rare to speak about her past. She had old eyes for someone in her early twenties.

Still, she was pleasant to look at, to watch break trail. Tall and curvy, dusky and exotic in ways Conrad had never seen, back home. He knew she had been a dancer in Yonin, an exotic performer lured here by the promise of good money and a new start from *something*.

They all had fallen for that one. Almost nobody was actually born on *Thuringwell*. That damned Duke had brought them all in on labor contracts that never quite paid enough to escape. Twenty years of hard labor and they would ship you home. Too broken down to be of any use to anyone and too poor to support here.

Elizabeth didn't talk about her past any more than he did. Than any of them did. It was enough that she knew the woods better than just about anybody in the troop. And while it was nice to follow five paces behind her and watch that hard butt wiggle, she had made it clear early on that she didn't want anything to do with any man.

Good enough. They were all dead men walking on this planet, just waiting for Haussmann and the rest of his goons to track them down and finish the job.

Suddenly, a clearing.

Elizabeth paused at the edge of the open space and looked around. Conrad joined her.

This would have been a perfect spot for a little cabin, on any other planet. Small creek flowing left to right. Nearly half a hectare of space in a rough ellipse. Good sun. Paradise. Totally wasted on that rat bastard Duke.

She turned and cocked a chiseled eyebrow at him. He hadn't actually heard a word from her in hours, just looks and hand signals.

"We should be far enough away from the others," Conrad opined obliquely, waiting for her to nod or scowl.

Nod, it was.

Conrad slung the shotgun over his shoulder, ran his hand through his short-cropped blond hair, and pulled a stolen radio unit from his belt.

"*Aquitaine* Forces Command, come in, please," he said.

He expected to have to repeat himself several times before he a reply.

Someone was awake out there.

"Who is this?" a woman's voice rapped at him. She sounded on the verge of flaying skin off his back with her tone alone. "This is a military channel."

"Understood, *Aquitaine*," he replied, taking a deep breath. "My radio callsign is Gold-Seven. I have information that should not be broadcast. I would like transport to you to negotiate."

"Gold-Seven, what are your coordinates?" she replied.

"What map are you using, *Aquitaine*?"

That got even Elizabeth to smile.

"Good point. Stand by."

A new voice joined the conversation. Conrad would have said older, if he had to guess. Also female, but not as angry. Quiet, but not soft. If the first woman had been sandpaper, this one might be a honing stone for sharpening a knife.

"Gold-Seven, this is Ground Command," the newcomer said simply. "Why do I care who you are?"

Okay, that was to the point. And definitely not Imperial. Those people would either be threatening or ignoring him right now. Probably while tracking the signal and sending a kill team after him.

But that was what Fraser had meant about command.

Risk and reward. He had two cards he could play. And they wanted one of them right now.

"Because there is a small, heavily armed, Imperial force around forty kilometers, zero-seven-zero from Yonin. My commander suspects mischief and tasked me with contacting you. There are other conversations as well."

In his head, Conrad could imagine the woman palming a little alarm button, like they did in the movies. Every pilot on the base would suddenly charge out of the shower, or the kitchen, or wherever, throwing on clothes and racing across the tarmac to their ships.

He had definitely watched too many movies as a kid.

"And your location, Gold-Seven?"

"Shawnee Valley. Little Golden Creek," Elizabeth suddenly spoke up.

Conrad nearly dropped the radio in surprise. How did she know that?

Still, he repeated it.

"You better be alone, Gold-Seven," the woman growled.

"Myself and one other, *Aquitaine*."

"Make yourselves comfortable. We'll be along shortly."

Conrad gulped in spite of himself. That had to be the most politely dangerous thing he had ever heard, even after surviving Haussmann's pet torturers.

"GOLD-SEVEN, this is Shawnee Patrol One. Unmask yourself."

Conrad had known they were coming. That many horses made the most interesting racket, echoing off the trees especially when they got deposited at the high edge of the valley by a small, red, space freighter that swooped back away like a fighter craft.

The new woman speaking on the radio didn't sound altogether friendly. None of them really had.

Conrad was amazed at how many women *Aquitaine* had under arms. The *Fribourg Empire* didn't allow women to do much of anything dangerous or exciting.

He glanced at Elizabeth and took one last drink from his canteen. Neither of them had been expecting *Aquitaine* to respond that quickly. It might have been thirty minutes, from first call to troops dropped.

These people were not fooling around.

"Mid-valley," he said simply into the comm. "There is a clearing on the creek. We're on the east edge, back under the trees."

"Understood," she said simply. "Walk slowly into the clearing."

They were already here?

Conrad checked his shotgun, slung across his back next to his backpack. The canteen went back on the belt, as did the radio. Elizabeth did the same, wary as a rabbit.

On a lark, he took her hand in his, like a couple of lovers on a hike. Hopefully, it would make them look less threatening.

She nearly balked for a second, and then relaxed with a soft growl that promised words later.

The clearing was suddenly too small. Pleasant and homey had given way to eerie and confined. Conrad took ten steps into the low grass and looked around.

"Hello?"

"Good enough," a man yelled. "Stand right there. And put the weapons on the ground slowly."

It came from his left. Maybe. Nothing but trees.

Nothing to do but obey. Conrad moved like a mime he had seen once, all over-sized gestures done slowly for people to observe. He really didn't want to die, today. Elizabeth was just as twitchy.

Once the guns were down, he took Elizabeth's hand again and stepped well away from them.

Silence. Eerie, delicate silence.

A man appeared. Big, bulky, intimidating.

He walked closer with deliberate paces, a pistol in one hand held low by his side.

The stranger smiled, but the face was not a pretty one. He looked like an ogre trying to figure out how to not scowl.

As he got closer, Conrad realized he might come up to the man's nose in height, and was maybe two-thirds as far across the shoulders.

Giant. Coming closer. Death.

Conrad took a deep breath and silently said a prayer in his head.

The risk and reward of command.

The stranger paused about ten meters away. The pistol came up and loosely pointed in their direction, more a statement of fact than a threat.

"Gold-Seven?" he rumbled in a deep voice.

Conrad nodded.

"Just you two?"

Again, a nod. Conrad didn't trust words. He could see movement emerging along the edge of the trees behind the ogre. Lots of movement. Mostly guns pointed in his direction.

A whole lot of guns.

A short whistle from the treeline.

The man holstered his gun and smiled. Kind of.

"I'm Centurion Vo Arlo, attached to Fourth Saxon," he introduced himself. "You wanted to talk?"

CHAPTER XXIII

"WHAT DO WE KNOW?"

Jessica felt powerless. Isolated.

It was not a happy feeling, watching her contingency plans fall apart. She had always had everything worked out several steps ahead of the other guy.

Here she was in close orbit, trailing the Imperial station as her engineers rebuilt it slowly. Nothing particularly interesting was happening at this altitude.

That was the primary reason she had chosen a dead-end place like *Thuringwell*. Almost no interstellar traffic, and all of it predictable enough that she might be able to capture everyone that blundered along. That would keep the *Fribourg Empire* in the dark far longer than an attack on *Iger* would have.

Hopefully, there was still a reinforced battle fleet still hiding at *Iger* for her to never come.

She would only get one chance to surprise them with this trick. It would work or fail under her hands. Well, hers and Wakely's. Plus Fourth Saxon, *LVIII Heavy*, Digger, Moirrey, and a whole cast of people history might never remember.

But it would all hang on her head.

Success has many parents. Failure is an orphan. That was what the ancients had said.

Jessica looked around her cabin. After so long on the Strike Carrier, she was still getting used to the quarters she had inherited aboard the Star Controller. This room, her single cabin, was only slightly smaller than her old Flag Bridge had been.

She had an attached private sleeping chamber with a personal head and shower. A walk-in closet that was huge.

The better for all those custom-tailored uniforms I'm probably supposed to have.

Jessica snorted under her breath. Former First Fleet Lord Loncar probably would have filled up that closet and overflowed into another chamber.

Out in the main room, a salon that could comfortably seat half a dozen people and a bar to serve them, plus a full conference table with broadcast electronics over in one corner.

She had considered stripping the place out and putting in a training dojo here, but she was the Fleet Centurion. She needed to command her people. That meant having their respect and not being too far out there. As she knew she was.

Not as bad as Alber' d'Maine, but close.

Deep breath.

On the screen Wakely was still reviewing her notes.

"When we landed, the Imperial Security folks at the various mining camps bolted like rabbits," Wakely said with a hint of a smile. "The Army Regulars didn't have orders to do anything stupid, so they kept order until we could put local troops in place and take charge."

Lop off the head of a snake, and it flops around. Decapitate an Imperial Army garrison and it will simply keep on keeping on. *Aquitaine* infantry troops probably would have done the same thing as Imperial Security, and almost as fast.

Still, the mines were intact and had started producing ores within three days. If the current rate was only half of what it had been before, Jessica had no doubt that it would ramp up once she got through to these men.

"As a result, we have all the records at the mines that were destroyed in Yonin," Wakely continued. "We also have a guest, of a sort."

"Of a sort?" Jessica asked.

"The man is Conrad Penztler," Wake replied. "Imperial records show him as a ring-leader who tried to organize a strike in the primary mine. He was tortured for a while before he was released. He disappeared into the forest, became what they call *bushmen* around here, and joined or started a small planetary liberation movement. He came to us to talk."

"And he just turned himself in?" Jessica had a hard time buying that.

On the one hand, gift horses. On the other, gifts bearing Greeks.

"They heard our offer of amnesty, Jessica," Wakely replied, looking straight at her on the screen for the first time. "That's what Penztler wanted to discuss. The gift he gave us was the location of a platoon of guerillas that were moving in to hit the starport again."

"Did we get them?" Jessica asked sharply, leaning forward.

"No," Wakely began. "Burdge put a patrol in front of them as a dam, and is currently chasing them backwards into the heavy brush."

"What? Why?"

"That's what I asked, Jessica," she replied heavily. "He said wanted to drive them hard and see where they went. He figured that they might call for help that he could turn around and mousetrap. We have far more firepower on call than they do."

Jessica rested both of her palms flat atop her thighs and bit back her first response. She would have annihilated them and dared the rest to challenge her. But you could do that in space, where there was no place to hide. You fought until someone surrendered or fled into JumpSpace.

War on the ground was far more messy.

"Good enough," Jessica growled. "What else can he tell us?"

"Actually, *Margrave*," Wakely said with a twinkle in her eye. "He wants to talk to you about the entire liberation movement surrendering, or possibly enlisting in our cause."

Jessica stopped and played that last part back again in her head.

"That easy?" Jessica asked with an edge.

"It is what we set out to do, Jessica," Wakely said with a serious, almost sepulchral tone.

Jessica let herself smile.

"I didn't actually think it would work, Wakely."

"Me, neither. But what do we have to lose?"

"Everything, *Palsgrave*. Everything."

Jessica took a breath before she continued.

"You think I should come down and meet with this man?"

"He is apparently the second-in-command of the largest force of rebels under arms," Wakely replied. "And he thinks that they might be willing."

"Good enough," Jessica said. "I'm already adjusted to Yonin local time. I'll come down first thing tomorrow and have a chat with his man."

Jessica keyed off the channel and leaned back to think.

No plan survives contact with the enemy. That's why he's the enemy. His job is to fuck it up.

And her original plan had gone right out the airlock anyway.

Orbital Control destroyed instead of captured. The station itself badly damaged. One of the ore freighters shattered into pieces all over the starport, just now being cleaned up. Imperial Security reacting far faster than they should have, to get under arms and disappear before she could bottle them up. If estimates were correct, there was nearly a full cohort of troops out there, possibly six hundred hard, angry men.

And they were going to fight her to the death on this one.

CHAPTER XXIV

IT WAS one of the benefits to the local planetary infrastructure Jessica hadn't anticipated, but was more than willing to take advantage of. The City Hall building on the planet below her, at Yonin, had been built like a veritable fortress by previous, extremely paranoid, mayors and planetary governors.

Not only had *LVIII Heavy*'s particle cannons not particularly damaged the structure, but it was actually still strong enough that an administrative shuttle could land on the roof with clearance on all sides. Instead of landing amidst all the mess at the starport, and knocking everyone there off rhythm with salutes and busywork, she could go straight to the capital to meet with Wakely.

Jessica had a particularly jaunty walk this morning as she came out of *Auberon*'s main corridor and entered the dramatically-overdone Ready Room for visiting dignitaries.

Again, unlike former First Fleet Lord Loncar, she didn't need to make a production of catching a shuttle to the surface. Denis Než had everything in hand here. The squadron knew what to do, and she could always command from the surface if an Imperial warfleet decided to show up right now, assuming they didn't give her time to get back to her Flag Bridge.

An Imperial commander was likely to be careful. Not everyone was willing to take the risks that Emmerich Wachturm, the dreaded Red

Admiral, did as a matter of course. He might charge in on her at full bore, like last time.

Live by the sword…

The ready room itself was overkill, but *Auberon* was a Star Controller, not just another warship in the fleet. This would be the first place a visiting Ambassador or First Fleet Lord would see when they boarded. As a result, it was built big and pretty.

Inside the airlock-grade door to the flight deck, the room was twelve meters wide and sixteen long, with a four meter ceiling for no better purpose than to impress scale on a visitor. The carpet was *Republic of Aquitaine* Navy Green, a dark, forest green, just this side of moss, thick enough to wade through, but durable enough to last through any kind of party, including *Auberon*'s pilots.

The walls and ceiling were raw metal that had been covered over with a paint the naval architect called *Celadon*, perhaps a shade more green than Ladeaux's sky in the morning. At least here, unlike most places, no pipes were visible, with only HVAC air vent outlets in the walls.

Along Jessica's left-hand wall, a row of bolted-down, cloth-covered sofas and comfortable chairs, were arranged into three little groups and done in a mottled gray pattern that would hide any stain. Across the way was a full-service bar with a small kitchen in the room behind it, in case she needed to throw a dinner party complete with cocktails and munchies, but didn't want to bother the Main Wardroom up three levels.

Decadence, writ in naval architecture.

Centurion Enej Zivkovic, her long-time Flag Centurion, was already there waiting, seated on a sofa with his computer on his lap and one of his Yeomen beside him, when Jessica arrived. He looked up from his conversation, saw her, and whispered one last set of instructions. The other woman nodded, turned, nodded deeper to Jessica, and flew from the room without a word.

Jessica walked close and smiled at the man who was as much her left hand as Denis Jež was her right. She nodded to indicate the woman who had just left.

"Anything I need to worry about?" she asked.

"They're big boys and girls, Commander," he replied, closing up the shell of his computer and standing. "They can handle it themselves, for the most part, once somebody makes a suggestion. If you have to get involved, I've probably screwed up. Yeoman Travere is already aboard and waiting for us."

Jessica had wondered where her *aide d'camp* had disappeared to. Normally, the tall woman was her shadow, following her everywhere except the head. An hour ago, she had said she would make the flight, and vanished.

Enej awaited Jessica's attention.

Jessica was struck suddenly by the changes in the man before her. Enej was as much taller than normal as she was shorter than average, but he was skinny. Not lean, like Tomas Kigali, or even average, but skin over bones. Even his uniforms tended to look baggy. He kept his blond hair very short, almost a buzz cut, and his green eyes didn't miss anything.

Originally, he had come from a very poor family, another Scholarship Student like Jessica. The kind that got into Fleet Boarding school, and later the Academy itself, on brains and not connections.

Kindred spirits.

But unlike Jessica, Enej had not impressed anyone enough along the way that they took an interest in his future career. She was where she was today in part because a future First Lord of the Fleet had been her first tactics instructor, twenty-five years ago.

Enej had ended up in the boonies of the Fleet, a brilliant young officer in a fleet of merely very smart ones. His problem was the lack of a pure killer instinct. An aggressive officer, even a dumb one, would advance, if he was lucky enough to survive. Enej played multi-dimensional chess, rather than poker.

Until Jessica had scanned his file before taking command of *CVS Auberon*, he was doomed to go nowhere. She had taken a chance on the young man, reading between the lines in his personnel file, and had never regretted it.

This morning, he stood perfectly still before her.

Jessica wondered if the semi-quiet relationship he had maintained with *Furious*, one of her top pilots, had influenced the man, or whether coming so close to death so many times had burned all the fidgeting out of the man.

Once, her Flag Centurion had fidgeted constantly, rocking his weight back and forth on his feet, or drumming his fingers on a countertop. Something.

Today, perfect calmness, like the surface of a pond in the first light of dawn.

Night and day, but they had all been through the fires at *First Petron* and *First Ballard*.

None of them would ever be the same.

Enej had gone from being merely a Flag Centurion to being her Chief of Staff. And he would probably continue in this role until she retired, or one of them got killed.

Having his solidity, along with Denis Jež and her other commanders, made it all possible.

Jessica let the moment stretch a bit longer, enjoying the calm competence the man exuded into the room. It was like the first warm sunlight rising.

"We ready?" she asked, finally.

"Shuttle's warmed up," he replied simply. "Pilot has a running calc going. Escort team will launch as soon as you step onto the flight deck. Everything else is waiting for us or in one of our heads."

He paused and smiled a mischievous grin.

"And *Gaucho*'s a bit put out that he's not flying you down this morning."

"I have no intention of going to this meeting smelling like a horse."

"That's what I told him, Commander," Enej concluded. "Plus, he's having fun playing taxi for Fourth Saxon, and the rumor mill says he might have a cowgirl girlfriend."

"What woman would be crazy enough...?"

Jessica paused and thought about it for a second.

"Dash Mitja? Scout Patrol, First Cohort."

"That would be the one, boss."

Jessica shook her head and turned towards the airlock-hatch. Those two getting together would either cancel each other out, or multiply the crazy. There would be no middle ground.

Heaven help us all.

Just outside of the big hatch was a small office. The transparent walls enclosing it kept the sound of the flight deck out, and, in event of an emergency, kept air in.

Seated at the center of the chaos, surrounded by a team of helpers, Command Flight Centurion Iskra Vlahovic looked like a queen. She was a former pilot who had been medically retired after they cut her out of the shattered remains of her fighter craft. Then she came back to service and recreated herself a second career as a flight engineer.

A small woman with an outsize personality, and a willingness to keep pilots in line. Something that Jessica had needed when she inherited the bizarre Flight Wing of old *Auberon*.

And it had worked so well she had kept the same strange configuration on the Star Controller. Instead of three flights of nine *M-6* fighters like the others, she had two, plus the old Scouting and Saturation Wing alignment: *da Vinci* in her little *P-4 Outrider* scout, augmented now with four *S-11 Orca* medium bombers, and four more *M-6* fighters. From a distance, it would look like the typical full wing of twenty-seven signatures, right until someone looked close, or the *Orcas* let loose.

Iskra nodded up at Jessica as she entered the room and leaned into a microphone.

"Sky Team Eight," Iskra said calmly. "Launch and form up."

Lights on her board went green so the Flight Centurion turned back to Jessica.

"We're all set for you, Fleet Centurion. *Petron* is loaded and primed."

Jessica frowned.

"I was planning to take an administrative shuttle down. The building's not big enough or sturdy enough for a DropShip to land on it."

"This is still an active war zone, Commander," Iskra said flatly. "You will be protected. I'm also sending *Sunset* along with four of the fighter jocks."

"And a GunShip, Iskra? What if I order you to break out a shuttle?"

"My Flight Deck, Jessica. My rules. If you don't like them, don't fly."

Jessica nodded. If that woman could somehow bottle stubbornness, she would be rich.

Still, it was good to be surrounded by professionals. If they thought the situation warranted it, they were probably right, and her job was to let them do their job.

Jessica nodded at her Flight Deck Commander, and then grinned.

Iskra let her serious face crack just long enough to grin back before she turned back to her boards.

Jessica passed through the next hatch and onto the flight deck itself,

Enej in tow. *Auberon* only had four DropShips, instead of six, partly to make space for the Orca medium bombers, partly because she had modified the overall design to carry things like an entire Construction Ala in addition to the eighteen hundred ground troops she normally transported. Star Controllers were big, but there were still limits.

Next campaign, she might strip out half the landing capacity and stuff the Flight Deck to the gills. And bring along another Transport Carrier like *Andorra*, currently sitting docked to the remains of the orbital station, slowly unboxing an entire Flight Wing worth of fighters to serve as a local defense force.

There were any number of ways to keep Imperial planners awake at night.

DropShips were big creatures. In private service, *Petron* might qualify as a medium freighter, except that she didn't have the legs for long sails in JumpSpace.

Jessica paused so suddenly that Enej bumped into her from behind before he could stop himself.

He started to say something, but she waved him silent and considered the evil plan that had inserted itself in her brain. Fighter craft were not Jump capable. GunShips and DropShips were, over very short distances.

Jessica had a sudden vision of one of the big, monster freighters, like the ore carrier that had died on *Thuringwell* below her, carrying a whole wave of GunShips to the edge of a planetary system and then launching them to sweep in ahead of a battle squadron. It would be an avalanche, instead of merely a sledgehammer.

Jessica smiled a warm, wicked grin at Enej and then started walking again.

"Is it safe to ask?" he inquired from over her shoulder.

"Next time we pull a *2218 Svati Prime*, someone's in for a very, very rude surprise," she replied, almost bubbling.

Some people played chess. Others liked to knit. Jessica solved tactical and strategic situations for relaxation. It was what she should have been doing earlier, when she felt so isolated and lost as her plans kept failing.

She should have gone back to the filing cabinet and made more plans. She would make up for it tomorrow.

The smell as she came up the stairs and into *Petron*'s airlock reminded Jessica of home. Just inside, Marcelle was seated with the

DropShip's Commander, Flight Centurion Branca Rocha, and the two women were sipping freshly made coffee. Jessica could see the pot, grinder, and press on a sideboard behind them.

Marcelle must really like Rocha. Or lost too much money to her playing poker.

Jessica couldn't think of any other reason the pilot rated freshly ground and hand-pressed coffee. It was Jessica's one serious indulgence. Marcelle was somehow always able to find beans. Jessica made it a point never to inquire how.

"Ready to launch, whenever you order, Commander," Rocha said, starting to stand, a flight bulb on her hand.

"Finish your coffee," Jessica waved her back down.

Since Marcelle had obviously come down early to set up the whole performance, the least Jessica could do would be to sit and be catered to. It wasn't like they could start the meeting on the planet below without her.

Jessica took the spot across from the pilot as Marcelle stood. The smell was enough to brighten her day even more than solving tactical impossibilities. Enej formed the fourth point of a small square.

Recently-roasted beans poured into the grinder and reduced to flakes by hand. Water already close to boiling in the pot. Grounds and water into the press and stir, until the first, perfect layer of foam formed, filling the air with that acrid tang of caffeine. Press slowly. Cut with a little water. Add locally-sourced honey liberated from the ex-Duke's former estate, along with fresh cream from a recently-nationalized cow.

It was amazing how friendly folks might get when you set down a whole patrol of heavily-armed cavalry on a horse and cattle ranch, with instructions to treat the place like they would have to pay for damages later.

Fresh cream in her coffee. Fresh vegetables from the Duke's own hothouse.

The man even had what Jessica's spies on the ground suggested might be the smallest, most perfect Japanese garden imaginable, though Jessica had not figured out how to steal it and install it aboard *Auberon*.

Yet.

Five minutes for the perfection of coffee was a moment worth wasting. Down on the ground, things were likely to get testy.

CHAPTER XXV

IMPERIAL FOUNDING: 175/05/09. YONIN, THURINGWELL

FOR A MOMENT, he thought it was a second apocalypse descending from the heavens. Then Metthias remembered that the first one wasn't over yet.

On a clear, cool morning, the sun disappeared, plunging him into sudden shadows as he stepped away from the coffee stand and back into the flow of traffic on the sidewalk. Many heads turned to look at the sky, but most of them went back to their day a moment later.

Only Metthias stood transfixed, an ebb in the current of bodies.

Quickly, he came back to himself and started moving.

Never stand out, or someone might ask questions.

Questions would be bad. Deadly. Suicidal.

Metthias found a quiet lee, a recessed doorway to a shop that would not open for another hour, and watched the sky fall in.

The thing was huge. A blue-gray steel whale bigger than a building, slowly descending from the stars and taking up a hovering position over the City Building. The galaxy's biggest hummingbird preparing to sip its breakfast.

Finally, his mind found words for it.

DropShip. *Republic of Aquitaine.* Nightshade-class.

Invaders.

Why was it hovering?

It was too big to land, and is delivering someone. Someone

important enough to be personally conveyed to the City Building, rather than landing at the port and coming over separately.

They waited patiently, the two of them. A minute passed.

The DropShip shivered once, rotated in place, and sedately ascended a bit as it flew in the direction of the port.

So. Taxi awaiting the return fare.

Metthias smiled, just a shade and just for a moment.

There should be time to get into position.

CHAPTER XXVI

DATE OF THE REPUBLIC MAY 9, 396 YONIN, THURINGWELL

IT CERTAINLY WASN'T *Gaucho* flying. Jessica and Marcelle could have broken out the fine porcelain for their coffee without risk today. Of course, *Gaucho* would have probably set a new sky-to-ground record doing this. He would have at least tried.

Jessica had gotten spoiled by the crazy man.

Still, the landing pad atop the building was clear. A team of marines surrounded the edges of the building as *Petron* gently settled into position and lowered her landing ramp, two of her landing struts deployed and just touching the stone of the roof.

Jessica moved quickly down a ramp designed for armored vehicles, Enej and Marcelle trailing two and three steps back. The Yeoman in charge of the marines nodded at her as she approached and gestured for her to follow him into the stairwell and down out of sight.

Behind her, the hum of *Petron*'s engines changed camber as the DropShip surged skyward.

Inside, out of the wind, she found one of Wakely's people, a young man she only knew as a scholar on loan from the University of Ladaux.

"Welcome, *Margrave*," the man said formally, turning immediately away and descending the stairs into the building.

Jessica and the others followed him down ten quick flights, nearly a third of the thirty-five story tower, before emerging into the reception area where Wakely had taken her offices. The spaces that were reserved for Imperial high officials, for the Mayor, the Governor, and the Duke's Castellan, comprised three of the top five floors and had been sealed off and preserved for now. At least until Wakely decided what she wanted to do to fill in three offices that each took up most of an entire floor with empty space and a single desk.

Ego.

The three men would have said power, if asked, but Jessica knew that true power could make do with a shoebox office tucked away in a distant, basement corner of the palace. The kind of man who could fill whatever space he entered. She had a fairly low opinion of the men who had been in charge here.

Miles Gunderson had at least been a gentleman, but his office still had window-to-window silk carpeting in a soft rose color that certainly cost more than most of the miners on this planet earned in a year.

Wakely met her in the oversized reception area stuffed with mismatched sofas, lots of desks, and maps tacked to every wall.

It was a vaguely jarring transition for Jessica, to go from being surrounded by the nearly identical uniforms of her people to the sorts of civilian mufti in this room. The man who had escorted her down the stairs was in a sedate blue. Wakely was wearing a flowing linen outfit with a mixture of salmons and oranges. Around the rest of the suite were a half-dozen others in everything except green. Only the four marines stationed around the edges of the large space wore green, but they were carefully keeping a low profile, here as guardians, not bodyguards, per se.

Jessica guessed that was an unconscious move by the civilians to distinguish themselves from the several thousand people in uniform around them.

Wakely had a spring in her step this morning almost as good as Jessica's. It was one of those days where everything seemed to be going right.

"So," Jessica said as she got close. "We have a prisoner?"

"Worse," Wakely replied with a droll smile. "We have an ambassador."

Jessica shrugged. The man could call himself anything he wanted. She and Wakely were the power in this system. The stranger was nothing more than the assistant to a small-town mayor come to the big city. The question would be to discover what he wanted.

"Is he ready for us?" Jessica asked.

"He is," Wakely smiled. "He had a visit with a doctor yesterday, dinner, breakfast, tea, and a good night's sleep. I've got him in a conference room with a guard right now, and I think it would be best if it was just the three of us talking."

"Good enough," Jessica agreed and let Wakely lead.

This was one of the reasons *Thuringwell* had been first on her list. Unpopular Duke. Armed resistance movement that wasn't big enough to be an existential threat by itself. That those men might be willing to deal was just a bonus, at this point.

Largely empty world on which to maneuver. Dramatic upside if all of her and Wakely's plans worked. The new plans.

Not that she had expected them to. Jessica had been firmly convinced they had all failed explosively in the first twelve hours, when the station blew and then the ore carrier followed.

She would never let on to anyone, but Wakely knew her well enough by now to guess.

The conference room was obviously intended for *little people*, and not the Duke or his favored. Industrial white paint over sheetrock. Bland taupe carpet designed to hold up to a lot of traffic. Pseudo-wood conference table a meter and a half by three, with ugly metal legs underneath. Nine mismatched chairs, mostly in black, with a shockingly-blue one that looked stolen and hidden out of the way.

And one prisoner.

Conrad Penztler. Former miner. Former labor organizer. Former political prisoner. Current armed resistance fighter. Proposed Ambassador to the Huns.

The other Huns.

He fidgeted in the same way that Enej had once. The two men were of a look physically as well. Tall, wiry blonds without a gram of spare flesh. But Enej had a calmness to him now that this stranger was lacking.

Penztler cast her a very wary eye as he stared at her. He rose as she came into the room, causing the marine in the corner to flinch for a second.

Jessica was more amused than anything when the marine relaxed on realizing it was the Fleet Centurion coming in, since she could supposedly take care of herself with any man, according to her marines. Apparently, stories about her fighting to the death with blades had made the rounds with the new unit, as well. She wasn't sure if she should thank Vo Arlo, or give him a stern talking to.

Penztler carefully held out a hand to shake, an interesting Imperial custom.

Jessica reached across the table and took it in hers.

His skin was leathery and calloused. A shower had gotten the man clean, but there was still dirt under his nails that would require a good manicure to eliminate. She considered suggesting it, but remembered that there were only three shops in all of Yonin, given the dearth of civilized citizens needing such a service.

One more mark of barbarity I need to address, one of these days.

Jessica added importing qualified manicurists to the list in her head.

"Sri Penztler," Jessica released his hand and sat, with Wakely taking the chair on the end, rather than sitting across from him. It softened the room.

He sat, or rather perched on the edge of his seat nervously.

She thought about making him wait. Silence could be just as sharp, just as effective as a saber, used expertly. But her time was valuable and this man had come to her. His folks could shave years off the effort, or drag it on forever if they chose to be stubborn.

More stubborn.

Easy-going men didn't fade into the bush and take up arms against the Imperial family.

"You asked for a meeting with myself and the *Palsgrave*," Jessica continued. "And provided us valuable intelligence about a pending Imperial attack. I am here. How can I help you today?"

Wakely had helped hone them, but it was really First Lord that had taught her the verbal tricks to get inside someone's skin without them realizing it.

Penztler reacted like someone had stuck a needle into his hand. Not much, just a shuddering flinch he couldn't control.

A woman in charge. Women in charge. *Aquitaine* women. And he was here to try to make friends, or at least common cause.

Fish very much out of water.

Jessica smiled to soften the blow.

Penztler let go a held breath audibly and settled backwards into his chair, just about the time the marine looked like he was willing to get twitchy.

"What is your mission on *Thuringwell*, Admiral?" he asked carefully.

Not exactly subtle, but Jessica hadn't asked about the weather or his family. This wasn't a social call where they might spend twenty minutes getting around to the topic at hand. This was business. More to the point, this was a war.

"*Margrave*," Jessica corrected him simply. "We control the system. We control Yonin and the mines now. The Imperial Army and the local government have surrendered on terms and been taken into custody for repatriation."

Her smile turned a shade more ugly as she leaned forward.

"There are two armed forces currently operating in the wilderness beyond my control," she prodded him. "At least one of them will need to be annihilated root and branch in order to succeed in securing *Thuringwell* as an *Aquitainian* planet."

"One?" he asked carefully, holding his cards close to his vest.

Again, not used to a woman giving orders. His mother had probably been the last one in his life, and maybe not even then, considering modern Imperial notions of culture.

"Colonel Dieter Haussmann of Imperial Security is currently in the field somewhere with several hundred men under arms," Jessica said simply. "I don't expect they are the kind of people who are willing to surrender on any terms. So I will hunt them down like vermin and extirpate them. I'm fine with making them martyrs, Penztler."

"And the liberation movements?"

Penztler had gotten perfectly still, but it wasn't calm self-assurance. Rather, it was the look a rabbit got when a hawk appeared overhead.

"You haven't committed any crimes against the *Republic of Aquitaine*, yet," Jessica said carefully.

This was the sort of conversation that would probably be recounted at a Court Martial. Her next one.

They didn't get any easier, but at least the *Republic of Aquitaine* Navy was careful to have public court proceedings when things got this complicated. It served to exonerate an honorable officer from any questions, and to provide a learning tool for others to know where the lines were supposed to be brightly drawn.

That the next one might be held before the Republic Senate was just a mark of scale and consequence, not style.

The man shook his head in vague agreement with her statement, but didn't speak.

"And also understand that poaching will be a serious crime shortly," Wakely spoke up suddenly.

Penztler was jarred even further off center. He had apparently forgotten about her in his concentration on Jessica.

Jessica watched him mouth the word without speaking it.

Poaching?

"Poaching," Wakely repeated firmly. "Fleet Centurion Keller has purchased and transported to *Thuringwell* several herds of livestock intended to expand the local food supplies. Those herds are privately owned, but will be managed for the good of the colony."

"And Fourth Saxon has a very dim view of cattle thieves." Jessica smiled warmly at the man.

Her smile was the promise of a long fall from a short rope.

He saw that, too. Whatever he had been expecting this morning, it had not been anything like this.

Jessica leaned back and smiled some more. It was probably still a little too much cat to his mouse, but that was the situation.

Moments of silence passed as Penztler got his bearings. Mostly.

"You plan to stay," he concluded quietly.

It was not a question, exactly. Perhaps if he said it out loud, that might make it more understandable. He had that look about him, right now.

Certainly, it opened a new chapter in diplomacy. If the Imperials had tried something like this, the whole planetary population might fade into the bush. The Imperials had discovered long ago that it was easier to simply command local space and coopt the locals. Several Republic worlds had been under their control that way for some time.

Prying an Imperial world loose, and doing it in this manner, was a new thing. A new threat to the *Fribourg Empire*. A crowbar Jessica intended to torque until something broke.

Hopefully, not her.

"I do," Jessica agreed, letting the rest dangle.

"And the other units under arms?"

She found it interesting, the way he phrased that.

Before, it was *liberation movements*. But the world had been liberated from Imperial control. And he dared not use the real term.

Rebellion. That would put him on the same side with Haussmann.

Some of the groups already out there in the wilderness might make that choice. She would see how much pull this man had.

"As I said, you haven't committed any crimes against the Republic, Penztler. Yet. That's likely to change, the longer your groups remain in the field. I will be less receptive as time goes on."

Jessica leaned forward again to drive her point home.

"At some point, the *Fribourg Empire* will figure out what we've done here, and try to stop us. If the world is on our side, we're far more likely to fight it out, than to simply cut our losses and retreat back across the frontier."

Or, you best understand that there are risks either way, Sri.

"I am not in a position to negotiate those stakes, Admiral. Governor. *Margrave.*"

It took him a moment to wrap his head around that title.

"May I return to my unit and make your case to my commander?"

"I look forward to it, Sri," Jessica said.

"Will you require assistance to get back to your base?" Wakely spoke up again. "Your associate, Elizabeth Guhathakurta, has asked for and been granted political asylum. Elizabeth thought that you might need help in the bush."

Jessica watched that bit of information get under the man's skin like a tattoo needle, a little staccato pulse counterpointing his heartbeat.

"We will provide you with maps and food, Penztler," Wakely continued. "Plus you'll have your radio and other gear. We appreciate you not being ready to share the location of your base. We would like to deal with you on faith."

On faith.

Wasn't everything being done here on faith? On luck? On timing?

"I would like to talk to her, to Eli, before I go, if possible," he said, still in a mild state of shock.

"Absolutely," Wakely rose gracefully. "I'll send her in shortly."

Jessica rose as well.

Everything had been said that needed to. Penztler would go back to his people and make the case. She would deal with the consequences, one way or the other.

Wakely surprised her by gesturing for the marine in the corner to depart with them as well.

Outside, Wakely gestured to a woman who had been working at a nearby desk.

"Eli," she said to the woman. "I'll let you two have a few minutes of privacy, and then I'll send you back with the *Margrave*."

Interesting. So this was the defector. Jessica studied the woman more closely than she had last time she had been in this room.

Elizabeth Guhathakurta was taller than Jessica. Darker. Curvier both in chest and hips. She had medium-length hair nearly black and eyes the dark brown of aged, stained wood.

It was interesting to watch her move. She had the same low center of gravity that Jessica saw in the mirror. In Jessica's case, close combat training with blades. Guhathakurta looked like she might have something similar, but it was more flowing, less compact. Given the planet, Jessica would have said exotic dancer for money, but there was also something wild and dangerous underneath.

Wakely must have had a very interesting conversation with the woman to already be willing to let her talk to Penztler without supervision.

In a moment, the two of them were alone in a side office.

Jessica had a host of questions she wanted to ask, but Wakely was unlikely to have any more answers than she did.

"Will it work?" Jessica settled on.

Dr. Wakely Okafor, PhD, Distinguished Fellow, Visiting Scholar, expert on Imperial governance, shrugged.

"Maybe?" she said. "Penztler is supposedly the second in command to a man named Fraser Cydelmynster, according to the files we have started to read. That man has a deep and abiding hatred of Imperial Security."

"How bad?"

"They killed his wife publicly," Wakely said. "Shot her in the street. He vanished before they could get to him. Most of the modern liberation movement came about in the last four years because of that man."

"And we don't know much?" Jessica asked.

"Almost nothing," Wakely said. "He might surrender and ask for asylum. He might become a patriot. He might decide to go after Haussmann personally."

"Keep me posted," Jessica decided. "He has until we destroy Haussmann and his people to make up his own mind."

After that, this Fraser Cydelmynster would be next on her list.

CHAPTER XXVII

DATE OF THE REPUBLIC MAY 9, 396 YONIN, THURINGWELL

JESSICA SMILED as she looked out over the rooftop.

It hadn't been all that long, dealing with Penztler. Enough for Enej and Marcelle to settle in and do paperwork, but not to get bored with it.

Now they had both followed her back up to the roof, gasping a bit at the climb. She considered suggesting that they spend more time stair-climbing and less time working on machines. *Auberon* had enough decks to get anyone in shape. Running stairs had long been part of Jessica's morning routine.

Nothing on the roof had changed, except the location of some of the men and women protecting it with crew-served weapons. They had apparently moved to cover different flanks of the skyscraper in the ninety minutes she had been below.

From the stairwell, Jessica had a good view of the starport. She watched four small dots detach themselves from the ground, followed a few moments later by the bigger bulk of the DropShip *Petron* leaping gracefully skyward.

Enej was on the landing with her, with Marcelle a few steps below, a marine below that, the defector, and another marine. The space was a bit crowded, but everyone left her alone to think. She could just hear her Flag Centurion speaking into a sound-deadening microphone, arranging their taxi ride.

Elizabeth Guhathakurta was an interesting find. Ex-prostitute, ex-dancer, ex-bounty hunter, ex-everything. A woman far older than her twenty-four years standard. She had a feral edge to everything she said, and how she moved, that kept Jessica's marines, both big men, nervous.

Marcelle could probably still teach the young woman a few tricks. There are things you don't pick up in bar fights for at least a decade. Or three, in Marcelle's case.

Right now, Guhathakurta was behaving like an Imperial Lady of the Court. One with a very mischievous twinkle in her eye, but few words. She had been unwilling to provide any tactical or strategic intelligence, beyond the Imperial Security attack that had been thwarted, so she still retained some level of loyalty to her former comrades, which was a good sign.

But this was a woman with an eye towards the main chance, and a willingness to gamble.

Her interview had been even more interesting than Penztler's. She wanted out. Away from *Fribourg*. Away from a male culture. But unwilling to commit to *Aquitaine*. Still, she would be taken aboard *Auberon* and given a job, if she wanted, or simply transported to *Ladaux* and kissed farewell on both cheeks.

The woman looked like she might be reading Jessica's mind. She smiled warmly for the first time, perhaps seeing her escape from a life of male-domination in the massive DropShip slowly sliding over the edge of the roof like a morning eclipse.

"*Margrave*," she called suddenly over the sound, causing the men in between them to twitch. "Can you really win?"

Jessica smiled back at her.

"What kind of man is Fraser Cydelmynster?" Jessica fired back.

They had had this conversation earlier, but nothing had come of it. Maybe the woman was finally relaxing.

"Gold-Four, the Captain, is a hard man, *Margrave*," Elizabeth said, her eyes drifting off to the horizon and unfocusing. "They killed his wife. You know that. But he still talks to her. Listens to her advice. Most of the men don't pay enough attention to realize that."

Jessica gave the woman a shrewd smile. Elizabeth kept sounding decades older than she was.

Still, that might be an opening she could exploit. Jessica figured she had a one in three chance of having to fight the man. He was probably most likely to go after Haussmann personally. Though he might be willing to come in from the cold.

Jessica had several industries and properties that she and Wakely needed to sell off to local investors willing to put up sweat equity to see succeed. Captain Cydelmynster sounded like the kind of man who could get himself elected Governor, if he wanted.

Now, she just needed to convince him that he wanted to.

Tomorrow.

Today, *Petron* was just touching the rooftop gravel, hovering sedately as before, ramp down like a mouth waiting to swallow them whole.

One of the marine Yeomen gestured for her to board. A light drizzle had begun to mist everything. Not enough to even wet her uniform, just dampen her hair. It got her aboard half a step faster and across the big bay of the DropShip to the officer's cabin.

Jessica sat on one side, with the rest of the group mostly seated across from her, Guhathakurta smiling at the two big men seated on either side of her, professional paranoia evident.

"Rocha, we're ready to lift," Enej said out loud as everyone buckled in.

Again, tea would not have spilled as the ship tilted softly away and began to hum louder.

Gaucho probably would have dropped the ship on its ass and lit the afterburners, trusting that everyone was serious about being secure enough to treat it like a hot drop.

He did that.

The alarm was almost simultaneous with the explosion.

Tea would have gone everywhere as *Petron* shuddered and lurched sideways, vibrating madly as it spun on the flat axis. There was a sound like metal tearing that approached apocalyptic.

"Mayday. Fleet, this is DropShip *Petron*, declaring an emergency," Rocha's voice came out of the speakers. "I am under fire and have sustained a hit. Feels like a ground-to-air missile."

"Acknowledged, *Petron*," Jessica heard Denis's calm voice on the comm. "What is your status?"

"Airworthy and evading. Stand by."

A second hit jarred the ship, nearly turning her turtle as the starboard aft corner was suddenly driven into the air by another explosion.

The engines stopped for a moment. *Petron* stalled into freefall like a character in a children's cartoon hovering over the edge of the cliff.

Jessica felt the big vessel right itself with a roar of defiance. Up front, Rocha slammed the engines to the stops and left them there. Everyone in the cabin was pressed into their restraints by the sudden acceleration. Up became up again, and then the aft of the DropShip became down as the ship stood on her ass and leapt for the sky.

"Fleet Centurion, what is your status?" Rocha said calmly.

Jessica looked around to be sure. The cabin where she rode was a mess, but it was also towards the bow of the DropShip, just behind the cockpit, inside the best armor. The hits had been well back.

Exactly where a DropShip was designed to take ground fire and still fly.

"We're fine, Flight Centurion," Jessica replied slowly, forcing the adrenaline out of her voice. "Can we make it to the starport intact?"

A calm commander infects her crew with calmness.

"Don't care, Commander," Rocha growled over the engines. "I'm going for sky."

Jessica could hear the woman's teeth grinding over the comm as the howling got louder.

"What is our status, then, Rocha?" Jessica asked.

"Two hits, Commander," the pilot replied. "Lost one engine. The others are intact. Escort wing is dropping flares and jamming electronics so hard that the iron in your blood might react down on the street. They'll probably start strafing if somebody fires another shot."

"Understood."

There wasn't a lot Jessica could do at this point that wouldn't inject more chaos into the system. Let the experts expert. The city would survive whatever incoming fire demanded the right of way.

"Please stay in your seats," the pilot continued. "The drop bay may no longer be pressurized, but the rest of the ship is and I'm going for orbit and rendezvous with the mothership."

Jessica nodded and turned to Enej, catching his attention as he spoke furiously into his microphone.

"I'm going to owe Iskra an apology," Jessica said.

"Nope," her Flag Centurion replied with a harsh smile. "That would be if you were dead. She's going to settle for a whole bunch of *I told you so*'s."

Jessica nodded.

War is chaos. Somebody down there had thought he could assassinate her.

Maybe, just maybe, that rat bastard would be stubborn enough that he could be taken alive.

CHAPTER XXVIII

"SO WHAT DO WE KNOW?" Jessica growled.

It was just her, Enej, and Marcelle in her office. She could have done this on the Flag Bridge, brought everyone up for a big staff meeting, but that wouldn't have gained anything except to take time out of people's busy days.

And let them watch her apologize to Iskra Vlahovic personally. As Enej said, nothing like a good *I told you so*.

Marcelle had done the same to Jessica a little more privately, while making her coffee before anyone arrived.

"*LVIII Heavy* didn't stop to ask questions," Enej said without looking down at his notes. "One of the tanks had a line of sight on the building that had launched the two ground-to-air missiles, so they hammered it with their cannon a few times. Ground troops got there four minutes later."

An image was projected, showing the room from a variety of angles, including badly-scorched shipping boxes with unarmed missiles inside.

"And?"

"And he got away," Enej continued. "The device was a camouflaged air-defense battery with two tubes and half a dozen more missiles secured close by. Apparently remotely-activated. Security footage on a nearby bank has identified a probable shooter and tracked his vehicle to the edge of town. Looks like he met some people there, presumably more sleeper agents, swapped land vehicles, and ran like hell."

"Into the forest?" Jessica asked.

"Affirmative," he said. "Fourth Saxon has a patrol headed that way to track them."

Jessica considered the situation. That room had not been put together in the last two weeks. Imperial Security had apparently been planning for this sort of thing for years.

It was entirely out of character for Imperial Security to be this prepared, this good, on a world this irrelevant. The only thing she could think of was Haussmann was so paranoid he had gotten himself exiled here to keep him away from the halls of power, and he had nothing better to do with his time than exercise his craziness.

On her.

That suggested that the men who had fled into the bush might be more heavily armed and prepared than her current plans anticipated.

This just kept getting worse.

Or better, if she wanted to look on the whole thing as a tactical exercise of the kind originally dreamed up by Nils Kasum to keep her on her toes.

Anything less stubborn than a DropShip like *Petron* would have been destroyed. Even one of the fighters would have been shattered at that range. There were probably more of those surprises out in the wilderness, just waiting for her to push troops out, supposedly covered by air support.

Jessica realized that Enej and Marcelle were quietly watching her, waiting.

At least they knew that her bouts of introspection were tactical, and not depression and self-doubt. Another reason they had stayed with her all these years.

"Get me Rebekah Kim on the comm," Jessica said with a leap of intuition.

Enej let an eyebrow come up, but he grabbed his computer and started typing.

Within thirty seconds, the semi-snarling face of *LVIII Heavy*'s Commander appeared in a projection. Apparently, the woman was in the field. The camera pickup was from inside *Freefall*.

"Fleet Centurion?" Kim asked, managing to convey an amazing

amount of disdain at the interruption of her day, just from the look on her face.

This was a woman of very few words.

"Kim, I want you to rearrange your forces a little to free up a team to push into the brush with a patrol from Fourth Saxon."

"Why?"

On any other officer, that was probably pushing the boundaries of insubordination. With Kim, it was literally the question she wanted answered, so she could plan her next move.

"You heard about yesterday?" Jessica asked.

"Legate Burdge covered it in his morning briefing," the Cohort Centurion replied simply.

Again, the minimum number of words necessary. Jessica appreciated dealing with Kim.

"I'm going to have Fourth Saxon send someone after the bastard that did it," Jessica said, trying to keep the hostility out of her voice. "I want at least a lance of your tanks to accompany them as heavy support. The locals have bigger guns than I was expecting."

"Do we know who Burdge will send?" Kim asked, bouncing in the camera pickup as *Freefall* lurched over something big enough to rattle that much tonnage of tank.

Jessica was amused that the commander of *LVIII Heavy* was in the field on patrol, but that was one of the reasons Jessica had asked for this cohort, a willingness of everyone involved to get their hands dirty. Fourth Saxon was the same way.

"Arlo is currently attached to Scout Patrol, First Cohort," Jessica said. "Since he's my ground coordinator, probably them. They'll still need someone from your team to back him up."

"Arlo?" Kim asked. There was something in her voice that didn't register.

"Centurion Vo Arlo," Jessica reminded the woman. "You sat next to him at the big dinner, and earlier when we went to meet Fourth Saxon on the ground."

"Right," Kim said breezily. "Let me review rotations here. I think I have everyone assigned to duties that I can't pull them off of. Might just send myself and 1-1-1 to do it."

"Let me know," Jessica said, cutting the line.

Enej and Marcelle both had grins on their faces.

Jessica considered the two of them before she spoke.

"Is there something going on between Kim and Arlo?" she asked.

Marcelle shrugged Gallicly.

"I don't think she's his type, based on some of what I've heard," Enej offered diplomatically.

The way he said it was not particularly convincing.

Marcelle chuckled.

"You think she'd give him a choice, Flag Centurion?"

CHAPTER XXIX

DIETER SCOWLED, insulted.

He had spent years on this planet, preparing. He had warned them, repeatedly, that this day might come, that they might wake up one morning and find an *Aquitaine* fleet in orbit overhead.

They had laughed.

Very few of them were laughing today.

Still, she had outraged his sensibilities, this woman, this *Fleet Centurion*.

Nowhere had he made plans sufficient to combat this latest threat. He had never imagined such a need.

That failure, of his own imagination, only made it worse.

Dieter lowered the binoculars and took a deep breath, crushing his teeth together so hard his neck hurt.

Around him, the rest of the patrol achieved perfect stillness, perfect quiet. There had been noise, so low as to be unconscious, obvious now only in its absence.

Dieter considered the nine men who had accompanied him here. He looked quickly around the little copse of trees on the morning hillside, glancing skyward once on habit. They were invisible from above and below, dropped down behind a small backslope where they could look over from their bellies and elbows, like he and Sergeant Stoltberg were doing now. The rest squatted nearby, wary and watchful.

Who knew what dangers might lurk here?

Stoltberg waited carefully.

"I would not have believed it possible," Dieter hissed. "She might be good enough to challenge me. We shall have to do something about that."

Stoltberg nodded slightly, more a placeholder than agreement. He was a big, stupid hound, an attack dog waiting to be turned loose. It took Dieter's genius to make a man like Stoltberg more than just a bully waiting in an alley.

Dieter raised the glasses once more.

Down below, a snake of destruction half a kilometer wide slithered through the valley. Not much was clear from this distance, beyond the fact that *Aquitaine* was leveling ground, filling things in, bridging creeks.

Apparently, building an entirely new railroad system.

Running to his left, the destination was obvious. They were perhaps forty kilometers to the edge of Yonin from here.

What he did not grasp was the other end.

Railroads are fixed infrastructure connecting two important points. There was nothing north of Yonin.

Nothing.

And yet, *Aquitaine* was connecting to something.

It would not be enough to attack the camp below. Even from here, Dieter could make out platoons of armed troops and armored vehicles defending the workers and their equipment. And *Aquitaine* could quickly ferry troops from orbit or Yonin to box him in if he launched a frontal assault.

Damn her!

Dieter's teeth clenched again.

I will not be beaten by a woman.

He stood slowly.

"It is a railroad," he observed in a voice as sharp as a knife. "We must find out what is at the other end. And then we will destroy it. And her."

CHAPTER XXX

IMPERIAL FOUNDING: 175/05/12.
BACKCOUNTRY, THURINGWELL

IT WAS WORSE than Fraser imagined. More painful than it could possibly be.

He was damned.

If he did, if he didn't. It no longer mattered.

Things had been ripped from his control. Not that he had ever had much to begin with.

Fraser sipped his warm, dark, instant coffee and glanced around the evening camp. Fires could be built out here, if they were small and sheltered from observation on all sides. Warm food went a long ways towards keeping the barbarism of the situation at bay, especially when the temperature faded in the late afternoon gloom.

Conrad had finished his story. He looked anxiously around the group of ten or so folks close by.

Nobody spoke.

Probably waiting for Fraser to make a decision. He was The Captain.

Horse shit.

Fraser had been expecting threats from *Aquitaine*. Possibly they would simply arrest Conrad and disappear him into a camp somewhere, never to be seen again. Maybe they would drive their tanks into the forests and try to run him down like a deer.

But no.

They wanted him to surrender? Politely?

Was she nuts?

No. She was playing chess, and everyone else was playing jacks. She could see that. He could as well. Conrad might have an inkling. Eli had leapt at the chance to escape, but that was Eli. He couldn't begrudge her the move. Anything would be an improvement after *Thuringwell* for a woman like her.

"We'll sleep on it," Fraser announced gruffly. "We have time. She won't catch Haussmann soon."

That got a chuckle. Everyone there had dealt with Imperial Security personally. A few still bore scars the man himself had left, like Conrad.

Fraser leveled himself upright.

"It's good to have you back, Conrad," he said as he lurched off to his tent.

Behind him, he heard the rest settling in. Some would stay up for a while. Most would be asleep shortly. Darkness came fast and the sun rose early at this elevation.

The little green and brown tent was small, no bigger than any of the others, and smaller than most, since he didn't want one big enough to share with anyone. Fraser loosened his boots and hung them upside down on a little wooden contraption he had made, just for the purpose.

He crawled under his blanket and let his thoughts wander. This was the time of day when he was his most creative, fading down into darkness and sleep. His mind could disassemble any question and spend hours while he slept, randomly putting pieces together until it found a connection that worked.

That had kept them alive.

And now he was dancing with a new partner. Colonel Haussmann was a predictable-enough opponent. Crazy and paranoid, but largely given to thinking on rails.

This woman, this Admiral Keller, no, Fleet Centurion Keller, get it right. She has already blown the rails entirely away and left everyone with an empty, green field upon which to play.

How do we survive her?

Fraser closed his eyes and let go of the day, hoping the darkness would drag him all the way to the bottom of the well and let him sleep untroubled.

It did that, occasionally.

Not tonight.

Jeannine was there, as he knew she would be.

One of the advantages to being dead was that you would always be as beautiful as you had ever been, at least in the eyes of your widowed husband. Her hair would always be that short, brunette, pixie cut she had tried out just before they had shot her. Her legs still had that long, slender silhouette in the afternoon sun, distracting every man on the street because they knew they couldn't have her.

"Hello, my love," she whispered as he faded into being in her little park hollow.

It looked remarkably like the one where he had gotten down on one knee and proposed to her, twenty-seven years before.

Fraser wanted to flee this dream, to find someplace safe, but there wasn't anywhere safer for his sanity than in her arms. The last waking part of his mind wondered if that made him less crazy, or more.

She held out a hand that drew him towards her like the pull of gravity.

"You could let go, you know," she continued in that slight voice normally reserved for murmurs in a sweaty bed. "Walk away like Eli did. Find happiness. It is never too late."

"And lose you?"

Fraser couldn't help his voice breaking, even in a dream.

She smiled ruefully and clenched his hand tighter. She pulled him in close and suddenly they were dancing, slow and warm, like that first night he ever laid eyes on this beautiful creature and knew no other would ever do.

"You will never lose me, Fraser," she whispered into his chest, letting his arms enfold her. "I will always be no farther away than your memory, than your dreams. I will be here every night when you want to dream."

"He killed you," Fraser agonized quietly.

"And he lost," her voice suddenly became a cold blade, a broadsword. "Now he can never have me. And you will have me forever. He did not defeat me. He suffered the ultimate defeat. He could only kill me."

"And me? What do I do? How do I win?"

"Oh, my love," she whispered, caressing his cheek with her right hand. "Every day you are alive you defeat him. Every one of your people who are alive with you are burning splinters under his fingernails, an itch he cannot reach. Every breath you draw diminishes him that much more."

"I swore I would see him dead." Fraser let the warmth of her hand embrace his raw soul.

"He is fallen, Fraser Cydelmynster. Let it go."

She began to fade, even as he clasped harder. Her spirit ran through his hands like water, like mist, like the morning fog in the hollows melting under the rising sun.

Finally, even the scent of her perfume was gone.

Fraser awoke in darkness, flat on his back. Something had thumped his foot hard enough to break him out of a dream.

"You awake?" Conrad called quietly from the tent's doorway.

Fraser laid there for a moment, finding gravity and place in the darkness, so different from where he had just been.

He felt a wet burn down both sides of his face, where the tears had drained back and run across the tops of his ears.

"Fraser?"

"Yeah," he sat up and wiped his face, glad that nobody could see him in the utter darkness of his tent.

Conrad knew, but Conrad knew most of it anyway.

"You were growling and moaning in your sleep. Roald had the watch and came and got me."

"Thanks."

Fraser jammed his boots on his feet and hooked them shut. He stood up out of his tent as Conrad stepped back. There was a rifle in a small storage crate to keep it dry. He grabbed it and checked the round in the chamber before turning around.

Maybe he had it together enough to talk to the living.

"You okay?" Conrad asked carefully.

"Yeah."

There wasn't much more coherence at this point. Fraser was slowly climbing up from the bottom of a very deep well and needed time to order his thoughts.

"You go back to sleep, Conrad," he said. "I'm going to go sit with Roald for a while and then maybe I'll be better."

Conrad gave him a dubious look, but said nothing.

The two of them went way back as friends. Nothing much more needed to be said.

Roald had a look of concern. There was enough moonlight to see a ways, especially from the little rise just outside their main camp. Fog crept around below, poking cold fingers into nooks and sleeping bags.

Fraser found a comfortable tree across from Roald and leaned back.

He knew he should take Keller up on her offer. Knew it in his bones.

But he would never be happy until he had Haussmann's skull on a pole in his front yard as a warning to future generations.

The galaxy had gotten as bad as it had because there were not enough men and women willing to stand up to men like Haussmann. And there were always men like Dieter Haussmann.

How many of his own people would Fraser lose when he offered them the chance to escape with *Aquitaine*?

It didn't really matter. He would go after the man alone, naked, with a sharpened stick, if that was all he had left. Even Jeannine knew that.

CHAPTER XXXI

DATE OF THE REPUBLIC MAY 22, 396 CAX
SHIVAJI. ABOVE THURINGWELL

HE DID HAVE to hand it to her.

The Fleet Centurion had managed to find possibly the most boring place Alber' could think of in Imperial space to invade. What was the term she had used to describe the planet below them? Company town, or something like that.

Isolated.

Predictable.

Dreary.

Alber' d'Maine sat in his command chair and scowled professionally at the universe.

Any other planet might have such a dynamic-enough economy that little tramp freighters would be running back and forth to nearby systems hauling goods.

But no. That idiot Duke had kept his greedy, iron fingers around everything. Even the asteroid belt was nearly virgin, under threat of Imperial imprisonment or a prison planet if anyone looked to develop it.

No, everything was on the planet below. One starport, one city. Nearly two-score open-pit mines sprawled like wounds visible from orbit on a clear-enough day. Rails connecting everything like a giant octopus or spiderweb.

Dull.

But on the brighter side, it also meant that he could pull *Shivaji* out of the defensive line and patrol near space, as long as he was careful. *Ballard* still frequently hopped out to the far edges of the system to look around, but that was a part of her job, the primary reason she was here in the first place.

Kigali would have been mutinous with boredom, by now.

Shivaji's purpose today was to turn off all active arrays, go dark, and slide into the area outside the edge of the gravity well like a leopard seal hunting penguins.

RAN's biggest stealth frigate.

Even aboard *Rajput*, Alber' hadn't been allowed this luxury. But his fierce, little heavy destroyer had still only been an escort. Nobody in their right mind would have believed she could kill a light cruiser. Let alone survive afterwards. With anybody else in command, she couldn't have.

But they didn't get it.

Shivaji was a very dangerous creature, all by herself. Heavy cruisers were designed to show the flag, frequently traveling on distant and potentially dangerous missions alone. They could generally outrun battleships and outfight anything smaller, at least long enough to slip into the safety of JumpSpace.

Alber' smiled. It was a harsh, cruel smile, entirely out of place on the big, friendly bridge of his vessel. *Shivaji* as she was configured today might duel an Imperial battleship on even terms, especially if one tried to stay right at the edge of the range for the big Primary beams, where they would expect an advantage against a *mere cruiser*.

And they would have one, right up until he turned away, slid outward beyond even that range, and opened fire with the two Type-4 beams on her dorsal fin.

Station-class firepower.

Shivaji didn't have any missiles, but she could kill things from a very long ways off.

Around him, things were quiet.

Running dark meant that sensors were off. Shields were down to the bare minimum for navigation. Emissions of all kinds were strictly curtailed.

As a result, the crew were doing little things like maintenance that normally was saved up for spring cleaning day, while paying attention to all the passive feeds and a tight-beam, two-way communications-laser from *CR-264*, who had been tracking them for the rest of the squadron, just in case.

Ping.

Alber' surfaced from his day-dreams. Most of the bridge crew came to a higher state of awareness with him.

"Commander," his Science Officer called. "A vessel just emerged from JumpSpace. It is approaching the edge of the gravity well at a speed that suggests a warship rather than a freighter. Albedo suggests a smaller light cruiser."

All that from three seconds staring at a screen. As well as years of preparation.

And the purifying fires of battle.

Alber' had initially been concerned when Centurion Zoya Najafi came aboard his command. Fleet personnel files listed her as a quiet, almost mousy officer. Nerdy in the way of many ivory-tower intellectuals.

He had been prepared to see her stick out from his crew of dedicated warriors like a sore thumb. For her to discover that she didn't belong here, and quickly request a transfer out to a quieter vessel. Many did.

Not everyone was cut out for war, not the way Alber' d'Maine understood the term.

Alber' was usually happy to send them off to greener fields.

Today, he wouldn't trade her for Tomas Kigali on the sensor array. *Warrior* didn't mean you had to hold a pistol or a knife to be dangerous. It was the vow of excellence you took every morning when you climbed out of your rack. It meant a dedication to your craft as an adjunct of war itself.

She was his eyes, his ears, just as he was her strong right arm.

Today, his instincts had served him right.

Alber' locked eyes with his First Officer as she emerged from the office where she had been doing paperwork. It was her shift, but Alber' was most at home on the bridge, so he was frequently to be found here in his spare time.

His Executive Officer, Senior Centurion Cruz Bösch, was an average woman in most physical respects. Medium height, medium build, regulation length blond hair. On the street, one might walk right by her without noticing her, one of thousands more who looked just like her. Pretty enough to be the girl next door on a good day, but nothing that demanded your attention.

The body might be average, the face rather plain, but the mind belonged to a back-alley, bare-knuckles brawler.

His Executive Officer looked at him for a nod, got it, and transformed herself into a Goddess of War.

"All hands to Battlestations," Cruz said simply, turning and taking her normal station on his right. She stopped and pulled out the emergency survival suit stowed for such a moment as this and started to slide it on as she watched the screens.

Cruz could have evicted him from the central chair. That was her prerogative as Duty Officer until he relieved her.

But she could fight the ship just as well from there. Hell, a sailor like Bösch could fight *Shivaji* just as well from the Forward Wardroom freezer, if push came to shove.

"Engines to full," she continued in her subdued tone. Today, her voice sounded like driving nails into wood by landing a DropShip atop it. Implacable. "Engineering, confirm all weapons charged. Navigation, plot an intercept course that passes above the enemy vessel when she decides to flee the gravity well. Defense Centurion, keep shields to minimum until they realize we're here, but unlock all defensive systems and fire at anything that approaches. Let's not let them Barn Owl us, today."

That last got a chuckle from everyone.

At one time, before she had gotten famous for it, then-Command Centurion Keller had frequently fired off a stealthy missile at the same moment she launched all her fighter craft, hiding the signal in the noise and letting the bird, a stealthy Barn Owl missile, run down its target ballisticly, not activating terminal guidance sensors until it was right on top of the target.

When it was too late to do anything.

It had been a very effective trick. But even Imperial gunners learn. The survivors did, anyway.

Bösch glanced back at Alber' for confirmation, asking if he wanted to change anything before she took them in.

Alber' stretched like a cat in his seat without standing. He had a fantastic crew, trained down to a very fine fighting edge, and then purified by the flames of *First Ballard*.

He keyed the shipwide comm and came as close to a genuine smile as he ever did.

"Ladies and gentlemen, cry havoc and let slip the dogs of war."

CHAPTER XXXII

IMPERIAL FOUNDING: 175/05/22. SEVENTH SON. ABOVE THURINGWELL

BACK TO *THURINGWELL.*

Another boring mail run from the sector capital.

This had to be the only place she knew that made Kittras look interesting.

Merryn sighed and settled herself into the left-hand chair as *Seventh Son* dropped out of JumpSpace.

At least this time, she wasn't smuggling the sorts of goods that would get her executed if they caught her. Not even outright rebellion against the Imperial order was that profitable. Next time, probably. By then, it would be about time for another crate of rifles or something.

There was a rhythm to these things, she had found over the years.

Today, Merryn had come out of jump a little farther out than normal. Well within acceptable, considering the distance she had just leapt, but far enough away that she needed to make up time.

She brought the big, twin engines on line. *Seventh Son* shuddered and came alive, like a bull getting ready to charge a red cape, as she boosted both of them to seventy-five percent and started downhill on the gravity well far faster than *Thuringwell* normally justified.

"*Thuringwell* Traffic Control," she pushed the record button on the comm. "This is TCL-100893471AJQ. Requesting lane assignment for docking. Cargo of mixed goods including sector mail from *Kittras.*"

And the message was away. Otto was probably not on duty today.

Most likely Lo. Hopefully he had enough caffeine and food in him to grind off his normal, surly edge.

For Merryn, another week of paying the bills and dreaming about what she would do without having to scrimp and save to keep this big beast in fuel and oxygen. Merryn reached out and laid a loving hand on the polished, baby-blue dash in front of her.

Space had been her whole life, living aboard this very vessel from her earliest memory. She had stayed aboard when her mother decided to give up and marry a lawyer so that she could stay on the ground.

Merryn had inherited the vessel and his crew when her father died. She had personally recruited all the replacements for when those people she still thought of as loving aunts and uncles and cousins had retired, being of an age with her father and not ready to keep it up with his rambunctious daughter after so many decades in the business themselves.

A strange voice intruded as she scanned the near-orbit and made adjustments to catch the station after a chasing pass.

"TCL-100893471AJQ," a man said harshly. "This is a secured zone. Stand down immediately and prepare to be boarded."

What the hell?

Nowhere could she hear the word *please* in anything the nasty man had said.

"Yan, Tyler, Hao," she said urgently into the PA system, waking her crew from whatever they were doing. "Something's wrong. Stand by for emergency maneuvering and maybe pirates."

She was technically the only one on duty right now, so the others could catch up on desperately-needed sleep.

It was *Thuringwell*. Nobody came to *Thuringwell*.

The crew could sleep tomorrow. Right now, she needed to get gone from whatever pirates thought they had her boxed in like a cute, little iceberg of a freighter, something as maneuverable as a pig on ice.

Catch this.

Merryn slammed the engines to the stops and felt the whole hull shudder as both engines went redline and began pushing her hard.

Nothing showed on close-in scans. There was a lot more traffic than normal around the station itself, but Merryn hadn't been paying that close of attention. It was *Thuringwell*, the most boring place she knew.

Or had been. Yesterday.

Seventh Son had come into the orbital plane a little high. The station was orbiting at about forty degrees north latitude, relative to the planet below. That meant that angling back up would be the fastest way to escape the gravity well of the planetary body so she could get far enough out to jump to safety.

They were probably counting on that.

Merryn pushed the nose of her little bird down at the same time she lit the engines.

Pirates were lazy. Nobody would be expecting her to go this way. Or this fast.

And they certainly wouldn't be prepared for the amount of torque her engines could deliver, diving down into the gravity well to slingshot straight out the southern pole like a diver entering water from the five meter platform.

Catch me if you can, buddy.

Merryn smiled. Still nobody close on the scanners. That meant probably a junkyard-rebuild fighter craft or two hiding somewhere nearby with sensors dialed down. The kind that thought they could intimidate her long enough for the mothership to show up and handle things.

Tyler would be in the tail gun turret shortly. Then a couple of punks in snubfighters would be chasing her right into his guns.

It was like I planned it this way or something.

"TCL-100893471AJQ," a new voice rang out.

This one was quieter. Still male, but a much more dangerous-sounding one. Thin and deep, like the wound a razor blade leaves.

"This is the *Republic of Aquitaine* Heavy Cruiser *Shivaji*," the man said simply, almost sounding bored. "*Thuringwell* is under martial law. You will stand down or you will be destroyed."

Aquitaine? Seriously? Get a better shtick next time. That lie was too outrageous to pass any sort of sniff test.

Merryn tried to coax a couple of extra dynes of power out of the engines anyway, sledding down the gravity wave of the planet. It would be like riding a rocket-powered rollercoaster at the bottom of this pass.

Seventh Son bleeped at her suddenly. A vessel had apparently been running dark out there, just waiting. Just like she expected. Typical pirate routine. He had lit his engines and sensors, and powered up his shields to give chase. Like he was going to catch her now.

Amateurs.

Nobody could catch her or touch her at this distance. Even fleet primaries were out of range. Their only hope would be lobbing a missile at her, and Merryn was just itching to try out some of the new counter-measures electronics she had installed over the last two years, just for this sort of pirate shenanigans.

For a moment, all of *Seventh Son*'s sensors overloaded as a flash of energy went past her nose, almost close enough for a decent sunburn.

She had never seen a beam that powerful. Neither had the scanners.

"That was your only warning shot, TCL-100893471AJQ," the man's voice drawled.

What the hell was that? Warning shot?

Merryn turned and took a good look at the scanner readings coming in.

That was no pirate. It was nothing she had ever seen before. It was too big. Hell, the energy signature of the shields alone was several orders of magnitude bigger than *Seventh Son*. And they had something they thought could kill her, even from that far away.

Merryn gulped, swallowed past a thick tongue, and dialed her engines back to idle.

What the hell was going on?

AT LEAST SHE had gotten taken down by professionals. That was cold comfort for Merryn, but cold comfort was better than nothing. She could still sniff at amateurs and pirates, assuming she walked away from this one with her hide intact.

There really had been an *Aquitaine* Heavy Cruiser lurking out there. And it had been her bad luck to stumble into his path, like a salmon swimming in front of an orca.

The one warning shot had been enough. Another one of those would have gone through her shields like tissue paper, and not lost much oomph punching starlight all the way through her hull.

At least they were acting polite. No bluster, no threats, once she shut her engines down and inserted the *Seventh Son* into a safe, high orbit.

Merryn took one last look at the board before she powered

everything into passive mode and got up, grabbing the leather satchel with all the ship's papers.

A quick check on the board to confirm where everyone was. That *Republic* ship trailing her in a higher orbit. One of the local cutters had detached from the station and was headed over to play customs games, but at a very leisurely pace.

The fun part was the administrative shuttle that had already separated from *Shivaji* and requested a docking lock. *Aquitaine* would be boarding her first.

Merryn keyed the ship-wide.

"Hao, Yan, Tyler," she said with some urgency. "Airlock one, right now. Dress nice. Don't be armed. These people mean business."

She closed the channel before anyone could argue and left the ship on autopilot for now. There was nothing she could do about what was going to happen next, except put on a pleasant face and try to talk those people out of doing anything irreversible.

Seventh Son was not your typical freighter in Imperial service. The halls were wider than normal, almost as wide as a passenger carrier. The soft green color covered most of the walls in an inviting tone, offset with gray floors and cream-colored ceilings. Lights were cheap, so she had added enough to make the place festive. Right now, they were all on.

Anything to put the invaders in a better, softer frame of mind.

She very briefly considered putting on some quiet background music, but figured that might be overdoing it.

Let's not make this look like a brothel.

Her crew met her down on the cargo deck. They were all younger than Merryn, but hard-working and well-recommended.

Yan Neumos, her navigator, was a little taller than her, and a little darker. He was originally from the border world of Madaripur, a hard-scrabble place that nonetheless turned out bright students who immediately left to find their fortune in the greater Empire.

Tyler Yi was ethnically Korean, from Yeoncheon. He was tall and strong, but no longer a young man at twenty-six. *And what did that make you at thirty-two standard, Merryn?* Still, he worked hard, and had been the connection that brought his little sister, Hao aboard.

Merryn had never worked with a better loadmaster, anywhere, than Hao Yi. For some, it was a lifetime of skill built up. Hao could study a random pile of irregular boxes and shipping crates for five minutes, and then pack them into the smallest space imaginable without a single wasted motion.

She was nineteen standard, looked sixteen, and cursed like a fifty-year-old retired Engineering chief. A petite, gorgeous, foul-mouthed, female chief with bright green eyes and skin the color of burnished gold.

Merryn took her place at the left end of the line. The hull was already rattling and pinging as the *Aquitaine* shuttle locked itself into place on the other side of the airlock and set up a seal around the door.

She had left the outer door unlocked. From the next set of sounds, they were using it instead of blowing the door apart and venting the ship to space, or cutting their way through.

Hopefully, professionals. As long as they maintained pressure and seal, both sides of the airlock could be open. It was only on a pressure drop that both panels would slam shut on emergency override.

The inner hatch hissed and whirred as someone pushed the button on the other side.

The panel opened slowly outward into the airlock corridor.

Merryn found herself facing two Republic marines in boarding armor, but at least they had left their faceplates open. Always a good sign.

The pistols pointed at her were just the cost of doing business with strangers.

"Is this everyone?" the taller marine asked. It was a female voice.

Merryn did a double-take. The armor did not reflect female curves, but she had never run into a woman as a guard or customs officer.

The *Fribourg Empire* didn't have any.

"Huh? Uhm. Yeah. All of us."

Or something like that.

Think harder, Merryn.

"Very good," the marine said. She stepped out of the lock and looked both ways, stopping to smile at everyone before holstering her weapon.

"All clear," she called.

Now what?

The answer strode out of the shuttle with a very serious look on her face. And no boarding armor. Just a green and black uniform with a single white stripe on the right arm.

Her inspection of the crew was less perfunctory. Merryn studied her back.

The stranger had the same dusky brown skin tone as Yan, what the ancients used to call South Asian, and piercing, brown eyes that didn't miss anything.

"I am Centurion Amala Bhattacharya," the stranger said simply. "The *Republic of Aquitaine* is holding *Thuringwell* and this system under martial law."

She paused and stared hard at Merryn. Merryn just nodded politely. This was not even remotely the kind of day she had been expecting. Best ride it out and take stock.

"As carriers of the Imperial Post, you and your cargo will have some measure of diplomatic immunity, but the vessel will still be inspected. I do not expect that it will be impounded or nationalized, but that is for the *Palsgrave* and the *Margrave* to determine."

Diplomatic Immunity? These people were serious? And possibly seriously deranged.

And thank the Creator I don't have a crate of rifles on this run. Suppose there will be any next time?

Merryn smile neutrally and held out her satchel.

"What's this?" Bhattacharya asked blankly.

"Transport documents," Merryn replied with a brighter smile than might have been necessary. These folks were warriors, not bureaucrats.

"Engineering inspections, crew certifications, proof of insurance and bonding authority. Also a manifest and a load receipt."

And all of it was dead accurate, this time. Small favors. Maybe, just maybe she could get to the station with a minimum of fuss, and then the ground. And then she and Redyert were going to have to rethink things on *Thuringwell*.

CHAPTER XXXIII

IMPERIAL FOUNDING: 175/06/26. IMPERIAL CONSERVATORY, ST. LEGIER

BOOKS. That was what Joh smelled.

Johannes Wiegand, His Imperial Majesty Karl VII, Emperor of Fribourg By Grace Of God stood just outside the doorway to the man's cozy office and sniffed quietly.

Old paper made from older trees, bound in cotton fabric and cardstock and then filled with a carbon-iron ink guaranteed to last for centuries.

It was a smell unique to libraries, and to small offices where the walls were covered over with stained, wooden shelves that were never dusted enough to keep the bunnies at bay. A place where a small window overlooking a courtyard was never opened in the winter, so no air circulated through it to freshen things up.

As a metaphor, it struck perhaps a shade too close to home. He would probably have to do something about that, and he might have to do it in an official capacity, because this man wasn't necessarily likely to listen to friendly advice, even from him.

But not today.

Today, he waited quietly. Out of sight.

The door itself was open. The man inside was keeping office hours for his students, but armed troops had quietly sealed off every hallway and instructed the scholars on this floor to remain where they were for the time being. Most had been at a late lunch together, and dutifully herded themselves off to the library instead.

Joh could do that.

Perks of power, as long as you didn't abuse them. That was what made them all the more powerful.

His Imperial Majesty requests…

And then magic happened.

Joh smiled to himself before settling into his serious face and taking a breath.

He came around the corner of the doorway and looked inside.

Sure enough. Books. Hundreds of them. Every color, every size, every topic, from what Joh remembered. The man didn't have many idiosyncrasies, but collecting physical books was one of them.

The man Joh was here to see sat behind a desk strewn with papers, neatly arranged into several stacks. He appeared to be editing a manuscript, as student papers would be electronic. Joh imagined he could hear the pen scratching the page.

A shadow, or perhaps a sound, caught the man's attention. He looked up from under fiercely brooding eyebrows. There were shadows in those eyes that had only appeared recently. Depths and pain.

The beard was new as well. The hair was perhaps two centimeters longer than it would be under regulations, were this man still on duty. And it had finally gone the rest of the way gray, while Joh's was still brown above his ears, at least for a few more years. At least Joh knew what he would look like, were he to grow a beard in a few years.

The man's time behind a desk had done the opposite of what one would expect, as he had apparently lost weight. Perhaps he had more time to eat right and exercise regularly. That would be a first, considering the need.

Only the uniform hadn't changed. That man had absolutely thrown a fit at the suggestion that he be promoted. Joh wondered if blue would be an insult after so much time in red.

So much of the man's legend wrapped up in the color red.

In the end, Joh had acquiesced. It was one of the few times this man had made serious demands on his Emperor, threatened him with retirement, calling in old favors, blackmailing him with stories that could be told.

And Joh owed this man more than either of them could ever possibly tally, let along repay.

The *Imperial Admiral of the Red* Emmerich Wachturm studied his Emperor silently for several more seconds. It seemed to stretch into minutes, or days.

They had been friends for nearly five decades. Words weren't always necessary.

"What's she done now?" Emmerich asked simply.

Joh blinked.

How could Em possibly know?

He didn't. He was *The Red Admiral*. The best tactician in the last century, *Fribourg*, *Aquitaine*, or anyone else.

He would probably know. Still…

"How did you know?"

"Anything else, from politics to show horses, you would have invited me to a quiet family dinner at the Palace and picked my brain over century-old brandy," Em replied solidly.

It was like listening to a mountain speak.

"The only thing that would blast you out of your palace to come here and see me, personally and without warning, is Jessica Keller," Wachturm continued. "It's something so outrageous that Naval Command and your staff have no response, and you can only think of one man who can help."

Emmerich Wachturm studied him hard, eyes like a predator lurking at the edge of the fire, blinking slowly.

Joh kept waiting for a growl to come from the darkness.

"There are days I would like to hate you, Em," *His August Imperial Majesty* replied sarcastically as he stepped further into the room, pulled a short stack of books out of the way, and placed them on the floor so he could plop down in the only chair and stretch his legs out to one side.

"But I'm right," The Red Admiral replied.

"Em, you're almost always right," Joh replied.

Joh watched a shadow of pain flit across the man's face.

Almost always.

Except when it came to Jessica Keller.

And then nobody ever seemed to be right, except perhaps Nils Kasum, First Lord of the *Republic of Aquitaine* Navy. The enemy.

Emmerich Wachturm, Joh's favorite cousin, had been his Best Man, his Sword, his Shield for decades now. Together, they had driven the *Fribourg Empire* to heights undreamt of a century ago.

And then Jessica Keller.

"You could have her assassinated," Emmerich said quietly.

Joh nearly snarled at the man who was his closest friend after his Empress.

"If that is how I have to win, to rule, then I have already failed, Em," *Johannes, His Imperial Majesty Karl VII, Emperor of Fribourg*, said sharply.

Joh considered other options. He reached back with a hand and flipped the door closed softly enough that it would latch, but not hard enough to make the hair-trigger guards outside jump.

Just enough to separate them from affairs of state.

"That is the one other great pity," the Emperor continued, almost murmuring to himself. "There is no man we could offer her in a dynastic marriage to broker a generational peace with *Aquitaine*."

"I greatly respect the man that the Crown Prince is becoming," Emmerich replied with a nod. "But Jessica Keller would consume him like a flame. What news of the *M'hanii Frontier*?"

"Your strategic changes have begun to bear fruit," Joh replied. "Not enough. Not yet. But I can see the improvements. That is one of the reasons you are here, instead of on the frontier."

Emmerich scowled darkly in response.

Inwardly, Joh cursed himself. He was a much better speaker than that. It was unnecessary to rub the man's face in the fact that he had been forcibly retired from field command.

By Imperial Edict…

Emmerich was too close. It was too easy to relax around him.

Unintended pain was occasionally the consequence.

"Keller," Admiral of the Red Wachturm growled into the hollow quiet.

He sounded like a mid-winter bear roused at the end of a short stick.

"They commissioned the new *Auberon* as a Star Controller," Joh replied carefully.

How much of that was an *Aquitaine* response to Emmerich Wachturm and his famed Battleship *Amsel*, the Blackbird? A Star Controller could take on a Battleship and win.

Another reason Em was in this office instead of command. He would try, and she might finally beat him bad enough to cost the Emperor his best strategist, his Best Man. His best friend.

"Instead of a work-up cruise to show the flag, like much of the Imperial High Command suggested, she went straight to the frontier and launched an attack," Joh continued.

Wachturm raised a single, beetling eyebrow, but retained his poise.

"On the off-chance you were right," Joh said, "I had ordered a fleet to assemble and hide at *Iger*. A few Admirals suggested that would be her target, to pay us back for the defeat they suffered there four years ago."

"*She* wasn't defeated at *Iger*, Joh," Emmerich laughed gruffly. "Only that fool Loncar. Where did she go?"

"*Thuringwell*. April 28." Joh replied.

It was a mark of all those years on a flag bridge. Joh had seen it many times.

Emmerich's face fell into confusion and a hand reached out automatically to pull a book from a nearby shelf, almost without looking. The Red Admiral probably could locate his copy of the *Imperial Gazetteer* half asleep and blind, stinking drunk.

Most of the good officers were like that.

The *Fribourg Emperor* sat patiently as Wachturm flipped the book open and devoured the page.

"Duke Waltev Damsell?" he asked with a furrowed, confused brow. "That fop?"

"I'm sure he thinks of himself as a dashing rake," Joh smirked. "He certainly was, thirty-odd years ago. But yes. Him."

Moments of hard silence stretched as Em read and thought.

Joh could see Em's eyes dance back and forth on some distant, unseen horizon.

"She's mousetrapped you, Joh," Em finally said.

"There is a reason I came here, Em, instead of ordering you to the palace, you know."

"No," Em countered. "It's worse than that."

"How?"

"Think about *Ballard*. What we did there," The Red Admiral said.

Joh could see the man practically leap from point to point, like lily pads on a deep pond, intuitively grasping something that had eluded everyone else. Joh seriously considered retiring Grand Admiral Huff, another of their cousins, just so Emmerich Wachturm could be promoted to supreme command of the fleet. It might be the only thing that kept the Empire alive over the next decade if they didn't stop Jessica Keller.

Joh shook his head in confusion.

Em nodded sympathetically.

"We let the spies know we were going for *Ballard*," Em continued. "Partly to destroy the *Sentience*, but mostly as a trap. Kasum couldn't risk sending Home Fleet to stop us, afraid that we might strike *Ladaux* instead."

"And?"

"Your fleet is trapped at *Iger* now," Em said. "*Thuringwell* isn't close, but *Iger*'s the only logical place to attack that frontier for military advantage."

"I'm aware of that, Em," the Emperor replied dryly.

"*2218 Svati Prime* had no military significance either, Joh," the Red Admiral replied, just as dryly. "Look what she did there."

Joh shuddered. There weren't words to describe the psychological impact of *Keller's Long Raid*, as history had taken to calling that campaign. The entire *Fribourg Empire* had convulsed, until the Red Admiral himself had chased her off. But even then, he'd only chased her off. Other worlds still looked over their shoulders when her name was whispered.

"What are we facing at *Thuringwell?*" Em asked in a hard tone.

Joh brought himself back to the present. *Thuringwell* was still a smaller problem than being the Emperor.

Today.

"A Star Controller task force," Joh said. "*Auberon*. Three cruisers. Half a dozen escorts, the heavier ones they call destroyers. Several support ships we haven't been able to identify, but presumably construction forces."

"And she's just camped at *Thuringwell?*"

"She is."

"Then we're missing something."

Joh smiled instead of replying.

"Can I return to the field?" Em asked.

His tone was light, but the words were very, very heavy. Certainly, having the Red Admiral in command again would help, but it would take him away from his duties to the rest of the Empire.

Was that what she had planned? Could she possibly know about the *M'hanii Frontier?*

"No."

That was one Imperial Edict that would not be revisited. Not today.

"Then you will need at least one entire battleship task force, probably two, if you want to dislodge her," Em said.

If he was disappointed, it didn't show in his tones.

"Two?"

"A Star Controller is a force of gravity, my dread Emperor," Em said, only partly sarcastically. "I will remind you that it is functionally equivalent to both a battleship and a Fleet Carrier at once. And under Jessica Keller's command."

Joh nodded.

This was why he had come here. That fear in the night, that Emmerich Wachturm would be right, again.

But he couldn't help himself.

What in blazes would she want with a place like *Thuringwell*?

CHAPTER XXXIV

DATE OF THE REPUBLIC JULY 1, 396 RAMSEY STARPORT, THURINGWELL

AND THAT, as the man in the video used to say, were that.

The 'road weren't done, not by a long shot, but the hard parts were behin' 'em nows.

Moirrey stood on the catwalk of her little personal watch-tower office and looked out over the field of the new starport they was just abouts to dedicate.

Give it three more days fer the last of the concrete to cure and all the witches to be exorcised from the wiring runs, and Lady Keller could come down herself and bless the place with her awesome ju-ju.

Behind Moirrey, the door to the main watchroom opened quietly. Moirrey sighed, knowin' it were too good to last. Saana were here to mother-hen her into paperwork, or som'tin'.

Why dinna they tells her aforehand how many trees a Centurion were required to kill on a daily basis? Even electronic ones? Reports, reports, reports.

At least she gots her own budget these days to build toys. First prize for all the time in the lab back home had finally come true yesterday, when she got to back the first locomotive into the flat yard with a stack of cars behind her and pinball them into a second stack of cars just waiting fer their load of rocks to get dug outs the ground fer smeltin'.

And it dinna even sound like porcelain crashing, fer all the tons of steel going bang.

Still, were awful quiet.

Something weren't right.

Saana would usually just start in with whatever needed doing, confident that her boss could absorb it all and play it back later at slow speed fer the interestin' bits if she needed.

Weren't Saana.

Moirrey looked over as Digger leaned on the rail next to her.

He smiled down at her. He had a gleam in his eyes.

"No," she said firmly. "I'm no' lettin' you tunnel throughs a mountain, Digger."

He just grinned and shook his head. It were an old conversation by now.

"That's later, Centurion," he said. "Tomorrow, we'll be submitting plans for a four-leaf clover subway system under the new starport."

"Seriously?" she asked. "Yer gonna mole the place?"

"A-yup. I brought the *John Henry* all this distance, Moirrey. I'll be damned if we don't use it somewhere."

She started to say something when a sound caught her attention.

Kinda a soft whomp.

Several of them.

Then a whistle like the wind coming up, 'cept it kept coming.

Digger got all twitchy, then grabbed her and pushed her to the door, ripped it open, and shoved her inside.

What the hell?

Moirrey started to say something, but he weren't listening.

"Saana," he yelled, grabbing Moirrey's hand and dragging her towards the staircase. "Get down. Incoming!"

Then he were pounding down stairs, pulling her along like a mom who stopped too long at the store on the way home and now were late fer her soap operas.

Slap, slap, slap.

Down into the office she shared with Saana.

At least Saana thought Digger were as daft as she did. She just stood there like a quizzical dog.

"Under the desk," he yelled. ORDERED. "Now."

Words became deeds.

Digger pushed Moirrey down and stuffed her under the desk, and then crawled in with her.

Not exactly how she envisioned their first date, but sometimes a girl's got to be open-minded. Moirrey adjusted into the little space and squirmed closer against Digger.

Just a bit. You know, fer safety and all.

Across the way, Saana were doing the same, no less confused. At least she had space on her side. Best to use it.

"Digger," Moirrey asked. "What…?"

And that, were as far as she got.

The whistling screams outside suddenly turned into booms.

Big booms.

Crap exploding everywhere booms.

Three of them. Two kinda dull.

One that sounded like the earth were ending.

Moirrey were suddenly glad there was a building around her. And a desk. And a Digger. Even if she were accidentally a little more wrapped around him than him protecting her.

Whatever.

Saana would just have to make do with a desk.

And then silence.

Eerie still quiet. Kinda like that first break of dawn.

Right before all hell broke loose.

Moirrey had been around the marines and ground troops enough to identify the sound of the big vehicle-mounted twin autocannons letting rip, like a giant duck farting.

The 66mm particle cannons on a trio of tanks sitting down at one end of the field had a whip-crack sound, like someone had snuck up and throwed a cat into a watering trough when it weren't looking.

Fer about two minutes, all the hounds of hell were baying.

Outside, a man's voice slowly broke through the noise.

"CEASE FIRE. CEASE FIRE. ALL UNITS STAND DOWN. READY DEFENSIVE POSTURE TWO."

It took a bit, but calm returned.

Digger looked over and kind of down at Moirrey. He had an awkward grin and a serious blush going.

Moirrey unwrapped herself from around him and kinda unsquished her boobs from his ribcage.

Mostly.

Enough.

I mean, you could get a ruler in there now. Maybe. At least a piece of paper. It's the thought, right?

Still, probably not the time to sneak a kiss. Outside, it were serious business. Quiet, but serious. Slobbering amounts of ordnance had been going down-range with smaller booms, but that were mostly over.

No necking on the battlefield, young lady.

Today.

Digger didn't look like he wanted to crawl out from under the desk any more than she did.

Trust Saana to go all mother hen and ruin everything. Nothing like getting caught out just as you were going to start necking on the couch, when the parents suddenly came home.

"What was that, Digger?" Saana called from across the way.

Digger flinched and leaned back. His hand stopped being wrapped around Moirrey's hip in a way that he could drag her in for a good smooching.

Moirrey wanted to growl at Saana.

Digger shrugged with promise and slithered out of her grasp.

"Somebody fired a mortar at us, Saana," he replied, rolling up on his knees in the empty space between the desks and standing.

Moirrey nearly leaned out and patted his bottom as he did, but caught her hand short.

No necking on the battlefield.

He turned after he stood and held out a hand that pulled her clear vertical in one swoop.

"Seriously?" Saana asked as she surfaced as well. "How did you know?"

"This was not my first firefight, Yeoman," Digger replied with dignity.

Outside, the gunfire had given way to that same calm that had surrounded them five minutes ago.

On a desk, the comm chirped.

Moirrey walked over and checked the name. *Security Force.*

"Hiya," she said as she keyed it live.

"Is everyone safe at your location, Centurion?" the woman asked with the kind of seriousness that was usually anathema to her day. "And how many people at your location?"

"We're good," she said. "Me, Digger, and Saana."

"Very good, Centurion. Thank you. Please shelter in place for the next thirty minutes unless you need to come to the command post?"

"Nope. We'll hang out here. Might order pizzas later."

The line went dead without another word. Security had no sense of humor.

She missed having Jackson Tawfeek around to kid.

"Digger," Moirrey turned back to the man and considered dragging him back under the desk. "What just happened?"

"I think, Moirrey," he replied wryly. "Maybe we finally found the Imperials. Or rather, they found us."

CHAPTER XXXV

DATE OF THE REPUBLIC JULY 1, 396 RAMSEY STARPORT, THURINGWELL

HE WAS FINALLY GETTING USED to moving around like this, but nobody had told Vo how weird it would be.

Warships were deliberate things. You worked with care and planning, so that when the bad guys showed up, everyone calmly raced to their station and did exactly what they were supposed to do.

Nothing was done on the spur of the moment unless the bad guys dropped out of JumpSpace on top of you. And even then, there was a plan.

There was always a plan. Especially with Keller in charge.

Still, he was getting to be a pretty good rider. Not as good as the long-service veteran line troopers of Fourth Saxon, to say nothing of the lunatic Cossacks of Scout Patrol that he had spent the last several months with, but not bad.

Vo smiled. Even Shevi had come around. At least as far as the horse was going to.

They all clomped quickly down the ramp of *Cayenne*. Not quite a running-start dead gallop, but the sort of canter where the next trumpet call would normally be to draw sabers and charge.

Scout Patrol, First Cohort was the Legate's fire team. When something went wrong, he sent Dash first. And these days that meant Vo was usually at the sharp end of things with them.

And at least they were at the new starport, even if it wasn't quite done yet. Out in the middle of nowhere, instead of at the edge of Yonin. *Cayenne* sat in one quadrant, vomiting forth an avalanche of horses and troopers. Across the way, the DropShip *Tamarin*, one of *LVIII Heavy*'s regular taxis, squatted like a malevolent gray toad. After all, nobody but *Gaucho* would paint a DropShip bright red.

Overhead, the GunShip *Necromancer* hung low in the sky, all weapons unlocked and every jammer handy cranked up to *stupid*. Nobody was shooting now, but Vo had no doubt what kind of response someone would draw right now if they did. There were also a half-dozen fighters from the fleet overhead orbiting at a fairly high altitude, as well. Visible, but out of immediate reach of missiles.

Hawks prepared to drop on uppity mice. If *Necromancer* left them any scraps.

Vo smiled as they closed on the command tower. It had been just under three hours, and not a peep from whoever had fired on the base.

They were still going to get an entire augmented patrol coming after them.

"AND THAT'S ABOUT ALL we know, until you actually find them," the man said.

Vo nodded. He had worked some with Senior Centurion Anton Wolanski of the Construction Ala, universally referred to as *Digger*, but the man was mostly coordinating fleet things through Moirrey. She was here as well, in the big conference room with mud tracked in on green plastic floors, along with about a half a dozen other folks from Digger's team.

Vo was seated directly across from Digger. Somehow he had ended up between Dash and Cohort Centurion Kim of *LVIII Heavy*.

It wasn't much to go on. Short range sensors had picked up three incoming mortar rounds in the air. Troops on the security perimeter had opened fire in return, but everyone had stayed inside the wire, waiting for reinforcements to get here from Yonin, aware that it might be a trap designed to draw them out of their safe place and into an ambush.

That was what Scout Patrol was for. And *LVIII Heavy*.

And who was supposed to be in charge for something like this was a little weird. Patrol Centurion Dash Mitja commanded, but could always be out-ranked by Vo in his job as Ground Coordinator for the

Fleet Centurion, or Cohort Centurion Kim. They rarely did, but Dash looked over at him now all the same.

They had developed something of an unconscious language by now. Dash reminded him too much of his baby sister Sonja, the wild one. And it worked if they handled things that way.

Kim left him a little more disturbed. There were looks, and occasional comments, that could be *interpreted* in ways that left Vo a little off-center. If he wanted to think about them. Vo was happier just pretending to not notice.

He wasn't sure how much longer that was going to protect him.

Kim was short and thick. Still curvy. Maybe if you took a regular-sized women, not a lanky pencil like Dash, and squished her down until she came up to the middle of his chest. Kim was abrasive and direct to most people, from all the stories he had heard, but she had always been friendly and a bit circumspect with him.

Almost flirtatious.

It made him nervous.

Vo wasn't the least bit ready for a girlfriend. Not after *Quinta*.

He nodded at Dash and glanced over at the Cohort Centurion. Those were not the eyes of an angry armor commander looking for Imperial troops to run down with her tank.

She even smiled up at him.

Vo cleared his throat and turned back to Dash. Safer. Much safer.

"You brought your own lance, plus a Support Lance, Kim?" Dash asked.

Her words weren't a direct challenge. Her tone might be.

Vo wondered if he had inherited another protective, baby sister.

"Keller wants them found, which is your job, Mitja," Kim fired back. "She wants them crushed, which I do. These men are far too prepared to just be a group of drinking buddies on a camping weekend. They're going to think they're a tough nut. I brought a bigger hammer."

Vo felt like he was on a beach, watching the waves roll in and out as his head rotated back and forth.

"And the Air Defense tank?" Dash asked. She was getting close to a sneer.

Kim just smiled serenely. If sharks were ever serene.

"Next time he tries that stunt, we'll shoot the rounds out of the air."

Vo leaned forward, just enough to put his elbows on the table. And, coincidently, break the rope of mad energy connecting the two women.

Dash backed off. A little. Enough. At least she took a breath.

"We have three options," the Patrol Centurion said after a moment, leaning back and turning to talk to Digger, Moirrey, and all the others who had maintained a low profile during the exchange.

"First," she continued. "They set everything up on a timer and ran like hell. Second, they fired and then started running. Third, we're dealing with dead-enders who thought you would rush out and engage them. They're looking to run like hell now."

"Are they?" Kim challenged. It wasn't blades at dawn, but Kim wasn't going to just let it go.

"Would you stay, after Digger called in the cavalry?" Dash fired back. "Or would you reconsider and try to get out before you got crushed like a bug underneath tank treads?"

Kim actually smiled at that. Dash smiled back at her.

That almost made it worse.

Vo wondered if they were going to suddenly draw belt knives and swear a sisterhood blood-oath, or something.

It had that mad feel to it.

Somebody out in the brush was about to have a very bad day.

VO HAD WATCHED as Dash sent Second and Third Squadrons out to explore the flanks. The local security teams had managed to triangulate the launch point to within about forty meters, but it was on the back of a hill from the camp that was about to turn into a starport.

Dash had a solution that was both perfectly reasonable and completely insane. One of her heavy weapon teams, the *ballistae*, had lofted a simple diamond-shaped kite up into the wind and was looking through a camera mounted on it. Cheap, effective, safe.

They could see the clearing. There was even early-afternoon sun glinting off what looked like the tube of the weapon itself. Past that, Vo was completely lost as to what he was looking at, but Dash and her team seemed pleased.

He had left Shevi tethered with the rest of the mounts and wandered over to where the seven tanks sat hunkered down in a laager, bows and barrels pointed outwards like snouts sniffing the wind.

"Want to ride with *LVIII Heavy* for a while, Arlo?" Cohort Centurion Kim stepped around from out of sight behind the Air Defense tank known as *Bloodhound*. It had the same low profile and block appearance as the rest, but instead of the single 66mm particle cannon, it had a pair of over-sized autocannons barrels on the sides of a blocky turret, one on each side of an oversized sensor bulb of a nose.

It even looked like it could shoot down an incoming round.

It wouldn't do much against a DropShip or a GunShip, even if their shields weren't all that great this deep in an atmosphere, but those kinds of ships had been built to take a tremendous amount of abuse anyway and keep flying. The Fleet Centurion had proved that when *Petron* got singed over Yonin.

"Next patrol sweep, maybe," he replied, only a little evasively. "Got a horse that needs taking care of. Wouldn't do to leave him here with folks that don't know how to curry him right."

She smiled up at him, like he had said a particularly funny joke.

"So what can I help you with?" she asked lightly, almost warmly.

Seriously, was this woman flirting with him?

The way she stood was completely at odds with every story he had heard about this hard-charging, pain-in-the-ass, tank jockey.

Vo decided to stay as safe and professional as he could.

That he could do.

"So the Construction Ala has armored scout cars on repulsors, and they seem to work just fine," he said, carefully, evasively. "Why do tanks have treads? I would think you could be much faster and more maneuverable that way."

Kim laughed. It was a hard laugh.

She reached back and tapped on the side of *Bloodhound* with a clenched fist, like knocking on the front door. It still sounded like she was tapping on stone.

"Because those things are egg shells, Arlo," she said merrily. "Fragile little birds in the afternoon breeze. The big gun on *Freefall* can kill one of those from as far away as I can track it."

"Seriously?" he blurted in surprise.

"Calm weather, cold air, low humidity, Vo, I can tag you at forty kilometers away. Hard enough to stomp on one of those little scouts like a bug."

Her face had transformed.

Get an expert on a topic they love and you can see what someone is really like. Kim was very obviously a tanker. Her face even turned from average into something attractive as she forgot to scowl.

"Tanks need a lot of armor to resist something like the 66mm particle cannon," she continued. "That's weight. The kind of repulsors you need to lift that amount of mass becomes counter-productive. Plus, every centimeter higher you get is another hundred meters away someone can see you. Tanks stay low, down in the mud where the ground itself hides you."

She leaned back against the armoured hide of the Air Defense tank now, as if she could draw sustenance from the metal itself. Vo wasn't entirely sure she didn't.

"Fourth Saxon's fine for finding the bad guy," she said. "But he's going to be too well dug in for them to dislodge. And you just know Haussmann's prepared for orbital strikes."

"Why?" Vo countered.

"I have money down with one of my crew that Dash will find a three-shot automated mortar with a timer when they get over there," Kim said confidently. "Line it up, account for wind, temperature, and humidity forecast right after breakfast the next morning, then disappear into the trees. Her job will be to find his trail. Then I get to play."

Her face was almost flushed as she spoke, even if her eyes weren't really focused on him.

Then she came back to herself and smiled warmly up at him.

That left Vo even more confused, but it wasn't like he had ever figured out how women worked, especially not after what happened on *Quinta*.

When had women started finding him attractive?

And what could he do about it?

CHAPTER XXXVI

IMPERIAL FOUNDING: 175/06/18.
THURINGWELL WILDERNESS

ALL IN ALL, Dieter found himself pleased. The *Aquitaine* response had been textbook in many ways, and off-kilter in others.

The mark of a truly professional military force.

Dieter even smiled.

He knew he wasn't going to get to duel with Keller herself. That woman was an Admiral of the Fleet. She would stay in high orbit, well beyond the reach of anything he had access to on the ground.

No, instead, he would have to contend himself with her minions, and use them as an allegory for the woman herself.

Deep in his heart, he knew that no woman could be his match. However, she was obviously very good, to be given this level of power by *Aquitaine*.

But they were run by women.

What did they know about the true order of things?

He rewound the image on his screen and watched it again in fast motion, safe in his little hideout three valleys away.

It had taken some time to arrange things properly. Secretly tracking the new railroad being built. A whole series of laser links to a set of cameras covering large swaths of the valley where *Aquitaine* was building a new starport that nobody else knew about.

Dieter had briefly wondered if this would become a new military base as well, until he realized that this particular valley was centrally located to five of the major mines producing the ores that were *Thuringwell*'s economy.

She wouldn't dare...

But she had. Just as she dared other impossible things.

Dieter was torn between giving his life to stop this woman, and abandoning his post in order to escape with the knowledge and insight that his Imperial masters might discount if he sent an underling. He might have the future of the very *Fribourg Empire* at his fingertips, if those people wouldn't ignore his warnings until it was too late.

Again.

Slowly, he breathed in and out and pressed play on the time-lapse video.

Two titanic Republic DropShips, one of them bright red, slipped over a nearby ridge at high speed, followed closely by a GunShip. Half a squadron of fighter craft well overhead, circling.

No familiarization run to downwind the port, just race in hard, barely over the wire, and slam the brakes on, drop to the ground, and drop the launch ramp. Tanks from the gray ship. Cavalry from the red one.

CAVALRY? Was there no limit to this woman's audacity? Who fought wars in an interstellar age from horseback?

And yet, it worked.

The horses had proven themselves faster than infantry and far more agile and devious than mechanized scouts or air cav.

More time lapse.

Most of the horses pouring out of the various gates, spreading out and seeking his troops, the first moves on the gigantic chessboard called *Thuringwell*. Those forces went to the corners and pressed in, bishops on the flanks.

Dieter made a mental note to locate a cache of spider-mines from his stockpiles and issue them to his pioneer troops. Men on horseback would not be as cognizant of mines with tripwires in the heavy brush, compared to simple infantry.

While spider-mines were designed to discourage pursuit in heavy terrain, they would also make a lovely surprise to terrorize and kill horses.

Dieter came to the end of the footage and powered the device down.

He came back to the present and stretched his back, seated too long in his chair, hunched over inside his little cave bolthole. It was dark, dank, and smelled of earth and death in here. It was crowded, even when he was alone, with a small desk, trunk, and a gray, fold-up cot.

But it protected him.

There were many ways to locate men in heavy terrain. Powerpacks could be detected on the right frequency. Sound itself could be used, if enough men were moving. From overhead, a passing listener could map things on the ground for experts to identify.

But even a few decimeters of soil and rock covering a sheet of plywood was proof against nearly anything. There were no square shapes to give him away. His equipment was fully shielded against leakage. He had no thermal signature, even as the earth above him kept him warm on cold nights.

If the stakes weren't so damnably high, this might be a game worth playing for years, just to see who could escalate the arms race of their skill to the highest levels fastest.

He had dreamed of having a worthy opponent. Fate had finally rewarded him with one.

First he would beat her. And then he would humiliate her.

Win.

Dieter smiled and stood.

The patrols coming from the *Aquitaine* base would go the wrong way. Misdirection had been built into their original approach, taking an extra three days to circle around, and giving his pioneer teams time to establish the lasers that let him watch his foe work.

He could watch them now as they blundered into the woods. Track them as they moved and learn how they fought. Lure them into ambush after ambush and grind them down.

Win.

CHAPTER XXXVII

IMPERIAL FOUNDING: 175/05/27. YONIN, THURINGWELL

MERRYN LOOKED AROUND THE RESTAURANT, conscious of being out of place in the amount of money, the absolute piles of it, that the rest of the people here embodied.

She was running late, and had messaged Ulaffson, but still she had expected to find him waiting for her in the bar. Instead, he was already seated at a cozy table in the corner, dabbling at an antipasti plate and sipping from a glass of something burgundy.

As Merryn approached, she noticed how much older Sri Redyert looked, like the last few months had aged him a decade. She knew him to be around fifty years standard, but right now he looked much, much older. And tonight he was dressed in his finest suit, while she was just in a clean outfit: gray slacks, gray ground shoes, three layers of shirt for warmth, and a blue jacket over top with pockets everywhere.

It did not leave her feeling secure. But then, nobody on *Thuringwell* really was.

Nobody could predict what *Aquitaine* would do next. They might all be broke tomorrow.

Meeting him here didn't help her nerves.

This wasn't his private club, but it was still among the nicest on the planet, catering to the flakiest bits of the upper crust. Merryn knew folks from the sector capital at *Kittras* who came to *Thuringwell* just to eat dinner at *Sfacciato*. She never had. Wouldn't, except on someone else's tab. A simple dinner party for four might run equal to her weekly operating budget.

But he had invited her. In words that let her know it was both safe, and serious.

Ulaffson Redyert rose from his chair as she got close and took her hand for a kiss. Old Imperial manners, even out here.

Merryn blushed, but not mostly from the embarrassment of the situation. She just didn't belong in a joint like this.

What was he up to?

He even seated her like a perfect gentleman before returning to his own chair and pouring her a small amount of wine.

His own glass had lost more than he put in hers, but he knew she rarely drank. Conscious, careful, gentlemanly, precise.

Just how bad was it?

"You might have noticed some things have changed," he cleared his throat evasively.

Merryn's eyes danced in both directions, wondering how many of the people around the two of them were the sort of staunch Imperial citizens that would take offense at a rebel and a gun-runner in their midst, if they ever found out.

"The *Aquitaine* fleet introduced themselves personally," she replied lightly, and with perhaps a hint of irony.

"And how did that go?" he asked with some concern.

She could see more in his eyes than just profit and loss. They had gotten deep into Imperial intrigue together. They might hang side by side.

"My papers were in perfect order," Merryn hinted. "*Seventh Son* has now undergone a most thorough and complete inspection by *Aquitaine* Fleet Engineers. It was more detailed than anything I've ever paid to have done."

Seriously. The Imperial yard at *Kittras* where she normally had maintenance and overhauls performed wasn't as comprehensive. Those people would have found everything. Anything. A crate of rifles would have been nearly first on the list, to say nothing of trying to ship illegal narcotics in a crawlspace or secret closet.

At least they had been polite about it. And put everything back together better than they had found it. That one, twitchy light fixture in the kitchen worked right for the first time in nearly three years.

But that was what you got when you dedicated twenty expert men and women to a task and handed them the original design specs for the ship, which were always included in her manifest paperwork. She still wasn't sure how frightened to be. They would know *Seventh Son*'s every nook and cranny next time they wanted to inspect her.

Merryn's gun-running days might be over.

If she wanted to live to see thirty-three.

Ulaffson nodded at her and fortified himself with another gulp of wine.

"How lucky you came along when you did," he said. "With the cargo manifest you had."

Yes. Lucky. Without the contraband.

Merryn nodded. It was almost Kabuki Theater to talk in a room like this. Public. On display.

Exposed.

The man in the corner on her right had been and probably still was the biggest shipping magnate in the sector, owning two of the four mega-freighters that hauled ore out, and several of the smaller ones that brought in grain shipments regularly. *Seventh Son* had done neither, since that market was sewn up by friends and relatives of the Duke.

A thought struck her.

"So what happens to all the contracts with the former government, Herr Redyert?" she asked, perhaps a little louder than necessary. And more formal. But for public consumption.

He blinked at her for a moment, and then leaned back and got a canny look in his eyes. Now he was sipping his wine for effect, rather than strength.

"That, my dear, remains to be seen," he pronounced. "I have had a meeting with the new Governor, and she is reviewing all existing contracts, as well as putting new tenders out for bid."

Merryn felt her soul grow cold. If you wanted to hire a vessel, especially a formerly Imperial one, or at least one in Imperial Mail service, it made perfect sense to do a naval assessment of the vessel. Especially under the pretense of a customs inspection. One with a score of professional engineers on the task.

She wasn't sure if she should feel honored or terrified.

"I was looking into the possibility of bidding on some of the upcoming contracts," Redyert continued in an august tone. "That was one of the reasons I wanted to meet you for dinner this evening,

Madam Teke. To discuss possible future business ventures, given that our regular sector mail contract is most indisputably terminated."

Terrified.

Redyert hadn't called her by her last name in years. Even in public. They were on stage here.

Or rather, she was. He was challenging all the other money in the room with his intent to change sides. To have her change sides as well.

Well, not change sides. Merryn had no intention of running guns to the Imperials. That was what changing sides would look like, to her. To the others, treason would be to take a contract hauling good and passengers to and from *Aquitaine*. Beyond that dark frontier.

Of course, the men in this room had never let politics get in the way of profit. It might, however, slow them down for a few months, leaving an opening for someone ambitious enough, nimble enough.

Crazy enough.

And if she had just had a major overhaul and tune job done by competent engineers, and hadn't had to pay for it, she might just be in the running.

For a very short moment, deep in the dark places where she didn't even whisper her secrets to herself, Merryn wondered how many other men in the room would try to outbid Redyert for her services. How many would try to buy *Seventh Son*, or her, or both outright?

She leaned back and took the slightest sip of her wine. It was amazingly good wine. It deserved better than the abuse Ulaffson had been subjecting it to.

Slowly she looked around the room. Several men were staring back. Electricity passed. None of them knew about the guns, but they apparently all knew about the inspection.

Just watching them, Merryn felt like she had just been delivered the best crème brûlée, the best cabernet in town. She was having dessert first tonight.

These men, these Imperial businessmen, would happily cut each other's throats for a quick shilling. She had no doubts about that.

Redyert couldn't doubt it, either. He was playing for the galleries, tonight.

How much money could she squeeze out of these people, if she wanted to dance?

Enough to retire? To buy a whole fleet of freighters and become a conglomerate?

Dad had invested his spare money over the years in a tavern owned by his best friend from school. It was supposed to be a place to live out his days in quiet, without the constant churn of travel and the risks of the life.

What did she want?

What did she want?

Up until this moment, Merryn had never gotten beyond the next quarter, the next year, the next major round of maintenance.

What is Redyert offering?

She leaned forward and put her elbows squarely on the table, resting her chin on her hands. He flinched briefly, but that was her not showing off the best Imperial table manners her mother had pounded into her from a very early age. Merryn could probably do deportment better than Ulaffson, if push came to shove.

"You present a very interesting conundrum, Herr Redyert," she purred.

Out of the corner of her eye, she could see several other men unconsciously lean closer as her words grew quiet. Ulaffson smirked very subtly. He probably saw the same things happening behind her.

"On the one hand, this world is under martial law," she continued. "*Aquitaine* law. They would likely prefer that all trade goes across what used to be the frontier. Especially if this is now a war-zone."

"Indubitably," he replied, letting his smile hang the rest of his comment in the air.

"But this colony would probably collapse in short order without all the myriad spare parts and equipment that can only be acquired from Imperial suppliers in the short term," she opined vaguely before pouncing. "Someone will have to go get those parts."

"Someone who was willing to go through a much more rigorous customs inspection than is the norm for *Thuringwell*," he agreed. "At a much greater risk, since either the Imperials or *Aquitaine* might confiscate cargo and vessel at any time."

"Tremendous risk," she countered.

"Tremendous need," he replied. "And possibly a short-term monopoly on the supply of such parts, since I cannot imagine *Aquitaine* would sanction more than a very few vessels plying that shadowed line."

Crap. How much money was he going to gouge the locals for?

A little light went on in her head.

Enough that they'll consider replacing their machines with Aquitaine *equipment over the next few years, committing them further to the Republic. Has he been a spy all along? A plant?*

Merryn smiled. No. He was merely a businessman. One with a very long memory of slights and insults at the hands of the Duke and his friends.

Paybacks are a bitch, aren't they?

A waiter interrupted her thoughts before they got too dark. He delivered salads and offered cheese with one hand and pepper with the other. Merryn hadn't ordered. Ulaffson had apparently prepared everything in advance.

Yes, he was playing a much longer game than she had realized ten minutes ago. Deeper. Sneakier.

Better.

She smiled at him. Cracking her knuckles right now would feel appropriate, since they were about to get down to brass tacks, however poorly it might look in a joint like this.

But yeah, there was suddenly a lot of money on the table, for a woman willing to dream.

CHAPTER XXXVIII

GÖLL WAS FEELING FRISKY. The roan mare sneezed at something and kipped her hips a little as they walked.

Dash flickered her wrist. Not much, just enough to twitch the bit in her mare's mouth and remind her that they were on duty today.

On Patrol.

Nobody was signaling with the bugle, not in a back country heavy with ticks and Imperials, but all the horses were at least as well trained as the men and women riding them. They knew the signs.

Hunting.

The back country of northern *Thuringwell* wasn't as heavy and impassible as it looked from the air. Not enough drizzle to support a full-on temperate rain forest, not like some of the places on *Saxon*. Just enough that tanks couldn't run roughshod and infantry would get lost.

Of course, most infantry units could be counted on to get lost in the middle of a highway on the way to the bar or the brothel, if left to their own devices.

It had taken half the afternoon, circling around the launch point for the mortars and getting scouts down on the ground. The Impi's probably thought they were being cute, coming in one way and heading out the other.

It made perfect sense if'n you were a city boy looking at things on a map from the air conditioned confines of your fine, expensive office. But most of *Saxon* was back country.

Her scouts had found both sets of tracks. Eight men. Five carrying heavy gear, the mortar team plus three men with ammunition boxes. Two more who were probably scouts and guards. Plus one officer in really nice boots. Expensive. Barely broken in.

Probably pulled them out of his foot locker when the flag went up five weeks ago and had barely worn them in the field before this. Certainly, the treads were still crisp.

Dash was pretty sure she'd be able to ID the man just from his feet, if they ever caught up with him.

Now, she had pushed out the whole patrol in separate groups. Ninety troopers, ninety-one with Vo, split into their nine lances, like fingers pushing through long hair, working out tangles and searching for ticks. Not that her brunette locks were ever that long. Usually just barely enough to pull back into a tail like Göll's.

But they'd find the Imperials who thought they were being cute.

She snickered. The Fleet Centurion had been right. Fourth Saxon was absolutely the best unit for a back-woods task like this. *Eleventh Xelni Rifles* was the only other Legion she could think of with enough skill to do this. And they were mostly mountain infantry specialists.

They'd have all their fun farther north and way west of here, up in the cold, rugged nastiness of hill country.

Arlo glanced sideways at her.

Dash just smiled.

"It wouldn't make any sense to anybody outside my head, Vo," she said with a wave of her hand.

He nodded at her.

She'd been a mite anxious when they added that city boy to the troop. Never seen a horse in person, didn't know a damned thing about them. But he'd turned out to be pretty good at it. And had been studying hard, mostly her from the bad habits he'd picked up. Shevi was doing fine, and Vo rode at least as well as her regulars, even if he'd never been in a hell-for-leather charge into enemy fire.

At least he wasn't going to hurt himself falling off his horse. That had been a worry.

And he had proven himself crazy enough for Patrol Squadron. That went a long ways to cementing his place in the column.

A rider cantered close. Dash identified Hawne Sherazi, Decanus of

3rd Squadron's Castle Lance, by his horse, Mitra. Her black coat was the single darkest in the Patrol, on one of the sweetest horses. He swung long ways around and ended up on her right, opposite Vo.

"Narwhal picked up something," he said. "Figured you should see it."

Nothing more than that. And that was a lot of words from Sherazi. Unless you wanted to talk music with the man. Then he might never shut up.

"Have everybody hold," Dash called back to Aoibhín. "Fifteen minute rest stop."

Mitra was already moving. Göll and Shevi followed, along with the rest of the lance.

She loved the Narwhal. Nobody ever gave it enough credit, thinking that her troopers were super-duper redneck hillbillies born with forest craft in their DNA.

Horse shit.

Saxon had running water and extensive public libraries.

Hard work and bleeding-edge electronics at every opportunity.

They had invented the Narwhal on *Saxon*.

Telescoping carbon-fibre rod that would bounce up to six meters with the flick of a wrist. Package on the top about the size of a lunch pail, covered over with every sensor a Legion Armorer could think of. Optical cameras, audio sensors, radio. The works. Plant it in the ground every hour or so and listen to the birds and squirrels, unless something made the little red light go ping.

Apparently, something had.

Castle Lance, 3rd Squadron was all dismounted when she arrived, splayed out in a rough circle with the horses to one side and guns pointed outward. Just like she had pounded into everyone's head. She made a note to give Sherazi a gold star later.

Two lances mostly filled the little clearing, so she pushed her team off to the left and followed Sherazi on foot, with Vo, Aoibhín, and the Draconarius in tow.

She found Trooper Yağmur Küçük up a tree. *Little Rain*, her name meant in one of the ancient tongues. Today, she looked like a squirrel. Being the smallest woman in the Squadron didn't help.

She was also a Pioneer, the explosives and electronics expert for her lance, and the bearer of that squadron's Narwhal.

Yağmur was intent on something. Her nose was almost pressed to the bark, as if she was sniffing.

"Little more left," Yağmur called. "There. Now put me a second post and we'll nail the line."

It took Dash a second to figure out.

One of the lance's troopers was up the way a bit. This was mostly a game trail, but deadfalls and age had cleared out some space as well. Not a highway, but also not a full-on bramble you had to shatter with machetes.

The second trooper had set one stick in the ground and was holding a second while everyone ignored them and watched the trees.

"A skoosh right," Yağmur continued. "Bit more. There. Drop that."

The little woman watched for a moment, then shimmied down to the ground and smiled up at the rest.

"Bastard thought he could get away with it," she announced in a tone that sounded like victory.

"With what?" Dash asked.

Yağmur looked at her blankly for a second.

"Oh, right," she said. "Hi, Dash. We were riding by and the Narwhal beeped. Went back and found a laser transmitter hidden in the tree. Nearly freaking invisible, but it's on so I could scan it. Got a line on the next one. Someone's being sneaky."

"How so?" Dash asked.

Talking to Yağmur was like talking to a squirrel sometimes. You had to let her run out of energy. Interrupting her explanations just made them take longer.

Yağmur pointed to her left, the direction Scout Patrol had been headed.

"Shooters went that-a-way, Chief," she said. "Nice and smooth and moving at a good clip."

She held out her other hand, pointed to the right. Now she was the world's smallest, cutest scarecrow.

"Laser's pointed the other way," she said. "They got us heading off after nothing but those eight goobers, and probably an ambush. Main force is north-east of here instead. Probably waiting for us to get lost so they can come in and hit the base again when nobody's looking.

"Can you track it?" Dash asked.

"Can your horse swim?" Yağmur fired back.

Dash chuckled. Göll would get a running start into any body of water big enough for her to float, if you let her. Whether you got off first or not.

"That thing come equipped with local video capabilities?" Vo asked from one side.

Yağmur started as Arlo stepped closer, like he had appeared out of the shadow of a tree or something. He did move quietly, when he was on the ground. Deliberate-like. Ninja, some of the troopers had decided.

"No, sir," Yağmur got formal quickly. "Single beacon laser transmitter only. Standard Imperial model. You establish the first laser on the line, and then walk plumb until the signal begins to degrade with atmospheric distortion. Drop a second unit and phase them into linkage. Second unit normally zigs in a different direction to throw off snoopers like me. Build an entire array and you can talk and watch secretly."

"Is Haussmann sneaky enough to redirect the line down the line?" Vo wondered aloud.

"Doubt it, sir," Yağmur said. "Imperials tend to be linear that way. The first marker line is usually within ten to fifteen degrees of the overall path."

Vo turned towards Dash now, looking down at her with a troubled look.

"Worth an overflight that direction to see if we find him?"

"Negative," Dash said. "Never let him know we're coming. You'll ask someone upstairs for recent scout imagery from orbit to see if they've left any clues. Otherwise, we sneak up on them. Aoibhín, let everyone know we're swinging around wide left and circling. Castle 3rd will follow the line and keep us on track."

You didn't salute in the field. That just marked officers to get shot by snipers. Everyone jumped to and started moving, which was good enough.

There were bad guys out there, thinking they had pulled a fast one on her.

Boy, weren't they going to be surprised?

CHAPTER XXXIX

DATE OF THE REPUBLIC JULY 4, 396 SC
AUBERON. ABOVE THURINGWELL

IT HAD TAKEN A LITTLE REMINDING, and a few arguments, mostly with Enej and Marcelle, but Jessica had mostly learned her lesson. Nearly getting killed in the field, over something stupid, could still be a learning experience. Creator knew she had nearly gotten killed enough times to be a genius by now.

Rather than spend as much time on the surface as she had planned, she mostly communicated by secured comm these days. Daily calls with Wakely. Weekly full briefings with a larger team. Regular reports from the Legate. Notes from Moirrey, usually filled with sparkles and unicorns, regardless of being official fleet memos. Terse, almost telegraphic reports from Vo.

Not being in control frustrated her, but Jessica had at least come to grips with that aspect of growing up. Of being in command. Sometimes, you had to send people into situations over their head, and hope that their training would see them through.

After all, wasn't that what she was doing?

Today, a long overdue chat.

Things on the ground were getting boring and routine. On the one hand, that idiot Duke had long since beaten everyone into at least conformity, if not submission. On the other, she hadn't upset their apple cart all that much.

It was fascinating how people could quickly adapt to an entirely new routine, once they got over the initial shock. One quick bow wake and everything settled. Wakely was still a novelty, a woman in charge. Jessica was the boogey-man come to get them in the night if they misbehaved. The locals had mostly shrugged.

Things had almost gotten boring again on *Thuringwell*. That was when she expected the anarchy to begin. Haussmann had not disappointed, but they had been mostly little raids and explosions. Nothing big. Cydelmynster had gone silent, but he would need time to decide how he wanted this to go down.

Jessica leaned back from her chair and looked around her office. She knew she would find Marcelle just outside the door when she opened it, probably waiting with all the magical implements to make fresh coffee.

Maybe she would need coffee later. Right now, it would just make her need to pee.

That could wait. She liked her office.

Star Controllers were monstrous beasts. Bigger than anything that moved. Staffed by thousands of the best crew in the fleet. Everything was done on a grand scale.

Except her office.

Technically, the design specs classified this as the workspace for a junior Centurion on her staff, but it was a perfect fit for her. Four meters on a side. Just enough for a desk, two chairs, and a sideboard, with a small sofa tucked into the corner.

It was only after she had claimed it and decorated it that Jessica realized how closely it matched Room 2304 at *Ladaux* Fleet Headquarters. The office of the First Lord of the Fleet, Nils Kasum.

The Dragon's Den.

Jessica smiled. She didn't need to have this meeting here. She would go to him. Security had already confirmed that he was as trapped in daily paperwork as she was, as late in the day as it had gotten.

Jessica rose and stretched, turning her shoulders ninety degrees left, and then right. Tomorrow, she had scheduled a bout with the training robot. Nothing exciting, just enough to keep her on her toes.

Like this next meeting might do.

She opened the hatch and emerged from her chrysalis. Sure enough, Marcelle was there, with her nose buried in a book.

By now, Marcelle knew her well enough to not even rouse. Jessica would have pinged her on the comm if she needed something. A single raised eyebrow spoke volumes.

Jessica nodded. Marcelle almost smirked in reply and went back to her book.

The novelty of having an adoptive big sister had worn off decades ago, but having someone who could almost read your mind never did. And it reassured her. Marcelle wouldn't hesitate to walk her right back into her own office and yell at Jessica if she thought it was necessary.

Not that it had been, recently. Not in days.

Jessica pulled her tunic straight and set out. Best to sneak up on the man.

The duty watch schedule was synched to Yonin below now. It was late enough in their day that most of his staff was off-duty, at least as off-duty as a starship ever got.

His door was open as she entered the outer office and signaled his Yeoman to silence with a finger to her lips. Jessica smiled at her, and gestured for her to depart.

The woman gulped, nodded, and stood up silently.

And Jessica was alone in the outer office.

She leaned on the doorframe and studied the man as he looked down and read something intently.

Jouster. Command Flight Centurion Milos Pavlovich. Tall, dark, handsome. Brilliant pilot. Unconventional pain in the ass. Flight Commander, *Star Controller Auberon*.

"How is it you never managed to get properly Court Martialed and grounded, *Jouster*?" she asked suddenly.

She had to give him credit. He barely flinched as he looked up from his screen.

He studied her for a moment before he responded, probably trying to figure out what he had done this time. The man had a history of pushing his luck. Becoming a Command Flight Centurion hadn't tempered him much.

"When I was young and stupid," he smiled wryly, "I was always the best pilot around by far. Later, I had a commander who forced me to behave and inspired me to even act like a professional occasionally."

Jessica nodded. Somewhere along the way, *Jouster* really had grown up.

She stepped into the office and sat in the only chair.

"You ever regret being in charge?" she asked.

It was a mark of his tempering that he could relax around her enough to tease her back.

"Nope. You?"

"I accepted it early on," she replied. "The cost of those two hours of combat was the weeks of drudgery that preceded it. Do you still get to fly enough?"

"Mostly," he shrugged in turn. "I have a good ground staff that takes care of most of that side of things. I hired my own version of your Flag Centurion to handle paperwork. I probably get to fly about twice as much as most men and women in my position."

That was a novel approach. But then, this man had always pushed the envelope, in life as well as in flying. At least he was doing it constructively these days. A bit like Jessica.

But at the same time, he was extremely young to be in this position of authority, and still be one of the best pilots around. Most had at least a decade on him when they commanded a force this large, and had begun to lose those fine edges that marked good pilots and helped them survive.

Jessica made a note to review the setup with Petia and Nils once she got home, to see if doing it that way would make the entire fleet more efficient, more dangerous.

Every little advantage that could be eked out.

"So what can I help you with, Fleet Centurion?" *Jouster* asked suddenly.

His voice hadn't gotten serious, but he had lost the banter. Again, a serious man recognizing the situation. Jessica Keller was in his office, unannounced, rather than having him come to her.

That would probably knock anybody a little off keel.

"I need to know how well the entire flight force will react," she said simply. "The *Fribourg Empire* won't wait forever for us to be successful here. They can't react with what they probably had waiting at *Iger*, at least, not all of it. But they'll come. I have no doubt of that."

"Is that why d'Maine is always practicing his stealth?" *Jouster* leaned forward and put his elbows down on the desk, sliding his computer screen to one side.

"Yes," Jessica said simply. "And *Wombat*. And *Ballard*. And everybody else. How ready will you be?"

Now he leaned back. His eyes got a distant look and flickered side to side as he began to read reports and panels in his head.

"The three wings off *Auberon* have been training together for a little more than a year," he said. "Because First Lord loves us, he let me have *Bitter Kitten* as the lead on Second Squadron and then let me stack it with the best I could recruit from across the fleet, as well as through your connections to *Petron*."

"*Petron?*"

Jessica was only a little surprised. They might be pirates by nature on *Petron*, but she had impressed the hell out of those pilots the day she became Queen. The survivors, at any rate.

"In addition to *Furious*, I was able to recruit one of the only other three women currently combat-qualified from *Petron. Kinnison.*"

"Only one?"

Jessica knew about Flight Centurion Mio Yoshioka, nicknamed *Kinnison* for the wreck of the ancient super-dreadnaught abandoned on the surface of *Bunala*. That planet had taken on some manner of mythic status in Jessica's legend, the place where she supposedly first swore her blood oaths with Arnulf Rodriguez, then King of the Pirates.

The man she would later avenge.

"I tried to get *Starling*," Jouster said with a shrug that turned into a grin. "But she decided to settle down and have a family and has gone into legitimate business. And *Wiley* has gone into line command instead and plans to eventually take over David's spot commanding *Kali-ma*, since he has to be a king in your place."

Jessica remembered *Wiley* from her last visit home. She could see the woman turning into just as good a Captain as she had been a melee fighter. And if Jessica wasn't home that much, that just meant that David could focus on acting as king in her stead, until everyone just accepted him in the position and she could abdicate in his favor. Or maybe become Dowager Queen and train up a whole generation of girls to not accept second-class citizenship.

The possibilities gave her something to plan for in another two or three decades. Assuming she lived that long.

"So where does that leave you?" Jessica asked.

"*Bitter Kitten*'s Second Squadron is entirely female," he replied, smiling like a shark. "With the exception of *Hànchén*, who has been adopted as an honorary sister after he outflew everybody but *Kitten* and *Furious*. I would stack them up against anybody else in the fleet and bet heavily. Third Squadron under *da Vinci* still looks like a normal melee force, until you get close enough to see one *P-4 Outrider* scout, four *S-11* medium bombers, and only four *M-6*'s. And I've been pushing First Squadron, telling them that Second Squadron's probably better. They are, but that gap is closing."

"Who are you?" Jessica said with a grin of her own. "And what have you done with that *Jouster* that I nearly convinced to resign in disgrace?"

If you took everything else away, her career might be judged a success, just for turning Milos into a proper Command Flight Centurion and pointing him at the Imperials, instead of where he had been headed when she met him.

"I had a good example to follow," he said, much quieter. "Lead by excellence. Demand excellence. Settle for nothing less."

The words came back to her. The words every Command Centurion spoke, even the pilots, when they took command.

She will exercise excellence and demand the same of her crew, that the whole reflect the greatest acclaim in serving the needs of the Republic and the will of the Senate.

Jessica had walked into this room with a few vague misgivings. Only a few. They were all gone now.

"What about the rest of the plague of locusts?" she asked.

"The Destroyer Squadron has been together for years," he replied. "Those three wings are used to operating as a single team. Depending on the battle, I'll either put them dead center and build out from that, or hang them way out on a flank as a crossing attack."

"And *Andorra*?" she asked.

"Now that the station is fully repaired and a little expanded, that sneaky little Transport Carrier has uncrated and off-loaded fifteen of her chickens. That leaves her with space to fly the other fifteen from her own decks, as long as you don't mind us taking ten to fifteen minutes getting everybody launched. You'll have a little more than six squadrons in flight when the Imperials come, maybe eight worth of firepower if you let me send all the Gunships out as well and keep the two escorts in to protect the station. Do we know what's coming?"

It was Jessica's turn to lean back and think.

"By now, they've probably crept into the system, hiding in the darkness, looking around," she spoke, mostly to herself. "If we're lucky, they missed *Shivaji* and don't grasp the significance of *Andorra*. But they're still going to bring enough ships to take on a Star Controller."

She fixed him with a tight stare and relaxed some of her natural reticence. This man was going to be a significant part of why she survived. Or didn't.

Three years ago, she had finally learned to build strategies around *Jouster* doing something tactically insane in order to give him something to do. To channel him in productive directions. *Bitter Kitten* and *Furious* were just as bad, and even better pilots.

She needed him prepared for what was coming, regardless of her not knowing. And this wasn't one of those situations she could assume he had done his homework. Nobody approached this topic as obsessively as she did. Nobody.

"Simulations of Imperial doctrine suggest three primary tactical options," she continued, ticking them off with her fingers. "Two battleships with task forces. Four Fleet Carriers with their escorts. One of each. So, aggressive, defensive, or sweeping."

"What else have you planned for?" he asked, his voice now as serious as hers. He knew her well by now.

"A wall of escorts and missile cruisers doing hit and fades," she replied. "Three squadrons of heavy cruisers and battlecruisers charging us like a barbarian horde and then racing out the back at full speed. Just about everything I could think of or that the Red Admiral had ever tried."

"Will he be back?" Jouster asked.

Their last battle with the man had been nearly apocalyptic. Two squadrons of warships wrecked. Thousands killed. *Alexandria Station* destroyed.

But he had failed. Jessica and Suvi both survived.

"I doubt it," she replied. "He's been in retirement since *First Ballard*. If Karl let him off the leash now, he would need at least six months to train up a crew. That's that much longer for us to dig in. In another three months, we might well have won *Thuringwell*."

"So they'll be here soon?" he inquired.

"Every day, I wake up expecting them," she replied.

That took him a bit aback.

"Are there any as good as the Red Admiral?" he asked finally.

"No," she shook her head. "Well trained, lucky, good, but nobody with his genius for maneuver and aggression. I've planned for crazy, but we won't know until they arrive. And then it will be messy, but not to the death. We're not the only campaign under way right now. If they strip the frontier to come here, they've probably left some other system wide open for First War Fleet to raid."

"We'll be ready, Commander," *Jouster* said simply.

Jessica rose from her seat and held out her hand. They shook. Not Command and Fleet Centurions. Not man and woman. Comrades atop the wall, waiting for the creatures of the night to arrive.

She smiled, wandering back in her mind to the times she had nearly ended this man's career. She didn't think she had ever given Nils Kasum as many fits, but now she was beginning to wonder.

She also knew that she had forged the right sword for this mission.

Because the Imperial Fleet would be here soon. And they would not be friendly.

CHAPTER XL

IMPERIAL FOUNDING: 175/06/03. YONIN, THURINGWELL

TODAY, Merryn had dressed a little more formally. Taken the time to break out a less comfortable outfit, the sort of thing she would wear for a meeting with a banker or new customer. She wore a sedate and fairly conservative indigo skirt that nearly covered her black lace-up boots. To go with it, four layers of overlapping silk tops, almost like kimonos, from lavender to cream at the inner-most. Her hair was up and swept back and over her right shoulder, coiled up like a small, fuzzy tail.

She had even brought out her father's old, battered briefcase with the leather-clad metal sides, filled with paper documents. It was older than she was, and dated to him first purchasing *Seventh Son*.

Merryn was aiming for a particular look today, although she was not sure if the effort would be wasted. On many worlds, looking like the upper-class widow of an important businessman frequently deflected the inherent sexism of Imperial men by playing on their own perceptions of nobility and rank, as well as their upbringing.

If you didn't know who a woman was related to, you dared not insult her, at least not in public.

It frequently worked.

Today, was a different story. Nobody had a handle on the new Governor.

Redyert had dutifully applied for a license to bring in a shipment of very specific repair and replacement parts for office equipment and consumer goods. The humdrum things that kept the lights on and the comms working. Infrastructure nobody noticed until it failed.

And it would, without regular maintenance.

The Governor, Lady Wakely Okafor, had summoned Merryn instead of Ulaffson to a meeting in her office.

Again, Merryn wondered if the man had really been a spy all these years. She could never ask him, or anybody else, but it would explain many things in a more satisfactory manner than him just being a cutthroat business type moving fast and settling old scores.

There was enough of that going around these days as well.

The front of the State Building had been repaired. The damage had been largely confined to the third through fifth floors. Merryn could only tell because she had seen pictures from the fighting and knew where to look for fresh paint and occasional dimples filled in.

To get here, she had already walked through two checkpoints. Both were friendly, but the men and women manning them left no doubt how serious they could be if pushed.

And the front of the building was guarded by a pair of tanks, crouched like the stone lions wealthy families occasionally sat on either side of the front walkway. Big, weathered, and mean-looking.

The guards at this door went through her briefcase as well as subjecting her to a thorough and hands-on search. Again, friendly and polite, but professionally paranoid.

Very much not fooling around.

The elevator quickly whooshed her to nearly the top of the building. There were more guards here. At the same time, there was also a range of office workers, all heads down typing, or talking quietly on comm sets.

Merryn was a few minutes early, but was quickly ushered into the Governor's office.

Again, a radical change, where she might have previously been kept waiting by the former Mayor or Governor for an hour, for no other purpose than to establish her place in the pack hierarchy of Yonin society.

Or perhaps, she had been upgraded. *Aquitaine* was a society that saw eye to eye on the sexes. Maybe just being a woman here had gotten her in the door. If so, she would need to play that for all it was worth.

There was the potential for amazing profit in the chaos and fog of war. Redyert had seen it, if he hadn't instituted it.

The new Governor looked just like her pictures, but they failed miserably to convey the depths and strength of the woman behind them. She was a few shades darker than the former mayor of Yonin in skin. And her centimeter-long ringlets were just starting to turn gray along the bases and edges in a way that somehow conveyed majesty and intellect on a body that still looked like she spent several days a week in the gym.

Certainly her hands and arms were stronger than Merryn's, but Merryn generally only worked the machines aboard *Seventh Son* just enough to stay in shape.

Governor Okafor was in better shape than Imperial women half her age, Merryn concluded. All of them. And many of the men.

Merryn wondered what that said about the Admiral overhead. Jessica Keller also had a reputation as being a hard woman, a warrior at least the equal of the best of the men.

She must be an ogre.

Merryn sat and steeled herself.

The fencing started with Tea.

Not tea, but Tea.

One lump only. A soft dollop of cream. Darkest black brew. Steam billowing off both cups.

Blow on it a bit to cool it. Sip as quietly as possible, eyes never leaving eyes across the desk, but otherwise silence.

Waiting.

Imperial society would fill the vague space with generalities of weather and health. Futile chatter designed to obscure the fact that nothing was actually being said. Long minutes of time wasted that might be more usefully dedicated to commerce in its myriad forms.

But Merryn was also accustomed to waiting in antechambers for stupid amounts of time.

The Governor was unlike any politician she had ever met. Or bureaucrat.

Okafor pounced.

"I have a bid from Herr Ulaffson Redyert to make a run across the new Imperial border to the Imperial planet of *Kittras*," she said suddenly, jarring Merryn from her idle lethargy. "A shipment that requires, *requires* mind you, the vessel *Seventh Son*, and no other."

Merryn managed not to choke on the sip of tea in her mouth.

Suck it in carefully. Swirl it around to cool it, regardless of the heat damage. Keep your mouth shut and your eyes down. Swallow before engaging. Breathe before choking.

Merryn managed to look innocent and surprised when she looked up.

She hoped.

"So he proposed, when I met him for dinner last week," she replied neutrally. "Even a colony as small as *Thuringwell* would suffer unexpected economic damage if they tried to shift hardware paradigms so quickly."

Hopefully, innocent enough. Nothing whatsoever about smuggling. Not that there was much need to smuggle if the merchandise on the manifest was so valuable. Just pack in as much as you could possibly hold and use it to print money here.

"I find it interesting that he requires the one ship in this entire sector owned and commanded by a woman to handle this task," the Governor countered.

Another sip. Swallow. Buy time.

"One of only three I know of in the *Fribourg Empire*," Merryn evaded.

"So I surmise, Sri Teke," Okafor purred. "Does that make you more or less reliable as an Imperial citizen?"

Do not react. Do not flinch. Remember to breathe. You have *not* just been caught with your hand in the cookie jar *unless* you let them think so.

"I have not ever known a home beyond the hull of *Seventh Son*, Governor," Merryn shot back, hoping she sounded confident and not panicked. "I was born aboard her, and with luck, will have children someday that I can pass her on to when I want to retire, as my father planned."

Imperial world? Republic world? Who'll be nicest to an old lady who hopefully has a lot of money put away?

Merryn made a note to withdraw a significant chunk of her personal savings from the Imperial Bank at *Kittras* and convert it to something she could deposit in a Republic bank against future need. Maybe third-party bearer bonds from one of the fringe empires.

Thuringwell had stopped being a quiet backwater where she could make her usual margins with very little risk.

"So you might be amenable to regular runs to *Kittras*?" the Governor asked lightly. "There would of course be complications, but even in a war-zone, commerce must continue."

Merryn still felt like a cockroach in the middle of the kitchen floor when the lights came on, frantic to scurry for the corner.

"I think we should consider a single run, Madame Governor," Merryn managed. "After that, we can reassess our options."

Like running like hell for the Imperial interior and never, ever looking back. Or maybe *Aquitaine*'s. Girls were still treated better on *Ladaux* than *St. Legier*. The commoners, anyway.

"And when Imperial Security asks you to be a spy, Sri Teke?" Okafor fired back. "Then what?"

As if *Aquitaine* won't make the same demand? With the same outcomes?

Merryn did not choke on her tea. She was a little more prepared now.

She smiled. Light at the end of the tunnel.

"Hopefully, the profit will be too great to consider it," she purred in turn. "After all, those are the sorts of things that disgruntled citizens undertake."

"Yes," the Governor agreed with a shark's smile. "There have been rumors and innuendo about yourself and Sri Redyert being bandied about. I chalk them up to sour grapes, now that it's possible the wyrm has turned and *Thuringwell* faces a much more interesting future."

Merryn managed not to sputter. Her tea cup barely shook. Okafor was watching her like a hawk.

"Yes," she agreed after a too-long beat. "Sour grapes, I'm sure."

"I thought as much," the Governor said, rising and holding out her hand. "I look forward to doing business with you, Sri Teke. At least as much as you're willing to undertake."

Merryn was never sure how she managed to get out of the room alive and not in custody. Most of it was a blur. Smiles, and nods, and words. Down an elevator. Out into the street. Down several blocks on autopilot.

Order a shandy from a yard-side bar she had frequented over the years. Someplace with honest booze at honest prices and a quiet booth in the back where the waitress would deliver a glass and go away.

How much did they know? And if I'm about to be hung, who's buying the rope?

CHAPTER XLI

IT REQUIRED every element of skill and luck Fraser had accumulated in the last four years to get this close.

He really missed Eli right now. Her skill. Her savvy. Her instinct for when to freeze and spend an hour pretending to be a particularly ugly tree, just before an Imperial patrol wandered by without realizing it.

With all of *Thuringwell* as a hiding place, just finding Haussmann's forces was enough of a problem. Doing it without them realizing it was another level of difficulty.

Doing it while gathering up the fragments of the various liberation fronts was even harder.

Very few of his people had turned themselves in to Admiral Keller. Fleet Centurion Keller.

That woman.

The rest had stuck with him. As other teams had disintegrated, and largely snuck back into town, a few had filtered in and joined him, men he trusted, or who were closely vouched for. Long-serving rebels.

There would be no more new recruits joining. Anybody trying now was either a spy or an Imperial patriot with foolish delusions about what Fraser was really up to.

He rested now, just on the lee of a ridge, with Conrad and Roald on either side of him. To an outsider, it would have been impossible to describe what he was doing.

Watching. Smelling.

Knowing.

They had found human tracks in the forest.

There were always tracks, generally from lone hunters. Occasionally from other liberation teams. Nowadays, even hoof prints from Republic patrols.

Truly, hoof prints.

These were different. Not amateur, but certainly not people gifted in forest craft. Hunters in the deep green, rather than those used to being hunted. Arrogant and dominating, rather than submitting to the will of the trees to hide.

Fraser considered just how far he had come from that first week he'd spent in the wilderness after Jeannine was killed. A city boy from the slums, barely educated by Imperial standards, eking out a life on a mining contract, far from home, with only his wife to keep him on track.

Now he was surrounded by a family he had assembled. Other survivors who looked to him to keep them alive.

Could he really demand that they potentially throw their lives away on one last raspberry?

It was forty men and women, taking on hundreds. Worse, two score intending to attack hundreds, not trying to escape.

Actively pursuing Imperial Security forces. And he had found them. Down there, below.

It wasn't obvious to the average person. Fraser had developed a third eye for these things. Eli had been born with it.

Haussmann was down there.

The maps would tag the valley as an old, played-out mine, thin to begin with and abandoned when the seams petered out. Sure, there was still ore to be had, but *Thuringwell* had so many places where it was easier to get at, and a Duke who really only wanted enough peons digging to support his lifestyle. At least the grandfather had been that way.

The next two generations were even greater dandies, spending most of their lives at Court and living on the rents their Households produced.

Aquitaine would never grasp what was down there. The tailing piles would tell a singular story, one of rust and despair. The two holes in the side of the mountain were nothing more than eye sockets in a hollowed out skull found by the side of the road.

But tracks had led to sensors mounted on trees. And Conrad had been an electronics tech in his previous life. He knew where to tickle the little bugs to get them to give up their secrets without crying for help.

Sensors led to communications lasers. Quiet, serene, invisible, right up until you found them and recognized them. Then they turned into searchlights illuminating the night.

It had taken a week to get this far with the entire team. Two people could have done it in two days, but it took time blinding the right sensors and creeping under them, like thieves in the night.

And there was still the entire valley below. The monstrous mouths of the mine, those eyes in the side of the mountain, were distant little holes from here, fifteen kilometers away.

Fraser assumed minefields and weapon emplacements below him. Anyone getting this close was certain of where they were going and would need to be engaged with force. Briefly, he considered digging out a telescope to see if he could get a better view, but his soul had already recognized the place.

Megiddo, if you will.

Was he really going to go down there and get himself killed? Was he about to ask all of his closest comrades to die with him?

Was he utterly deranged?

Fraser looked over at Roald Dreyfuss, laying close by and watching the sky and trees with a close eye. He was a former mucker from the same mine that Conrad had fled. A man of few words but quality deeds.

Roald stared back at him now. It was a calm look. Not placid in the way of cattle or sheep, but simply waiting.

Calm, but there was anger hidden carefully away, awaiting expression when the moment arrived, as it had not yet. This was a man with a cross to bear, and an axe to grind. Intelligent brown eyes attested to that.

Roald wasn't here because his Captain had ordered him. He was here because his Captain needed him.

Fraser suddenly realized that he would see the same thing if he turned the other way and asked Conrad the same, silent question. Or the rest of the team, hidden carefully down the slope and waiting for his words.

This was the other burden of command. These men and women would be willing to die for him, because they knew he would be at the forefront of the charge, striving to make the world, the galaxy, a better place.

And he wasn't about to throw away those lives on a pointless act of suicidal defiance. Not when there was another way. A better way.

Fraser nodded.

"I've seen what I need," he whispered. "Roald, back us out and away. I need to make a call."

"To who?" Conrad asked quietly.

"To Keller," Fraser said. "It's time she and I talked."

CHAPTER XLII

HE DID NOT WEAR his full dress uniform often. Not the one with all the good ribbons, and the loop of braid around his left shoulder. And the sash and the saber.

And Emmerich had never worn this one before.

In the last year and a half, he had lost nearly ten percent of his overall mass, mostly around his belly. More walking to and from his office across the Fleet Conservatory's large campus, combined with more quiet dinners with his wife and fewer grand banquets with too much food and alcohol.

Emmerich suspected that the Duchess Freya was in league with her cousin-in-law, the Empress, to make him take better care of himself. Certainly, he hadn't been in this good of shape in decades, regardless of all the exercise he used to get when he was aboard a starship.

He stopped dead as he arrived and took a deep breath.

Em wondered if he would ever command a warship again. He stared hard at the door in front of him as if he could divine his future in the grains of oak.

From this side, a simple wooden panel with a conference room number. But on the other side, his former life. One that might be lost to him forever. Would it be worth existing, if he had to live the rest of his life grounded?

Could he?

Enough. Be The Dread Red Admiral today, regardless of what you might feel. The Empire requires it.

He pressed the old-fashioned latch handle and pushed the door into the room.

Inside, he was the guest of honor. Everyone rose from their places around the long oval table and came to attention. Heels clicked and spines popped as shoulders came back.

Em knew every man in here. They were all his in some manner, either his students and former team members, or men that had been trained by his acolytes.

At the long end of the great table, where the Emperor would sit if he were to join, they had left the space open for Admiral of the Red Wachturm. Twelve captains filled the long sides, with an Admiral of the White at the lower end of the table.

The other Admiral had shaved his head clean as he had gone bald. On some men, the look was a touch pathetic. On this man, it added a level of fierceness to his otherwise pale skin, complemented by green eyes that shown like emeralds.

Admiral Saveliy Kozlov. An exceptional tactician, if a bit linear in his thinking. But that could work, if you had a big enough hammer. Kozlov might.

Without a word, Em grasped the entire strategy and battle plan behind the attempt to liberate *Thuringwell* from its new-found masters.

It was difficult even thinking of the five primary captains around Kozlov by their names, as he automatically placed them on their respective bridges and thought of them simply by the names of their vessels.

Captain Iohan Pavelovski of the Fleet Carrier *Europa*.

Captain Nelson Amavaraia of the Fleet Carrier *Hokkaido*.

Captain Reinhart Snelling of the Battleship *Varga*.

Captain Dietrich van Aakken of the Flag Cruiser *Novo Daysahn*.

Captain Alain Toma of the *Varga*'s Light Cruiser Escort *Wintergold*

The other seven were Frigate Captains, three from *Varga*'s wolfpack, and the other four being the regular Task Force escorts for the carriers.

Two teams, each capable in their own right, but not used to working together. Plus a Flag Cruiser used to operating solo on various diplomatic and exploratory missions all over the Empire.

Would it be enough to defeat Jessica Keller?

Was anything?

And in that moment Em finally understood why Joh would not let him command again.

She had gotten under his skin, made him wonder at his own abilities.

She had made him *doubt*.

He might never forgive her for that.

Em took his seat and gestured the rest to sit. An Admiral of the Red had that privilege with these men. Doubly so, *The Red Admiral*.

He fixed Kozlov with a hard stare. It was the kind of glare the man had once faced defending a thesis before a Board chaired by Wachturm himself.

"Wolfpack or avalanche?" Em probed the room in a voice bordering on rude. "I see no ground forces commanders."

The rest of the men were there as window dressing, as much as some of the top captains in the *Fribourg Empire* could be considered such.

Only Kozlov mattered.

"This will be settled in orbit, Admiral," Kozlov fired back, just as hard. "Whatever happens on the surface will be desultory."

Em nodded.

He wasn't about to correct the man. Not publicly. These men needed absolute iron self-confidence.

It was enough for him to be filled with questions.

Communications surveillance had picked up the name of the appointed Planetary Governor. Em had even read two of Dr. Okafor's books, with two more on his shelf to get to in his spare time. He had spare time these days, but not enough to consume all the books he had acquired over the decades.

Wakely Okafor was not a random selection on an *Aquitaine* mission. Not for an undertaking this big.

Not with Jessica Keller in command.

Dr. Okafor was one of the Republic's experts on Imperial Systems. Planetary governance. Culture.

Psychology.

Over breakfast this morning, Em had played a mental game with himself, pretending to be Nils Kasum and trying to outguess the *Fribourg Empire*'s response to such a provocation as *Thuringwell*.

Wakely Okafor might be subtle enough, ambitious enough, think big enough, to try to wrest a world away from Empire.

With Jessica Keller, she might succeed.

"What are you facing?" Em prodded.

It was easy to fall back into the Socratic Method. Nothing better had proven its worth in one hundred and fifty centuries.

"A Star Controller Task Force," Kozlov replied quickly. "The equivalent of a Battleship and a Fleet Carrier flying on a single hull. Three Cruisers. Six Destroyers. Whatever defensive fighter squadron she has brought with her as a permanent force."

"And assaulting?"

"One Battleship. Two Fleet Carriers. Forty-eight type A-8a melee fighters, eighteen type A-3g fighter-bombers, six B-9 heavy bombers. One Flag Cruiser. One light cruiser. Seven Frigates. Four D-class escort scouts."

Kozlov admitted no doubt in his voice. That was good.

After Emmerich's raid on *Ballard*, after his failure to kill the three most dangerous women in the galaxy, both sides had considered the weapons and associated tactics Moirrey Kermode had invented. A few had been adopted. Those would no longer be a surprise, merely an adjustment.

Kermode would have come up with something else by now, but Em didn't bother asking these men to think that many moves ahead. It wasn't that they weren't smart enough or capable enough. Nobody but Kermode could guess at what she might do.

And against this much firepower, it might not matter.

At the same time, he still knew *doubt*.

This many vessels assembled in one place represented more than two full Task Forces not available elsewhere on the Empire's vast frontiers. Worlds were left unguarded. Sectors softened.

Already, pinprick raids had occurred as *Aquitaine* probed for weakness.

They knew.

These men were the shining broadsword of *Fribourg*, upholding the martial honor and might of the Emperor himself.

It was left to Em to figure out how to protect the rest, that soft, weak underbelly of worlds, with the greatly reduced resources that his personal war with Jessica Keller had caused.

"And?" Em asked again.

"Avalanche, Admiral Wachturm," Kozlov replied. "We have her out-massed, out-gunned, and trapped at *Thuringwell*. Unless she has brought another squadron from *Aquitaine*'s First War Fleet, she will be annihilated."

Em wished he could know such certainty.

He dared not suggest to these men his own theories for what Keller was really up to with a place like *Thuringwell*. They might scoff at him. They might ignore him. They might even believe.

But as Kozlov had said, it would be decided in orbit, so it would be better for them not to try to think beyond that battle.

He would never show it, save perhaps to his Duchess, but tonight, he was going to go home to get very, very drunk and mourn what he had lost.

Somewhere along the way, he would toast Jessica Keller, and then, perhaps, he would seek a way to be free of her ghost.

CHAPTER XLIII

DATE OF THE REPUBLIC JULY 2, 396
BACKWOODS, THURINGWELL

THE COUNTRY HAD GROWN ROUGHER with elevation.

Dash figured it was something to do with the distant sea and close hills and mountains. The locals had very little to do with all the oceans on this world, concentrating inland to work the mines, but there was still a lot of drizzle and occasional monsoons through here.

Scout Patrol was tightened up now. Three hard columns with only a few scouts outside that. Third at the center as they followed the signal line.

Everyone had a firearm in their hands now, too. Trouble was coming.

Little Rain signaled a hold and dismounted.

Küçük carried the Narwhal like a lunch box in her left hand, and her revolver in her right.

Rather than flip it up on its pole, she rested it briefly on her shoulder and turned slowly in place. After a moment, she walked to her left and repeated the action. Finally, she moved to a fallen log and put her nose close enough to sniff.

Moments passed.

Küçük rose and signaled to Dash to come over from her spot on the near right. Arlo came alone, plus the Cornicen and the Draconarius. This was probably going to be official business.

"What's the latest, Küçük?" Dash asked.

The tiny woman squatted down and tapped a bump on the log with the barrel of her revolver.

"Bastard just changed direction seventy degrees," she grumbled.

Dash nodded, but Vo asked anyway.

"I thought you said that they tended to go in nearly straight lines?" he said.

"Yes, sir," the scout replied. "They do."

"And?" Arlo prompted.

"It's a trap, Vo," Dash interjected.

She could feel that in her bones.

The ground ahead suddenly opened up into something approximating a prairie. The horses would love it, after so much time pushing through scrub and bramble, but they didn't think about things like enfilading lines of fire and mine fields.

That much clear space was an invitation to meander in, look around, and get chopped. Couple of square kilometers, at a dead minimum, with her troops right on the edge of one long axis. The transmitter line had originally been set to skirt along one edge. Instead, it had turned and leapt straight across the middle of the longest part, as if drawn with a compass.

"Did he know we were coming?" Arlo followed her line of logic quickly.

For a city boy, he had picked up on horse combat tactics remarkably quickly. Must have had a good teacher sky-side.

"Küçük?" Dash asked.

The woman leaned forward and sniffed the beacon again. Or whatever magic she was doing.

That one might honestly be the kind of crazy redneck that everyone assumed made up the whole Legion.

"Naw, just a paranoid mind, PeeCee," she replied after a moment. "Guessing he was running his lines and saw this lovely pasture on a map, so he set a killzone right in the middle of it. This log is a stupid place to put a transmitter link, unless you want it found."

"And you want the trackers to ride right out there following it," Arlo concluded her thought.

"A-yup. PeeCee?"

PeeCee. Patrol Centurion. Boss. Dash.

Her troop. Her decision. Arlo was just a ride-along at this point, but he could call in help if they needed it.

LVIII Heavy wasn't that close either, but close enough, in a pinch. *Tamarin* could drop them handy in under twenty minutes. Less if all hell broke loose.

It still felt wrong.

What would I do, if I was him?

Dash dismounted and handed her reins to Charpentier. The Draconarius was the only person here without a gun out, but the standard was on a pole with a sharpened spike, worst came to worst.

Arlo joined her as she studied the field. He brought out the glass optics.

"What would you do, Arlo?" she asked.

Vo had talked about someone called *Navin the Black*. Dash wondered if a marine who did a career aboard starships would be any good at field maneuvers.

Vo stood perfectly still for several seconds.

"Spider-mine the whole damned place," he said finally. "It would take an entire pallet of them, but I would actually run them heaviest along the port edge from here, second heaviest to starboard, and just enough in the middle to spook horses and make you turn and try to run for an edge through the heaviest bits."

He studied the path behind them for a bit, and then the field again.

"Probably add a box of plasma mines for the tanks," he continued, pointing. "There, there, and there. Just to be an ass. Three or four cameras to watch. Maybe a couple of laser sensors two and a half meters off the ground, where an elk won't set them off, and a cowboy will."

Dash was impressed. City boy apparently did know something after all. Or he was paranoid enough. She wouldn't have come up with the laser high enough to paint a cavalry trooper while ignoring native fauna.

That just made the killzone worse. The only way to be sure was to ride someone right out in the middle of it and set the damned thing off. Or try to ride around it.

She could go crazy playing chess against herself, trying to outguess Haussmann's paranoia and skill.

She considered letting him win this round. There were other ways to skin this cat.

"We were headed that direction when we got here," she announced loud enough that close lances could hear her. "I'm guessing he's prepared for us to miss this line and keep circling to the left, or to cut straight across. We're going to back off a few kilometers and circle this place in from the far right and see if we can catch his line."

Dash drew a breath. It was rare that she had to say this, especially to these people. But that was part of being in charge. Thinking the hard thoughts.

"It may be that he gets away with it," she said. "Gets away from us. Better safe than sorry. This is a guerilla war. We have to catch him, and not keep walking into his traps."

She could see some of the air leak out of her people. The disappointment couldn't be helped. In about ten minutes, that would probably turn into a slow-burning anger that would fuel people to be on him hard.

One of these days, Haussmann would screw up.

Dash hoped she was the one to catch him when he did.

CHAPTER XLIV

IMPERIAL FOUNDING: 175/07/03. KITTRAS PORT, KITTRAS

IT WASN'T surprising that they came for her, only that it took them so long to get organized.

Merryn had even taken a slow approach to the planet, coming out of JumpSpace well clear of the gravity well and sort of idling her way in and to the ground, taking nearly twice as long as was her usual wont.

And still, *Seventh Son* had been on the ground for nearly a day. The local merchants who generally bid on filling Redyert's orders had already come and dickered before retiring and beginning to send trucks round filled with boxes.

There was going to be a lot of money on the table.

Those containers that weren't still factory sealed were going to get opened up manually, but only after Merryn had gotten into JumpSpace and put on a suit with its own air supply. And the locals could be damned if they had anything to say about that.

Still, she knew the man as soon as she saw him on the bridge monitor, approaching the primary airlock ramp. *Seventh Son* might be a medium freighter in size, but she still had enough landing struts to keep the entire vessel three meters in the air when it landed. And since she was buttoned up right now, the only ways aboard were the loading ramp, which was up and locked, and the primary airlock ramp, which was deployed and inviting, right until you got to the locked inner hatch. That was it, unless you wanted to pretend you were a ninja.

He even looked like a spy. Merryn suspected she had watched too many cheesy videos in her time, but the man had that tall, elegant grace, lean without being cadaverous, that she expected. She wondered if they all went to the same school to learn to dress and walk.

Certainly, casting directors had nailed this man without ever meeting him. Or he had watched too many of those same vids and was working to emulate them.

Six months ago, she would be terrified right now.

Instead, she just keyed the ship-wide with a tired hand.

"Yan," she called quietly. "We have company. Can you take over the bridge watch? Hao, report to airlock one. Without a weapon *visible*, please."

Hao would have a gun of some sort tucked away. She was just like that. Beautiful, petite women tended to develop survival instincts in the big, bad galaxy. Hao's usually involved firearms. Merryn was happy to bite and kick.

The *Fribourg Empire* had come for her. She wondered if they would treat her like a man, a Captain/Owner on his own deck, or like a silly little girl that could be ordered around because she was incapable of taking care of herself.

Merryn forced the snarl off her face as she rose from her left-hand seat and made her way off the bridge.

Deep breaths. Calm heart. Relaxed hands.

You are not a spy. Aquitaine *barely even hinted at recruiting you.*

That would come after she returned from *Kittras*. If she returned.

The spy was waiting patiently in the airlock when the inner hatch cycled back into the hall. There was a lot of space here for the door to swing, physics demanding that it would slam shut and be held in place like a cork if something happened to the airlock itself.

Up close, the man was tall and skinny. Well dressed, tailored, perhaps, but still only fifteen or eighteen kilos heavier than Merryn, with a whole head of height advantage.

An average face. Short brown hair in a neutral cut. Clean shaven.

Forgettable.

"Captain Teke?" he asked formally, hands crossed behind his back at some vague approximation of parade rest.

Merryn held onto hope. The man could just as easily have addressed her as *Madame Teke*.

"That's right," she agreed without committing to anything.

"I represent certain personages that would like to have a meeting with you," he continued smoothly. His voice was remarkably rich for such a skinny frame. "Would you be available to talk?"

"We've been awaiting your arrival," Hao replied. "Shall we?"

He paused. Merryn actually saw emotion cross his face. Indecision, mixed with a hint of disdain, and a dash of concern.

Apparently, even Imperial spies might be human.

"This invitation is for you only, Captain Teke," he said.

"And this is Hao Yi, my loadmaster," Merryn smiled glacially up at him. "*We* will go. Or we won't."

Hao suddenly transformed into a fierce little creature, like a teacup Chihuahua that had gone rabid. She never made a sound, but her eyes suddenly glowed with angry fire and Merryn could see her roll her weight forward onto the balls of her feet.

A pretty, little, foul-mouthed loadmaster, who wasn't the least bit intimidated by drunken rowdies in a yard-side bar.

The spy blinked. Twice.

Merryn smiled cruelly.

He deflated. Ever so slightly. Rolled onto his back in the secret confines of the *Seventh Son*'s airlock and bared his belly to the tiny girl. It was enough.

He nodded and preceded them into the late afternoon sun.

Hao smiled with a mouth that wouldn't melt butter.

IMPERIAL SECURITY on *Kittras* was apparently housed in a converted Georgian palace on the edge of the central district. It was a white, granite mansion that was too big for a family, and too small for a business. The sort of thing a banker would build for himself when he was getting ready to put his name on university buildings or hospitals.

Apparently, he had subsequently fallen on hard times. Or crossed the wrong people, if Imperial Security owned the building now. The foyer still screamed money, though.

Men downstairs had thought to separate Merryn and Hao when they arrived. Force Hao to wait behind while her captain was escorted upstairs and possibly to her fate.

Merryn was fairly certain she actually heard the faintest growl come from Hao's throat this time.

They eventually let the loadmaster pass.

Upstairs, down the long, oversized hallway, Merryn was led to what was probably a formal salon in its previous life. Wide double-doors in white that opened into a medium sized space, too big for High Tea, not large enough for dancing.

One desk. One man. No chairs for guests. It wasn't that kind of office.

Merryn would have said shark in shallow waters, but the man reminded her of a sudden cobra in a wood pile, rearing up and flaring his hood at her. At them.

Unlike the spy who had brought them here, this man was very, very dangerous. Even Hao recognized that and retreated behind a shell of polite *bonhomie* after they entered.

Promises and other silent questions passed over the women's heads to the spy who had been their escort, before he retreated and left them alone.

The silence stretched. Cobra was unhappy. And yet, he needed something from her. Had to even ask politely. Had to treat a woman as a Captain, and not a female encumbrance.

For the briefest moment, she could see the wash of anger in his eyes at the entire situation, before he crushed it and asserted his dominance over the room. It was like musk filling the air, without a single word.

Merryn was singularly impressed.

"We have just returned from *Thuringwell*," Merryn decided to open hard and fast on the man. "I'm sure you were aware by now that a naval force from the *Republic of Aquitaine* is currently occupying the system under martial law."

The cobra studied her closely, like she had turned into a mongoose. Merryn kept expecting a tongue to flicker out.

"And yet you escaped, Captain Teke?" the man finally spoke.

He had a voice like eighteen-year-old scotch. Warm and smooth and caramel, until it got to your center and erupted briefly. She could almost taste the knife in his words.

"Admiral Keller demands that commerce continue, sir," she countered. "Apparently, the shipping houses are all making deals. My vessel was simply the first to be allowed to depart."

It even sounded plausible.

"And what information can you provide?"

He was suddenly much less hostile. Here was a proper Imperial citizen running to the authorities with stories of monsters in the night. Exactly the sort of thing the Imperial Security Bureau was empowered to handle.

"Not much, sir," Merryn took care to sound helpfully distressed. "My ship's records were wiped of all militarily-useful data in the process of my vessel undergoing a thorough inspection by *Aquitaine* military engineers. I suspect spies."

And she didn't need to mention that she had wiped those records herself. She might yet be considered a spy. If that nasty cruiser sneaking around was a shock to her, it would be doubly so to everyone else who wasn't expecting it.

Maybe she was a spy. Certainly, not a patriot, considering all the guns and things she had smuggled in for Redyert over the years.

"It will be unfortunately necessary to subject you to a very intense interrogation, then, Captain Teke," he purred at her.

It sounded almost wistful, like he really wanted to get out the honey and the ants, or the electrodes for her nipples, and would have to just settle for bright lights and mental abuse.

She had experienced Imperial Security confined to *polite questioning* when they couldn't prove she had done anything. They still couldn't prove it.

Merryn flashed back to Governor Okafor in her office, offering tea and sizing her up. No threats. No bluster. Was that what it was like to live in *Aquitaine* as a woman? To not have to be twice as good as any man to be considered half his equal?

"Your associate will not need to be detained while we question you," he continued.

For the slightest moment, Merryn lost her grip on the anger she had been holding on to.

"Funny," Merryn countered with an edge to her voice her mother had taught her. "I thought I was a loyal Imperial citizen, voluntarily attempting to help. I hadn't realized I was to be treated like a common criminal."

One did not run guns to rebel groups in a fit of pique. At least, not for that many years. That was a calculated intent. But one might still be possessed of a great and terrible anger that convinced them to do such a thing in the first place. And to keep doing it in the face of deadly risk.

Outwardly, she was as loyal as the day was long. If they could have proven anything, she would have simply disappeared along the way, with little more than a footnote in a quarterly report filed away somewhere.

She had rights. Hao as well, but *Fribourg* counted a man, or a woman, extra when they captained a vessel as large as hers.

The spy, the cobra, recoiled, ever so slightly, under the lash of her tone, rather like the previous man had. Perhaps they had both known high-borne women who would brook no nonsense. It was a common enough Imperial archetype that she knew how to exploit.

"Not at all, Madam Teke," the man countered quickly. "My apologies for a poor choice of words. Your assistance is most valuable. I will find you a comfortable room and a good secretary to aid one of my men in directing your conversation towards useful topics."

He pushed a button on his desk that must have been wired to a siren in the hall, from the speed with which the tall man returned.

THEY TOOK her and Hao to a small office downstairs, barely big enough for four people around a table.

In the end, it required take-out from a competent Italian restaurant: several kinds of pasta, containers of sauce, and small boxes of meatballs, washed down liberally with fresh tea; to get through the ordeal. Merryn could not remember ever talking for so long without a break or a nap.

Hours had passed. Night had fallen to utter dark, broken only by the waxing light of the smaller moon, not much better than a flashlight to see as they made their way from the Security agent's ground transport to the base of the airlock ramp.

No one had spoken on the ride back. Merryn from exhaustion. Hao from overall twitchiness. The agent from his training, or watching too many vids.

Once outside, in the cool air, Hao took her hand like they were schoolgirls and practically drug her up the ramp. Still, without a spotter, Merryn rated it fifty/fifty she would have tripped and slid back down, or managed to pitch herself over the side, since her eyes kept wanting to cross.

At the top of the ramp, Tyler met them, a carbine rifle carefully tucked away by his side and a look like the little, rabid Chihuahua's angry, big brother. Go figure.

They got her inside and got the airlock door sealed without a word.

"Will they actually buy any of that squamph you were peddling back there?" Hao finally asked in an excited giggle.

"I don't care," Merryn replied tiredly.

She looked up and saw Yan had joined them. She had her whole crew, her whole family here supporting her.

"So now what?" Hao continued.

"Pack well for our departure," Merryn said. "Get as much material as we can carry. Then I'm going to the bank and converting three-quarters of my saving to negotiable instruments to bring them with us back to *Thuringwell*, en route to *Aquitaine*."

"Only three-quarters?" Yan perked up.

"If I close the account, right now, it will set off all sorts of alarms and they might arrest us on general principle," Merryn explained herself. "If, however, I have a great story about an investment opportunity, cash only, back on *Thuringwell* with a trading house about to change sides, they might not flinch."

Hao had a gleam in her eyes.

"You'll need to sell it just right," she purred. "Maybe they'll want in and hand you a briefcase filled with money on the spot."

"We can only hope, Hao," Merryn said. "Fifteen minutes after the fleet gets to *Thuringwell*, they'll know they've been had and we can never come back to the Empire."

"What did you tell them, Captain?" Yan asked.

"That cruiser that nearly smoked us? *Shivaji*?" she replied. "They missed it when they were scouting. They're only expecting the one Battlecruiser and a couple of light jobs. And they sure has hell aren't accounting for all the fighters Keller packed away in her Winter Stocking. Or that industrious, little minelayer in orbit. A good little Imperial citizen would have corrected their notes."

Right now, however, she just wanted sleep. In another twelve hours, they might be ready. Hit the bank first thing, run like hell, and get across the border before anybody was the wiser.

Despite her exhaustion, Merryn had never felt so alive.

CHAPTER XLV

JESSICA KNEW it would be interesting when Enej knocked on her door with his knuckles, and then opened the hatch two beats later without her doing it. When everything could be sent electronically, human contact was unnecessary.

That made the message itself important.

Jessica closed the document she was reviewing and looked up, eyes wide with inquiry.

"Fraser Cydelmynster is on a secured comm, asking specifically for you," Enej said simply. "Fourth Saxon picked it up and patched it to us through their network."

Jessica could think of a number of reasons the man might be calling her instead of the Legate or the Governor. All of them were rather interesting.

"I'll presume they know where he is, by now?" Jessica asked.

"Probably within meters, boss," Enej replied. "Should they do anything about it?"

"No," Jessica decided abruptly. "Send a signal to the Legate that he may want to drop his Heavy Scout team close by, and to prepare, but not to move without my explicit orders."

"Got it."

And Enej was gone.

Jessica sucked the last few drops of warmth from her nearly-empty coffee mug and settled herself into her chair. Just because, she cleared everything off of it as well, which involved putting her tablet computer in a drawer and adding the clipboard with a pen.

She already lived lean.

Jessica reached out and triggered the call button on her comm, waiting there patiently for its current moment of glory on one side of her desk.

The air got scratchy as the call was patched through so many links.

"This is Keller," she announced.

She waited.

"Fleet Centurion, my name is Fraser Cydelmynster," the man replied slowly.

She could hear a vast weight in his tones. He had a mellow voice, somewhere between tenor and baritone normally, she would have guessed.

Today, he was just dog-tired.

"I realize that I am not in a position to strike a hard deal," he continued in that slow cadence. "However, I am generally acknowledged as the leader of the forces dedicated to liberating *Thuringwell* from the *petit aristocracy* of stupidity that rules us. And I need your help."

Well, that was certainly novel. Invoking the brotherhood of command. The Legate would appreciate the move, as would several other people she had no doubt were monitoring the channel on mute.

"The Duke no longer rules here, Cydelmynster," she replied carefully.

She doubted he was including her in his classifications. Certain phrases become ingrained and must be excised over time. And certainly, the previous Duke had been a blind fool, but that was not an uncommon trait in a world of vast, inherited wealth and power. *Fribourg* was stronger than *Aquitaine*, but far more brittle.

"No," the man replied with worn care. "But his lackey still roams."

"And what help could I provide?" Jessica challenged. "You have not yet accepted my authority."

"I accept your power, Admiral. Fleet Centurion. Most of my people have chosen to return to civilization and accept you."

"And you, Fraser?" Jessica took a chance and pushed the conversation into the personal. "What will you do?"

The *Fribourg Empire*, like *Aquitaine*, maintained a level of discipline around names. Strangers, and even co-workers, would address each other by their family name, frequently for years, until invited.

Only friends, lovers, and comrades in arms would generally be free to use a given name.

The Brotherhood of Command.

"I swore an oath, Fleet Centurion," he replied after the briefest pause. "One that has nothing to do with you. But today, I cannot execute on that oath without dying unsuccessfully, stupidly. I have a hard kernel of troops under my command. We have located what I believe is Haussmann's primary base, but in attacking it, we would be forty against hundreds, in someone else's bloody war."

Jessica could almost hear the Legate and Primus Pilus yelling at her to make a deal, any deal that would get them those coordinates. She expected text messages to start chirping on her tablet any second now. That was one of the reasons it was tucked away in a drawer.

This conversation was just between the two of them.

He might have forty. Intelligence analysis was pretty firm that Haussmann had around five hundred. Jessica had an entire fleet at her command, with Fourth Saxon, *LVIII Heavy*, and all of her own marines available in a pinch. A force as much bigger than Haussmann's as his was over Cydelmynster's.

"What was your oath, Fraser?" she asked, again pushing into the personal.

If rumors were to be believed, the man had personally conjured the entire liberation movement himself from thin air. Certainly, he had taken small bands of roving outlaws and turned them into a full-on guerilla force, however small it might be.

A few years from now, he might be the kind of man who could get himself elected Governor of *Thuringwell*, and be a good one, if he didn't get himself killed today.

"When they murdered Jeannine, my wife, I swore I would not rest until Haussmann and his kind were destroyed," Cydelmynster replied.

Jessica could hear the pain in his voice, the unimaginable loss he carried with him every day, even years later.

It was something else she shared with the man, beyond the hollow rigors of command, even if she doubted a man like that would know it.

Jessica hoped he would find a way to survive. Too many people chose to die in circumstances like this. She nearly had, until Desianna had gotten through to her, held her when she cried, anchored her enough to maintain her balance, long enough for her to stand on her own.

"And what did you want from me?" she asked again.

It was necessary for him to speak the words now. This might be what it took for the man to break out of that place where grief had driven him. Certainly she would not help without him asking, either in the field or in the mind.

"I would like my force to be an independent command under your cavalry's orders when they get here to go down there and crush the man," he said heavily. "If that means we take the point and get used up opening the way, that will be enough for me, and for the men and women under my command. They are all here for much the same reason."

So, death and glory in battle?

Jessica could see the Legate and the Primus Pilus nodding to each other across whatever table they shared. They would happily destroy Fraser and his troop to protect their own. Grind the strangers like hamburger. Simple math. Less important ex-Imperial rebels instead of highly trained cavalry troopers.

She would have to break the two of them of that thinking. Perhaps even nicely.

Winning *Thuringwell* over the long term depended on exactly this man and his most loyal soldiers surviving the coming battle.

Jessica was about to speak, to offer the man some reassurance in accepting his offer, when Enej opened the door silently and walked to her desk. He handed her an actual printed piece of paper while he pushed the button to mute the conversation at this end.

Probably something very rash from Fourth Saxon, since they couldn't get hold of her directly.

She read the words and felt her heart stop.

She looked up at Enej, and he simply nodded.

Jessica took a moment to get her voice and adrenaline under control.

She pressed the button and brought the conversation live.

"Captain Cydelmynster, I accept your offer," she said firmly. "However, you will not be attacking that base today."

"Why is that, Fleet Centurion?" he asked carefully.

She could hear the weight lifting off his back as he spoke.

"Because Haussmann and his Security forces have just launched a major assault on the new railroad yard that is about to connect the old mines and the economy to *Thuringwell*'s future," she replied. "I want your force in place to intercept them when they retreat to their base."

"At your command, Fleet Centurion," his voice snapped to attention.

"Stand by for my Flag Centurion, Captain Cydelmynster," Jessica said.

She keyed the comm closed, and then connected directly to the Legate's office.

"You've heard about the attack on Ramsey Starport?" she asked as soon as he answered.

"Affirmative, Commander," Burdge drawled simply. "We presumed another hit and fade, but this one is much bigger. I'm already vectoring as many ground forces in as I can spare."

"Where are Dash, Vo, and Rebekah?" she continued.

"Already loaded," he said. "Was expecting you to drop them on Cydelmynster."

"Get Fraser's coordinates, then drop Dash on Haussmann's best line of retreat," she ordered. "Then get the locals integrated as scouts and be prepared to be the cork in the bottle."

"What about air cover?" Burdge asked.

Aquitaine owned the sky and orbit.

Something didn't feel right.

"Would you pull an attack like this if you were worried about airstrikes and GunShips, Burdge?"

"Hell, no, Fleet Centurion," he snarled back. "I'd be camped on a bunch of defensive artillery just waiting for some stupid throttle-jockey to buzz me low enough I could stuff a missile up his ass. Hell, I might launch an attack like this just draw them in so I could kill them."

"Then you and I are thinking the same way, Legate," she answered. "Can the base hold until you can get there?"

"Not if Haussmann pushes hard, Commander. But I can drop people close enough to push him sideways before he does too much damage to people. Hardware is likely to be used up."

"It's your battle, with one exception, Burdge," she said carefully. "I want Cydelmynster and his forces to come through as intact as possible. That man might be the key to winning the whole planet, and I don't want him dead."

Even if Fraser demanded to become a martyr, dying for the cause of liberty. Enough people were going to die today, and more when the Imperial Fleet finally arrived. Very few of them had the possibility to turn the tide of history like Fraser Cydelmynster might.

CHAPTER XLVI

DATE OF THE REPUBLIC JULY 18, 396 RAMSEY STARPORT, THURINGWELL

IT WERE ALMOST BEAUTIFUL, for all that it were a big, ugly, black-iron-looking log on rails. Still, it did the job. And did it with big, mean stuff.

And nobody were gonna touch her high score for docking rail cars on the flat ground of the new starport. Moirrey were sure of that. Oz and his silk scarf be damned.

Moirrey stood inside her little watch tower office and enjoyed the view out her big, second-story, picture window of the whole yard beneath her. It had finally stopped that damned drizzling a bit ago, just about the time the sun had gone down, and now it were kinda just wet and miserable, but the sun promised to boil every'tin' clean'n'dry in the morning.

The tea were almost gone, and her tummy was all warm and happy. Maybe another fifteen or twenty minutes and she'd be all good to slip into her bunk with all the blackout curtains pulled down and go to bed.

Below, the big, black monster were resting. *Yonin/Ramsey Engine Number One*, colloquially named *City of Brani*, fer the capital of *Ladaux*, 'cause it were bad luck not to give an engine a personal name.

Numbers were fer inventory. They dinna convey souls.

Tonight, she needed some soul. Moirrey couldna put her finger on it, but things was amiss. Bad ju-ju kinda strange. More than just staying up late killing more trees for the Gods of Bureaucracy.

Sumtin'.

Tea had only kept the beasts at bay fer a bit. They hadna slain 'em.

So she were at the window in her already-dark office, enjoyin' the view o' the yard. *City of Ithome* and *City of Saxilby* in their spots out across the way. *City of Brani* close below her, waitin' the morning when they would finally be ready to join up to the main line and blowed this planet's economy sideways.

Maybe that were it. Tamarrows, when they would test the last link in the spur and she could drive *City of Brani* out to Mine #14 direct-like. Then nobody would have to go all the way in to that cramped, little yard attached to the starport to unload ore. They could bring it here and unload. A third of the time, and ya didn't have to answer to bankers in town.

See? That were the problem. Nobody done gived the mines names like places got. Even if they was stupid names. At least that gave them souls.

Moirrey smiled. She had already invested a goodly chunk o' her retirement money in a company that were all set to build a smelter here, just down the creek from the brand, spanking new starport she were about done building. Then folks could ship out big metal bar stock instead of hauling off megatonnes of rock to be broken down somewhere else.

Stupid, stupid idea. Stooooooopid, even. Wasteful. Unless you were a lazy git of a Duke and owned a smelter on some other planet and it were easier to pay yer friends to haul stuff for you.

Moirrey smiled fit to light the morning.

Next, we make Digger build me a passenger rail line to Yonin so folks can live there and ride to work in the morning, and head home in the evening, just in time fer the starport to opens. Yonin were a boring place today. Weren't always gonna be. Not if the Republic needed to build 'emselves a great big base here to push the frontier back.

Lotsa money to be made. More when the locals got in on the act and invested sweat and soul for a slice of the pie, like whats Lady Keller and Doctor-Governor Wakely were plannin'.

And maybe, just maybe, make a little lady from Ramsey rich in the process. Weren't always gonna be fleet. One o' these days, I'll have to go get a real job and everything, instead of just playing around in the engineering labs.

Movement caught her eye. Where weren't supposed to be none.

Peeples. Too close to wire. Alarms shoulda been hootin' and stuff. They did that when the fool deer wandered too close.

And lotsa people. Way too many. Couple of rugby scrums o'folks out there, doing something that dinna make any sense.

Moirrey set her tea mug down and grabbed the big optical lenses from the cute, little decorated holder she had made pretty.

Something really weren't right.

There was one guy seemed kinda in the middle of things. Small. Bantam cock looking kind of fella.

She brought them folks into focus and something in her head went *click*. Them fools was wearing gray, not green.

Little guy nodded to a big, ugly mog next to him. Big mog flipped a rocker switch open and pressed it.

Ten years in engineering saved her eyesight. Moirrey slammed her eyes shut as fast as she could and then lowered the lenses outta her face. She could always go back and watch tape later, if'n she rilly needed to. She dinna figure she would.

Through her eyelids, the night lighted up. Heartbeat later, the room went boom. Not bad enough to knock her tower over, but big. Shake the walls 'n' rattle the windows kinda big. Broked glass she were any closer.

Moirrey opened her eyes in time to see a long section of fence fall in, along with the two big watchtowers on that side of the yard. It were on the wilderness side o' th' base, so they was the only two.

Tweren't none now.

Gray men were pouring over the line that used to be the outer fence. They weren't shooting much yet, but that wouldn't take long. This weren't no cheap mortar stunt.

These dorks were serious. Alarms finally started wailing fit to wake the dead here.

Moirrey got the lenses back up and found the bantam. Something about him screamed *In Charge*, in spite of him looking not much bigger than her. And he weren't in that front surge of yahooligans coming over the wire.

Instead, he lifted up something big and flipped it over his shoulder, like a hunk of plumbing pipe. Moirrey couldn't identify the thingee, until a missile flamed outs the near end, growing huge like it were coming right for her.

Before she could think, or duck, or nothing, the fire lance slammed into the side of *City of Brani* and lit the entire night on fire again.

Anti-tank missiles work just peachy on train engines. Good ta knows.

City of Brani, that humongous lump of black, bad-ass steel, rolled onto her side and died. Just like that. Weren't no ammunition aboard her to make pretty secondary explosions, and no liquid fuel. Just a big, dead snake.

Son of a mud-dauber. Ya jes killed my train, you bastich.

Moirrey saw red.

Lady Keller had insisted that she have the cute little pistol in the custom-glittered holster on her at all times. Navin the Black and Vo Arlo had insisted she learn to use it. Apparently neither of them had read too closely about her and Lady Keller's adventures on the surface of Ramsey. An' Vo'd been too-near-deaded above *Ballard* when she started playin' ninja games with the bomber wantin' ta kills Suvi.

Moirrey pulled her petite pistol out now and checked the charge. Crazy Saxon cowgirls might be all about old-style six-gun revolvers, but Moirrey had herself a cute, little pulse pistol instead. Matte black with silver unicorns etched into either sides of the barrel.

'Cause, you know, unicorns.

She slid the pistol home, grabbed her dark green over-jacket, and slid into it as the bantam started to move forward.

You killed my train, buddy. Yer a dead man.

CHAPTER XLVII

IMPERIAL FOUNDING: 175/07/18. AQUITAINE'S NEW STARPORT ON THURINGWELL

THE SUN WAS JUST DOWN. The rain had tapered off enough to make a difference.

Had the weather kept up, Dieter might have canceled the assault and come back another day. His force was well equipped with pulse rifles, but he was beginning to appreciate the simple, slug-throwing weapons that the invaders wielded.

Rain would not hinder them. Only darkness.

Dieter filed the thought away and considered the almanac in his head. Spring was ending. Summer would see warmer, drier weather. The next attack would need to take that into account.

Beside him, Sgt. Stoltberg nodded. The last saboteur was in place. The charges were set.

Aquitaine might have brought an entire battle fleet and a Legion of Cossacks, but the security teams around this new starport were hardly up to that standard. Dieter had managed to sneak more than one hundred men into close proximity of the outer fence. There were almost two hundred more dug in on the ridges around them, all set to enfilade the responding forces when they came in. Better yet would be the commander of the Legion flying in more DropShips to deliver reinforcements.

The one DropShip over Yonin had gotten lucky. Neither hit had gotten home through the armor, because both were fired by passive sensors and auto-homing lasers. Tonight, he had live gunners prepared to unleash hell.

Now he just needed to entice *Her* into overreacting.

It shouldn't be hard. She was just a woman, after all. They were drastically under-equipped to handle something as complex and stressful as modern war, all silly *Aquitaine* propaganda to the contrary.

Everything was in place. Sgt. Stoltberg waited.

Dieter nodded and turned to the armorer on his other side. He opened his mouth to spare his sight and hearing from the coming blast.

A moment later, a whole series of torpedoes exploded, special shaped charges designed to clear barbed wire or mine fields, depending on which direction you laid them on deployment.

Both towers went over backwards, along with nearly three hundred meters of razor-topped fencing.

In chess, he had just cleared the entire wall of pawns and taken out both Rooks.

Now it just remained to *goad* her. Mayhem and devastation should do nicely.

The armorer handed him the launcher, already keyed live and set to yellow for standby.

Professional.

All his men were professionals. That was why *Aquitaine* would lose. They did not treat war like a vocation.

Dieter turned in place and lined up the shot in his mind. He and a handful of others were on a small rise. Not much, but enough that he could fire over the lead team's heads as they charged, and the trees behind him would absorb the back-blast.

He took a deep breath and considered his role tonight as dragon-slayer. There were three of them down there to kill.

He could set back the invasion for a very long time by murdering them.

Dieter set the missile launcher on his shoulder and found the beast's heart in the red cross-hairs. A tone sounded in his ear.

Joshua's Trumpet calling perhaps, even if nobody else on the field today would understand what that meant.

The recoil was surprisingly light. That was yet another sign of rightness.

The beast died in an angry blaze of light and sound.

None would dare question his commitment after tonight. The rest had surrendered and let *Her* have the world. Only Dieter Haussmann had dared resist.

Perhaps the Emperor would finally admit Dieter had been right.

That conversation would have to wait.

Dieter handed the launcher to the armorer and reached back for his auto-carbine on the sling behind his hip. The man would wait here with the rest of the support force while Dieter showed these troopers what it meant to lead, as the first wave had just cleared the wire and begun to destroy *Aquitaine*'s base.

There was nothing that could stop him now.

CHAPTER XLVIII

DATE OF THE REPUBLIC JULY 18, 396 RAMSEY STARPORT, THURINGWELL

ABOUT THE MOMENT she were thinking some darkness would be nice, someone blowed up a transformer relay.

Moirrey's world went from dimly lit to moonlight behind clouds in a heartbeat. With the flash boom of sometin' overloading.

Imperial Security goons was right proper punks.

She watched pulse rifles strobe through the mist and yuckiness.

Imperial bolts left a redder aftertaste. Fleet rifles were more blue. Hers would be gold.

Glitter-kissed, as she had explained to the guy when she tuned it. Gots to be pretty. Nothing else worth havin'.

And now, ninja games.

Weren't as bad as that rat bastard trying to blow up Suvi aboard her station, but there was a bunch more folk running around tonight. Only advantage a girl had were a dark green jacket and black pants, when the goobers was wearing slate gray. That woulda blended better if'n they was still lights ta be had. They becomes gray ghosts floatin' 'round in this flavor o' darkness.

Maybe it were one of the friendlies that dropped a blanket o' dark on everytin'.

Worked in her favor.

Something needed to.

She reached out a hand in the dark and touched the metal of the train engine's side.

Yup. She'd gotten good'n'dead.

Moirrey still had to check. *City of Brani* might have held on, but that bastich had put his bolt through her heart.

She were past mortal wounded now. LanderShip would need to run out the cranes and lift her upright after this. And maybe just fly her skyways so she could be rebuilt like an angel in heaven afore coming home.

That were job number one, tamarrows. Tonight, snipe huntin'.

But fer the things getting boomed, and all the folks liked ta gettin' killed in the stupid tonight, it were almost like those times she 'n' Dina used ta sneak out and play games in the fields at night. Before boys, anyway. Different games after that. Still sneaking out. Not as much hiding, except from parents and watch geese.

She snickered under her breath.

Whoda thunk watch geese would be good training for Imperial dipshits with guns?

Moirrey peaked around the corner.

First run of losers were past her now, back on her right as she looked past *Brani*'s bow.

Where were that bantam cock hiding?

There.

Group of them moving with the second wave. Him pointing and sending folk thither and yon to do stuff.

More booms.

Big, ugly mog were still with him. Dumb hound trailing his footsteps, but this one were carryin' another missile launcher, which meant *Ithome* or *Ramsey* were next in line for the chopping block.

Over my dead body, bucko.

Rain were mostly gone. Dark night, high humidity, clear field.

Moirrey kneeled and braced her left hand and the pulse pistol on *Brani*'s cowcatcher atop her right hand. 'Twere good to let the lady's ghost help with the shot, dead if she mights be.

Sixty meters, give or take. Five goobers with guns facing the wrong way, kinda trotting in formations, left to right like they was on a mission from God, 'r sometin'.

Moirrey let the unicorns take charge, horns downrangin' like a finger o'doom.

Deep breath, calm heart, just like Jackson Tawfeek had taught her.

Let them move and let the movement draw the eye.

Blow out, pull trigger.

Moirrey figured she should shoot the big mog first, on accounts him having the next missile launcher 'n' all. Knock him down and throw stuff sideways fer the rest, fox in the henhouse kinda night, only backwards.

Chickens attacking the fox.

Click.

Nothing.

What?

Crap. Safety, dummy.

She flipped the little switch and found the dude downrange again.

There.

No time fer pretty. Seventy meters and about to get to cover between buildings.

Snap shot.

Pulse.

St. Andrew's Unicorn riding to the rescue.

Except something went wrong.

The dude blowed up.

Moirrey were staring right at it, so the after-flash carved channels in her night vision.

More usefulness. Pulse bolts do naughty things to solid rocket fuel weapons if you hit the missile insteads of the dudes carrying 'em. And he were kinda boomed all over the place. Like, red mist splatter.

But *Ithome* were safe now.

And they's looking this way.

Bantam.

Hiya, bastich. You keep laying there and I'll come over and kills you next.

Moirrey leaned out and popped off a couple more shots. She could barely see from the spots in her eyes, but she only needed to annoy them at this point.

Whoops. They gots guns too. Shootin' back kind.

Moirrey let loose another quick barrage.

Gettin' a mite hot around here.

Hide behind Brani.

Peek out.
Crap, they're gone. Betcha they's huntin' me now.
More ninja games.
Ya thinks yer as good as a goose, princess?

CHAPTER XLIX

DATE OF THE REPUBLIC JULY 18, 396 CAX
SHIVAJI. ABOVE THURINGWELL

"SQUADRON, THIS IS KELLER ABOARD *AUBERON*," the voice rang out of Alber's comm and filled his nearly-bare personal cabin. "I have the Flag. All hands to battle stations for possible attack coinciding with the ground assault on Ramsey Starport."

Alber' nodded to himself and sipped the last of his iced tea. *Shivaji* had gone stealth at the first reports of gunfire, even as he had slid on his emergency suit. He imagined winning a great deal of money betting that he, Tomas Kigali, Denis Jež, and Robbie Aeliaes had all gotten there within thirty seconds of each other, if he could find a sucker willing to bet on the four of them merely waiting for orders from Jessica.

Keller might be a Goddess of War, but she was not the only one here today.

"Najafi," Alber' called into the comm.

"Aye, sir," his Science Officer replied a beat later.

"We are a leopard seal, Science Officer," he said. "Hunting penguins from beneath the pack ice. We'll do it by smell and not sight today."

"Exec's already lined us up, Commander," the woman replied. "Kigali has *CR-264* in tight against the carriers like a sheep dog. We've got a reciprocal laser comm going with him until we need to unmask."

"Very good. Put Bösch on," he continued.

Shivaji's Executive Officer was there a moment after that.

"Go ahead," she said quietly.

"Since nobody has jumped out, Cruz, I'm going to take a nap and then relieve you in a couple of hours. If they were coming, it would have been smarter to hit us first, to turn our attention skyward, then go after the ground when nobody could help."

"My thought too, Commander," she replied.

Alber' smiled. His instincts for battle were always good. Nothing spoke to him of need today.

Tomorrow, an Imperial Fleet might come calling, might come a-courting. Leopard seals hunted Imperial penguins just as happily as they did Chinstraps. One of these days, *Fribourg* would discover that, hopefully the hard way.

CHAPTER L

IMPERIAL FOUNDING: 175/07/18. AQUITAINE'S NEW STARPORT ON THURINGWELL

NO BATTLE PLAN *survives contact with the enemy.*

It was an ancient maxim.

Dieter had spent a career trying to prove it wrong by out-planning, out-working, out-paranoiding the other man. If the eventualities were covered by a contingency, one was not surprised. One simply evolved the attack by following a new wrinkle already spelled out in detail on page twenty-seven. Or page nine hundred and six.

Aquitaine's security teams for this base had not demonstrated a particularly high level of paranoid sophistication in his three days of observation. Dieter had to put this current impasse down to bad luck and not bad planning.

Sgt. Stoltberg was dead. There was no doubt whatsoever about that.

Private Killinger had not been all that impressive of a soldier under his command. The best Dieter could say about the man now was that his death had saved Dieter Haussmann's life, however incidentally.

Perhaps Dieter would write him up as a hero later. The man might have a family somewhere that would appreciate that.

One moment Stoltberg was there, auto-carbine up and taking the occasional shot as the group closed on the next dragon.

The next, a flash of light and pain that left Dieter on his side, mildly charred and tattooed with a fine red mist that was probably mostly made up of Killinger's blood.

He levered himself to a sitting position and shook his head to wobble the cobwebs loose.

Stoltberg had exploded. Correction, his missile launcher had exploded. Stolberg had been collateral damage. As had Killinger.

Dieter drew a breath and pulled it all the way down to his toes. The other men of this squad were still horizontal, although he could not tell if that was shock, fear, or death.

Movement caught his eye.

At the front of the dead train engine.

Incoming fire.

Stoltberg had been shot, possibly by the man over there.

For the briefest moment, Dieter wondered if the ghost of the dragon had returned to flesh as an avenging angel, set to protect her other two comrades from his wrath.

Focus, damn it.

He flipped the safety and aimed in the general direction of the man by the train. A quick burst forced the man to cover.

Dieter drove himself to his feet by pure will. The others in the squad were just now stirring. Casualties so far had apparently been limited to Stoltberg and Killinger.

Another burst caused dirt nearby to explode, like an angry, carnivorous vole attacking his feet.

Dieter shook his head again, concerned that he had a concussion impacting his perceptions. That would not do.

He couldn't hear anything, so he fired a quick burst and pushed the other three to their feet. At least he could get them to cover before any more fire came this way.

Movement again. It was hard to identify. Certainly a man with a pistol. Probably an officer who had managed to react faster than his troops.

It was what officers were supposed to do. Lead.

Be better than the men they commanded.

It wouldn't save that man. He had killed Stoltberg and destroyed the launcher. Killing the other two dragons would have to be done by hand now. Dieter had the explosives and experience to do that.

But first, that *Aquitaine* officer needed to die. The rest of the attack was on schedule, possibly ahead. The local security forces were only now beginning to respond. They could be pinned down long enough to damage the other two train engines terminally, before Dieter's forces needed to withdraw and draw them into the next trap.

Dieter scanned the area. The officer had gone to ground.

Good enough. If he stayed down longer than thirty seconds, Dieter and his squad would have him.

He edged to his left and drew his men with him. The rest of the attackers had their orders. Dieter was going to kill the paladin protecting the dragons.

CHAPTER LI

DATE OF THE REPUBLIC JULY 18, 396
BACKCOUNTRY, THURINGWELL

ONE OF THE advantages to working with Dash and Rebekah's teams so much was that everyone was starting to think and act like a single entity.

Vo had gotten a direct message from the Flag Centurion on *Auberon* to supplement the messages coming through Fourth Saxon's HQ.

Gaucho had apparently gotten a similar message, because he was already on the ground, bays open and ready to load horses when everyone started to arrive, pulling on boots and tightening cinches.

Across the big field they were using as a temporary base, the DropShip *Tamarin* was also loading up with the seven tanks of Cohort Centurion Kim's combat team.

Rather than ride up the ramp, like about half the rest of the Patrol, Vo led Shevi by the bridle. Or rather, he was in front and the horse was headed aboard. Vo had no doubt if he dropped the reins right now and stopped walking, his horse would probably find his way to the right stall and back himself in.

The inside of *Cayenne* these days always reminded him of what lungs were supposed to look like. Big tubes branching off to smaller and smaller ones, until you got to the little sacks that would hold a single horse, with space for the rider to stand close by, and to mount up, safe and secure in the event of weird maneuvering. The whole

Patrol could come charging down the ramp like an avalanche in a hot landing.

They practiced it frequently.

Right now, the order was to mount up and hold for coordinates.

Scout Patrol wasn't going to ride to Moirrey's rescue today. Most of the rest of First Cohort was going to be vectored in and dropped on the Yonin side of the base to drive the attackers towards Scout Patrol and the rebel force who were now allies.

It was going to be a strange day. Everything was pretty much turned around sideways.

At least Shevi knew where he was going.

Dash and Göll were already waiting.

"You know, Vo," Dash smiled as she scritched her mount under the chin. "We could probably get the armorers to build you a stall aboard *Tamarin*, so you could ride with Kim."

Butter wouldn't melt in her mouth right now.

"That would be great, Dash," he countered in an equally-sweet tone. "But Shevi would surely get awful lonely without any other horses. You'd probably have to come with me."

And not spend any time around *Gaucho* went unsaid. It didn't need to be said. Most of the Patrol teased her about having a crush on the pilot. She didn't exactly dispute them.

A noncommittal grunt was his only answer, which was far less profane than Vo was expecting. He got his horse turned around and backed into the stall, hooking up the side straps to keep them both safe in sudden maneuvers.

"Any idea where we're going?" Dash asked suddenly.

Vo started to say something, and realized that everyone expected him to have a channel straight to the top lady. To know *The Truth*.

Truth was, he had no idea what the Fleet Centurion was up to. He got orders and messages from Enej Zivkovic at best, and that was usually it.

"Saddled up and ready to be dropped in front of the bad guys as they start to run," he said.

"Story of my life, Arlo," Dash replied.

A voice over the address system ended all conversations before he could add something witty.

"All hands are aboard," the loadmaster called.

Vo could visualize Takouhi Nazarian seated next to *Gaucho* up on the bridge, looking at all the various balance readouts with a jeweler's eye. She was like that.

"Stand by for ramp closing in ten seconds," the woman continued.

Even the horses perked up at that, but they knew the flight sequence at least as well as their riders did at this point.

Big, ringing sound as the outer world was cut off suddenly, followed by the internal air systems ramping up to handle the heavy smell of horse.

"All hands brace for liftoff."

Again, the horses spread their legs out a little and leaned one way or the other. Cowboys and cowgirls did the same.

And then *Cayenne* was in the air.

Vo held on tight as the ship tilted into the air and raced away, forcing him and all the rest into the backstops built to catch them.

Having *down* move around from inside a ship was still a weird thing for Vo. The big starships had enough gravplates that *down* was always *down*, or you were in freefall. Here, he was in a massively oversized air-taxi, flying low and fast over the terrain instead of bouncing high in the air to land on the other side, like civilians traveled.

Civilians weren't expecting to charge headlong into combat at the other end of the trip, either, just a quick jaunt down for coffee and a pastry, or whatever civilians did in the other world. Vo hadn't been one in so long he had no idea what they were like anymore.

And Creator willing, he wouldn't for a while yet.

But today, bad guys with guns were playing hide and seek in the trees.

And Fourth Saxon had to go find them.

CHAPTER LII

DATE OF THE REPUBLIC JULY 18, 396 RAMSEY STARPORT, THURINGWELL

SHE KNEW BETTER than to stay in one place. Geese had taught her that.

For the briefest moment, Moirrey considered climbing up *Brani*'s side and ambushin' the Bantam from up there.

If 'twern't four on one, ya git…

Instead, she bolted for a stack o' wood ties thirty meters away, close enough to a couple pieces o' big, metal pipe to protect her butt from strays n' keep goofball an' his friends from stumblin' o'er her in th'dark.

Deep breaths, young lady. Ya been running yer squares ever'morning inside the wire. Yer in better shape than most o' Digger's teams. Yous can out-jackrabbit all them fine shits all days. And Lady Keller's counting on you to stop jackknobs like this. Digger won' get here soon enough to save the other twos *Cities*.

Is up to you.

Explosions had mostly died down. World were startin' to light up with a couple o' autocannons sendin' coppered lead downrange, so Digger'd final got his folks woked up. Help's a-comin', however slow.

Y'all keep that over there fer now, m'kay? Gots enough trouble here without yer incoming fire, thankyouverymuch.

Almost on cue, Bantam popped around the corner and killed a patch o' grass with red pulses.

Grenade right now'd'a'been daft fun.

Moirrey considered taking a shot, but they all popped back and hids quick 'nough. She settled for kneeling in the wet muck and pretendin' ta be a bush some landscaper'd missed.

Ten seconds o'nothin' an' they popped out again, fit to kill that same patch o' grass. Sod done boomed under the sudden-like witherin' fire. One even shot the top o'*Brani*, right 'bouts where she'da liked to been hanging.

Them folks weren't total incompetent.

Jes not watch geese.

Moirrey gargoyled. Movement rights now were what triggered the eye, not color. Pa's favorite gander'd taught her that, once upons a time. She were just another lump of darker in dark if she kept still. Four o'them Grays was moving against *Brani*'s black hull, makin' Kabuki ghosts.

Auto-carbine rights now and you'd be dead men, Bantam.

The four only paused for a second before moving to her right.

Yup, ya figered I'd go fer my tower and hide in a death trap, like a silly-ass princess from a fairy's tail, didncha?

Bantam were second in line, head on a stick looking all directions at once.

Door to the tower were shut, and locked with a keypad. And a sparkle bomb in the overhead light fixture.

That were just fer Saana, who occasionally fergot to enter the right passcode before pullin' on the door, having to remember so many different combinations.

But tonight, a wee bit of glitter might be the silliest things ever.

Moirrey moved like a sand dune, creeping up and lining her unicorn's horns with the last man in line.

Wait fer it.

Bantam an' front dude sidled up and shot the door lock, just like in all the bad videos. Chewed up the door jamb like her favorite pooch once done her shoes. Number one grabbed the handle and pulled, just as number three charged into the dark all set to fire.

And the Glitterbomb in the overhead light went *BOOM*!

Moirrey couldn't suppress a giggle, so she pushed it out as she pulled the trigger.

Her gold strobe of light were hopefully hidden by an entire tube o'glitter the size of her thumb gettin' blasted all over everywhere and everyone.

And glitter were forever!

Three glitterpimps was really pissed now. 'Specially when they turned abouts and see'd that number four somehows done gotted himselfs dead when nobody was lookin'.

Whoopsie. Were it poisonous glitter? Are we alls doomed?

Moirrey nearly lost it with a giggle fits. She had to suck air an' grind her teeth ta keeps from movin' an' givin' herself away. They mights be mad enough to charge across forty meters of slushie gravel and crap to where she were hidin', fire er no fire.

Gargoyle.

Okay, they's realized this is bad an'r going fer better cover. Tower's a trap.

Hey, what's th'big idea tossing a grenade in my office, ya git?

Crap. That's that. Hopefully the glitter lab upstairs is no' dead, now. Saana woulda been gacked if'n she were still in the tower, instead of bunked in safe over in the main barracks.

Moirrey counted eleven and then lined up with the other end of *Brani*. 'Tweren't many places to move o'er here without running across two sets o'tracks and a bunch of flat, open, killing ground.

Sure 'nuff. Someone popped out at a dead run, zigsn 'an' zagsn. He were to draw fire fer whoever were dumb nuff to shoot right now.

But I's not here. Done runned off fer Digger or the tanks. Y'all's all safe now.

Right?

Five count and number two popped out. He were only jogging, so her first shot weren't as hurried. Click and zip.

The target dropped. 'Twere no big thing to snag the other one, just coming out from cover and running right into her line. She fired several more shots into the darkness, wicked little pulses of light and sound like an angry hummingbird.

I'm a gonne be's a right, proper dead-eye, I keeps this up. Maybe I need to become a marine, after this.

The wood in front of her exploded with a wet squelch.

Moirrey flopped onto her side, happy the ties was deep enough that only one layer had gone boom.

Couple more shots and the whole thing's gonna be burning.

From the ground, she peeked. Bantam were standing over there, hosing the area around her with red pulses. Angry pulses. Pissed-little-Bantam-done-lost-all-his-playmates pulses.

And he gots grenades. 'Er did have.

Diffinititely times to bug out.

Moirrey pointed her left hand in the Bantam's direction and pulled the trigger a couple of times. Not really aiming. Almost giving him an aim point, but also driving him to ground.

He flopped forward and fired a few random shots back.

Standoff.

Moirrey was up and running, wishing the rains would start up again. At least then, getting shot in the back with a pulse pistol might not be lethal. Fire suppression system done saved her ass on *Alexandria Station*. Weren't none here.

Gots maybe half a power-pack worth o'shots, and one spare on the belt. Not enough fer a serious firefight with crazy peeples.

Maybe the weather gods will look down on me with favor.

At least the ground were all wavy an' stuffff. Digger'd n'r gotten 'rounds to leveling everything to snooker regulation. I'd be deads if'n he had.

She jumped down into a small drainage run. Short as she was, the grass was over her head for the most part. She loped, parallel to the tracks, hoping nobody were coming uphill towards her. In the dark, it would be shoot and pray, and hope the other guy were in gray and not green.

Moirrey ran.

CHAPTER LIII

IMPERIAL FOUNDING: 175/07/18. AQUITAINE'S NEW STARPORT ON THURINGWELL

IMPOSSIBLE.

Dieter's entire command squad had been killed. Annihilated by one man.

Worse, the man was getting away. If he did, that man might be competent enough to upset the entire attack plan.

Dieter marked the location where his radio corporal had fallen as he got to his knees and watched his foe disappear from sight.

There. Gone to ground. I must kill you and then I can come back for the rest of the base. We are ahead of schedule, but I cannot allow you to survive.

Dieter's anger drove his legs and roaring lungs.

No Republican officer would rout him.

It was not in his lexicon.

Defeat was what he did to others. Usually followed by banishment or death, depending on his whim.

Dieter circled to his right as he moved. Closer to the tower if he needed cover. Not rushing blindly into a foe that was expecting him.

Tactics.

Overhead lights to his far right came alive, followed shortly after by the hideous buzzsaw of a vehicle-mounted twin autocannon. It was an *Aquitaine* weapon. He had brought nothing so heavy. All of that was dug in outside the base waiting for reinforcements to try to rescue the engineers.

Dieter glanced over. If that sound was the leading wave of the attack, they were also ahead of schedule, and deeper into the base than they should have gotten.

They might also all be dead now. That was the sound of an ambush springing, like a loop trap catching a rabbit and flipping it into the air.

Those men were forlorn. Hopefully they had extracted a good price for their death. Shortly, Phase Three would come into play, as the attackers finally met a solid resistance and immediately began to withdraw to the back of the base, where the second wave would be lightly dug in to bloody the nose of counter-attacking troops. He would need to get back to the radio in another five to seven minutes to coordinate the many teams in motion.

Dieter smiled coldly at the night.

Sacrifice a pawn to draw out a bishop. Weaken the entire defensive line.

Strategy.

The ground began to give way at his feet as Dieter rushed up on the ditch. He fired a short burst at the darkness, just in case, but his foe had already fled.

Movement on the left drew his eye. Assholes and elbows racing away in the drainage ditch, and then only a head as the man rounded a curve before disappearing completely.

Dieter considered the map of the base he had constructed by daylight.

Yes. He will come out over there, but not directly. First, a long loop around, staying out of sight and effectively blind.

I can cross directly and cut you off.

Dieter's smile turned to a cold snarl.

You will not survive this night. I promise you that.

He set himself a hard pace across the uneven ground, a man-killing stride that lesser men would fail at.

They did that.

Fail.

Dieter Haussmann did not. He would prove himself the master of all men.

CHAPTER LIV

IMPERIAL FOUNDING: 175/07/19. BB VARGA. ROBISSON WAYPOINT

VARGA'S FLAG Bridge was not one Kozlov had commanded from before, but he had no doubts that it would work out. His own Flag Crew had spent better than a week integrating with *Varga*'s staff and working out various idiosyncrasies on the flight here.

And if *Varga* wasn't quite the equal of the battleship *Amsel*, Wachturm's legendary Blackbird, she was still a close enough second. He would be able to improve on the master and do something the Red Admiral had not.

Beat Jessica Keller.

Admiral Saveliy Kozlov took the seat at the head of the big conference table and looked at each of his captains individually. He knew some commanders would hold an electronic conference before an attack such as this, but he believed in maintaining the personal relationships. That required these men getting off of their comfortable bridges and taking a shuttle here.

That would be doubly important at *Thuringwell*. Every day that woman held the system, she grew more powerful, more dangerous. There was not time for a long, leisurely cruise, mixed with combat simulations and training missions.

Already, she had been running rampant for three months. Creator only knew what kind of damage she had done to the planet. At least she had not bombed it into oblivion. Intelligence reports indicated she was leaving the planet itself largely alone, so obviously she was lying in wait for him.

She would not be prepared for this onslaught.

Saveliy rapped his knuckles on the table top to draw all eyes.

"You have read the mission, gentlemen," he said in a smooth, baritone voice. "Instead of organizing at the edge of the system, where she might spot us before we are ready to attack, the entire Task Force is assembling here, tuning everything, and then we will jump right to the edge of *Thuringwell*'s gravity well and initiate our attack."

Saveliy looked around at his commanders.

Jessica Keller was the stuff of nightmares to men like this. Everyone had read about her exploits, her luck. Her legend.

Frankly, the woman was insane.

And her vessel, the *Aquitaine* Star Controller *Auberon*, was *Varga*'s equal in pure firepower. But she was limited to a single flight wing on her ship, and probably a reinforced squadron of fighters. At most, forty fighter craft.

This Task Force would field forty-eight melee fighters alone, plus twelve medium and six heavy bombers.

In addition, he had *Varga*'s wolfpack, a Light Cruiser and then three battle frigates that were each at least the match of one of *Aquitaine*'s Destroyers. He could charge down the gravity well at her with *Varga* and the cruisers, with all seven frigates out front, and leave the smaller D-hull escorts behind to protect the Fleet Carriers.

It would truly be a battle fit for the legends, like an avalanche of fury racing down the mountain, looping once around the planet, and hitting them again while climbing out. He would have enough momentum on his side, after a gravity slingshot, to catch any vessel that thought to escape by running for the edge of the gravity well.

The only thing that would save them would be to scatter to the winds and hope a few survived. Certainly, the lesser vessels could be largely ignored at that point, in favor of destroying her.

And then Admiral Saveliy Kozlov would be a name all the Empire would know.

"Questions?" he continued.

"Are we ceding tactical initiative by coming in at this speed, Admiral?" Captain van Aakken inquired politely.

That sort of thinking was normal from a Flag Cruiser. Their job was usually more diplomatic in nature, rather than the pure combat of

Varga and her wolfpack, or the two Fleet Carriers and their escorts. *Novo Daysahn* was a lone vessel much of the time, pursuing missions along the *Fribourg Empire*'s frontiers and borders.

Trade, diplomacy, exploration. Not combat.

"On the contrary, *Novo Daysahn*," Saveliy replied. "We will be seizing the initiative. They must respond to us."

"I appreciate that, Admiral Kozlov," the man continued. "We will charge at them, make a fencing pass, and then circle and catch them as they try to flee. But we cannot slow down enough to respond to surprises."

The man was at pains not to sound like he was challenging his Admiral's expertise. Kozlov would grant him that. But he obviously did not understand fleet tactics.

Saveliy leaned forward and smiled to soften the blow of his words. An admiral who did not listen to his captains would eventually lose them.

"They cannot stand the amount of firepower we will bring to bear," Kozlov reiterated. "Their formation will be shattered on our first pass. The only thing that will save them will be to try to run. At that point, we will have a stern chase, our speed against their head start. It will probably be close, but the siege will have been broken and Keller's fleet in disarray."

"As you say, Admiral," van Aakken replied, ceding the point.

The man was the stranger here, anyway. *Varga*'s five ships, and the carrier Task Force, had each operated together for a long stretch. Fleet High Command had determined that adding a full cruiser to the mix would be enough to push them over the top, being the equal of at least any one of *Auberon*'s cruiser escorts and able to fight either of them to a standstill while the fighters swarmed and stung them to death.

Saveliy looked around to the other captains at his table. Their faces were marked by hunger, rather than doubt. And he would only need to deal with van Aakken for today. Perhaps he would put the man on point, just to give him a taste of the true glory of battle.

Jessica Keller was doomed.

CHAPTER LV

DATE OF THE REPUBLIC JULY 18, 396 RAMSEY STARPORT, THURINGWELL

OKAY, *adrenaline wearing off. Times t'breathe.*

Moirrey stopped as she crossed a small side cut where a concrete drain pipe appeared. It were cover, of a sort. Good enough, anyway.

She squeezed her tiny frame into the barely-larger pipe and let her lungs catch up. In her mind, she had crossed almost one hundred meters of ditch from her tower. If goofball was still chasin', he might run right by without realizing she was there.

If she could breathe quieter-like. Not an easy task, right now. At least her pistol didn't wobble as she pointed it. But nothing jumped out.

After a bit, her breath started to come back t'normal, as wells.

He'd'a been here by nows, if'n he were comin' this way. Must not.

Slowly, Moirrey crept out of her tunnel and peaked around the edge of the ditch.

Nothing coming.

She turned and gargoyled her head up and over the top of th'pipe molasses-like.

There.

Damn it, he's good.

I'd'a run smack dab inta him if'n I'd kept goin'.

Moirrey watched the man stop and creep up to the edge of the ditch, down 'rounds the farther corner.

Yup. Deaded but good.

He were too far 'way to shoot from here. An' he knows I dinna make it that fer, so he's like to come back this way.

She watched the man vanish from sight suddenly, like hell had opened up and took him.

An' none too soon, neithers.

Crap, he's in the ditch wit' me. Ain't gots nowhere to run, 'less I turn tail and head back inta his folks.

Not good.

Moirrey looked at the pipe beneath her. It were dark and wet, and prolly runned straight fer a piece.

Just bouts perfect fer a death trap. Mine. But he thinks he's all that an' a chocolate sundae.

Moirrey considered her options.

She could sprint across the open field now, while he was down, and maybe get away. She could sit down here in her little pipe an' wait fer him to pass, hoping he dinna look too close.

That bastich killed City of Brani. *He donn gets ta get away.*

Moirrey smiled as she swapped powerpacks in her pistol and considered glitterbombs in the darkness.

CHAPTER LVI

IMPERIAL FOUNDING: 175/07/18. AQUITAINE'S NEW STARPORT ON THURINGWELL

DIETER KNEW HE WAS CLOSE. Explosions and lights to his left revealed the dark emptiness where the drainage ditch ran. He crept close, auto-carbine sniffing like a bloodhound.

Nothing.

The man could not have gotten past him. Ergo, he was still back up the way, probably resting and plotting his next ambush, expecting Dieter to continue chasing.

You have another thing coming, young man.

He skulked forward and hopped into the ditch, landing with a barely audible squelch in the mud. He was safe from stray fire here, as long as he let his ears become his eyes, confident that the sound of steps and gasping breath would alert him in time.

The auto-carbine was pointed forward, just in case, but he was the hunter tonight.

The *Aquitaine* centurion might have destroyed Dieter's command squad, but he would never defeat Dieter Haussmann. He was simply prolonging his death by running, not escaping.

Death was his only escape now.

Dieter let his mind become one with the canal. His foe was here. He knew that. Now it remained but to find the man, and kill him.

Slowly he moved, letting the sounds of fighting elsewhere mask the sound of his steps in the mud, the rasp of air in his lungs from running so hard.

Movement would be death. A slight twitch on the trigger and a pulse of fire would erupt, perhaps even before his conscious mind registered the man.

His only fear was that they would both reach a corner at the same moment and be to close-combat in the mud instantly. Dieter considered pulling a trench knife, but the path straightened out and led like a plumb line. No one would find him off-guard.

Constantly, he scanned the rim above him. Sometimes, the soil was above his head, sometimes low enough that he could peer into the semi-darkness.

The ambush across the way had apparently been thwarted. Fire from that quadrant of the base had tailed to almost nothing. For the briefest moment, Dieter considered letting this man live and retreating to where his radio corporal had been killed.

This attack was more important than one man. His troops needed him in command right now, moving pawns and knights with authority and conviction.

And yet, he was in too deep now to simply walk away.

Honor demanded blood. He would not be bested by any man from *Aquitaine*. Ever.

A deeper darkness intruded as he slid forward.

There was a cross-canal feeding into this one. Just the perfect space for his foe to lie in wait, probably hidden and waiting for him to appear at the mouth of the intersection.

Dieter considered leaving the ditch. He paused and looked above.

Nothing but grass in any direction. Either he is there, or he has managed to escape.

So be it. One last duel and we will consider it good. You will die now, or you will be the one that got away from Dieter Haussmann.

He slithered down, belly-flat into the muck, and approached the fateful corner. Human eyes would be looking at man-level. They would not be looking for a viper coming around the bend.

An ear. An eye. A barrel came around the edge of the mud and rock.

Nothing.

Well, nobody. There was still a concrete tube running into darkness. A grenade now would be perfect, but would expose himself too much if the man was crouched in the dark waiting, as Dieter would be.

Silently, he confirmed the fire select on his auto-carbine at fully automatic.

Pull the trigger and empty the rest of the powerpack until I release it. Fill that tunnel with death.

Dieter drew a breath and exploded to his knees, leaning into the weapon as it pulsed repeatedly. There was so much fire going into the tunnel at one point that he could actually see the concrete itself reflecting the pulsed red light.

Nothing.

False alarm.

Still, a worthy idea. Anything in the tube would have died.

He snapped the depleted powerpack from his weapon and stuffed it into his pocket before reaching for a spare.

"Good idea," a voice chirped at him from the darkness. "Bad lucks."

Before Dieter could move, eyes appeared at the top of the ditch, above the tunnel, where the man had laid in wait, face down and skin covered in mud.

The hand appeared as if in slow motion.

Dawn exploded, a golden pulse of energy liberating itself on his chest plate like a hammer. A second struck him in the shoulder. The third caught him in the face.

Darkness began to engulf him.

A voice began to carry Dieter Haussmann's soul to hell.

A woman's voice.

"Ya killed *City of Brani*, you sombitch," she said.

Hell claimed him.

CHAPTER LVII

DATE OF THE REPUBLIC JULY 19, 396
SOMEWHERE, THURINGWELL

VO KNEW BETTER than to grumble. In space, you had a year of boredom that would get punctuated by an hour of insanity. Hopefully, with the bad thing happening to the other guy.

Right now, night was thinking serious thoughts about giving up and letting day have a little fun.

Then the serious stuff would probably happen. And probably pretty quickly.

It was a story as old as organized warfare, from all his studies and personal experience.

Hurry up and wait. Everybody get ready for the ball to drop, for the rocket to go up.

Wait.

Nothing happens.

At least they had a nice view and fresh tea. The terrain hereabouts was a series of rolling hills. It reminded him of a fuzzy green blanket laid out flat, and then pushed together from one side. Maybe frozen waves. He'd never been far enough north on any planet where he served or visited to see eternal ice.

Maybe.

Morning would be coming soon. He couldn't wait to rack out and sleep, assuming everything worked out.

Cayenne had dropped them to one side of the high end of a valley midway between the new Ramsey starport and Cydelmynster's coordinates for the main Imperial base, with explicit instructions to steer clear of that place until all of Fourth Saxon and *LVIII Heavy* could be brought to bear.

Intelligence at HQ suggested a hundred men had come over the wire before being repulsed. Or maybe annihilated, from the descriptions the Legate had passed along.

Digger and his folks had apparently been sandbagging a little.

The Imperials had made it as far as the main rugby pitch when a whole squadron of angry repulsors-scouts with twin autocannons popped up from cover.

That was the price of warfare.

Another hundred had been dug in along the fence waiting to rescue the first group. They would be waiting for a long time.

Something had apparently gone wrong with the attack. One of the first times Vo could say that in all honesty. Up until now the Imperial troops had been dangerous wraiths in the darkness. This was the first time Fourth Saxon or *LVIII Heavy* had been able to inflict significant casualties.

And it was *Auberon*'s marine detachment and Digger's Construction Ala that had done most of it.

Vo grinned to himself. Not a topic the rest of his current team would probably find nearly as funny as he did. Army troops could be like that.

The sun was just about to come up over the hill behind him.

Scout Patrol was dug in like a nine-pointed star. Well, close enough. Nine deadly arrows pointed outward, surrounding the four combat tanks of 1/1/1 plus *Bloodhound*. The nasty air defense chassis was pointed west with the barrels raised, protecting the two support tanks tucked in behind it.

He doubted they were putting out any emissions, but *Bloodhound* would fire up the targeting radar at the first hint of incoming fire and let loose. Rebekah's team had shown themselves to be every bit the crazy counterpart to Dash's.

Freefall got his attention, twisting her turret around with a noisy, grinding squeal, maybe ten degrees and depressing the barrel enough that any shot was likely to sunburn any part of Scout Patrol that wasn't dug in deep enough.

Good reason to put the horses at the center, with the support tanks.

"*Aquitaine?*" a man's voice called. "We're coming in."

Dash popped up from behind a nearby downed tree thick enough to stop most incoming fire.

"Arlo," she quietly called. "You're on."

Either Cydelmynster had lied about his coordinates when they picked out this landing space, or those people had moved like deer through the trees.

He hadn't been expecting them to rendezvous for another hour.

Still, time to earn his keep.

Digging into wet soil for protection was not second nature for Vo, any more than it was for the rest of Scout Patrol. But they hadn't had that hammered into them by Navin the Black.

For all Vo's size, he was still deeper than anybody else. One did not argue with *The Viking* about useful skills.

Vo levered himself upright and slung the carbine across his back. He had left the damned sword with the damned horse today. The pistol would be enough. If it wasn't, five tanks and a whole squadron of maniacs better be. There were only supposed to be two score coming. And they were supposed to be friendly.

"Here," he yelled back as he walked forward.

Conrad Penztler emerged first.

The man hadn't changed much. Maybe a little more drawn. Preparing to walk into the shadow of death would do that to a man, he suspected.

The other man he knew from old pictures and recent descriptions.

Fraser Cydelmynster. Legate of a very small force of men and women who had decided to take on the entire *Fribourg Empire*. And smart enough to call for help from the Fleet Centurion when things got out of hand.

Vo liked him already.

"Centurion Arlo," Penztler called as they got close. "It's good to see you again."

"You, too, Penztler," Vo replied.

Up close, Fraser Cydelmynster was a bear of a man. Almost Vo's height, and broader across the chest and shoulders. Vo could see him being a successful miner, a job that required compact strength.

"Captain Cydelmynster," Vo continued, taking the man's hand and sharing a firm grip.

He hadn't lost anything in the years on the run. The man might give Navin the Black a challenge at arm-wrestling.

"Centurion," Cydelmynster replied.

Vo could see something in the man's eyes.

It took him a moment to place where he had seen that look.

She probably hadn't realized anybody was paying that close of attention, but Vo had seen the Fleet Centurion with that amount of pain behind the eyes a few times. And he knew why, in both instances.

"Arlo," the Captain continued. "Unless it's an emergency, my folks would enjoy some down time right now for naps and breakfast. We've been moving all night to get here before Haussmann and his men could break contact."

"That's the purpose of this bivouac, sir," Vo replied. "Plus, the Imperials have not withdrawn as fast as the Legate of Fourth Saxon expected. It's almost been a fighting withdrawal from the starport."

Cydelmynster studied him closely for a moment, as if he spoke in jest.

"That's not Haussmann's style," the man pronounced.

"I'll bow to your greater expertise with the man, Captain," Vo shrugged.

More people were appearing now. Green and brown ghosts suddenly made flesh, weapons slung across backpacks.

The final count was thirty-seven men and four women, each of them just as hard and rugged as the men, maybe more so.

This was not a place that soft women survived.

VO WAS SEATED around a compact cooking stove with the inner core of the combined team. Dash, Rebekah, Alban holding the colors, Aoibhín with radio. Penztler and Cydelmynster had joined them this morning, after food and over coffee.

Vo didn't figure he was getting to sleep anytime soon.

The Legate just made it worse.

"Digger and his team have confirmed the identity," he drawled from the security of his headquarters tent, somewhere warm and comfy. It hadn't been drizzling on him, tucked safe inside. "Colonel Dieter Haussmann was killed during the raid. Pretty early on. That's probably why it fell apart when it did."

It was interesting watching the reactions around the group. Penztler and Rebekah Kim seemed mad. Cydelmynster was phlegmatic. The rest were looking forward to the next set of orders.

"Do we know how he died?" Captain Cydelmynster asked.

The Legate smiled into the camera pickup.

"Apparently, he got on the wrong side of Centurion Kermode, according to the reports."

Vo snickered before he could stop himself.

Yeah, Vo could see that. He had read the reports from Alexandria Station. And the Fleet Centurion had filled him in on some things that never made it to the report.

"Orders, sir?" Dash leaned into the pickup.

"We're pushing out from the starport, Dash," the Legate answered. "And encountering platoon-sized forces and rolling them up. Looks like Haussmann was expecting a rolling ambush walking backwards. Except they haven't moved fast enough or with any coordination."

He paused to take a sip of something from a mug as he stared at the group on his own display.

"Your orders are to move closer to that valley we expect is their base, and locate the forces defending it. Pin them down and keep whoever is in charge there from coming to the aid of the pieces we're swallowing at this end. We do that and this campaign might be over. Questions?"

"How soon, Legate Burdge?" Cydelmynster spoke for the first time.

"DropShips are enroute, Captain," he replied. "The sooner we can get this done, the sooner your folks can come home."

CHAPTER LVIII

IMPERIAL FOUNDING: 175/07/22. YONIN, THURINGWELL

GOVERNOR OKAFOR'S office hadn't changed. The tea was better this time. Perhaps Merryn returning from *Kittras* rated the better stuff.

She could only hope.

Back at the port, Redyert was furiously sending more trucks and people over. *Seventh Son* had never hauled this much material from the sector capital, former sector capital, whatever it was now.

That place.

And she would be done and gone shortly.

And Hao had been right.

The story about a sudden, cash-only investment opportunity had caught someone's ears at the bank as they converted her savings to negotiable bond instruments.

More money had shown up. An entire second briefcase full, in the hands of a man whose suit screamed private banker to very wealthy individuals. Very few questions asked. Handed into her custody to hopefully make this man's principal a great deal more money.

Merryn wondered if she was swindling the Duke of *Kittras* this time.

Governor Okafor shared her smile, as if she could read Merryn's mind.

"So where is your next destination?" Okafor asked quietly.

Merryn put on her innocent face.

"You imply that I won't make another run to *Kittras*?" she asked.

"Storm clouds are gathering, Captain Teke," the governor replied. "But they aren't ready yet, or they would have prevented you from returning. Too great of a risk, especially if they still view you as a loyal citizen."

"I do not believe that *Kittras* or *Thuringwell* will be on my itinerary in the near future, Governor," Merryn said closely.

"Oh?"

Merryn took a few moments to tell this woman about the spies on *Kittras*. About the faulty intelligence someone had gathered. About the man in the suit.

She wondered why she was telling so much until Madame Okafor began to laugh out loud.

Then she understood.

"Would you mind telling that story again?" Okafor asked after a moment. "I have someone who should hear it."

"Please."

Merryn waited for a moment as the Governor picked up her handset, activated her comm, and locked in a secure channel to *somewhere*. She put down the handset and brought up a small holographic projector.

"Captain Merryn Teke, of the freighter *Seventh Son*, late of *Kittras*, may I introduce you to Fleet Centurion Jessica Keller, the *Margrave* of this system."

Merryn suddenly felt tiny and a little scared.

This was Jessica Keller. Evil incarnate. The devilish, demonic woman who was going to destroy the *Fribourg Empire* if she wasn't stopped.

And then Merryn realized what had been missing in her life, all these years.

These two women were in charge, and assumed that they should be in charge, something no Imperial woman would dare conceive of, unless she were high-borne, and only then to handle her late husband's affairs until a male relative could be brought in to take charge for her.

Or the daughter of a life-long shipping captain, who refused to settle down and pop out children for some man.

Merryn Teke was never, ever going back to the Imperial side of the border. Any border.

"Fleet Centurion," Merryn said in a tiny voice, taking in the other woman's image in the projection.

Jessica Keller wasn't that much older than Merryn Teke. Perhaps a decade, at most. Just on the other side of that divide where her hair was starting to go gray, and she wasn't going to do a damned thing about it. Sharp, penetrating green eyes that seemed to be weighing Merryn from the sky where she sat. The beginnings of crow's feet around the eyes.

"Captain Teke?" Keller said. "How can I be of service today? I presume Wakely has a very good reason that I need to talk to you, considering the state of things."

Wakely.

Not Governor Okafor. Or even Doctor Okafor.

Just *Wakely*.

What would it be like to live that free? If petticoats were no longer a fashion requirement these days, the thinking behind them hadn't changed much. She had heard about such a place, talked about it, even dreamed about it. And here it was, right in front of her.

"The *Fribourg Empire* is coming, Admiral," Merryn said flatly. "Here's what they asked me at *Kittras*, and what I told them…"

CHAPTER LIX

DATE OF THE REPUBLIC JULY 19, 396
SOMEWHERE, THURINGWELL

EVEN THE UNIFORM was a little outside regulations, but by this point in his career, people put that down to eccentrism and not insubordination. Instead of having his last name on his collarbone, like the other pilots, his just read *Gaucho*.

After all, there were only three people in the galaxy who called him by his real name anymore. The Purser only did when he was drawing cash for planet-side needs. The Fleet Centurion when she wanted his undivided attention. And his sainted mother, when she wrote the occasional letter to update him about his ex-wife and daughters, Ahalya somehow inheriting his own kith and kin as well in the divorce.

He still wasn't sure how that happened.

But that was acceptable. His real family was here anyway. Chief Takouhi Nazarian, his loadmaster, sitting next to him on the bridge. First Rate Spacer Murphy Alexandru manning the Ventral Tower Gun. All of *Auberon*'s Flight Deck in orbit above him. And now all of Fourth Saxon's First Cohort Scout Patrol, still the only group never to bitch about his flying.

Good people.

Gaucho twirled both ends of his handlebar mustache first, and then lifted his cowboy hat and ran a hand over his shaved pate. Well, mostly shaved. Lot of bald up there these days. At least the mustache was still a nice dark ginger.

Nazarian just glanced over and grinned. His nervous habits probably kept her calm. She only got nervous when he became perfectly calm. And that only happened under fire.

"Status?" he queried.

"Last lance at the ramp now," she growled back.

He nodded and popped all of his knuckles by turning his laced fingers outwards over his head. It sounded like popcorn ripening.

Three count, and his hands came to rest on the flight joysticks, fingers falling into their cradles and transmitting flight information in bumps and pressure so he never had to take his eyes off the sky to check something.

"Clear," Takouhi continued.

He brought the engines hot quickly and settled on thrust alone as the last horses got far enough away that he wouldn't singe their tails.

Probably.

Part of him was sad as he tilted the big, red DropShip's nose into the sky and started to get clear. This might be the last time he ever got to hot-drop Fourth Saxon. A more pleasant group of folks would be hard to find.

One of these days, he would be back to the whiny marines that traveled aboard *Auberon*.

Although, now that she commanded a Star Controller, a whole fleet, *Gaucho* had no doubts that the Fleet Centurion would be in the thick of things frequently.

She was a sword with luck. You used that sort of thing as long as the luck held, like a magic talisman, and then hoped that you didn't break it too bad when it was finally time.

Even before the little sound beeped, or the sensor tag under his left ring finger wiggled, *Gaucho* knew his own luck had just run out.

Nobody had ever proved psychic powers that were reliable and testable. And *Gaucho* never talked about those moments of improvisational inspiration that had kept him alive this long.

He still wasn't going down without one hell of a fight.

Every imaginary hair on the back of his neck stood straight up. His angle was wrong, his engines laboring at lift instead of speed, he was completely out of position.

Anything he did right now and *Cayenne* might turn turtle.

At this elevation, he'd hit the ground before the planet even knew he was coming.

Time for crazy.

Gaucho slammed the engines to the wall and cut all output from the forward thrusters. *Cayenne* bucked like one of those wild horses he had just delivered to the valley below as her nose dropped.

The radar lock warning finally caught up with rest of the universe and beeped loud enough to get Takouhi's attention, not that she could do anything at this point except fire off flares and chaff, but the machine was already doing that for her.

Movement at two o'clock resolved itself into a missile riding a cloud of gray smoke into the sky, like a crossbow bolt aimed at his heart.

Someone over there knew what he was doing. Any sooner on the shot and *Gaucho* could have landed hard but safe. Any later, and he might have been able to maneuver enough to dance around the first shot.

The second missile coming up was just icing right now. The first one was going to spike him like a bug hitting a windshield.

Gaucho counted three and cut everything off: engines, thrusters, the works. Everyone was buckled in tight, so nobody would bounce off the ceiling, and there was nobody back in the bay to fly.

Cayenne had all the flight characteristics of a brick right now. It was probably the last thing the guy on the controller for the missiles expected. Nobody in their right mind would try a stunt like this.

Cayenne started to fall out of the sky.

"Brace for impact," he yelled, just in case Murph wasn't paying attention down in his turret, looking down at the up-rushing ground. Hopefully this stunt wouldn't squish him.

Explosion.

More like an earthquake than anything else.

Happily, the Imperial gunner had caught him with an empty bay instead of so many tonnes of horseflesh. Temperature sensors down in the bay went off the charts for a few seconds as the missile tore a hole in his side.

Gaucho slammed all the engines on his starboard side to the stops, and all the thrusters on the left wide open. Everything else was quiet. *Cayenne* was ringing like a bell right now.

It worked.

The second missile was far enough behind the first that *Cayenne* managed to pivot her ass around to it as it closed.

Instead of threading the needle into the hole the first one had punched, she took the explosion in the starboard engine well.

It blew everything to hell, but it also absorbed all the blast.

Power dropped to almost nothing in a heartbeat as secondary generators were unable to keep up with the demand. But that was fine. *Cayenne* was a flat rock right now, spinning ever so slightly counter-clockwise as she fell out of the sky, instead of flipped over and trying to drill a hole in the upcoming planet.

Two trees shattered first. Then the planet itself reached up and slapped him upside the head. *Cayenne*'s armored shoulder took the brunt of it, plowing into the ground and gouging a path through trees, rocks, and anything too slow or stupid to get out of the way.

Wagner couldn't have done a better apocalypse with all the kettle drums available. Followed by silence, and then something metallic pinging that reminded him of nothing so much as the *Entry of the Gods* aria.

He looked over, but Chief Nazarian was fine. She was tougher than anybody he knew.

"Mayday, mayday, mayday," *Gaucho* said rather laconically. "*Cayenne* has taken ground fire and is down. Repeat, *Cayenne* is down."

Gaucho pushed a button on the dash and let *Cayenne* transmit her own cries for help with coordinates. At least Dash and Vo knew where he was.

"Murphy, what's your status?"

"Needing a new pair of pants, old man," the call came from below.

That was good. If something were really wrong, Murph wouldn't be bitching.

Now, hopefully the good guys would get here first.

CHAPTER LX

DATE OF THE REPUBLIC JULY 19, 396
SOMEWHERE, THURINGWELL

FREEFALL HAD JUST SETTLED into what would be the new laager while they organized for the next round. *Tamarin* had slipped away low and into the horizon, and *Cayenne* was about to follow.

Rebekah popped open the top hatch and stuck her head out as she waited for the horse troops to canter over.

Overhead, the scream of engines redoubled suddenly and *Cayenne* began maneuvering wildly. Rebekah dropped her seat and slammed the top hatch shut.

"All units," she yelled into the comm. "Incoming. Stand by."

She lit up every sensor *Freefall* had just in time to see the first missile wrap the stern of the DropShip in a wreath of flames. A second missile a moment later caused all sound overhead to stop.

"*Bloodhound?*" she called into the comm.

"Tracking," a man's voice called back. Patrol Centurion Park sounded a little harried, but that was the perfectionist in the man, not the panic of a newbie in combat.

Even with the heavy suspension of a tank, Rebekah Kim felt the impact as the DropShip slammed into the forest clear across the valley. The trees were a little thinner there, rockier soil and less rain keeping things more grassland at this elevation. Still, it was a small earthquake.

"Contact," *Bloodhound*'s Commander followed up a moment later.

Rebekah's scanner screen lit up with a feed from the other tank's better sensors, showing a big red circle on a semi-distant hillside, smoke ebbing away in the light breeze.

Even as thin as the cover was, there were too many trees in the way for her tank or its cohorts to do anything at this range. Except blow up more trees than the big, red DropShip had just done. That was the downside to energy weapons.

"I have a reverse trajectory," Park continued with a cold, vicious snarl. "Engaging."

Rebekah watched a feed from *Bloodhound* on one screen while she scanned for charging infantry on another. There was nothing in the sky right now, so whoever had shot down *Cayenne* didn't have any heavy artillery to back it up. They were about to learn what a dumb idea that was.

Bloodhound's guns began to cycle, like two T-Rex-sized woodpeckers attacking a tree. Eight rounds per second went downrange, just fast enough to type the letters on a keyboard if she wanted to follow along.

Long range. Slight tail wind. Mid-day warmth making the air lighter than night. Minimal cover except camouflage.

After three seconds, *Bloodhound* fell silent, twin barrels still sniffing the sky, daring someone, anyone, to try something else.

The first autocannon rounds impacted on the distant slope. Explosive rounds, not armor-piercing.

A tree was engulfed in flames, for just a moment, before the next several rounds in line shattered it. Explosions started on the slope behind it. Small ones. Fifty millimeter explosive rounds set to proximity detonation, finding ground, or trees.

Or someone's ammunition stores.

That was the only thing that Rebekah could think of that would make a secondary explosion that big. Maybe someone reloading a missile launcher when incoming fire hit the armoured storage shed with the door open.

The whole top of the hill turned into a very small, very short-lived volcano, spewing fire and wood chips in all directions.

"Choe," Rebekah called into the relative quiet. "Full speed. Get us to the wreck now."

"On it," the call came back as *Freefall*'s engines suddenly screamed.

"Dash. Vo. *Freefall* has point," she called into the unit-wide comm as the vehicle lurched into motion.

In this terrain, the horses might be able to outrun her, but only if they went full-tilt into unknown territory that might be crawling with Imperials. But they could keep up, and if it was another ambush, better to have the heavy armor taking fire. Men and women with sabers would do a fine job on infantry coming out of holes to shoot at her going by.

CHAPTER LXI

"ALL UNITS ASSUME ATTACK FORMATION," Saveliy intoned gravely into the air of the room. "*Hokkaido* and *Europa*, launch your wings."

His Flag Bridge was ordered, calm, prepared. A single master display showed the system, with every vessel color-coded and established with a vector. Other screens zoomed in on various elements he wanted tracked close at hand. His men were all poised over their screens, ready to move the entire fleet like a rapier seeking his enemy's heart.

Saveliy Kozlov was the Sword of Vengeance today.

Everything had been planned except the actual disposition of *Aquitaine*'s vessels when *Fribourg*'s scourge arrived. And in the ten minutes or so it would take for the combined *A* and *B* wings to launch and assemble, everything else would be organized.

Saveliy would have liked extra time to hang perched at the distant edge of the system, a light hour or more out, listening to traffic and taking the temperature and measure of the system. It was a technique Keller herself had mastered. All other commanders were, of necessity, forced to mimic her now, in an arms race that had no end save death.

Even today, it was too risky to attempt. From the waypoint, they had jumped less than a single light year, having completed a quick tuning and calibration check on all vessels, so that the entire fleet would arrive in-system nigh-simultaneously.

Landing farther out, the risk was that they might have blundered into someone intent on spotting them, someone who might then jump down to the edge of the gravity well and sound the alarm, a midnight rider to ruin the surprise.

No, better to come out in a fighting stance, right atop his foe. He did not expect her to run, not the woman who had charged into certain death with Wachturm so many times during the *Battle of Ballard*. But he might be able to catch her out now, vessels orbiting at different velocities that left them awkward as he arrived.

Not that it would help, with the edge he had in mass and firepower, but he preferred a clean death for the woman.

This would be the last time he spoke directly to the assembled vessels. All future orders would be routed through his command staff and broken down into vectors and firing assignments.

"Our foe has gambled everything on one bold stroke," he said, speaking as much to eternity as to the men under him. "She believes that she can drive back the entire weight of the *Fribourg Empire* here at *Thuringwell*. The Emperor has chosen us to dissuade her. We shall not rest until she has been driven back across the border, or destroyed. The choice is hers."

On the screen, six blue lights separated from the two Fleet Carriers at the top of the gravity well. Six more would be launching close behind them, until sixty-six craft were arrayed like raptors around a pack of hunting wolves, racing downhill at the *Aquitaine* squadron in an avalanche of destruction.

"All vessels prepare to engage."

CHAPTER LXII

"*AQUITAINE* SQUADRON, this is Tamara Strnad, aboard *Auberon*. I have the Flag," the voice emerged calmly from the wall speaker in her day cabin. "All hands to battle stations."

Jessica had been expecting them yesterday. She didn't even bother running to the Flag Bridge. It was just across the main corridor from her suite, another advantage of helping design this vessel from the keel up.

Instead, she made sure everything was in place and that she exuded an air of calm as she put on her slippers, strode across the hall, and looked around.

Enej had probably taken his Flag Centurion role a little too seriously. Other than trips to the head and shower, he hadn't left the Flag Bridge in several days, with food being delivered regularly and naps in a nearby office.

At least now his own staff would be able to pry him loose.

"Bridge, Keller," she called out as she entered, letting the systems route the call. "Tamara, what's our status?"

"Enemy fleet just dropped out of JumpSpace, Commander," the big ship's Executive Officer replied instantly. "Right at the edge of the well, forming up, and getting ready to head this way. *Ballard*'s hammering them with her sensors and I expect updates shortly."

Jessica smiled. The cruiser force that accompanied a Star

Controller into battle was supposed to be a well-balanced thing, according to all tactical and strategic theory. Three to five light and heavy cruisers that could be moved around like interchangeable knights on a chessboard.

Instead, she had brought a massively over-gunned, experimental heavy cruiser, with Alber' d'Maine commanding and no missiles whatsoever, and a veteran Battlecruiser under Robbie Aeliaes. Solid castles to hold the corners of the chess board against any comers. And far more firepower than she was supposed to have.

Instead of matching and balancing, she had added a knight and a bishop.

First, the Light Missile Cruiser *Ishfahan*. Two generations ago, her class had been heavy cruisers, and she, a weapons platform capable of unleashing her own version of Agincourt. She could still put up a staggering flight of birds, compared to anything else on the field today.

And lastly, the Survey Cruiser *Ballard*. The very vessel Tomas Kigali had turned down command of, since *they didn't kill things*, to quote him. And he was right. Even as light cruisers go, desperately under-armed. Instead of primaries, she had extremely expensive sensor arrays at least an entire order of magnitude better than anything any other warship carried. Often much better than that. But she was a fantastic escort when tucked in close around the carriers and not expected to carry her tonnage in combat.

And the rivalry with *CR-264* along those lines had just served to make both crews strive that much harder to be better at their jobs.

"First scan coming up, Fleet Centurion," Tamara called.

As Jessica reached her chair at the big table and settled in, all of the projectors came live with their different bits of visual information.

In the center of the enemy formation, just starting to turn in her direction, one blue star stood out, made her double-take.

No. Not the Blackbird.

That had been her one fear. That somehow she and Fleet Intelligence had guessed wrong. That the Emperor had changed his mind and returned the Red Admiral to active duty, *Nemesis* come down to settle their score finally.

Instead, the battleship *Varga*, along with two Fleet Carriers spewing fighters into the night like fall oak trees firing acorns hither and yon. Two cruisers. A swarm of frigates. Even a double pair of close escorts circling the carriers like hummingbirds.

For the briefest moment, Jessica knew a spike of utter jealousy. First War Fleet would have a field day, raiding a frontier with so much firepower pulled off the line, just to face her here.

Hopefully, they were making the best of it. The Red Admiral would put a stop to this sort of nonsense at some point. All he had to do was convince the *Fribourg Emperor* to offer a five or ten-year truce, and make the man honor it.

Fribourg was hurting far more than *Aquitaine* right now. The Senate might even accept the offer.

"Squadron, this is Keller. I have the Flag," she said quietly.

All the planning had come down to this. All the nights and weekends spent gaming out various political and military scenarios and storing the results where she could get to them instantly, cataloged and broken down for her commanders. All the possible permutations, based on the levels of aggression of the Imperial commander facing her.

Every sneaky trick she or Moirrey could come up with, along with Nina Vanek, Robbie Aeliaes, or Oz down in Engineering. And Command Centurion Enfys El-Amin, commanding the Republic Minesweeper *Wombat*.

Nobody used mines offensively.

But Jessica stopped being on the offense five minutes after the last of the little gunboats had surrendered instead of being annihilated in the face of the invading fleet. Three months of quiet execution had passed, atop nearly a year of planning.

The Red Admiral would have never fallen for it. Not a second time. *Qui-Ping* had nearly done him in. He had learned a great deal more care in where he flew, after that.

He wasn't here today.

"*Jouster*," she continued speaking conversationally, knowing her words now were going fleet-wide. A good team knew what everyone was doing, or going to do, so they could plan accordingly.

"Two Imperial Fleet Carriers have arrived with the enemy formation," she said. "Expect four squadrons of melee fighters and two of heavier units. Launch everything and ignore defending the station. Leave that to the two cutters. Remember that *Wombat* is holding your moat."

"Roger that, Flag," came the reply. "Flight Wing, execute Formation Six. Repeat, Formation Six. Form on 3rd Wing."

"Enej," Jessica turned to see his disposing of the last of his coffee and buckling himself in. "Where's Alber'?"

"Dark, Commander."

Jessica cursed under her breath. When things were boring, having him out there sneaking up on people was a useful thing. Certainly, Merryn Teke had been surprised, and she was probably the closest thing to a smuggler this system ever saw.

Now, an Imperial Admiral had arrived, and done so with what he thought was enough force to make her give way. Without *Shivaji* on the line, he might be right, depending on what *Ballard* had to say about the closing force.

This would require finesse. *Shivaji* could do a great deal of morale damage, especially if Alber' got lucky, but there was trouble coming.

Just once, she would like to walk into a battle with overwhelming firepower on her side. The original attack on *Thuringwell* didn't count. Nor did most of her *Long Raid* four years ago. Those were anti-pirate forces facing a small battle fleet.

This was another Imperial Admiral. Not Emmerich Wachturm, but someone probably trained by him.

She would have to settle for damaging the man's morale, his *certainty*. His battle plan designed to go up against someone like Jessica Keller.

She would keep Alber' d'Maine shadowed.

Dark.

Stealth games in a heavy cruiser. A creature in the night, suddenly howling for blood, where there had been only darkness before.

Jessica shared a smile at him.

"Have Kigali vector him in on the carriers first," she said. "They ought to be sitting ducks out there."

"On it," her Flag Centurion said as he started typing.

That might be an awful surprise. It might even turn into a *Surprise Reversed* version of *Third Iger*.

If she was lucky.

Now she just had to hold on long enough.

"Squadron, this is Keller," Jessica continued. "Execute Primary Plan Warspite. I repeat, Warspite. Situation Three. Prepare to receive a charge."

He had that look about him today, this new Imperial Admiral. The force wasn't as organized as they would have been, if they had short-jumped down in tight from somewhere farther out in the system. But they were quickly forming up with a line of frigates barely preceding the heavier vessels. Everyone would start to range with heavy weapons at about the same time.

This was going to be messy.

Jessica leaned back and scanned the faces around her. On the Strike Carrier, she had shared her Flag Bridge with four other people. Here, more than a score, all of whom would contribute to *Auberon*'s legend, her legend, in some vitally important way.

Rather than say anything at this moment, she just smiled. The most rousing speech she could have made was the one simply reminding them that they were the *Republic of Aquitaine*. The Fleet. Those men and women standing atop the wall, to quote First Lord Kasum, and protecting the innocent from the darkness.

Instead, she nodded. Most nodded back. They understood.

They had volunteered for this duty, to be here, doing this.

To face this with her.

"Bridge, Keller," she said simply. "Take her out."

CHAPTER LXIII

DATE OF THE REPUBLIC JULY 19, 396 CAX
SHIVAJI. ABOVE THURINGWELL

"AQUITAINE SQUADRON, this is Tamara Strnad, aboard *Auberon*. I have the Flag," the voice emerged calmly from the very bones of the vessel. "All hands to battle stations."

The sound filled *Shivaji*'s bridge with an energy someone else, a stranger, might classify as excitement.

Alber' knew better.

His instincts had stood him right. Up until an hour ago, a relatively junior Centurion with a very bright future ahead of her had held the bridge, gaining useful experience in the everyday decision-making that went into eventual command. She had even begun to impress his own people with her competence.

Not an easy thing to do.

Right now, Centurion Komal MacInerney would be grabbing some coffee on her way to the Emergency Bridge, where she would hopefully wait patiently for nothing to happen to the ship that would require her to take charge.

Alber' still made his people re-fly variations of the battle of *Qui-Ping* in simulators, just so the Emergency Bridge folks were prepared to engage an enemy battleship at short range, while tumbling oblong. Tobias Brewster, Emergency Tactical Officer aboard *Auberon* that day, had certainly taught everyone the benefit of being able to do that. And he still held the high score.

But there was no need for excitement. Today, he had command from the moment the flag went up.

"Science Officer," he growled quietly. "Passive read only. It will take time for *Ballard* to identify everything and route it to us."

"Roger that, *Shivaji*," she replied. "Coming up now."

Alber' smiled. It was out of tune with the modern age to refer to the Command Centurion simply by the name of his vessel. Had been for a generation or more, except in a few, isolated pockets of the Fleet.

Every day, Zoya Najafi reminded him why she belonged on his deck.

Alber' smiled at the heavens and made sure he was secured in his command chair and his emergency suit was charged.

One of the other goddesses of war in his life emerged from the day office and looked around.

"Bridge, this is Bösch," his First Officer announced with a challenge in her voice as she moved towards her station. "I have Tactical."

The chorus of assents might have been mistaken for a pack of wolves growling.

By a stranger.

Alber' made eye contact with Bösch across three meters of space.

"Navigation," Alber' said conversationally. "Plot us a course up and over them, outside the gravity well, so we can drop like hawks from the darkness. Nobody should be looking this way until it's too late."

Bösch shared his smile.

Shivaji turned like a leopard seal and slid away under the pack ice.

CHAPTER LXIV

IMPERIAL FOUNDING: 175/07/19. BB VARGA. THURINGWELL ORBIT

THE CHOREOGRAPHY WAS SPLENDID. This battle would cement Saveliy Kozlov as a force to be reckoned with, a tactical commander whose peers were the best in the Empire.

Varga held station at the rear of the formation, a warhammer coming in behind a solid shield wall to crush the upstart Keller and finally destroy her legend once and for all.

Up front, the three frigates from *Varga*'s wolfpack led the way, with the four who were usually the carrier's escort split two each on the flanks of the formation as protection, almost a horseshoe of lethal fire and steel wrapped around his front hemisphere. Mixed in and trailing, protecting everything, the four squadrons of melee fighters tasked to engage the defending squadrons and keep them from running rampant through the Imperial formation. Behind that, twelve medium bombers on his right and six heavy bombers on his left, for no other reason than the places *Hokkaido* and *Europa* had held when they came out of JumpSpace. The two cruisers, *Novo Daysahn* and *Wintergold*, on his front corners, properly aligned with the bomber squadrons.

It was a bullseye ring of Imperial might, with *Varga* at the center.

Above him, right at the edge of the gravity well, *Hokkaido* and *Europa* began to turn and make their way to a safe distance, with the four little D-class escorts like fireflies around them.

They would need the speed and distance. He was about to charge downhill firing, doing as much damage as he could, and then slingshot around the back of the planet and catch Keller trying to climb out and flee before him. Recovering the squadrons to reload them would be far easier if the carriers were already in motion on the right vector.

He would likely need them for a second run at Keller's scattered forces.

She could not run. She would never escape him.

Saveliy was willing to let every other *Aquitaine* vessel here escape today, as long as he could trap *Auberon* and crush her beneath his boot.

On his primary display, something went wrong. The crisp detailed readouts suddenly got fuzzy. Everything was degraded to the animated estimation mode his computers used when the sensors lost a signal and began showing a best-guess.

"Sensors," he bellowed across the room. "What just happened?"

Not the most auspicious way to start out a battle, but nothing he had seen before the sensors went haywire led him to believe Keller could thwart him today.

Auberon, just breaking orbit and turning in his direction, with the two Assault Carriers that transported her ground forces starting to run directly perpendicular to his movements.

They could flee. Their troops would be trapped on the ground and easy to round up, once he was done here in orbit.

Saveliy was more interested in the three cruisers. With *Auberon* coming out to fight, the Battlecruiser was facing his own Flag Cruiser. But for all the fighters and bombers, that would be a mismatch he would need to cover. On the other side, one of the light cruisers was lining up with *Wintergold*, while the other was hanging back.

That made no sense at all.

At least the six enemy destroyers were behaving rationally, forming up into two arrows pointed in his direction. By tonnage, they would match well with his seven frigates, and should just about neutralize each other.

Again, Saveliy wished he could have taken more time to train up this force. The warships under his command had a small but distinct edge on the defenders. *Varga* had roughly the same firepower as *Auberon*, but his Battleship was much smaller and more heavily built and armored, since he did not need to carry flight decks. He would happily get into a short-range slugging match with her, especially a new ship entering her first serious combat since her Builder's Trials had ended.

But it was the fighter squadrons that would tell, today. He should have almost double Keller's force of fighters and bombers, six squadrons used to operating together, against two and half squadrons from *Auberon* and another one from the defense platform.

And he wasn't going to simply sail up and open fire.

Who knew what tricks a woman like that might have come up with?

No, first a fast fencing pass to concentrate fire on *Auberon* and the Battlecruiser. Use the planet itself as a ramp to slingshot his entire force around and catch her from behind and below as she realized she was out-gunned and decided to run.

But the scanners were not behaving.

"Sensors?" he repeated.

It should be unnecessary but perhaps the man had not realized who spoke.

"Acknowledged, Admiral," the man said by way of placeholder. "We're getting an unexpected level of static on our targeting channels. Triangulating now."

Static?

How?

Every ship generated some manner of counter-measures, blips and blurs and noise designed to make it look like they were moving in other directions, so that beams missed and time was wasted.

What has she done?

"Could this be a scout jamming us?" Saveliy asked sharply.

"That is an option, Admiral," the man replied. "But the signals seem to be emanating from the Light Cruiser closest to *Auberon*, the one not preparing to engage *Wintergold*."

Light Cruiser? With that level of jamming power?

How?

No, that was a Republic Survey Cruiser.

What fool brings a Survey Cruiser into a fleet action?

One who wants to blind everyone with a thousand times more electronic fog than they are prepared for. Missiles should still generally work, using a reflective laser targeting signal coded to a vessel, but yes, beams would be fired into the smoke and confusion of battle.

The Admiral snarled to himself as he studied the readouts.

He had more than enough beam weapons to overwhelm a Survey Cruiser, packs of little wasps flying forward in angry, little groups of twelve. He just needed to retask a squadron of fighters that would have otherwise been moving to engage *Auberon*.

"Admiral, I have the Captain of the escort frigate, *Toriyama Sekien*, on line for you."

Saveliy checked the flight layouts to be sure, and he was. *Toriyama Sekien* was on the farthest port of his front line.

"This is Admiral Kozlov," he said, biting back the emotion in his throat. "Go ahead, Captain Villhaus."

"Commander, we are picking up a large number of new signals," the man said. There was emotion under the voice, but Saveliy couldn't place it. "Three of the destroyers are launching fighter craft, as is a freighter currently orbiting near *Thuringwell*'s orbital platform."

"How many?" he asked, willing to grudge his foe at least one surprise. This was Keller. She would have something unexpected.

"Twenty so far, Admiral."

Twenty? How?

No, it didn't matter.

He could place the emotion in the man's voice now.

Doubt.

CHAPTER LXV

ON THE DISPLAY, Command Centurion Enfys El-Amin did not look like a woman who appreciated the interruption. She might not have taken the time to personally talk to anyone else who called, save the Fleet Centurion.

Jessica could appreciate that level of commitment. That devotion to a task. She had to deal with it regularly with Alber' d'Maine, Tomas Kigali, and a whole host of others. Even Denis Jež, in his own quiet way, was dedicated to staying one step ahead of her, regardless of what she did.

Never an easy task.

El-Amin was a woman of few words. Jessica could reciprocate.

"How much of the final plan did you get installed?" Jessica asked quickly.

"All of Phase Three and sixty-three percent of Phase Four, Fleet Centurion," the quiet commander replied.

"If we start from scratch tomorrow, how much material do you have stock-piled?" Jessica continued.

That brought out a smile that reminded Jessica of Moirrey Kermode, or maybe Oz. Engineers were like that, even commanding warships.

"We have enough to get approximately forty percent of Phase Two completed again," El-Amin said. "I'm expecting a Fast Fleet Transport in the next five to seven days, with enough materials to get us into Phase Five if we went from scratch, or half of Phase Eight otherwise."

Jessica rotated the three dimensional map in her head, plotting the layers of the minefield like a giant onion.

"One last question and I'll let you go, El-Amin," Jessica said. "Are your Phase Four coverage gaps done port and starboard, or as a net with gaps being filled in?"

"Tis a spider-web, Fleet Centurion." El-Amin smiled. "We can hit someone almost anywhere, just perhaps with not much emphasis, unless he blunders into one of the heavier spots around the station."

"Thank you, Command Centurion," Jessica concluded. "You should prepare to evacuate with the Assault Carriers to the edge of the system. I will either need you again tomorrow twice as much, or not again until the Court Martial."

"Will do, Fleet Centurion. Best of luck."

And just like that, Jessica was alone again, at least inside her head. She was still surrounded by her staff, waiting for her commands, or words of wisdom.

Not that she had much today. Right now, everything was too evenly balanced. That in itself was a small win.

Maybe.

Robbie had an edge on the enemy heavy cruiser. *Ishfahan* was probably a bit outgunned by the light cruiser. *Auberon* and the battleship, identify confirmed finally by *Ballard* as *Varga*, were well matched, but battleships tended to be tougher, by their nature. He could take more damage than she could.

And he didn't have to win today. Just do enough injury to force her withdrawal from the system for long enough that he could take control again.

They would figure out her game quickly at that point, especially if they captured Wakely. She wouldn't even have to say anything. Just being here would tell them enough.

Best it didn't get to that stage, then.

"Signal from *Ballard*, Commander," Enej broke into her concentration. "Enemy squadron is blue-shifting."

Blue-shifting? Interesting. The Admiral over there wasn't going to trust his ability to absorb more incoming fire than she could. He was closing hard and fast, and apparently starting to speed up, just when he would begin to slow down if he wanted to start throwing punches.

Jessica plotted the man's current path against variations of Warspite she had calculated and saved to the file.

Best match, he was going to blast right through her formation, like galaxies merging, and then do one of two things, and he would have to commit quickly. Either he would slow down so he could annihilate the station, or speed up, loop once around the planet, and come at her with speed, like Fourth Saxon going after infantry in the open field.

The station could not be that important. That left a loop.

Maybe Enfys Al-Amin would save her bacon today. If the Imperial Admiral went low and fast, he might bumble into her minefield.

Jessica hoped she had never met the man commanding over there. Didn't have the sort of personal issues with him that Emmerich Wachturm had with her and Suvi.

The first major space battle ever fought in the *Ballard* system had been nearly apocalyptic. Nothing like a normal battle, where even crippling a single frigate might be enough for a fleet to shear off, depending, completely opposite of the fantastically expensive battle that *First Ballard* had been, in terms of ships and crew.

Hopefully, Jessica didn't have to destroy this man.

The only man she planned to utterly crush sat on an ornate throne on distant *St. Legier*.

CHAPTER LXVI

DATE OF THE REPUBLIC JULY 19, 396 ABOVE THURINGWELL

"DA VINCI," *Jouster*'s voice came through her headset like he was sitting behind her. "Everyone is in formation. You make the call."

Senior Flight Centurion Ainsley Barret grinned to herself inside her helmet. She and *Jouster* had been teammates for a good long time. Since he had first been banished to the boonies after that one escapade with that Fleet Lord's youngest daughter.

Jouster trusted her to keep things organized. She trusted him to keep her alive.

The rest of the team, including all the newcomers, were flying brand new hulls. Either they had upgraded to *M-6* fighters, or the *S-11*'s were brand new off the manufacturing line.

Only her little *P-4 Outrider* hadn't changed, other than a little bit of polish here and there and replacing a few parts inside. It was a slightly updated *M-4* chassis, a design older than her mother. It still worked just fine, since you didn't generally need all the extra capabilities of a top-of-the-line dogfighter when they pulled most of your guns and welded two big sensor pods permanently onto the missile rails.

And she didn't even need to do much scouting today. *Ballard* had everybody over there functionally blind from the massive, twin spotlights she was using to hash-blast anything Imperial that moved.

Nope, today, *da Vinci* was commanding Third Wing, and, because

Jouster had picked Option Six, anchoring the entire flight line from the exact center.

A Star Controller like *Auberon* normally flew twenty-seven melee fighters, six DropShips, two GunShips, and four Administrative Shuttles. Normal, predictable.

Boring.

da Vinci was so glad the Fleet Centurion had kept the strange alignment she had inherited from the old *Auberon*. Two regular Wings of nine melee fighters each, in triads. And Third Wing that was the odd duck. Or she was and her Wing reflected her.

Maybe.

One little, ol' *P-4* in the middle. Four *M-6*'s flying escort and protection on the front corners. Four *S-11* medium bombers inside that, loaded to the gills with missiles.

Today, something extra special was planned.

The Fleet Centurion had almost always allowed old *Auberon*'s GunShip, *Necromancer*, to fly with the Wing. Today, she had also added the other GunShip, *Sunset*, as well, tucked in deep and pretending to be just another fighter craft, like the rest of the signals around her.

And all the heavier craft were flying with their targeting systems cranked way down so that they just happened to look like melee fighters from this range. If you had *da Vinci* close enough to feed you real-time targeting data, it would work. Doubly so with *Ballard* backing her up.

And it did.

Additionally, the Transport Carrier *Andorra* could normally only fly a total of three fighters from her decks, the rest of her space being packed to the gills with boxed-up melee fighters being transported to new stations or hauled out to the big carriers for resupply in the field.

She could still hold thirty.

Once you off-loaded fifteen of them to their final berth aboard the orbital station, you could uncrate the rest. And fly them from *Andorra*'s deck. Especially if you were being sneaky, like today.

Somewhere, higher in the gravity plane, someone would be registering, right about now, that what had been forty fighters coming out to play, significantly outnumbered by the bad guys, had magically morphed into sixty.

Surprise!

Ainsley managed not to giggle over an open comm line. The veterans of *Ballard*, and *Petron*, and *2218 Svati Prime* wouldn't mind. The newbies were still absorbing what kind of a unit they had managed to get themselves promoted into.

"All craft, this is *da Vinci*," she purred instead. It would absolutely ruin her reputation if they thought she was anything but cool and laconic. Can't have that, my friends. "Formation Six complete. Prepare for Surprise Strike."

Again, nearly giggling.

Get control of yourself, girl.

She had never been able to pull a stunt like this. Wanted to. Thought about it. Dreamed evil dreams like this.

You had to have a full-on scout vessel backing you up. Imperials would be able to punch their own scanners through anything less powerful than *Ballard*'s searchlight right now. Even this would have failed if they had their own scout, which they apparently forgot back at the truckstop.

Live and learn, bubbles.

"*da Vinci*, this is Keller," the call came. "Warspite variant four in play. Repeat variant four. Stand by for the first incoming wave."

Variant Four?

Ainsley looked down and quick-keyed through the Warspite plans. The options planning page was extremely detailed. Keller had apparently been doing nothing else but wargaming this for the last two months.

Here we are. Four.

Really?

In a snowstorm? Are they nuts?

Gods, I hope so.

Ainsley managed to kill the comm before more giggles escaped. Someone else on the line wasn't fast enough. Sounded like maybe *Furious* from the pitch and tone. That woman had an arch sense of ironic humor.

Keller gave everyone ten seconds to read the key points, and probably stop laughing at what was about to happen. Those with any sense of humor. Okay, maybe both of them. But, still.

"Squadron, Flag," Keller said suddenly. "Incoming missiles. Imperial forces have opened fire. Stand to your defensive solutions."

da Vinci watched the number of signals coming forward multiply as the Impies let loose with their birds, steel tubes of solid fuel softly ejected into space, tumbling on high-power gyros to get to the right alignment, and igniting. From the fighters, a wave of missiles suddenly leapt into the darkness, sniffing.

It was about to get ugly around here.

"*da Vinci*," Keller continued. "All yours."

Ainsley took a very deep breath, yoga-like, and held it for two seconds.

"Flight Wing, this is *da Vinci*," she said. "Going Ghost now."

Ainsley didn't have to reach her long fingers to get to the controls she wanted. They were under her pinkies, and had already been programmed. Evil little weasels, hiding under her wings, about to wreak utter psychological havoc.

Moirrey Kermode swore that Chief Engineer Ozolinsh had come up with the original idea, but Ainsley didn't believe her one bit. The Engineer was far too straight-laced for something this silly, this far outside the coloring lines.

da Vinci pressed both buttons and watched her board dim significantly.

For the next two minutes or so, less if someone over there got smart, her little fighter, with one little pop-gun, would suddenly look like a light cruiser on fuzzy Imperial sensor readouts.

Let's see you respond to that.

CHAPTER LXVII

"CONFIRM," Saveliy barked savagely at his Sensors officer. "That can't be right."

The Flag Bridge was quiet enough that Saveliy actually heard the man gulp before speaking.

One did not challenge an Imperial Admiral on his own deck.

Moments of silence turned into a longer stretch. Missile officers counted down to impact. Gunners tracked primary and secondary targets, still well outside of range. Missiles began to shed their outer skins and separate into submunitions.

At the *Battle of Petron*, Keller had built a variant of a shot missile that contained short-range, Type-1 beams with small aiming engines attached. Perfect against junkyard fighters with minimal shielding.

Saveliy did not expect the same trick here. His craft were top of the line, expert, and could flip their shielding to a heavy forward array, just for exactly that sort of encounter. Most were, right now.

That would fail.

Keller would have dreamed up something else. It was her nature to use artifice instead of tactics to win.

What she would do this time remained to be seen. But he still had the upper hand.

At least half of the missiles going down-range right now were of the shot variety. How better to disarm a carrier than to shoot a covey of quail with a shotgun? If she had more than she was supposed to, that just meant more targets for his missiles.

He would adapt.

"Admiral," the Sensors officer repeated. "The new target, designated *Lion*, appears to be roughly the size of a light cruiser, according to the sensor readings we are able to pick up and his own targeting systems."

That a Light Cruiser had just appeared out of nowhere on his scanners, however, was a different beast altogether. It sat right behind the swarm of fighter craft that was the middle of the *Aquitaine* formation.

As he watched, it began launching missiles. A great many missiles.

On his port corner, the light cruiser leading was also launching an *impossible* number of missiles.

So, Keller had brought saturation cruisers with her, instead of combat warships. And yet, she still came out to fight him on the line.

"All vessels prepare to receive missiles," Admiral Kozlov commanded. "Shift to Defensive Posture Three. We will let them waste all their ammunition now, when it will do little good. After this, we will be chasing them and they will have no beam weapons to engage us."

That got a good chuckle out of the crew on the Flag Bridge. Missiles only worked if you could utterly overwhelm a target with them.

Keller could not.

And yet, she had to know that. Was this just a charge to build up speed for her escape? Had she already abandoned the system?

No. Those vessels were accelerating, but not madly so. Just enough to maneuver at him, to close the gap quickly, to reduce the number of minutes he might be able to fire at her before he returned.

Standard tactics. From a decidedly non-standard opponent.

What was she up to?

CHAPTER LXVIII

DATE OF THE REPUBLIC JULY 19, 396 SC
AUBERON. ABOVE THURINGWELL

SO FAR, *so good*.

Jessica watched the two fleets blossom and begin throwing seed pods at each other, like angry, opposing dandelion armies in a light breeze.

Big missiles, turning into smaller ones, turning into short-range sub-missiles. A few would get through, either way, but not enough to turn the tide, unless something went terribly wrong for someone.

It was the nature of such a battle. The first mistake was costly, so everyone strove not to make it.

You fired your missiles at him. He fired his missiles at yours. Or vice versa. Repeat. Eventually, the fighters run out of missiles and close to gun range. These would not be back-line militia pilots, chickens for the hawks to strafe. These would be balanced groups moving in tight concert.

Again, the two groups would probably neutralize each other, itself a victory for her, since the Imperial Admiral over there had probably been expecting to overwhelm her.

Should have brought nine heavy cruisers and nine frigates, my friend.

That would have hurt. This was a predictable scenario. Number three on her original list of expectations. The only problem with planning for something like this was she could not just flee, like she might have, had this been another raid.

Moirrey was down there. Wakely. Vo. Digger. Fourth Saxon. *LVIII Heavy*. People counting on her to pull this off.

If he was smart, the Imperial Admiral could have just stood off and worn her down with his own hit-and-fade runs. His supply lines were far shorter than hers were. He could retreat and return, while she had to hold the line until First Lord was convinced that this battle was won.

But probably nobody over there save the Red Admiral thought that way.

If they did, she would be in trouble right now, instead of just a fight.

I can win a fight. With odds this even, all I have to do is force your first foot fault, and then push.

Jessica took a deep breath and centered herself. It wasn't quite like facing the fighting robot, but there was little she could do at this point. Everything hinged on the men and women under her command executing flawlessly.

Robbie had a small edge on her left. Command Centurion Doriane Matveev, aboard *Ishfahan*, was just as much at a disadvantage. *Auberon* and *Varga* could unload the same amount of fire, but *Varga* was going to be heavier built. She could take more damage and keep flying.

And *Shivaji* was so far out of position that he could not significantly contribute to the battle at hand. His effect, hopefully, would be psychological.

After all, the Great Marshal had once said that the Morale was to the Material, three servings to one.

She needed it to go just right.

da Vinci suddenly turning herself into a warship on everyone's scanners went far better than expected. The line of frigates escorting the Imperial warships all began to fire missiles in her direction, nearly simultaneously.

Even a light cruiser would have problems staving off that level of firepower alone. Well, anybody but *Ishfahan*, which would still have a couple of tubes left over, just targeting incoming missiles.

It was the reverse of the Siren trick she had pulled on the Red Admiral at *First Ballard*. There, hiding suddenly and redirecting fire towards a shuttle masquerading as a carrier. Here, appearing suddenly, as if hidden by all the fighters in front of it, and unleashing a withering barrage of missiles.

If that was just a fighter squadron, it wouldn't have been able to launch that many missiles simultaneously alone, so it must be a warship, right?

The Red Admiral wouldn't have fallen for it. He would have been expecting some *S-11 Orca* bombers in the mix, with nine launch rails each.

As Jessica watched, the entire Imperial line shifted. Not much, but enough to suddenly engage another missile cruiser all set to pass through the middle of their formation on the fencing pass. The ships flared out a shade, just to get that extra second for defensive shooting.

Little things. Hopefully, it will work.

Again, not much. A precious, extra second of response time, if that. But suddenly she was facing two separate, smaller fleets coming at her instead of one. In their excitement, they almost appeared to have lost track of what *Ishfahan* was, treating her like a simple light cruiser and not a Manticore of Persian legend.

A second wave of missiles began arcing towards the warships, aimed ballistically to get around the wall of melee fighters closing, instead of passing through the scrum where they could be picked off.

Time for the defensive gunners to get to work.

CHAPTER LXIX

DATE OF THE REPUBLIC JULY 19, 396 ABOVE THURINGWELL

DA VINCI HELD it as long as she thought was prudent, and maybe a few seconds after that.

There was a LOT of crap coming her way right now.

She shut down everything she had all at once, then dumped flares and chaff and whatever out the rear of her little bird.

"Flight Wing, this is *da Vinci*," she said coolly. "Returning to normal operations. Ghost mode is over. I repeat, Ghost mode is over."

And just like that, the little light missile cruiser that had been all prepared to engage an Imperial Battleship at spitting range disappeared.

"*da Vinci*, this is *Necromancer*," Senior Centurion Anastazja Slusarczyk said in her ear from the command deck of the GunShip right behind her. "Shift your flight line to the port wing and stay dark. Heavy Wing will handle the incoming."

"Roger that, Ana," Ainsley replied. "Thank you."

Ainsley dutifully adjusted her flight. The incoming missiles would search helplessly for a bit, unsure of what to do. If she was lucky, some Imperial gunner had locked them in to hit a light cruiser and ignore all the fighters in front of it. Those would just fly randomly on at this point, maybe finding the Survey Cruiser *Ballard* back there if they flew far enough.

The rest would eventually give up and target a nearby *Aquitaine* signal. Any signal. Something to be useful before expiring.

Heavy Wing would have to handle it from here.

Necromancer and *Sunset* had both Dorsal and Ventral Tower gunners to shoot back.

And the *S-11*'s: *Starfall*, *Del*, *Balor*, and *Wingdance*; each had a single Tower gunner as well.

And a whole bunch of spare shot missiles on the launch rails, for just exactly a stunt like this.

Maybe not such a bad idea that the Fleet Centurion had spent so much time gaming this out and preparing everyone.

Old-days *Auberon*, with that dumb-ass Augustine Kwok in charge, would have been splattered if he had to go up against anybody who was any good.

Who wants to die in bed, anyway?

da Vinci checked her readouts as she fit into line , the last little chickadee on the left. The first barrage of missile madness was about done, except for what was going to happen above her. The two armies of melee fighters would soon begin to scrum. She couldn't do much damage, but you had to get a lock on her to hit her. And that was not going to happen, with as much noise as she could put out.

Something caught her eye.

"Squadron, this is *da Vinci*," she called. "Enemy force has just upped the blue-shift."

Why in blazes would they do that?

CHAPTER LXX

"WHAT DO YOU MEAN, GONE?" Admiral Kozlov growled at his sensors officer.

That man was being transferred to a garbage scow after this.

Apparently, the man intended to go down fighting, though. That alone might redeem him.

"Admiral," the sensors officer actually turned and looked at him from across the Flag Bridge, instead of politely yelling into the room. "There was nothing there on our scanners before, but they were very badly degraded by the amount of random static the Survey Cruiser is generating and aiming at us."

Saveliy could actually see the man's anger build. Anger at his Admiral? At the situation? At his fate? Kozlov did not know.

"Then a large signal appeared in the noise, the fog, if you will, and fired far more missiles than a squadron of *Aquitaine* fighter craft is capable of," he continued, grinding fine points out of a presentation deck. "That means there was something."

The man took a breath, suddenly conscious of where his response had led him, that precipice opening under his feet.

Imperial gentlemen did not duel.

Anymore.

The rules of etiquette and the laws of the *Empire* did still allow it.

Still, the man seemed to have realized where his steps were taking him.

"And then the signal vanished," the officer continued anyway, apparently throwing caution and destiny to the winds.

At least the man could laugh in the face of death, even if it was just his reputation, and not his being.

"Keller used a mixed squadron at both the *Battles of Petron* and *Ballard*, Admiral," he ground on. "Medium bombers and a scout, plus a GunShip, rather than just melee fighters."

"So how did she do this, sirrah?" Saveliy's anger was just on the cusp of razors.

Seconds would be needed shortly.

Give the man credit. He took a breath, considered his words, and then threw down the gauntlet, anyway.

"If a scout fighter put everything into broadcasting a targeting signal, we might interpret it wrong, especially given our blindness here," he said, not backing down one millimeter to his Admiral. "In that, we would have failed you. If there are bombers in there, instead of just the fighters we have been expecting, that is enough enemy launch rails to appear to be a missile cruiser, if we are already expecting one. She led us to a river. We drank the water. Admiral, I believe we have been misled by that woman."

The man fell quiet, obviously waiting to be relieved of duty, confined to quarters, and publically castigated.

Had he been wrong, had he been diffident, he probably would have been.

Even Imperial Admirals can admit to being fools.

As long as nobody calls them that publicly.

"All vessels," Saveliy called to the various tactical communications officers around the room. "Increase speed five percent. Assume the center of the enemy line is empty and continue to engage your original targets. Fighters will strafe only on this pass, withdraw though the rear of the enemy formation, and prepare for the second half of the battle."

If the sensors officer was right, he deserved a commendation when this was done, not a reprobation.

If not, there were a great many garbage scows to pick from.

CHAPTER LXXI

"SCIENCE OFFICER?" Alber' called to the corner station where she was hard at work.

"Negative, *Shivaji*," Najafi replied instantly. "No indication they've spotted us. I doubt that will last much longer unless they're drunk over there."

Alber' nodded. She echoed his own assessment. This woman belonged here, another Goddess of War in her own way.

"Tactical?" he continued.

"If we accelerate now to full speed," Bösch said. "We'll be in Primary range before they can do anything about it. We don't have missiles for those little escorts, but they won't survive the Type-3's very long."

"Save the big beams?" Alber' challenged.

"This is only Act One, Commander," Bösch purred back. "There's still a battleship out there to tangle with at some point."

"Agreed," Alber' concluded. "Navigation, initiate maximum acceleration. Tactical has the bridge."

Alber' could almost feel the energy in the room begin to vibrate at a higher pitch. Playing games as a leopard seal, hiding under the pack ice, had paid off better than anyone had imagined.

Two Imperial Fleet Carriers sat there in the rich, sable darkness, backlit by distant stars on the scanner screens. Even with the best telescope available, not much more than two flat blades, surrounded by fireflies in the night.

Long minutes passed as *Shivaji* raced forward.

"Tactical, Science Officer," Najafi called loudly. "Hard ping. Targets have realized we are not just space junk. Targeting locks incoming."

"Roger that," Bösch said clearly. "Defense, expect a flight of missiles. You are free to engage with all weapons. Gunnery, prepare to sequence the Primaries onto *Hokkaido*. Navigation, keep the helm steady through the first barrage."

Alber listened to the crew acknowledge the commands. This was their first time flying *Shivaji* into true combat.

All the times in the simulators, all the lanes at *Simeon*. Nothing compared to this.

But this was just *Shivaji*'s first blooding. Nearly everyone on this bridge right now had been with him at *Ballard*, when they took an over-gunned heavy destroyer and killed a light cruiser.

Against a small task force like that, almost a fox in the henhouse. Sure, they had more missile tubes and more little guns over there.

He had more Primary mounts.

And surprise.

Shivaji's hull rang like a bell as her first Primary ever fired in anger went downrange.

And the Otrera, the Goddess of War, smiled on him today.

Hokkaido was a Fleet Carrier. A long, slender tube of gray steel with a distended belly for launching and retrieving her flock of dangerous children. She was not quiet perpendicular as *Shivaji* closed, but close enough.

That first shot caught her in the ribs. Shields held, but that first blow had still landed.

Five more followed quickly, circling out from that first shot in a cone pattern designed to range the big guns so the Gunner could center in on the second barrage.

A total of four beams hit. Alber' would give the Gunner that one. It had caught enough of a corner of Hokkaido's shields to outline the boat like St. Elmo's fire. That alone would overload the shields, even if the shot itself would have missed hull.

It caused the shields on this side to fail, just in time for the sixth and final shot fired to get home.

Metal exploded. Oxygen erupted from shattered compartments. *Hokkaido* began to shed pieces larger than rivets.

"Nav," Bösch followed up. "Come left to three-five-zero, down ten, roll thirty. We'll entice them by aiming for their stern. They can turn towards us to bring the big beams to bear, or turn away and try to flee. If we caught them cold, they'll need a few minutes to get the JumpSails ready if they want to leap clear."

"*Hokkaido* is rolling to port," Najafi called from her corner.

Alber' nodded. That got an undamaged shield in the way fastest. *Hokkaido* was hurting right now.

He wondered if they would just flee and abandon their entire flight wing below. After all, in a complete worst case scenario, the fighters could all land safely on the planet below. If *Aquitaine* won today, they would be simply taken prisoner for a while and eventually traded home. If *Fribourg* conquered, they were safe until their transports returned.

Alber' did the math in his head and wondered if it would be better to cripple both Carriers now or destroy one and let the other escape.

Somedays, Bösch seemed to be reading his mind. Or perhaps they were all part of one higher consciousness called *Shivaji* right now.

"Commander," she said to get his attention from the screen. "Two halves or one whole?"

Alber' let the thought stew for a moment.

Shivaji rocked herself as an Imperial Primary caught her soundly. Pretty good shooting for an Imperial Carrier. Perhaps someone else who had learned a useful lesson from *Qui-Ping*.

"Damage *Europa*," he decided.

Dry-docking two Imperial Fleet Carriers for a year was almost as good as destroying them, after all, considering the nature of what the Fleet Centurion had set out to do.

"Gunner," Bösch called quickly. "Cycle to *Beta*. Fire when ready."

The Primaries were not as fast to fire as the Type-3 beams. Those lesser emplacements were simple beam emitters that just needed to be recharged from the generators and fired.

A Primary beam was itself a misnomer.

Centuries ago, some suicidal lunatic had intentionally overloaded a Type-3 beam emitter. He had destroyed the entire beam emplacement when he did so, but not before he bored a small hole into a nearby moon.

Afterwards, once they sifted the wreckage, the boffins had figured out how to replicate the weapon.

Now, you loaded an entire cartridge into the array and triggered a small implosion/explosion that powered a very short-lived generator. All the energy was routed through something like a Type-3 beam emitter, at least for the quarter-second that it survived, and then lased downrange in one destructive pulse.

Upside, tremendous range enhancement and greater damage.

Downside, Primary shells were like bullets, and had to be individually loaded, fired, ejected, and then reloaded.

At this range, only the Primaries even mattered, unless *Shivaji* opened up with the Type-4 beams in the turret, which were even bigger, heavier, and slower to fire. But those would be a lovely surprise later.

Hopefully.

Alber' watched the battle below continue to unfold.

The vectors on the screen told him everything he needed to know about keeping the Type-4 beams in reserve. The Imperials weren't about to slow down and slug it out with *Auberon*. At this speed, they would keep going, circle around, and come back for more.

That would give him time to get there for the next round.

Another round of Primary beams leapt from *Shivaji*'s bow, sniffing for *Europa* next.

The second Carrier had gotten enough warning to get her shields rearranged and reinforced. She had even begun to maneuver evasively.

Not that it would be enough as Alber' closed.

His Goddess of War, Goddesses, stalked the field today.

Shivaji hammered *Europa* with five of six shots, two of which hit almost the exact same spot on the shields, from the way the second one fluoresced everything briefly and then burned metal and oxygen in a tremendous halo of destruction.

Even from here, he could see *Europa* stagger and begin to tumble.

At *Qui-Ping*, it had not been necessary for one, little, outgunned *Aquitaine* carrier to win, only to escape before being destroyed. The Imperial Captains apparently came to the same conclusion here.

Hokkaido vanished first, fading like fog as her JumpSails came on line and got her clear. *Europa* took longer. Alber' was almost convinced he had damaged the carrier enough that he would get a second salvo in, when she jumped as well.

Three of the little escorts fled as well.

One, identifying itself as *D-743*, fired a pair of Type-2 beams at him before she disappeared last.

At this range, those weapons were about as effective as flashlights, but Alber' had to give the man credit for pure audacity.

No one would ever accuse that Imperial Captain of shrinking from his duty.

Alber' could respect that.

Bösch turned to him with a smile.

"Tactical, returning the bridge," she smiled.

"Roger that," he said. "Damage control parties are primary for the next fifteen minutes. "

He studied the battle plan the Fleet Centurion had been using, as well as the Imperial maneuvers in response. He picked out a spot on the map and sent it across the bridge.

"Navigation, plot us a course to get here."

That should be where the Imperial Battleship would emerge.

Then, they would see what a *Heavy Cruiser, Experimental* could really do.

CHAPTER LXXII

SAVELIY KOZLOV DID NOT KNOW doubt. It was not in his nature.

He did know rage.

Imperial Intelligence had provided very detailed notes about the forces protecting this planet. They had placed spies in the area, and interviewed captains who had been here as recently as a few weeks ago. Had provided the names and commanding officers of many of the warships today.

Nobody had mentioned a heavy cruiser.

It would not have just shown up here alone. No, it would have come with a small squadron. Every other ship was accounted for.

Ergo, it had always been here, and all of the spies had somehow missed it.

The original balance of forces had favored him, favored this attack. Even the additional forces Keller had brought in, all those fighters, did not change that.

An extra heavy cruiser would.

Keller had an edge now.

For the briefest moment, Saveliy considered the blow to his reputation were he to simply fly through the *Aquitaine* formation at full speed and retreat out the back. All the warships would be preserved. Nobody could do enough damage on a pass like this to cripple.

But he would lose two entire flights of fighter craft to go with all the damage *Europa* and *Hokkaido* had taken before they managed to flee to deep space. And he wasn't even sure how well they would be able to repair things, until he spoke with those captains themselves.

He rolled the video feed back again and played it at high speed, even as the two armies of fighter craft closed and passed.

There were a few moments yet, before his wolfpack and the destroyers would begin to engage in earnest.

Just as before. Darkness, and then suddenly a new signal appeared where there should have been nothing. This cruiser, this *Shivaji*, to read the transponder name from the screen, could not have gotten to that position without being seen.

No, it had been waiting.

Lurking.

Invisible until just before it came into range, as the two Carriers were spending every effort to break through the electronic fog and noise generated by the Survey Cruiser, and not paying enough attention to their own surroundings.

Saveliy would have finished the one rather than risking both escaping with minimal damage. But that was his nature. Kill one foe, rather than wounding several who might later recover.

The second missile cruiser had been a lie. The sudden heavy cruiser had not.

Damn than woman.

Saveliy returned his attention to the main screen.

His warships were on a lower plane than the two waves of fighters, just merging. Her warline was roughly conforming to his.

Good enough. There was an opening he could exploit.

"Wolfpack to pivot starboard and engage the battlecruiser now," he ordered sharply. "Support *Novo Daysahn*. Starboard escort, cross to center and protect *Varga* from the fighters and *Auberon*. Port wing, maintain current formation and proceed."

In his mind, Kozlov could see the risks involved in crossing his five frigates around each other so close to an enemy like Keller, but he needed the ferocity of his wolfpack to help the more-lightly-armed Flag Cruiser. *Varga* could add a little supporting fire as she went by, as weapons came out of targeting arc on *Auberon*. But he needed to smash that battlecruiser now, before *Shivaji* could rejoin the formation and provide something heavy enough that he risked defeat attacking.

Slowly, *Cerberus*, *Yokohama*, and *Ayakashi*, the Wolfpack frigates, turned, crossing bows on *Bernardo Aki* and *Darbyshire*, *Europa*'s normal escorts, as everyone slowed and came to new headings.

The three *Aquitaine* Destroyers on that flank had launched fighters at the start of the battle. That hull design, an Escort Carrier, usually sacrificed their own Primaries for more missile tubes, and generally more missiles, but mostly of a defensive nature. Less well armed than the three on the other flank.

Sure enough, the three erupted with a wall of missiles as his own ships closed, mostly focused on killing all of the Imperial missiles inbound, with just enough left over to keep his frigates and fighter craft honest.

Not much of an edge, but presumably enough for now.

But three extra Primary mounts on his frigates would weigh more heavily, since everything was already degraded by all the static in the air.

The two cruisers began to hammer on each other like angry titans.

They were, however, only a sidebar to the main action.

Ahead of him, *Auberon* was just about to come into reach. The battle would be decided here.

Or rather, this would be the beginning of her end. She might be able to flee fast enough to hide behind the defense of that heavy cruiser while he circled the planet. In that case, he needed to slap her hard enough now to get her attention.

"*Varga*," Kozlov snarled loud enough that the right officers heard. "Pass *Auberon* on our port side. Concentrate all fire on her as you go. Any weapons no longer ranging may fire on the battlecruiser instead."

This was where his legend would be born.

CHAPTER LXXIII

DATE OF THE REPUBLIC JULY 19, 396 SC
AUBERON. ABOVE THURINGWELL

IT WAS SO SUBTLE, so wrong, so risky that Jessica nearly missed it until it was too late.

The Imperial Admiral had done everything by the book up until now.

Textbook, if you liked classical music.

Jessica had grown up appreciating jazz.

First Lord Kasum had always taught that maneuver was what separated the merely proficient from the dangerously-exceptional commander. There was a science, after all, to the ordering of battle fleets.

But there was also an art.

Emmerich Wachturm was the acknowledged master of that art, by all sides.

The man over there had just made a mistake.

A subtle one.

She doubted he would even consider it one, even watching the logs back later.

The crossing maneuver was a very good gambit to bring the three frigates into *Nyamboya*'s flank. Jessica presumed they were the more veteran units, with the two racing to get to the center probably being escorts most of the time. Imperial Carrier task forces usually had four such frigates, so two on each attacking wing as escorts and three hunters in the middle.

Again, a perfectly acceptable formation and a reasonably successful maneuver.

But he had waited too long to spring his trap.

"Flight wing, this is Keller," she called, cutting straight through to her pilots, rather than waiting the precious extra seconds for the commands to get filtered through. "Heavy Wing to fire everything you have left at the battleship, right now. Every offensive missile on every rail that can bear."

The departing hunters might pick off a few. The closing escorts might as well.

There was still going to be a gap in *Varga*'s protection for too long, even if he went completely defensive right now and dove down and away from her and her fighters to gain space.

The man didn't seem like that type of warrior.

"*Nyamboya*, this is Keller," she continued.

Robbie Aeliaes was already on her command board. His face came live and filled a screen.

"Fleet Centurion," he said tightly.

Nyamboya was about to be facing a lot of messiness. He already knew that from the look on his face.

"Robbie," Jessica replied. "I don't need you to win right now. Just hold. Get them past you while you remain intact. He's coming back for a second round and I'll need you and Alber' when he does."

"Roger that, Jessica," he replied with a faint smile. "Bringing *BrightOak* in now?"

"Affirmative," she said. "This is what you get for being promoted."

"*Nyamboya* can take it far better," he shrugged. "Counting on you to pull a rabbit out of your hat, again."

"Stand by and watch, Robbie."

She cut the line and turned to her Flag Centurion.

"Enej, bring *BrightOak* and *Vigilant* in close to engage the battleship when we do, with *CR-264* providing covering fire everywhere," she said. "Leave *Rubicon* on the flank protecting *Ishfahan* and order *Ballard* to move to that flank immediately. Both of them have permission to move as far off that flank as they need to, to get clear. Questions?"

"Negative," Enej replied, turning to the staff around her and issuing orders.

In a way, it was like being on a bridge again, commanding, while the Tactical Officer handled the actual fighting. She gave orders, and let others execute them.

Hopefully, it would work.

Denis Jež appeared on her main screen right now, banded in red to get her attention and everyone else's.

"All hands stand by," he ordered sternly. "Enemy battleship closing to engagement range. Damage control parties to priority alert."

Because all hell was about to break loose.

CHAPTER LXXIV

JUST BECAUSE IT was a nice day was no reason for people to be shooting at him.

After all, *Cayenne* was already a mortally wounded duck waiting for the damned dog to come retrieve her. *Gaucho* smothered the profanities rattling around his head before they found his mouth and snuck out.

He and Takouhi had sidearms. Hell, Fourth Saxon had left a whole armory and gunsmithy in back if he wanted, assuming it hadn't been blown to hell or tossed around and crunched in the slide into second base under a tag.

"Murph," he called into the general comm as he stood up and put action to words. "Grab your go-bag and your gun and meet us in the primary airlock. We're skeedadling."

Takouhi gave him a look a lot like his ex-wife used to. *Gaucho* wondered if the two women had met or if it was a universal thing.

"What?" he said bluntly.

"Lot more armor around us inside, *Gaucho*," she replied evenly.

"And a lot smaller target for people with more guns than brains if we're outside. Not like Dash and Vo can't find us down here."

He grabbed a backpack from a wall locker and pulled a pistol as well, peeling a label-kind of thing from the back and sticking it to his thigh as he worked.

He turned to find her still standing there.

"Move it, woman," he ordered. "Boogie-man's coming."

Outside, the air was hot and rank in the zenith sun.

That was probably the smoke still pouring out of *Cayenne*'s ass, even after he had shut everything down. Even wire insulation would burn if you did it right. Apparently, they had.

At least he had managed to mostly hit a clearing. Or carve one.

Hard to tell from the ground.

Lots of downed trees to hide behind. Hopefully, nobody would manage to blow the big, red beast completely up. He would miss that old thoroughbred.

Murph met them at the lock, strapping himself into an identical emergency field kit, although he had added a helmet of some sort. Looked kinda like a construction type, except made from steel instead of rigid plastic. And painted purple.

Gaucho could not think of any army that used purple helmets, anywhere, anytime in the last couple of centuries. He also knew better than to ask with Murphy.

They found a nice little spot outside but nearby, where *Gaucho* had managed to shatter two trees in such a way that left a cozy, little gap they could all drop down into and be out of sight.

It had gotten quiet, except for he and Murph's laboring breath. They were air crew, not ground pounders. Why did they need to be in shape to run a hundred meters with packs?

"Because you occasionally get your lazy ass shot down and have to take cover in the rain," Takouhi replied.

Gaucho made a note to think quieter and with his mouth closed, next time.

CHAPTER LXXV

SAVELIY HAD NEVER FOUGHT anything so big.

As an Admiral of the White, he had commanded Battleships like *Varga* before, and once, even engaged in the body of a Battleship Task Force during a raid on an *Aquitaine* Sector Base.

But never against a Star Controller.

Auberon was only the sixth ever built, a fact borne out by the *SC-0006* on her bow, visible on scanners as they closed. *Aquitaine* was a museum now. *Arcadia* had been destroyed a generation ago in battle. *Amaravathi* was the Flag of their First Border Fleet. *Archimedes* commanded their First War Fleet. And *Athena* was the Flag of *Aquitaine*'s Home Fleet.

That left *Auberon*. Here. Now.

He felt like a shark swimming against a whale, as she was nearly twice his size, but with only the slightest edge in beam weapons. And shields that had to protect a much larger hull.

His missiles were worthless now. The Survey Cruiser was still jamming everything that moved, and she had retained the little escort corvette close in, but riding on her opposite bow. Not far enough away to avoid his weapons, but every shot he sent that way was a waste, and only the heavy guns ranged, while the escort could swat down every missile he fired.

And he had made a mistake.

Saveliy could see that now.

His left wing had orders to assault the missile cruiser and her escort on that wing. And they would, but the two cruisers and their destroyer escort had shifted that flank extremely wide on him while he was concentrating on the nearer battles.

Instead of moving with them, his force had maintained their formation. Fire had been exchanged, but desultory and at a long range. Little had been accomplished, and the closure rate was too great to correct the maneuvering error in any meaningful manner.

He ignored that flank. Nothing useful would come of that battle.

Auberon was nearly atop him.

Kozlov reviewed his boards.

Keller had responded too quickly. It was as if she knew in advance what he was going to do and had been waiting for him to open his lines.

By sheerest luck, only four missiles had gotten through the wall of fire from his escorts and defensive gunners. And those had been spaced out well enough that none had hit an unshielded part of the vessel.

Still, *Varga* had been stripped nearly bare of protection along a whole flank until his engineers could regenerate those shields.

He had settled for rolling nearly onto his back, relative to the plane of battle, and diving away from her a little. Not much, but he had the unfortunate psychological feeling of turning his belly to a predator.

Unsettling.

"Continue firing," he ordered when asked. "Use Type-3 beams defensively if necessary. Use all missiles defensively until ordered otherwise."

Varga was hurting. He knew that.

But *Auberon* had been kicked savagely as well. His Gunners were experts, and had continued to pound on the gray behemoth as they passed.

Now they were both through the valley of death. Only rear-facing beams were able to range, unless someone turned and disrupted their own formation.

At his speed, they could not catch him anyway.

And suddenly, silence.

Well, defensive guns continued to chirp, little tones indicating the size and placement of the turret, so commanders could listen to the music of battle and know the flavor of it without looking at other screens.

But the two fleets had merged, passed through each other, and were headed away from each other.

Saveliy reviewed the damage logs. And nearly cried.

Auberon had a series of hotspots scattered across her hull, the mark of his own gunnery team's excellence.

But just as many tattooed *Varga*'s hull.

Both of his cruisers had come through nearly unscathed. That made no sense. *Novo Daysahn* should have been badly damaged by a battlecruiser at that range, even as *Wintergold* traded soft slaps at long range with her opponent.

Ah. There.

Saveliy Kozlov knew rage again.

The *Aquitaine* Battlecruiser, *Nyamboya*, had almost completely ignored the Flag Cruiser, and concentrated his fire on the wolfpack, to devastating results.

Yokohama was a wreck, barely managing to hold formation. Toothless. Blind. She might not even be able to escape the system. *Cerberus* had been bloodied as well, although not as badly. Just what you would receive if a battlecruiser decided to hit you with everything she had, after first savagely mauling your teammate. The speed of closing had probably been all that saved *Ayakashi* from a similar fate. There had simply been no time to go after the third vessel.

Even one of the escorts, *Darbyshire*, had been hammered after flying too close to the line of the two *Aquitaine* destroyers suddenly moving in and escorting *Auberon*.

Only the fighter squadron had come out ahead.

His squadrons had lost five fighters destroyed and eight badly damaged enough to force their withdrawal, although he was unsure where they might go. *Aquitaine* had suffered eight losses and another dozen were fleeing back to their various carriers as the two fleets moved out of range.

"Squadron, begin orbital maneuvering," Kozlov ordered. "Waypoints four, seven, and fourteen."

Deep in his heart, Saveliy growled quietly.

It was probably impossible to win outright at this point, but he could always withdraw and repair his vessels. If Keller left, she lost.

This was still an Imperial world, close in to Imperial space. They could not hold it if Keller was driven off. If he could not destroy her, perhaps on the second pass he could punish *Auberon* enough to push.

He just needed to convince her to leave.

CHAPTER LXXVI

SHE COULDN'T TELL if the man wanted to cry, or rage, even after as many years as she had known Denis Jež. Jessica leaned closer to the screen to study his face.

He was closed off in a way she had never seen before. His eyes had grown shadowed. There were lines in his face that hadn't been there an hour ago. Jessica could even see a few gray hairs starting to peek out above his ears. He had a ways to go to catch up with her on that score, however.

"How bad, Denis?" she asked simply.

He had been on ships damaged before, but never ships he commanded. This was a first for him, and was probably as traumatic as *BrightOak*'s first major battle had been for her.

"Worse than *Petron*," he replied quietly, as if the volume could hide the rage running like a cold tide underneath. "Not as bad as *Qui-Ping* or *Ballard*. But we left after those two. Recognize we aren't leaving now."

Jessica silently agreed with him.

Nyamboya had been through the wringer, but had given worse than she got, since all Robbie's foes had been blasting different parts of his shield walls. And those could all be repaired before round two. *BrightOak* was mildly scorched, but her previous two commanders, both here on the field of battle today, had taken her through worse.

Auberon had fared the worst.

Jessica had to agree. Any other time, and she would have gladly called it a day and retired across the border.

She couldn't do that now. This was her side of the border now, and *Fribourg* needed to be pushed back. Two Primary mounts on her port side were currently wrecked. A third of her beam emplacements were damaged enough not to count, and she had suffered significant casualties on the flight deck when a shot got through downed shields. Iskra was still in command from her armored little box, but she was down a third of her crew between those killed outright, those fighting fires, and those being transported to medical bays.

It was ugly down there.

At least *Varga* was limping.

And of the seven frigates he had brought with him today, at least three would be in long-term dry-dock after the battle.

And two Fleet Carriers currently missing in action, badly damaged but not lost.

What was it about Jessica Keller that caused *Fribourg* commanders to lose all sense of proportion?

A decade ago, battles were rarely this bloody and protracted. Planets could not be conquered and held. It was simply impossible to bring enough troops to occupy a whole world. You simply held orbital space and controlled things, at least until you were driven off.

But now, her presence on the field of battle seemed to guarantee an insane disregard for casualties. It was almost like a religious crusade.

Jessica stopped.

That was exactly it. A religious crusade.

Jessica wondered if she had already won her personal war with the *Fribourg Empire*, on that score alone.

But wasn't she here, right now, trying to upset the old order of things by proving that you could conquer an enemy planet if you brought enough honey with you?

Nils Kasum, years ago, had ordered her to commit economic warfare on *Fribourg*. To cost them men, ships, and resources, at a faster rate than they cost *Aquitaine*. Four years later, she had certainly succeeded. The cost on both sides had been atrocious, but *Fribourg* still faced a bill at least an order of magnitude larger than she did.

Was this the endgame? Would Imperial commanders grow suicidal in attacking her? Try to win at any and all costs?

Jessica kept those thoughts to herself and off her face.

"*Shivaji* will be with us next time, Denis," she said into the gap. "And *Nyamboya*. You won't have to win alone."

"Can we win?" he asked quietly.

Of all the men and women here today, Denis might understand her if she said they already had, but she didn't want the rest to hear it. They would misunderstand, thinking she meant the battle.

Jessica meant the War itself.

After all, *Thuringwell* was a meaningless, little planet, in and of itself. There was nothing about it that rated the costs this battle had already racked up.

But it wasn't about *Thuringwell*. It was about changing the nature of the war between *Aquitaine* and the *Fribourg Empire*.

And *Fribourg* was dancing to her tune. Badly.

"Patch her up, best you can, Denis," Jessica replied. "Fly everybody who needs it to one of the other carriers for repairs. We'll ignore reloads for now and get everyone safe. They can't reload at all with their carriers gone."

Jessica took a deep breath and fixed her closest friend aboard with a cold stare.

"I intend to send this man home with a personal message for the Emperor."

CHAPTER LXXVII

DATE OF THE REPUBLIC JULY 19, 396
SOMEWHERE, THURINGWELL

"DAMN IT, DASH," Vo yelled over the sound of pounding hooves. "Slow down."

She wasn't listening.

This was hell for leather into the valley of the shadow of death.

Half a league, half a league, half a league onward…

At least Shevi could keep up. But Vo had no intention of running full-tilt into this mess.

And if Dash wouldn't listen, he did know someone that would.

Aoibhín was close, looking like a damned centaur atop her Arab stallion *Thorsten*.

Vo edged his own black monster close.

"Curator," he yelled across the terrible rumble of charging hooves. "Sound *Hold and Withdraw*."

She looked at him like he had grown a second head. "What?"

"*Hold and Withdraw*," he yelled, probably far louder than necessary across a meter of space, but he was beginning to lose his temper at this point.

"Why?"

Vo grabbed Thorsten by the bridle closest and leaned about as far out as he thought his own mount could hold.

"Because I gave you an order, Curator," he snarled savagely.

That seemed to break through the layer of crazed rime frost that had surrounded everyone else and turned them all into northern berserkers. Aoibhín pulled the horn from her hip and sounded the notes.

It had the intended effect.

The riders might not be willing to listen, certainly not that one crazy woman on point, but the horses knew those tones at least as well. They dropped from a hard canter to a walk in twenty steps.

Dash rounded on them like a dragon as she pivoted Göll.

"What the hell is going on?"

If a woman could stomp from horseback, Dash had managed. Maybe the roan mare picked up her rider's anger.

Aoibhín took the easy way out and pointed at Vo, still holding loosely onto her own horse's head.

"I ordered it," Vo said, probably louder than necessary right this moment, but he was tired of yelling at the back of her head as she ignored him in her charge down into the valley.

"You don't command here, Arlo," Dash snarled. "This is my unit."

"And it's my mission, Dash," he said back quietly.

Right now, his butt and his back hurt from the unaccustomed hard bouncing. His humor had long since gone out the window.

She looked like she wanted to make something of it.

Vo fixed her with a cold, angry stare.

"Try me, Centurion Mitja," he said with a cold, lethal edge. "Just try me."

Something got through to her. Maybe the look in his eyes. Maybe the set of his shoulders. Perhaps the way his hands flexed when he got this angry. His sisters had always been able to read that fine line and know when enough was maybe too far.

Something human came into her eyes, replacing the wild-eyed demon that had been there a moment ago. Around them Scout Patrol turned back into a military unit, no longer a pack of baying wolves.

"*Gaucho*'s down there," Dash said.

It was quieter this time. Less hostile. Almost plaintive.

Vo knew why. And he understood.

He was here to keep her from doing something stupid.

"And we're going to get him," Vo agreed. "But we're going to do it right."

He patted Shevi on the neck and dismounted. Horseback, he had to pay attention to not falling off, even after this long. A-ground, he could think and speak clearly. He could be a proper officer.

That was not something his parents or his siblings would have ever expected. His old mates either, but most of them were dead or in prison now, a fate he probably would have shared but for a lenient judge on a good day.

"Curator," he turned to Aoibhín and fixed his determination on her. "Contact *Freefall* and have them hold as well. Not to dig in, but prepare for maneuvers that do not include a dead charge into an obvious ambush."

"Acknowledged, sir," came the immediate response, followed by a hard blush that went all the way to the girl's hairline.

Dash even seemed to be breathing normally by now. That was a good sign. She had been burning white hot.

Vo could see maybe twenty troopers clearly in the brush and scrub. The rest were probably close enough to hear if he yelled, but he was sure they would all get the message, as if by magic. Probably secured pocket comms.

"That is a trap," he snarled loudly and pointed into the bowl below them.

There was remarkably little smoke visible, but he could see the top of *Cayenne*'s hull from here, so he knew which way to go.

Vo had no idea how many Imperial Security troops were down there. He didn't really care.

They thought they had enough to shoot down *Gaucho* and then rough up whoever came to his rescue.

It was his job to dissuade them of that notion.

"You are the Scout Patrol, First Cohort, of the Fourth Saxon Legion," he continued, pitching his voice to carry.

If there were bad guys close enough to hear, let them know what hornet's nest they had riled.

"You are meaner, sneakier, and crazier than they are," Vo challenged the men and women around him.

They growled at that. Maybe a few of the horses too. It was hard to tell.

"They think you are dumb enough to walk right into their hoof trap and break a leg," Vo said.

That did get a growl. Injuring horses intentionally was just about the fastest way to piss these people off.

"I would rather not," he considered aloud. "But I don't know a damned thing about how to maneuver Hussars in the field. Dash?"

If he had poked her in the hip with a cattleprod, she probably wouldn't have started as hard as she did. Maybe.

She did come into herself. Hard.

"Seventh Lance," she hollered loudly across the field and pointed.

A group of men and woman howled back.

"I want a sniper team on that rise yesterday. Third Lance, put your anti-tank missiles on the slope in front of them. Eight and Nine, roll right and swoop. Five and Six down the middle. One, Two, Four and the tanks circle left. Move it people."

It looked like ants in a kicked-over hill, but resolved itself by the time Vo had climbed his weary legs back into Shevi's saddle and drawn his pistol. Sabers were for Cossacks. He could still probably outshoot nearly anyone here.

He had done his job.

That much he could promise the Fleet Centurion tomorrow.

The mad energy was back, but this time it was focused, controlled.

Intent.

Mean.

Dash might have the hots for *Gaucho*, but that just meant that there was an entire Patrol looking out for the pilot and his crew.

Vo rode forward in the wake of First Lance.

And hell followed with him.

CHAPTER LXXVIII

IMPERIAL FOUNDING: 175/07/19. BB VARGA. THURINGWELL ORBIT

VARGA COULD BE REPAIRED.

The damage was not even particularly bad, once enough men had cut away the shattered and twisted metal to get at the bone underneath.

Kozlov's anger went deeper.

He would be a laughingstock now if he retreated. At best, he could look forward to retirement in disgrace, and not the sorts of Imperial protection that cloaked the Emperor's cousin from scorn.

That *woman* had done this to him.

He would not grind his teeth. Not here. Not on this deck. Someone would report his every word and tic to someone higher up, at this point.

How had he responded to pressure? Was he all used up? Should he be put out to pasture?

Never.

Saveliy Kozlov would die like a gentleman if he had to, but she would not make him crawl.

"Squadron, this is Admiral of the White Kozlov," he intoned firmly into the microphone. "For the second half of the battle, we will concentrate all fire on the enemy flagship. Without it, they cannot remain, and our flight wing will be able to take possession of the planet below. The Emperor has chosen us to drive the barbarians back across the frontier, and he is counting on every man to do his duty."

Saveliy cut the input and stared down the rest of his Flag Bridge from the moment of silence that had bubbled up.

"Wardroom," he said out loud, knowing someone would relay the message. "Dinner for the Flag Bridge now, and then the fighting stations. We will have some time before the next act."

And then he would take the battle to *that woman*, and do something Emmerich Wachturm never had.

Kill Jessica Keller.

CHAPTER LXXIX

DATE OF THE REPUBLIC JULY 19, 396 SC
AUBERON. ABOVE THURINGWELL

DENIS'S FACE filled part of one screen, next to a schematic of the minefields that *Wombat* had been weaving above *Thuringwell*.

Jessica watched his face, and her other commanders on the secondary screens, as the two Imperial forces began to coalesce back into a single fleet and begin their slingshot run around the planet. They could get a reasonable amount of speed going since there were no ships in any orbital plane at this moment.

Abbotsford and *Achaemenes* had gone straight down at the first sign of trouble, along with *Wombat* and the rest of the support force. Even *Andorra* had fled once she released all her dangerous little hawks. But she had no guns to speak of.

They would be safe out on the edge of the system for a few hours. At least until this mess was resolved one way or the other.

"Is there enough firepower to seriously hurt that formation?" Denis asked first.

"No," Jessica replied simply.

One heavy cruiser would be in deep trouble. Even a small squadron, if they were low enough and slow enough to attempt to hold orbit. This force was too big, and moving too fast, and not interested in getting down into the sort of range where all those little mines could detonate warheads and fire the resulting lased beams upwards at the nearest target.

Varga was just surfing the orbital well right now. Down, around, and back up full tilt. Coming after her.

"If the fighters had stayed with the warships, I would have lit the whole net up at once," Jessica said. "Even with the gaps, it would have been a rising tide eating a sandcastle made of melee fighters."

"So a waste of time?" Robbie asked from his screen.

"Not at all, *Nyamboya*," she replied. "There are missile satellites in there as well. Once he commits to climbing up at us, we'll open up with everything and both soften him up and distract him. He has nowhere to go with nearly fifty fighter craft, except to either land on the planet or get everyone to deep space and abandon the vessels themselves and pick up the crews."

"Would he do that?" Denis asked.

"Red Admiral would," Alber' barked sharply. "But the Red Admiral wouldn't have gotten himself into this mess in the first place. Hardware is far cheaper to replace than men."

Spoken like a true berserker. But Jessica knew Alber' was also right. Most of six squadrons of men would be prohibitively expensive to lose for a couple of years while they rotted in prisoner camps waiting to be traded home. The fighters themselves could be replaced far faster and far cheaper than training up new crews.

"So what's Act Two, Jessica?" Denis asked.

She smiled. Robbie had gotten used to calling her by her first name in certain circumstances. Kigali did occasionally. She doubted Alber' ever would unwind that much.

But it meant a great deal to her that Denis Jež, a man long nursing a small grudge at all the times he had been overlooked, was relaxing. Was willing to accept that he was not just a part of this team, but perhaps the steel skeleton upon which everything else was built.

She was just the Flag Officer. Denis commanded *Auberon* now.

She might not have been here without the support of the Senate itself, but Jessica Keller would have never considered attempting a stunt like this without men like these beside her.

Jessica smiled. These men might be mere footnotes in her legend. She had no doubts that the historians would concentrate everything on her and ignore the rest. But that legend would rest on their shoulders today.

"*Simeon*," she replied simply. "Lane Seven."

It was a measure of the men, of their temperament, or their experiences, in how they responded.

Denis nodded workmanlike, already deep in his own planning.

Robbie scowled, but he did that.

Kigali literally sneered in contempt, but he probably doubted the Imperials could be as challenging as Lane Seven itself was.

Alber' d'Maine smiled like Aphrodite herself had risen from the waves and offered herself to the man.

The others simply held their peace. Command Centurion Doriane Matveev, *Ishfahan*, hadn't been with Jessica long enough to find her niche with these men. Command Centurion Kanda Lungu, *Ballard*, had a disdain for warfare anyway, but she had been willing to commit all manner of petty delinquencies along the way. The six Destroyer commanders were all aggressive men and women in their own right, happy to add their swords to those on the table.

But *Auberon* would carry the flag. And probably suffer the greatest for it. That might break Denis's heart, but you would never, ever, see it. That much she was sure of.

Now she needed to teach the Imperials to respect her as much as they feared her.

CHAPTER LXXX

DATE OF THE REPUBLIC JULY 19, 396
SOMEWHERE, THURINGWELL

IF HE HAD TO PICK, it was probably that damned trumpet that was the most eerie part of the whole scenario.

Gaucho was used to the occasional sound of gunfire. If projectile weapons were so much louder than beams and particle cannons, it was still a predictable thing.

And he could hear the sound of engines pushing transmissions to the metal's edge as a group of tanks maneuvered around, somewhere to his right. They were even getting closer.

But that damned trumpet seemed to be coming from everywhere. Or nowhere.

Gabriel might be coming for him. But *Gaucho* had his doubts that his just reward would be a nice one.

Takouhi tapped him on the leg, and then pointed to the left when he looked.

Ghosts, moving through the trees.

Well, not ghosts. Ghouls, maybe. Come to munch on the corpse of his lovely flying machine.

She pointed a weapon at them.

Where in Hades name had she been hiding a pulse carbine, anyway?

Gaucho went back to his watch area and paid attention. Murph was poised and silent as well, but he never spoke much.

Not sober, anyway.

An explosion in *Cayenne*'s airlock nearly made *Gaucho* wet himself.

This was nothing like flying. Some jackknob had just lobbed a grenade into the airlock by way of saying hello.

That was rude.

Takouhi waited a few seconds, apparently for them to grow confident, and then opened up with the pulse carbine.

Gaucho couldn't tell if she got anybody, but all hell broke loose a second later.

Murph moved so little that *Gaucho* wondered if he was asleep over there. At least until he fired a single shot at something unseen.

Hopefully, he had gotten the guy. Murph was hell on wheels in flying combat simulators. Maybe he had also spent enough time in Hogan's Alley sims to be useful today.

Gaucho was just a pilot. Let Takouhi and Murph kill things.

Nobody moved in the area he was assigned to watch. That was fine with him. At least they had a direction to bug out if they had to.

More pulse fire.

Gaucho couldn't tell if anything good or bad resulted. These were single shots or short bursts. Nothing like in the vids where the heroine stood up and ripped the whole charge pack off from the hip.

He suspected Takouhi was that crazy. Hopefully, nothing today would bear that out. There were tanks and horses coming. That much he could hear.

Apparently, she had gotten somebody's attention. A grenade came this way. Sort of.

Not close but definitely not lobbed at *Cayenne* this time. It went off with a soft *whoomp* in the forest soil.

Takouhi responded with a longer burst. And then silence.

Again, kinda eerie.

He could hear men over there, yelling back and forth at each other.

Murph fired again. A single shot. Nothing more. No clue what he saw.

And that damned trumpet.

Louder this time.

Hopefully that meant closer.

Ta-TA. Ta-TA. Ta-TA.

The triple note that cute brunette in Dash's Lance played when they went balls out across an open field.

Screaming metal as well. Hopefully there was a tank coming to save his ass.

It would be nice to have some armor between him and the bad guys again. Dead trees just didn't cut it. Not against crazy people with guns.

Movement.

Gray against the green and brown.

More ghouls.

Imperials. In his zone. Trouble.

Gaucho raised the pistol and steadied it on the log, like Murph was doing. He stopped and turned off the safety, before Murph could get in another *I-told-you-so*, and aimed.

Three men.

Not exactly coming at him, but coming this way.

A projectile weapon right now would be more useful. The sound would at least hopefully drive them to cover. There was so much noise right now they might miss him shooting at them.

Hopefully, he could hit something at this range. It wasn't like he was crop-dusting or something.

Maybe that was the thing.

Think crazy, trick flying. Crop-dusting at full speed, through a canyon, because why the hell not, with a bridge. And people fishing off the bridge.

Spear-fishing. Let's make this a challenge.

Gaucho smiled and squeezed the trigger, aiming for the tourist on the left in the funny hat as *Gaucho*'s wood and canvas biplane blew past at too-low and too-fast.

The man dropped cold.

Crap. That worked.

Gaucho got excited and fired again. Maybe he got another one. Maybe not. Both fell forward.

And things started exploding off of his log.

Gaucho ducked, thinking thoughts about tree branches and iron bridges.

Crop-dusting and gun fights.

He could do this.

He got as flat as he could and found a gap at ground level.

A flying squirrel would have to be insane to try to thread this needle. Paint-your-aerial-wagon-bright-red crazy.

Fortunately, there was just such a squirrel handy.

Something over there moved.

Maybe a boot. Polished black leather would look like that with some mud on it.

Guacho went crop-dusting again, and then popped up and fired three shots into the trees so entirely at random as to constitute insanity.

Always let Lady Luck have a few rolls to herself. Otherwise, she gets jealous.

CHAPTER LXXXI

IMPERIAL FOUNDING: 175/07/19. BB VARGA. THURINGWELL ORBIT

THEY HAD CLEARED *Thuringwell*'s dark side and gotten organized.

Kozlov approved.

They would be climbing out of the gravity well, but were moving at a high speed and would continue to accelerate as they went.

Keller had arranged her forces into the most useless formation he could imagine. Apparently, *Auberon* was more badly damaged than he had imagined, if she had put the battlecruiser up front and kept the completely uninjured heavy cruiser back to protect her.

He would have to consider a savage braking maneuver to loop around her stern at this rate. Instead of retreating from him, she was diving down the gravity wall to meet him halfway.

Alternatively, he could ignore the cruisers and pour everything into Keller's hide as he went by, and then reach deep space and turn around.

Perhaps she would flee after that. Perhaps there would be an Act Three worthy of the name.

Certainly, the choreography demanded it.

Keller had her six destroyers in two arrowheads, with the Escort Carriers behind the line vessels. The two light cruisers, missile on the back and Survey Cruiser on the near side, escorted the battlecruiser at the back.

Perhaps *Nyamboya* had also been hurt worse than he thought, and needed protection from the oncoming Imperial vengeance.

Shivaji sat at the front of a diamond with the other three cruisers, just ahead of the battlecruiser and escorting both *Nyamboya* and *Auberon* as much as that damnable corvette. The one that had utterly annihilated any of his missile waves that had gotten through the static and fighter screen.

Tomas Kigali had lived up to his diabolical reputation today.

Facing, Saveliy had shifted all of his intact frigates in an over-lapping line of battle between his heavy vessels and Keller's force, with the two injured ones on the back of the formation. *Varga* had the van, exactly the opposite of before, but it would put him even with *Auberon* as the two fleets drifted into and past each other. *Wintergold* was in the center, and *Novo Daysahn* at the rear.

This would be a classic engagement on his side. He would rendezvous with all the fighters and use them to screen his frigates, as before. Everyone was out of missiles at this point among the flights, so there was little the two forces could do except neutralize each other.

At least until he hammered *Auberon*. Because that was the plan. While any missile would be fired at the nearest target as the two lines passed, every Primary beam was going to be held for *Auberon*.

Saveliy was happy to let the rest escape with only minimal damage at this point.

He was absolutely going to destroy Keller before he left the field.

It would be undamaged starboard to starboard this time.

Time for you to die, Keller.

"Admiral, hostile scan lock from below," the sensors officer called, routing a new image to his screen.

It was as if two hundred little fireflies had emerged from their slumber in *Thuringwell*'s orbit. Except there were no friendly, little bugs in orbit.

The signals turned into missiles separating from housings and beginning to accelerate after him.

Keller had planted a minefield for him, but used it all wrong. He could probably outrun all of those missiles, laboring as they were to get to the higher gravity planes he would be on.

Still, better safe.

"Squadron accelerate five percent," he ordered. "Drop *Yokohama* and *Cerberus* back as well as *Phineas Kervitch* and set them on defensive duties. Sensors, plot missile plan estimate on screen five."

A small change required, but nothing significant. If *Auberon* and *Nyamboya* were damaged enough that they needed *Shivaji* to protect them, he had enough firepower at his command to do the job.

353

CHAPTER LXXXII

JESSICA WATCHED the Imperial fleet adjust. *Ballard* not only kept their missiles blind and their scanners fuzzy, she also had a hard lock on every red and blue-shift almost as soon as it happened.

There. Distraction enough. The missiles would be chasing him. He would want to get clear, while looking back over his shoulder constantly.

Briefly, she considered matching the man maneuver for maneuver. Line her own destroyers nose to tail like the Imperial frigates. Put her cruisers into line to tango.

The good old days.

Except that *Ballard* had barely any offense to begin with, and *Ishfahan* has expended a truly staggering number of missiles in distracting the light cruiser who had wanted to maul her.

For a man so aggressive before, perhaps the Imperial Admiral had gotten too conservative now. His fighters were flying escort, rather than attempting to swarm her. His frigates had begun to launch missiles, but few and mostly it looked like an attempt to keep her at bay.

Plainly, he did not expect those two weapons to figure heavily in what was about to come.

The Red Admiral would have put his own Battleship, the *Blackbird*, in the middle, with a cruiser ahead and another behind.

Putting *Varga* up front gave him the most firepower at the start, but it would quickly taper off as the two lines blew by each other. Unless he was planning to hook around her stern as hard as he could and pour everything into *Auberon*.

No other tactical layout made any sense. She may have just forced another back-foot maneuver from the man.

Jessica made adjustments to the plan displayed in front of her and transmitted.

"Squadron, this is Keller," she said out loud, trusting Enej and his team to get everything routed right. "I have just sent an update to plan *Illumination*, Situation Six. Implement immediately and acknowledge."

Alber' d'Maine had surprised the hell out of her and all of her crew the first time he had turned off half his gyros and spun *Rajput* on her long axis to fire all her Primaries back along her flight path as she coasted backwards through space.

Jessica wondered what the look on the Imperial Admiral's face would be when *Auberon* accelerated forward at the same time the two cruisers pointed their snouts in his direction without coming about.

It would be harder to do with all *Auberon*'s mass. Not impossible, but the flight deck did not need a sudden loss of gravity and down to go with everything else.

Robbie and Alber' could handle it.

CHAPTER LXXXIII

DATE OF THE REPUBLIC JULY 19, 396 CAX
SHIVAJI. ABOVE THURINGWELL

IN THE END, ALBER' must have known Keller would go for the obvious solution.

She was still, at least comparatively, sane.

Rational.

Not fully dedicated to the Goddess of War in all her incarnations.

Not like *Shivaji*.

Keller was an excellent Fleet Centurion, diplomat, and commander. Well respected across the entire galaxy, beloved of the entire fleet.

But she still followed Athena, goddess of wisdom in battle.

Alber' d'Maine looked around his bridge.

This day, he would dedicate to Odin, the great northern berserker.

On his immediate right, Senior Centurion Cruz Bösch, Executive Officer. On his forward left, Centurion Zoya Najafi, Science Officer.

His own Goddesses of War.

Around the three of them, most of the old crew of *Rajput*, transplanted into fertile soil and allowed to take root.

Disciples of death and devastation in all its myriad forms.

But he would need to take them to a higher plane of existence today.

"Tactical," he called from that grand throne. "I am taking command."

Bösch turned on him like a cat bereft of a mouse, until she saw his face.

As wars of wills went, it lasted but a heartbeat. She bowed and bared her neck before him.

"Acknowledged," she said simply. "You have the bridge."

Alber' d'Maine would not be denied. And he would not destroy their careers by letting them take responsibility for this.

The day required it.

Keller would grasp that, eventually.

She would not order it. Would never demand it.

She would even understand it. Had done it herself.

She had faced the Goddess of War unleashed.

"Navigation," he ordered sharply. "Come right zero-seven-zero, down ten, maintain plane, accelerate to maximum. Acknowledge."

If his crew had any doubts, any reservations at all, he could not hear them.

But then, they would not be on his deck if they did.

This was a warship, a vessel dedicated to *War*.

"Acknowledged, *Shivaji*," the man replied promptly. "Zero-seven-zero, down ten, maintain bow plane, maximum acceleration."

And it was good.

"Defense Centurion," Alber' continued. "We are the Light Brigade. *Half a league, half a league, half a league onward*…You will shield us into the valley of death."

"Acknowledged, Commander," the man just ahead of Bösch said with a lilting challenge in his voice.

"Gunnery Centurion," Alber' concluded. "We are Achilles, challenging Hector himself before the high walls of Ilium. Your strong, bronze sword will guide us."

"Roger that, *Achilles*," the woman just before him on the left called over her shoulder without ever looking up from her screens.

Alber' d'Maine looked over the bridge of *Shivaji* and smiled.

"Ladies and gentlemen," he said quietly, by way of fiery speech to rouse his troops. "Charge."

This vessel was not just a ship of war.

Today, she was its Avatar.

CHAPTER LXXXIV

CROP-DUSTING DIDN'T SEEM to be working any more. Or maybe *Gaucho* had dusted all the crops that were willing to lay there and take it.

They had started getting fussy.

And smart.

Nobody had popped out in while, but shots kept chipping away at his log.

Gaucho had come to appreciate Takouhi hiding behind trees they had just knocked over, all wet and much less likely to burn. She was leaving smoke around them as she put potshots into downers that had dried out over the winter.

That just made the field even weirder, as a fake bar-fog rolled over everything else and blurred details. Fortunately, there were just enough branches and crap overhead that nobody would get a really good wicket run going and pitch a grenade this far, nor bowl one across the bumps and holes between here and there.

Apparently, his loadmaster knew her shit.

But he already knew that.

Movement drew his eye, kinda back in the trees a little. Gray on blue, maybe.

Somebody had just come out from behind a great big tree, moving like moss growing.

Gaucho would have missed him but for already staring that way and watching shapes do unnatural things.

As he watched, the guy over there pulled a big, gnarly, black tube up from his side and rested it on his shoulder.

Missile launcher.

Loaded even. *Gaucho* could see the orange warhead when it was suddenly pointed right at him.

The guy flipped out the little view-finder glass and started tracking.

About that point, *Gaucho* broke out of his stasis and realized he was about to be hit with an anti-tank missile.

He brought his pistol up and fired.

A shot exploded about head-high on the tree beside the guy over there, but that one was kneeling.

Gaucho pulled the trigger a second time and nothing happened.

He looked at the gun in his hand.

The little red charge marker had popped out to warn him he was out of shots and needed to change clips.

Over there, the guy had recovered from his flinch and lined things up.

Gaucho could see a laser line connecting his little bolt hole with the launcher on the guy's shoulder.

Time stood still.

Gaucho was still stuck in flying squirrel mode, crop-dusting and maneuvering.

All he could think of at this moment were sudden power lines.

Crap.

CHAPTER LXXXV

DATE OF THE REPUBLIC JULY 19, 396 SC
AUBERON. ABOVE THURINGWELL

"REPEAT THAT, ENEJ," Jessica said sharply, unsure she had processed his words properly the first time. There was a great deal going on around her on the Flag Bridge. She might have missed something.

Enej took a breath and looked down at his own screens before proceeding.

"*Shivaji* has broken formation, Fleet Centurion," he said again. "He has turned inwards towards the Imperial formation and begun to accelerate."

Jessica wanted to curse. To rail. To spit and claw and bite.

It was bad enough in the old days when *Jouster* had done stupid things like this. Pilots were supposed to be crazy and invincible, it was practically in the job description. At least *Jouster* had to deal with his own headaches these days from *Bitter Kitten* and *Furious*.

But Alber' d'Maine was supposed to be more rational that that.

Jessica laughed, mostly to herself.

And then, louder, at the entire situation.

Her, here, calling him crazy.

It made a nice symmetry.

"Bring him up on my main projection," she said simply.

There wasn't a lot that could be said now. Alber' had made his choice. Knowing him, he was adamantly committed and his entire crew with him.

Willing to go past the Gates of Hell itself, if necessary.

They were like that.

His face appeared, calm, composed. Only the fire in his eyes betrayed him as she studied the projection.

"Thermopylae, Command Centurion?" she asked briefly, taking him all the way back to the ancient Hellenes that undergirded so much of modern *Aquitaine*.

"Horatius, Fleet Centurion," he replied with a smile and slight shake of his head, equally calm, equally quiet.

Silent moments passed. There was nothing to say.

Alber's eyes were dark green. Jessica wasn't sure she had ever stared at him long enough and hard enough to register the color. If fire could be dark, his green eyes were lit right now with black fire.

"Squadron, this is Keller," she raised her voice loud enough to rattle it off the far walls of her Flag Bridge. "All vessels, priority override. Launch all available missiles and retarget all beams at the Imperial frigates and fighter escort. *Shivaji* is sailing into the wind and we must open her a passage."

Around her, very quietly, cheers. Perhaps they were just coming across the comms, and not from her own staff.

She would not look. She would not ask.

"Thank you, Fleet Centurion," Alber' said once.

And then he was gone.

CHAPTER LXXXVI

IMPERIAL FOUNDING: 175/07/19. BB VARGA. THURINGWELL ORBIT

CLEARLY, *Aquitaine* had gone mad.

Saveliy Kozlov could think of no other explanation.

One moment, a standard, starboard pass between battle lines. Predictable, rational.

Normal.

The next, that damnable Heavy Cruiser, the tormentor of his Fleet Carriers, the reason he had fallen so far this day, was turning towards him and charging across his bow, like a wild bull seeing a red sweater.

At the same time, the entire *Aquitaine* fleet opening up with everything they had, like a blizzard, but all of it focused on his line of escorts. There was not a single enemy weapons lock on any one of his cruisers. Only that doubly-damned Survey Cruiser so much as looked at the anchors of the Imperial fleet.

And it wasn't even the entire warfleet charging him.

Just *Shivaji*.

A lone wolf. A maddened bull.

Kozlov rechecked the flight vectors on a secondary screen, but *Shivaji* was not on a collision course. That might have at least made the commander's behavior marginally understandable.

This was utter madness.

And Kozlov's own cruisers were out of position to help, trailing behind him when *Shivaji* looked to cross his bow at high speed. Plus, the frigates were suddenly concentrated on stopping a barrage of missiles that threatened to shadow the sun.

This would be a slightly-damaged battleship against a newcomer heavy cruiser.

Insanity.

"All vessels," Saveliy called. "Continue defensive measures against the missiles. Retarget all Primary beams for the heavy cruiser and fire as you range."

Green lights started to come on around his main screen as vessels acknowledged his new orders.

He would kill *Shivaji* first, and then he would come back for *Auberon*.

CHAPTER LXXXVII

DATE OF THE REPUBLIC JULY 19, 396
SOMEWHERE, THURINGWELL

FOR A CITY BOY, Vo was beginning to relax around trees. Shevi seemed to appreciate low branches and generally managed to pick the side of the tree least likely to dump Vo on his ass.

Somewhere, he had gotten separated from the rest of First Lance and Dash. Aoibhín was around here from the calls, but the trees echoed strangely, so he couldn't tell from where she was sounding her horn.

That might be on purpose. It would certainly unnerve most folks, especially if they had no idea how many squadrons of cavalry were coming for them.

Scout Patrol must be close to the Imperial troops. Vo could hear the sudden eruption of brush carbines, that flat crack of a bullet going hypersonic at half a meter, and then slamming into something solid not far away.

But at the same time, he was completely alone.

Nothing moved in his line of sight except trees and smoke.

Weird.

Shevi cantered around another tree and Vo saw the red wall of *Cayenne*'s shoulder where she had plowed a furrow in the valley floor, pushing a small wall of dirt and rocks in front of her.

It was like he was in a bubble as silence fell everywhere.

White smoke. Blue shadows. Brown bark. Green leaves.

A quick chirp on his right turned Vo's head.

A head popped up from behind a log, wearing a battered, old cowboy hat over a bald pate, with a ginger handlebar mustache, looking to one side.

Gaucho.

Vo smiled and heeled Shevi in that direction.

Gaucho fired a shot into the trees on Vo's right, and then pulled his trigger on a depleted pack. That model pistol was lousy for visual cues when it was empty. Vo preferred a different maker, who had added a bar that popped from the top of the pistol telling you needed to reload.

Battles got messy. It was useful to not have to turn the gun sideways to realize why it wasn't shooting.

Gaucho cursed.

Vo realized that the man was trying to shoot something back in the trees, and was out of charge.

Vo spotted movement.

A man kneeling on one knee. A missile launcher deployed on his shoulder.

Targeting lock.

Forty meters.

Shadows.

Man-thick trees for cover.

Shevi was moving at a rising canter that threatened to break out into a full gallop. Vo had one hand in a death-grip on the saddle horn, and was desperately trying to hold his right hand steady with the revolver as his damned horse decided to take matters into his own hands.

When in doubt, empty the clip. Thank you, Navin.

Vo fired six shots as quickly as he could pull the trigger. He dropped the pistol, knowing the annoying lanyard connecting the handle and his belt would keep it dangling without falling to the ground.

Shevi was at a full charge now. And there were trees coming.

Vo reached down and drew that nasty saber from the saddle scabbard, feeling like a Mongol hordesman.

The world silently lit up white and dumped him on his ass.

Then everything went black.

CHAPTER LXXXVIII

DATE OF THE REPUBLIC JULY 19, 396 CAX
SHIVAJI. ABOVE THURINGWELL

"TIME?" Alber' asked the room, as if there was any doubt in his mind.

This was battle. His instincts were true. His crew had come to that highest place with him, the plane of pure battle.

He was Achilles. Hector stood across the shield wall from him.

"Sixty seconds to Point Alpha, *Shivaji*," the Science Officer called from her corner. "We are beginning to suffer ranging fire from the escorts, but we are well ahead of their line and most shots will be soft at this distance."

Alber' nodded.

It was one thing to charge directly into the middle of an enemy warfleet, daring them to shoot him with everything they had. It was an entirely different proposition, and much smarter, to blast across the Imperial's bow at high speed, a tigershark attacking a killer whale.

Shivaji would suffer a terrible mauling, just from the amount of destruction a battleship could vomit forth, especially against someone swimming across the longest arc of his Primaries. If Alber' was wrong, the rest of the Imperial fleet would pile on and pummel him into the sort of flaming wreck *Rajput* had been, after *First Ballard*.

But they were counting on a simple heavy cruiser. A Founder-class vessel, designed for exceptionally long cruises in comfort, as prepared for diplomacy and scientific exploration as for warfare. In her youth, a vessel remarkably similar to the Flag Cruiser at the far end of the Imperial line right now.

Alber' wondered if anyone over there had noticed that he had not fired a single missile during the entire battle.

He had none.

The tubes had all been removed, along with all the storage for the ammunition.

In its place, a whole group of decks had been cut out, with a wall of auxiliary power reactors and banks of capacitors and batteries put in, all wired to the new dorsal turret that First Lord wanted put through its paces.

And even those were not enough for what Alber' had planned. He was confident his engineering staff could get him six shots before something got so overheated that he would have to shut it all down. The cooling fins could only handle so much heat before they melted.

He would be dangerously close to that limit.

But he was Achilles, standing before the gates of Ilium, challenging Hector to single combat.

There would be no Patroclus, nor Paris.

Only *Shivaji* and *Varga*.

And at this speed, he doubted there would be time for more than six shots, anyway.

"Engineering," Alber' called loudly, as though Priam needed to hear this as well. "Stand by."

Alber' took a deep breath and pulled it into himself.

Live by the sword, bronze though it may be.

"Gunnery," he continued. "Fire the Type-4 beams as you bear and reload. Hold for the command to fire again."

Centurion Lauma Ikeda turned her head to look at him and nodded. She had killed a light cruiser, once upon a time. She had been with him since she earned her first broken stripe, a young cornet fresh from school.

She was his sword arm now.

Perhaps, she was another Goddess of War.

He seemed to collect them.

"Firing One," she said, pressing a single blue button on her console without looking, eyes locked with his.

The entire bridge dimmed significantly and hummed loudly for nearly a second, before everything returned to normal.

"Firing Two," she continued.

Again, *Shivaji*'s entire soul cried out, a sound that ground its way down into his own.

"Navigation, maintain turret arc, but begin evasive maneuvering," Alber' commanded. "Defense, we will have everyone's attention now. Gunnery, cycle the Primaries as they bear."

CHAPTER LXXXIX

IMPERIAL FOUNDING: 175/07/19. BB VARGA. THURINGWELL ORBIT

SAVELIY KOZLOV HAD NOT KNOWN that it was possible for the hull of a battleship to ring like a bell. They were built too solidly.

Varga still did.

At least he had been prepared for madness. For Keller. For her devious Weapons Technician and the things she had done at the Battles of *Petron* and *Ballard*.

With no other incoming risks, every erg of power had been routed into the shield facing as the cruiser charged.

The shot had still gotten through.

Some fool, some maniac, had actually mounted Type-4 beams on a warship? Station-grade firepower, designed to range beyond Primaries and engage hostile warfleets from a point of superiority?

The first one alone had nearly kicked in the shield. The second had finished the job. But for the reinforcements, there might be a perfectly round hole all the way through *Varga* on a diagonal right now, like the entry and exit of a bullet through soft flesh.

"Maneuver, damn you," he cried, uncaring who executed the command. "Shear off and roll."

Anything to bring a new shield facing to bear, and to get some distance before the cruiser could repeat herself. Another of those volleys and he might not make it out of this system alive.

The proud sound of Primaries and the weaker tone of the Type-3 beams suddenly seemed like three-day-old kittens batting at a ball, rather than supremely dangerous implements of war.

On his screen, *Shivaji* began to rotate on her axis, but that was *Varga* twisting like a crocodile onto her left flank to protect her savaged nose. At least *Varga*'s own fire was getting home.

Shivaji lit like rime-fire under the hail of energy.

"Where's Keller?" Kozlov turned to his sensors officer.

"Maintaining her line, Admiral," the man replied. "Beginning to open fire on our escort line and apparently ignoring the battle line completely."

Of course she would ignore him. At *Ballard*, she had crushed Wachturm's escorts as a surprise appetizer before going after his heavier vessels, a pattern than had made no sense, until you knew what she had done next.

Saveliy Kozlov had no intention of being *next*.

"All vessels, this is Admiral Kozlov," he ordered. "Down seventy and maximum acceleration. Rendezvous at Point Seventeen and prepare to withdraw from the system. *Aquitaine* will hold the field."

Varga rocked again, and the entire room went dark for nearly four seconds, lit only by emergency strips and consoles along the wall.

Kozlov found his hands clenched into painfully-tight fists when he could see his officers again.

"Gunnery," he growled. "Finish that bastard off before we go."

He may not have guns that heavy, but he still had more guns, and that vessel was too close to get away easily.

If nothing else today, he would kill *Shivaji*.

CHAPTER XC

LANE Seven at *Simeon* was an old friend. Alber' had flown it any number of times in real life, and hundreds of passes in various simulators in his career.

When he got home, he would make a case for a new lane, one where a Command Centurion did something as amazingly audacious as attack a battleship with a heavy cruiser.

And expect to win.

"Defense Centurion," Alber's voice sang across the bridge. "Continue targeting incoming missiles with all of the Type-3 beam emplacements. We'll use the Primaries and the big guns on *Varga*."

The man glanced back over a shoulder and nodded. Centurion Saša Perko was normally a quiet man. He did not approach his guns like a diamond cutter, as some did, but as a blacksmith. A simple craftsman willing to use brute force when elegance itself wasn't enough.

Right now, even words might be too complicated, as Alber' watched Perko's hands dance over the console like a pianist exercising Rachmaninoff. All around them, gun crews would be sighting, maneuvering, firing, and repairing the guns as combat wore them out. Centurion Perko managed to hold every target, every vector, and every charging cycle in his head.

At least the fighters were out of missiles, so they could only fire soft shots into *Shivaji*'s flank as she had blasted through their formation at high speed. And that, while they themselves were evading all the fire *Auberon* and her mates were pouring into the line.

Alber' even smiled a little.

It was entirely possible, at this speed, that they would survive this encounter. Not that he had cared one way or the other.

There was a job to do. And nobody else in the fleet better suited to performing it than the men and women who had chosen to fly with him.

Varga was moving now, rolling on her side and shifting her bow down and away.

It was the exact maneuver called for in this situation.

Textbook.

Amateur.

"Gunnery," Alber' said quickly as he saw the point of perfection. "I want you to sequence the Primaries first. Let him roll on the hook before you gaff him."

Ikeda smiled at him. She looked like a hungry gator meeting a weakened impala in the water.

"Sequencing," she replied.

Some command centurions had all of the Primaries identified by the same tone on the bridge. The vibration and rattles in battle were too fuzzy to help, but a single, bell-clear tone could tell tales. The Type-3s would be a different tone, to help differentiate.

Alber' d'Maine did not believe in half-measures.

Each Primary, and every single beam emplacement, was a different note, separated by a whole step on a keyboard and tuned regularly. Training simulations often sounded like experimental jazz symphonies of a-tonality.

Today, *Shivaji* was committing art.

Perhaps he should think of Centurion Ikeda as a Muse, rather than a war goddess. Melpomene would be honored at the comparison, standing with her deadly sword in one hand as she danced.

As *Shivaji* blasted across *Varga*'s bow, Melpomene sounded her scales, running uphill from the lowest note on the starboard wings to the highest note to port.

And then two crashing timpanies, terrible thunder to accompany the lightning as the gods themselves took the field.

Alber' d'Maine felt like a god. Odin seated on his high throne, watching the entire world, twin ravens at his shoulders as Goddesses of War.

Beneath him, incoming fire from all directions reminded him of a tide crashing in. He would pay a terrible price for this. They all would.

But he had made that decision already.

Sane humans addressed their mortality once, then tried to put it out of mind as much as possible. They wanted to live well.

Alber' lived by an entirely different motto.

You are going to die. Die well.

For Alber' and *Shivaji*, perhaps that meant dying today in such a way that Keller's grand strategy to unmake the *Fribourg Empire* took one more solid step to completion.

He had given his entire life to the practice of war.

He could give his death to it as well.

Bridge lights flickered and the hull rumbled briefly, a man-made, metal earthquake.

Somewhere, a shield had failed, but only at the trailing edge of a bolt.

Shivaji had been kissed, not backhanded.

That was coming.

Had the Imperial Admiral stayed calm, the shields that *Shivaji* had destroyed on *Varga* would have disappeared around the curve of the battleship's prow before *Shivaji* could fire a second salvo.

Now, he was rolling too fast for his defense centurions, or whatever they were called, to reinforce the next shield ahead of incoming fire.

Varga looked like a pig being gutted, but at this speed, they would pass and be gone before Alber' could gift the man with an apple.

For the briefest moment, Alber' even considered turning some, or even rotating his bow backwards to keep firing, but he needed to be gone before the other two cruisers got close enough for their fire to do real damage.

All of *Shivaji*'s shield readouts on his screen looked like *Varga*'s hull metal. Degraded, leaking, and prone to rupture.

Two more cruisers getting close would finish him off, even with every shield overloaded and set to burn out.

"Navigation," Alber' ordered over the sounds of music. "Redline the engines and get us gone from the field. We can always take our time decelerating later out in the cold darkness."

"Acknowledged," came the call.

In his bones, Alber' could feel the ship change. *Shivaji* herself came to that higher plane he and the crew were inhabiting as they were apparently going to survive this day.

On the screen, the big turret continued to track as they recharged.

There should be time for one more shot, Parthian, before battle was broken.

Melpomene's sword hung poised.

CHAPTER XCI

DATE OF THE REPUBLIC JULY 19, 396
SOMEWHERE, THURINGWELL

"YOU AWAKE?" a voice called from a great distance.

Vo swam back towards himself and felt like Atlas uplifting the world, just to get his eyes to open.

Sky.

Trees.

Faces.

Dash. Rebekah. *Gaucho*. Takouhi.

"Vo," Dash said as he started to sit up. "That was the craziest damned thing I have ever seen."

Rebekah leaned into his shoulder and helped push him upright.

He smiled at her as he shifted his butt around and found a rock he could hold down.

Shevi whickered at him from a few meters away.

"What happened?" he grumbled.

The world seemed awfully loud today. And red, but that was *Cayenne*'s hull in front of him, and not blood leaking down his scalp.

He hoped.

Things slowly began to reassemble.

"Arlo," Dash continued. "You are not a horseman. We can all agree on that."

Vo shrugged. He'd never touched a horse a year ago. He and that stupid gelding got along pretty well, these days.

"However," she said. "I have never, ever, seen trick-shooting like that from the saddle."

Things were still not coalesced enough to make sense.

Or maybe she was the one that was not making sense. Dash could be like that.

"What did I do?" he asked Takouhi.

She was likely to give him an answer that made sense.

Takouhi smiled down at him and squatted. It put them on a level when looking up kinda hurt.

"You shot the guy dead at a dead gallop," the petite loadmaster said. "You galloping, not him. Well, your horse at a dead charge, and you shooting. And him lining up with a missile launcher to shoot me and *Gaucho*."

"Yeah," Vo agreed. "Remember that much."

"So I presume he was dead and pulled the trigger anyway," Takouhi continued. "But he was falling forward when he did, and the warhead was already armed."

"Yeah?"

Still not making sense, but hopefully the punchline was funny. He needed a beer.

And Shevi needed a good currying.

"So it hit the ground about three meters in front of him and went off," she said. "Killed the rest of his team, right about the time Scout Patrol got here."

"How'd I end up here?"

Rebekah laughed.

"I can show you the video, Arlo," she said with a warm smile. "You dropped the pistol, drew your sword, and slammed face first into a tree branch that knocked you on your ass. The vet and the medic both agree that nothing's broken."

This being a cavalry troop, Vo was more likely to trust the vet, but he wouldn't say that out loud.

"Then what?" Vo continued.

Things were starting to settle back into coherence. Cohort Centurion Rebekah Kim still had her hand on his shoulder, but that didn't make him twitchy, so maybe it was an okay sign on his part.

"Forty of them decided they didn't really want to play rough with ninety of us," Dash said. "'Specially not with heavy armor kicking the door in. Rounded up the rest and called for the Legate to send backup, but apparently, the idiot Imperial Fleet decided to show up today. Keller's got her hands full, sky-side, so nobody will worry about us until probably tomorrow."

Vo looked up at the blue sky, and wished he could be there with his friends.

But thne he looked around and realized he already was.

He let Kim easily pull him upright. She had muscles in places where most girls didn't even have places.

And that wasn't necessarily a bad thing.

CHAPTER XCII

"LAST ONE JUST JUMPED, FLEET CENTURION," Enej announced.

Jessica looked up from the damage reports she had been studying. *Auberon* could be repaired in the field, but Jessica might have to build a small dry-dock in orbit of *Thuringwell* to do it. And that might turn into a viable business in a hurry, if she could find enough locals, trustworthy enough to work in it, or recruit folks from back home.

The fleet could do field repair and replenishment here, instead of heading back to one of *Aquitaine*'s core systems. And handle civilian vessels in need.

War by accountants was turning into an even more dangerous place than the one waged by the fighters.

"Get me d'Maine," she said simply.

There had been nothing she could do but watch.

Shivaji racing across *Varga*'s sailing line like an impala hunting a rhinoceros, slashing while being gored as the rest of the Imperial fleet dropped down and raced for safety, leaving behind all of the bereft fighters.

Those pilots had at least had the sense to withdraw to a safe orbit and wait once their commander had decided to flee. There was nothing else they could do once their ride left, except die gloriously in battle.

Jessica wanted to make them understand the unnecessity of that task.

Enej routed the image to her primary projector, making Alber' d'Maine's head appear nearly a meter tall. There was smoke in the background of his bridge, presumably from an electrical fire somewhere close.

At some point in the just-ended battle, something burning had either dropped onto the shoulder of his emergency suit, or something else had thrown a hot roostertail of sparks at the man from short range. His face was covered with soot, as well.

He had a very somber and serious look on his face now.

"What is your status, *Shivaji?*" she asked.

His bridge crew was moving calmly around in the background, and seemed to be in relatively good spirits.

Kicking an Imperial battleship nearly to death would do that. Especially with people like this.

"We can fly, Fleet Centurion," he said proudly, but quietly. "By tomorrow, the JumpSails should be operational enough to get us home."

"And the rest?" she asked.

There was something off in his voice.

"My Chief Engineer suggests that we would be better served to cut the hull at frames forty-three and eighty-nine in dry-dock, and replace everything between them with new construction," Alber' replied phlegmatically. "Both ends are in remarkably good shape, but I melted much of the middle of the warship. The coolant system design could use some rethinking."

Jessica knew what the specifications were for the experimental beam installation. She also knew that you were never supposed to fire it six times in that short of time, even if needs must and the devil was driving.

He had hit *Varga* square four blows and glanced a fifth off her ass before the big ship had managed to escape.

Battleships could take a tremendous amount of damage in battle and keep flying. *Varga* had just proven that. Alber' d'Maine had just held a master class in how much damage a determined foe could do to a battleship if he didn't necessarily plan on surviving the battle.

"Casualties?" Jessica continued.

Shivaji had been the single point of fire for two battle lines. Even at speed and fog and evasive maneuvering, she had been hammered as she went.

Alber' grew deadly serious suddenly.

"Forty-eight confirmed," he replied. "Eighteen more likely. One hundred eighty-three on medical report. My First Officer, Senior Centurion Cruz Jo Bösch, was among those killed."

Jessica grimaced.

Bridge hit. That explained the burns on his shoulder and arm. And his solemnity.

"I'm sorry, Alber'," she said.

"Being a Goddess of War does not grant immortality, Fleet Centurion," the man intoned, sounding like a Dorian priest of a sudden. "Only legend. Cruz's legend will live on as long as this crew does."

Jessica nodded.

A galling price, but it could have been much, much worse.

And *Auberon* still held the field.

"Stand down and begin repairs in orbit," she ordered. "We'll route you home first with the message packet, unless someone else arrives first."

"Roger that, Fleet Centurion."

And Alber' d'Maine was gone.

If he had functionally melted the middle of *Shivaji* after just one battle, it was likely that the Fleet would not modify any more Founder-class Heavy Cruisers into Super-Heavies. But trust that man to push a weapon up to and beyond the point of breaking.

At least they knew now. That was money saved over the long term.

In his own way, Command Centurion d'Maine was just another one like Moirrey. Not comfortable with what was. Always pushing for what could be.

"Enej," Jessica said after taking a deep breath. "Put me on the primary Imperial channel in the clear."

"Go, Fleet Centurion," Enej replied.

He must have already expected the command. But that was his job.

"Imperial flight squadrons, this is Fleet Centurion Keller," she said.

They knew what was coming, but best to remind them. Hammer it home.

"The battle is over and your carriers have fled," she continued. "You will land at the starport at Yonin on the planet below and surrender on standard terms for internment and transportation. Any vessels still in orbit in ninety minutes will be considered hostile and destroyed without warning."

She cut the signal and twisted her shoulders to the right ninety degrees to pop everything loose. Hopefully, the shock had worn off by now, and the squadron commanders and veteran pilots would nip any patriotic stupidity in the bud.

"Enej," she said in a quiet voice. "Loop that and follow up with any threats and promises necessary to put it into effect. If they have medical issues, send marines, medics, and a DropShip over and route them eventually down to planet-side hospitals so everyone stays close together."

"Roger that," her Flag Centurion replied.

Jessica keyed through messages, but there was nothing that she needed to do right now. She keyed a call to the planet.

Wakely was there instantly.

"Your Flag Centurion is already making arrangements to take over a local hotel," her partner in crime said immediately. "What do we do with all the fighter craft themselves?"

Clearly, Wakely had not spent the last hour worrying about potholes and such.

Jessica leaned back and thought for a moment. In a regular battle, captured gear was taken home and stripped for parts, nobody wanting to return it to the rightful owner, His Majesty's Government at *St. Legier*.

But that was a military solution.

Thuringwell had a civilian governor now, appointed *Palsgrave* by the Senate.

"Once the pilots land and surrender they are my problem," Jessica considered out loud. "At that point, one could make a case that the fighters and bombers abandoned on the field could be declared a nuisance and be impounded by the local government."

"Sell them to a breaker for parts?" Wakely asked. That was the normal step.

"Perhaps," Jessica agreed. "I suspect I know a buyer who might pay well to get them back intact. That would be cash that belonged to *Thuringwell*'s government."

"Back, Keller?" Wakely asked slyly.

"Anything else we do costs us time and money, Governor," Jessica replied. "A great deal of both."

"That's insane, *Margrave*," Wakely opined. With a very impish smile on her face.

"Any more insane than invading a hostile planet and expecting to hold it, *Palsgrave*?"

"So how do we contact them with such an offer?" Wakely asked after a few moments of intense silence.

"*Seventh Son*?" Jessica asked.

"No," Wakely said. "Merryn Teke is already across the border into *Aquitaine*, and is never going back to *Fribourg*."

"Pity," Jessica sniffed. "I rather liked her."

"As did I," Wakely replied. "Let me contact Ulaffson Redyert and see if he has other contacts we can exploit."

"I will leave it in your hands, Governor," Jessica said. "Let my staff know what you need."

Jessica cut the line and got back to the aftermath of battle.

When she was a young pup cornet, just out of the Academy, it had still been a time when two battle squadrons might put on martial displays and threats, and then back off after a few shots.

She was reminded of spring bucks showing off.

In the twenty years since, the Great War had gotten more intense, more violent. More expensive.

Four years ago, First Lord Kasum had told her in secrecy that *Aquitaine* was losing. Slowly being pushed back by *Fribourg* one planet at a time.

Everything she had done since taking command of the original *Auberon* had been military effort focused on economics. Bleed the Emperor and his government. Make them pay a greater price.

Force them to a standstill while *Aquitaine* got back on her feet.

Today had been a high price to pay for *Aquitaine*. But *Fribourg* had suffered twenty times as bad.

Somewhere along the way, she had turned into a demon from their darkest nightmares. Being a woman in command could not fully explain it, even as it did play on some of their darkest cultural touchstones.

She was the monster in the night that was coming for them.

Hadn't she just proved that?

Below her, *Thuringwell* was going back to being boring. Reports from Legate Burdge confirmed that Colonel Dieter Haussmann had been killed in battle, and his force shattered into isolated bands that

Fourth Saxon was either rounding up or hounding deeper into the forests.

And Fraser Cydelmynster had survived, according to the reports. That might go a long ways towards making *Thuringwell* a viable planet for the Republic, assuming he could be brought round.

Some men never came back from being pirates.

But that was tomorrow's problem.

All of her squadron had been damaged, but everything could still fight, save *Shivaji*. However, Jessica had no doubt that Alber' d'Maine would be at standing on the bow in an emergency suit, with a pulse pistol in one hand if he had to, should another Imperial force arrive to contest local space. And more help was coming.

If she could hold another two or three months, *Thuringwell* might forget that it used to be an Imperial world. That was one of the reasons she had chosen it in the first place.

She stood up and opened a line.

"Bridge, Keller," she said. "I'm going to get dinner and a shower. You have the flag."

Tomorrow's problems.

EPILOGUE: CITY OF SAXILBY

DATE OF THE REPUBLIC AUGUST 14, 396 MINE #14, THURINGWELL

It weren't *City of Brani*. That Engine were too badly killed to be repaired in any sort of useful time. Maybe not 'til Moirrey took it apart up on *Auberon* later.

Instead, Moirrey had put her foot down and told Digger to get *City of Saxilby* ready.

Just because they had blowed up her first chariot didn't mean Moirrey weren't going to do this, even if they did hafta delay things a bit fer security, cleanup, and preparation.

It were a good thing, too. Yonin Port's yard were nothing but slightly singed fighters right now, parked kinda ragged and slowly being lined up fer storage and maybe transportation.

That were a wee silly trick, maybe selling th'Emperer back his own stuff.

But today were about *City of Saxilby*. And Mine #14.

She really would have to work on makin' 'em give places right proper names. Silly, and poetic, and more inspirational than another durned hole in the ground with nothin' but a number.

Wouldn't do, no sir.

Moirrey enjoyed the view as she rolled slowly down the track. Digger was resting in the other pilot's chair as *City of Saxilby* approached the party, but Moirrey were driving the big beast.

Two iron rails, disappearing back into the trees. Lots of trees.

Up ahead, everything slowly cleared out and then it were tailing piles everywhere.

Beside her as she rumbled down the rails at a slow jog, six big, ugly tanks from *LVIII Heavy* rolled, three on each side as honor guards. Behind and around them, near a hunnert boys and girls on horseback, like some of the better parties back home in *Lincolnshire*.

Scout Patrol, First Cohort.

Vo Arlo and all his friends. And maybe a girlfriend, if rumors were true. She dinna ask yet. Everybody deserved a little happiness, now and again, and Vo more than most.

Moirrey smiled over at Digger and considered a roll in the hay later. Might hafta sneak up on him though.

Up ahead, a cute little reviewing stand had been throwd t'gether from rough-cut timber, with a glitter-splattered Welcome banner she had made herself slung across the front.

If'n ye were gonna have a party, ya gots to do it right.

Glitter.

And Unicorns. 'Cause, you know, unicorns.

Lady Keller were there, along with a whole heap of marines and more cowfolk. Doctor-Governor Wakely, too, along with a bunch of locals, and yahoos, and other misfits.

At least they had strung a proper piece of blue crepe paper across the rails, a finish line fer her great big iron horse to cross first, ahead of the other iron horses, and then the fleshy ones.

Just fer fun, she sounded the horn again.

The civilians jumped way higher than the horses did.

The cowcatcher caught the paper tape first and sliced it neatly. Jes like it were supposed to.

Railroad engines were big things that went through little things, especially when you was pulling near to fifty empty ore cars to load up and deliver back to Ramsey Starport for export.

One of these days, a smelter would be there, and all the rock would just be turned into bars right here and shipped off. Hopefully, that would make a little lady from *Lincolnshire* rich.

Moirrey let go the dead-man-switch and leaned forward into the brake lever. They weren't going fast, but there were a lot of tons of push behind her that needed to settle down and behave.

The brakes screamed worse than the air horn had, but *City of Saxilby* ground to a quick halt.

Moirrey grabbed Digger's hand and made to drag him to the hatch, but he made her emerge first with a smile and a warm hand on her shoulder.

She liked to blush sumthin' fierce at all the cheers and whistles as she did come out. And people chanting her name were just weird.

Still, she had done this thing. And other things.

She climbed down *Saxilby*'s steps as Lady Keller come up close. Her sister were good for a big, fierce hug, which made all the rest okay. Even the Doctor-Gov'nr hugged her, which was weird, but worked, too.

Digger went to give her his hug, but she wrapped him up and snogged him pretty good while everyone else watched.

And maybe they cheered a little louder when she did.

GODDESS OF WAR CAST LIST

Auberon

Name/Rank/Position

- Jessica Marie Keller (F)/Fleet Centurion/Commander, First Expeditionary Fleet. Margrave.
- Marcelle Augustine Travere (F)/Chief/Jessica's Personal Aide
- Enej Zivkovic (M)/Centurion/Flag Centurion
- Wakely Okafor/PhD/Palsgrave
- Denis Jež (M)/Command Centurion/Com*mander,* Auberon
- Tamara Strnad (F)/Senior Centurion/First Officer
- Tobias Brewster (M)/Senior Centurion/Tactical Centurion
- Aleksander Afolayan(M)/Centurion/Gunner
- Nina Vanek (F)/Senior Centurion/Defense
- Nada Zupan (F)/Senior Centurion/Pilot
- Daniel Giroux (M)/Senior Centurion/Science Officer
- Vilis Ozolinsh (M)/Command Engineering Centurion/Chief Engineer
- Moirrey Kermode/Centurion/Engineer, detached duty

- Phillip Navin Crncevic (M)/Command Marine Centurion/Dragoon
- Vo (Vojciech) Arlo (M)/Centurion/Marine
- Nadine Orly/Yeoman /Flag Marine
- Jackson Tawfeek/First Rate Spacer/Marine
- Nicolai Aoiki (M)/Master Chef/Master of the Wardroom

Pilots, Auberon

Name/Rank/Position

- Iskra Vlahovic/Command Flight Centurion/Flight Deck Commander
- *Jouster* - Milos Pavlovich/Command Flight Centurion/Flight Commander
- *Uller* - Friedhelm Hannes Förstner/Flight Centurion/Jouster's Wing
- *Vienna* - Avril Bouchard/Flight Centurion/Jouster's Wingmate
- *Bitter Kitten* - Darya Lagunov/Flight Centurion/Wing Commander
- *Hànchén* - Murali Ma/Flight Cornet/Bitter Kitten's Wingmate
- *Furious* - Cho/Flight Cornet/Bitter Kitten's Wingmate
- *da Vinci* - Ainsley Barret/Senior Flight Centurion/Scout Pilot
- *Gaucho* - Hollis Dyson/Senior Flight Centurion/Commander, *Cayenne*
- Takouhi Taline Nazarian (F)/Yeoman/Loadmaster, *Cayenne*
- Murphy Alexandru (M)/First-Rate Spacer/Tower Gunner, *Cayenne*
- Branca Antía Rocha (F)/Flight Centurion/Commander, *Petron*
- Anastazja Slusarczyk (F)/Senior Flight Centurion/Commander, *Necromancer*
- Leila Ketevan (F)/Flight Centurion/Commander, *Damocles*

Command Wing (RAN)

Name/Rank/Position

- Tomas Kigali (M)/Command Centurion/Commander, *CR-264*
- Hường Haukea (F)/Command Centurion/Commander, *Abbotsford*
- Tódor Zviadi (M)/Command Centurion/Commander, *Achaemenes*

Cruiser Force (RAN)

Name/Rank/Position

- Alber d'Maine (M)/Command Centurion/Commander, *Shivaji*
- Cruz Jo Bösch (F)/Senior Centurion/First Officer, *Shivaji*
- Zoya Najafi/Centurion/Science Officer, *Shivaji*
- Lauma Ikeda (F)/Centurion/Gunner, *Shivaji*
- Saša Ufuoma Perko (M)/Centurion/Defense, *Shivaji*
- Komal MacInerney (F)/Centurion/Asst. Tactical Officer, *Shivaji*
- Amala Bhattacharya (F)/Centurion/Marine, *Shivaji*
- Robertson Aelieas (M)/Command Centurion/Commander, *Nyamboya*
- Doriane Matveev (F)/Command Centurion/Commander, *Ishfahan*
- Kanda Lungu (F)/Command Centurion/Commander, *Ballard*
- Elzbet Aukley (F)/Senior Centurion/First Officer/Science Officer, *Ballard*

Escort Force (RAN)

Name/Rank/Position

- Teuta Uzodimma (F)/Command Centurion/Commander, *BrightOak*
- Yezekael Jarogniew (M)/Command Centurion/Commander, *Rubicon*
- Siranush "Siran" Akpabio (F)/Command Centurion/Commander, *Vigilant*
- Tonći Östberg (M)/Command Centurion/Commander, *Andover*
- Calista Katsaros (F)/Command Centurion/Commander, *Albena*
- Ionuț Yannic (M)/Command Centurion/Commander, *Advocate*

Support Force (RAN)

Name/Rank/Position

- Waldemar Ihejirika (M)/Command Centurion/Commander, *Mendocino*
- Illiam Kovack (M)/Command Centurion/Commander, *Duncan*
- Anne Holgersen (F)/Command Centurion/Commander, *Andorra*
- Guiomar Zelenko (F)/Command Centurion/Commander, *Ladysmith*
- Enfys El-Amin (F)/Command Centurion/Commander, *Wombat*

The Grand Army of the Republic: Fourth Saxon

Name/Rank/Position

- Declan Burdge (M)/Legate/Commander, Fourth Saxon Legion Cavalry
- Eko Tri (F)/Cohort Centurion/Primus Pilus, Fourth Saxon
- Dashyl Mitja (F)/Patrol Centurion/Patrol Commander, First Cohort, Scout Patrol

- Tariq Arazola (M)/Decurion/First Lance, Scout Patrol, First Cohort
- Aoibhín Hult (F)/Curator/Cornicen, Scout Patrol, First Cohort
- Alban Charpentier/Curator/Draconarius, Scout Patrol, First Cohort
- Hovsep Khachaturian (M)/Curator/Ballistarius Gunner, First Lance
- Magdalena Borislavov (F)/Centurion/Commander, 2nd Squadron Scout Patrol
- Hawne Sherazi/Decanus/Castle Lance, 3rd Squadron Scout Patrol
- Yağmur Küçük/Trooper/Pioneer, Castle Lance, 3rd Squadron

Equine Forces of the Republic

Name/Rider/Troop

- Göll/Dashyl Mitja/Scout Patrol, First Cohort
- Shevi/Vo Arlo/Scout Patrol, First Cohort
- Mitra/Hawne Sherazi/Scout Patrol, First Cohort

LVIII Heavy

Name/Rank/Position

- Rebekah Kim (F)/Cohort Centurion/Commander, LVIII Armored Ala Heavy
- Chea Tola Soun (F)/Trooper/Gunner, *Freefall*
- Ki Jun Choe (M)/Senior Trooper/Driver, *Freefall*
- Marina Soto(F)/Trooper/Loader, *Freefall*
- Bong Park (M)/Centurion/Commander, *Bloodhound*

Construction Ala

Name/Rank/Position

- Anton Wolanski (M) "Digger"/Senior Centurion/Commander
- Eric Musial (M)/Centurion/2IC, Construction Ala

Imperial Forces

Name/Rank/Position

- Dieter Haussman/Colonel/Imperial Security Bureau
- Otto Vollelk/Orbital Traffic Officer/Thuringwell Station
- Jacob Arnholdt/Captain/Commander, Thuringwell Station
- Gunter Walsh/Lieutenant/Commander, *CML-1596*
- Yanis Koppanen/Lieutenant/Commander, *CML-1688*
- Edgar Horst/Master Sergeant/Platoon Commander, 189th Division Honor Guard
- Metthias//Assassin, Imperial Security Bureau
- Saveliy Kozlov/Admiral of the White/Thuringwell Task Force
- Nelson Amavaraia/Captain/Commander, *Hokkaido*
- Iohan Pavelovski/Captain/Commander, *Europa*
- Dietrich van Aakken/Captain/Commander, *Novo Daysahn*
- Alain Toma/Captain/Commander, *Wintergold*
- Gregor Villhaus/Captain/Commander, *Toriyama Sekien*

The Republic

Name/Position

- Indira (Chastain) Keller/Jessica's mother
- Miguel Keller/Jessica's father
- Calina Szabolcsi/President of the Republic of Aquitaine
- Nils Kasum/First Lord of the Fleet
- Kamil Miloslav/Personal Aide to First Lord Kasum
- Judit Margrét Chavarría/Premier, Republic Senate
- Tadej Marko Horvat/Senator, Republic Senate, Chairman
- Hennigan McCandless/Chair, McCandless & Daughters
- Petia Naoumov/First Fleet Lord. Commander, Home Fleet
- Dr. Torvald Kijek/Husband to Wakely Okafor

- Thana Kijek/Daughter to Wakely Okafor
- Viriato Kijek/Grandson to Wakely Okafor

Thuringwell

Name/Rank/Position

- Merryn Teke (F)/Captain/Commander, *Seventh Son*
- Yan Neumos (M)/Navigator/*Seventh Son*
- Tyler Yi (M)/Gunner/*Seventh Son*
- Hao Yi (F)/Loadmaster/*Seventh Son*
- Fraser Cydelmynster (M)/Captain/Thuringwell Liberation forces
- Conrad Penztler (M)/2IC/Thuringwell Liberation forces
- Roald Dreyfuss (M)/Private
- Elizabeth "Eli" Guhathakurta (F)/Private
- Ulaffson Redyert (M)//Shipping Magnate
- Justin Hender (M)//Shipping Magnate
- Jose Wardson (M)
- Jeffry Johnson (M)
- Miles Gunderson/Mayor/Yonin Starport

ABOUT THE AUTHOR

Blaze Ward writes science fiction in the Alexandria Station universe (Jessica Keller, The Science Officer, Phil Kosnett, etc.) as well as several other science fiction universes, such as Corsac Fox, Operation Marrakesh, and more. In addition, he is the Editor and Publisher of *Boundary Shock Quarterly Magazine as well as Thrill Ride Magazine* . You can find out more at his website www.blazeward.com, as well as Patreon, bluesky, Facebook, Goodreads, and other places.

Blaze's works are available as ebooks, paper, and audio, and can be found at a variety of online vendors. His newsletter comes out regularly, and you can also follow his blog on his website. He really enjoys interacting with fans, and looks forward to any and all questions —even ones about his books!

Never miss a release!
If you'd like to be notified of new releases, sign up for my newsletter.

http://www.blazeward.com/newsletter/

Buy More!
Did you know that you can buy directly from the KRP website?

https://www.knottedroadpress.com/shop/

Connect with Blaze!

Web: www.blazeward.com
Boundary Shock Quarterly (BSQ):
https://www.boundaryshockquarterly.com/

ABOUT KNOTTED ROAD PRESS

Knotted Road Press publishes dynamic fiction set in exotic locations and unique non-fiction voices in genres such as autobiography, business, cookbooks, and how-to. Our authors cover a wide range of genres including science fiction, fantasy, mystery, literary, and poetry, appealing to all readers. We offer both DRM-free ebooks and print books for a global readership.

Knotted Road Press
www.KnottedRoadPress.com
www.KnottedRoadPress.com/Shop

www.ingramcontent.com/pod-product-compliance
Lightning Source LLC
Chambersburg PA
CBHW070733190726
48292CB00002B/249